"There are other ways than clothing to warm a man," he said gruffly . . .

As she opened her mouth to protest, he claimed it, his hand tangling in her hair to hold her captive. His beard brushed against her cheek and her throat. She pressed her hands against his chest and ordered them to push him away. But as they flattened against the solid wall of hair-roughened muscle, heat shot up her arms, sapping them of their strength.

Gently Travis caught her bottom lip in his teeth, then released it. She trembled with delight as tiny tinglings of pleasure filled her.

Deserting her mouth, he trailed kisses to the hollow of her throat. With his tongue he greeted her breast, and she moaned with pleasure.

All reason was gone . . .

VIRGINIA BRIDE

ELIZABETH DOUGLAS

DIAMOND BOOKS, NEW YORK

VIRGINIA BRIDE

A Diamond Book / published by arrangement with
the author

PRINTING HISTORY
Diamond edition / December 1991

ISBN: 1-55773-629-4

Diamond Books are published by The Berkley Publishing Group,
200 Madison Avenue, New York, New York 10016.
The name "DIAMOND" and its logo are trademarks
belonging to Charter Communications, Inc.

PRINTED IN THE UNITED STATES OF AMERICA

10 9 8 7 6 5 4 3 2 1

ONE

The Virginia Colony, June 1676

REBECCA Mercer sat primly in the small church that served the scattered plantations and smaller land holdings of the sparcely populated region along Virginia's upper Mattapony River. They were so isolated, they qualified only for a circuit preacher one Sunday in four. The other three Sundays Mr. Theodore Loyde and Colonel Howard took turns giving the sermon. Mr. Loyde was the younger, being in his early forties. As a man who ruled his home with an iron hand, he generally centered his talks on obedience.

This Sunday, however, it was Colonel Howard's turn. The colonel was near seventy and badly stricken with the aches. Having been a military man all his life, he concentrated his talks on battling the devil. His was the more interesting of the two as far as Rebecca was concerned. He organized his forays to save the human soul as if leading a campaign against the Spanish.

Generally, she found his enthusiastic call to battle entertaining, even inspiring. But today she could not keep her mind on what he was saying. Her time was almost up. It was better than a year since her husband, Thomas, had died. But even dead, his power over her remained.

Her jaw tensed as she remembered the reading of his will.

"And to my faithful wife, Rebecca, I leave all my worldly goods. However, because there is still much of the stubborn child within her, I feel she needs a man's firm hand

1

to guide her. Therefore, to keep her inheritance, after a suitable period of mourning she must remarry and with God's good graces provide heirs for Green Glen. If she does not rewed, all my holdings shall go to my cousin, Jonathan Mercer of London, England, with Rebecca receiving nary a pence. I realize my dear wife will see this as harsh, but I know her stubborn streak is strong, and I do not wish to give her leeway to avoid my wishes for her future."

She would have to pay dearly for Green Glen. But there was no other place for herself and her brother to go. They had no parents to turn to, and neither her maternal nor paternal grandparents in England would have anything to do with them. Her parents had been disowned by their families when they had married. Her eyes narrowed with purpose. She'd not give up Green Glen. She would choose a husband.

Finding a man who would be willing to marry her was not a problem. While she was not vain, she knew her features were pleasant enough and her figure sufficiently curved to invite a man's attention. In age she was only twenty-six. That was not ancient. Besides, there was Green Glen with its beautiful three-story brick manor house and the surrounding acres of fertile soil. It was a property few men would turn their backs on. Her finger went up to absently brush an ebony curl away from her face, and her brown eyes darkened with frustration. The problem was, she didn't want a husband. She had been barely sixteen when the marriage to Thomas Mercer, a man who was twenty-four years her senior, had been arranged. She did not want to face another forced marriage.

During the past year she'd gone over and over her choices. Theirs was a small community, thus the possibilities were limited. Shifting slightly, she caught a glimpse of Jason Garnet's pallid face framed by the thick brown wig he wore. Mr. Garnet was a neighboring landholder of moderate means and one of Rebecca's three most acceptable suitors. He was in his mid-thirties, tall and slender with a pale complexion and an effeminate air. He was very much a champion of the fashion of the day and wore the beauty patches so popular in court. She even suspected that a part of his paleness was due to a light dusting of ceruse.

He had called upon Rebecca several times during her period of mourning. Clearly he was interested in being her future husband . . . future master of Green Glen, she corrected. In truth, she doubted he had the strength to be master of anything. He was a weak-willed man. This would have suited her well, since she had no desire to be ruled again by any person other than herself. However, his mother, Mistress Harriet Garnet, was a very strong deterrent against choosing him for a husband. The woman controlled her son like a puppet on a string. She was a widow and thus devoted all of her attention to her son. No doubt she would move into Green Glen and attempt to take charge as though mistress of the house, something Rebecca would not tolerate.

Kirby Wetherly was another of the most reasonable choices. He'd also called upon her several times. He, too, was in his mid-thirties and a small landholder. However, whereas Jason Garnet was foppishly pretty, Mr. Wetherly was mannishly handsome. His thick, curled wig fell past strongly built shoulders and framed a face with dark brown eyes that danced with amusement. And he had no mother who ruled him. But he liked his liquor, and rumor had it that he liked variety in his women. There was even some talk that he might have fathered a few of the local children unbeknownst to the fathers whose names they bore. She knew of at least one husband who had sold his land and moved his wife away because he suspected her of being unfaithful, and while the illicit suitor had not been named, glances had been cast in Mr. Wetherly's direction. Through the years Rebecca had observed that marriage did not, as a rule, bring about any great reform in a male, and she had no wish to be humiliated by a wayward husband's antics.

Then there was Mr. Loyde. He had been widowed within

the same month as she. He'd explained that while he mourned his wife, he did not relish raising four children alone. He also confessed to finding himself attracted to Rebecca and to feeling a bit guilty because it was so close to his wife's death. "But the living must go on," he'd concluded. She had been quite moved by his manner. He was most definitely a charming man, with an honorable reputation and a strong-featured face that had aged well. He had the strength and build of a man half his years. But on many a Sunday morning Rebecca had caught the glint of steel in his eyes when he glanced toward one of his children who was misbehaving, and she had no desire to be ruled by such a glint.

Rebecca breathed a frustrated sigh, and as the colonel called his fellow parishioners to wage the war against sin, she went over the list of faults and good points she had devised for every available male she knew. It was not a happy choice.

Again she considered traveling to Jamestown to search for a suitable mate. But there she would be choosing blindly. At least here she knew the men and what to expect from them.

At least, most of them, she corrected. The service ended, and as she rose to leave, her gaze fell on Travis Brandt. Although he was not antisocial, he was a man who kept his own council. He had been her tenant for nearly a year. About a fortnight after her husband's death he had appeared at her door and asked to purchase the log cabin on the west side of her property and a few acres of surrounding land. But the cabin had been her childhood home. Even more, it had served as a sanctuary when she had need to seek solitude during the years of her marriage. Because of this, she could not bring herself to sell the property but had agreed to rent it to him.

He was a tall man with broad shoulders and a sturdy build. Other than that, she had no idea what he truly looked like. Contrary to the popular fashion of the day, he not only wore his own hair but a full beard and mustache as well. With his dark brown hair hanging thick to his shoulders and the facial growth obscuring the cut of his jaw and his mouth, she had a clear view only of his nose and eyes. His nose was good enough. It was average in size and fairly straight. But it was those midnight blue eyes of his that truly captured her attention. They were such an unusually deep shade of blue. Several times she had caught him glancing in her direction, but his gaze was always guarded and there was a coldness in those blue depths that reminded her of a winter storm.

He was a trapper and trader by profession. All people had been able to discover about his past was that he had come to the colonies some ten years earlier at the age of eighteen. He had begun his life in the New World as a vagabond trader, dealing in whatever commodity would turn the most profit. During one of his treks he'd been captured by Indians and had spent five years as their prisoner. It was with them that he learned his trade as a trapper.

Rebecca's brother, Daniel, liked this silent, bearded man and was always shirking his chores to go hunting or fishing with Mr. Brandt. Rebecca, however, found herself tending to avoid his company. She hated admitting it, but he intimidated her.

Abruptly, as if he felt her gaze upon him, he turned in her direction. He raised a questioning eyebrow in a way that seemed to ask why a woman of her standing would be looking toward him, and she saw the dry humor in his eyes. Then they became cold, as if he found her attention distasteful, and he turned away.

What I do know of him is that he's a bore, she decided, and making certain her bonnet was securely tied, she left the church.

Outside, she made her way toward her horse as swiftly as possible. But luck was not with her.

"Mistress Mercer, Rebecca, dear," Harriet Garnet called

out and, with her son in tow, hurried toward Rebecca. "I must have a word with you."

Coming to a halt, Rebecca smiled stiffly. Remembering her manners, she curtsied as they approached. " 'Tis so nice to see you, Mistress Garnet, Mr. Garnet."

"You're looking lovely as usual," Jason said, bowing as his mother returned Rebecca's curtsy.

"I'd say she's looking a bit too brown," Mistress Howard, the colonel's wife, observed sharply, joining the group. "She's been getting too much sun." Margaret Howard was nearly as old as her husband and much more nearsighted. She leaned forward, her watery blue eyes studying Rebecca's face even more closely. "Comes from having to oversee her land herself. That's man's work, dear."

"I'm sure my Jason would be pleased to help in any way he can," Mistress Garnet offered quickly.

"How kind," Rebecca replied. "But I would not like to waste his valuable time. My fields are doing very well, and the animals have survived the winter in good health."

"It takes a man's eye to make certain of that," Mistress Howard interjected pointedly.

Rebecca shifted uneasily. The colonel had been named executor of Thomas Mercer's will. Could his wife be letting her know that he'd decided the time had arrived for her to wed?

"If Mistress Mercer is in need of a man's eyes to inspect her crops or animals, I would be most happy to accommodate," Kirby Wetherly offered, quickly joining the gathering and bowing deeply toward Rebecca, then politely toward the others.

"Are you certain you can spare the time from your other pleasures?" Mistress Garnet questioned sharply.

Rebecca forced herself not to smile. Clearly Mistress Garnet was willing to fight dirty to gain the wife she wanted for her son.

Kirby smiled charmingly. "Madam, I would find my greatest pleasure in being able to aid Mistress Mercer."

Mistress Garnet gave her son a nudge.

"It would be *my* greatest pleasure to serve Mistress Mercer," Jason said quickly.

Obviously wanting Jason to have the last word on this subject, Mistress Garnet quickly changed the direction of the conversation. "And where is that energetic little brother of yours?" she asked Rebecca. "I thought the two of you might enjoy taking dinner with us today."

"Yes, where is he, indeed?" Mistress Howard demanded in a strongly reprimanding tone. "I didn't see him sitting with you. I hope he's not skipped church again to go fishing. It'll take more than payment of a fine to set it right this time."

"He was ill last night and had a fever this morning," Rebecca explained. "I felt it prudent to make him stay in bed. Mildred Taylor is with him. The aching in her joints was great this morning, making her unfit for even the shortest journey."

"I have heard it mentioned that this winter has been particularly hard upon your cook," Mistress Howard said with sympathy. Nodding her head, she added, "And 'tis wise not to take a fever lightly. Summer is almost upon us, and this heated air does seem to encourage illness."

A look of concern spread over Mistress Garnet's face. "You must let us know when Daniel is better so that Jason may come over to inspect your crops."

Clearly Mistress Garnet wasn't going to take any chances on having her precious son exposed to disease, Rebecca thought dryly. Well, at least Daniel's mild cold would give her a few days' reprieve. "I really must be going," she said apologetically. "I promised Daniel I would be back as soon as possible. He is quite miserable."

"Give him our best wishes," Mistress Garnet requested.

As Rebecca moved toward her horse, Mistress Howard scowled reprovingly. "You rode alone?" she questioned sharply, glancing toward the river where Rebecca's servants were gathering at her skiff for the trip back to Green Glen.

"I find the woods soothing at this time of year," Rebecca replied.

"Soothing?" Mistress Howard shook her head, in disbelief. "The Pamunkey lurk in Dragon Swamp while that queen of theirs no doubt plots to murder us all in our beds. And," she added pointedly, "it has not been that many months since the Susquehanna came through this area raiding our plantations and massacring our people."

" 'Twas the lucky ones that died quickly," Mistress Garnet interjected. " 'Twas terrible the tortures they put the captives through."

"But does not the governor have control of the queen, and did not Mr. Bacon and his men roust and conquer the Susquehanna," Rebecca questioned in her defense.

"The governor deals too easily with the Indians," Kirby Wetherly scoffed. "If he had not listened to their promises of peace, many of our people would not now be in their graves."

"And Mr. Bacon deals too rashly," the colonel said sternly, having arrived a few moments before and heard part of the conversation.

Mistress Garnet looked shocked. "Surely you have no sympathy for the Susquehanna."

" 'Tis not the Susquehanna that concern me," he replied grimly. "Mr. Bacon himself did not even fight them. He enlisted the Occaneechi to conquer the Susquehanna while he remained on the Occaneechi's island and ate their food and enjoyed their comforts."

"But he was forced to fight the Occaneechi when they returned and reversed their loyalties," Mistress Garnet pointed out in Mr. Bacon's defense.

The colonel shook his head. " 'Tis not what I heard. By many accounts it was Mr. Bacon who provoked the confrontation. He wanted the prisoners the Occaneechi captured, and he wanted the plunder. I understand there were a thousand beaver pelts." His expression grew grimmer. "They were our friends, and now they, too, are our enemies."

"If you ask me, no Indian can be trusted." Mistress Garnet spoke with firm conviction. "And the governor is a fool to think thusly."

"What do you think, Brandt?" the colonel suddenly demanded, turning slightly to include the dark-haired man who was standing a few feet away in unobtrusive silence. "You've spent time with them."

The tight little grouping opened up to include Travis Brandt, and Rebecca found herself closest to him. She had the feeling he was annoyed at having been drawn into their number, but his voice was polite enough when he spoke.

" 'Tis my belief that when Major Trueman killed the five chieftains he had invited to his camp under a flag of truce, he forever made it impossible for any Indian to trust the word of a white man," he replied.

"Just so." The colonel nodded his agreement.

"They had no right to hold us responsible for what that man from Maryland did," Mistress Garnet snapped.

"Virginians were there, as well," Brandt pointed out in an easy drawl.

Rebecca glanced toward him. He was baiting Mistress Garnet, and there was actually a hint of mischief in those blue eyes of his. She felt the most curious curl in the pit of her stomach. *The man is a bore,* she reminded herself tersely.

"Well, what's been done is done," Mistress Garnet replied with self-righteous indignation. "Now we must all fear for our lives so long as there is one Indian still living in Virginia."

"I am afraid Mistress Garnet is correct," Mistress Howard interjected, her attention again squarely upon Rebecca. "You cannot know where they are lurking or what foul deeds they have in mind. You should have come by boat with the rest of your people."

Rebecca knew the woman was right. It had been the anxiety of knowing she would soon have to choose a husband that had driven her to travel alone. She'd hoped the quiet ride would help her reach a decision. In truth, she admitted grimly, she would almost rather face the Indians than a new husband.

Mistress Howard's expression grew even stronger. "And the forts the governor has erected at our expense . . . they are a joke . . . a jest! The men are not allowed to ride to our aid until they contact Sir William first for permission."

"I, too, came by horseback," Kirby Wetherly interjected, again bowing exaggeratedly low toward Rebecca. "I shall be pleased to see Mistress Mercer safely home."

Rebecca felt a prickling on the side of her neck, and glancing to her left she saw that the amusement in Travis Brandt's eyes was now directed upon her. Rewarding him with an icy glare, she turned her attention back to the others.

Mistress Howard was looking relieved while Mistress Garnet was flushed with anger. Clearly unwilling to give Mr. Wetherly an advantage, she said, "Perhaps it would be best if Mistress Mercer were to accept a ride with us in our skiff. One of her male servants could see that her horse gets back to Green Glen." Her gaze traveled skyward. "One must not disregard omens. Not when there have been three of them in the past year. 'Tis a warning to us all." She clutched the Bible she held in her hand more tightly. "At night I still dream of the comet streaking westward across the night sky. Then there were the pigeons."

"I rightly remember those." Mistress Howard glanced skyward, as if in fear the birds might again appear. "They was so thick, they was like clouds in the sky. Nearly scared my cook to death when a flock of them decided to rest in the big oak just outside the kitchen. 'Twas so many of them, their weight caused a huge branch to come crashing to the ground. And the sound of their cooing when that happened could have been heard by a deaf man."

Mistress Garnet nodded until her curls bobbed. "Then there were the flies."

"Ain't never seen nothing like them," Kirby Wetherly admitted. "A good inch long and as thick as my little finger."

"They just came right up out of the ground," Mistress Howard added with awe, as if she still found this invasion of insects difficult to believe.

Rebecca, too, remembered the huge flies. They had eaten the freshest leaves on the trees and then within a month had disappeared.

"You cannot overlook such omens," Mistress Garnet warned again, her gaze fixed on Rebecca. " 'Tis something most grievous brewing in the air." Her expression became motherly. "You must come with us."

Rebecca could not deny the omens, but she refused to accept Mistress Garnet's offer. The woman wore her nerves thin, and they were already thin enough as it was. "My horse is equipped with a sidesaddle," she pointed out. "I will not ask one of my men to walk all the way to Green Glen. It would take far too long, and he would miss the major portion of his Sabbath. And what if he was attacked by Indians? He would not be able to ride to safety, and any harm that came to him would be upon my conscience for the rest of my life." Then, before Mistress Howard could second Mistress Garnet's suggestion, Rebecca added, "I really must be getting back to see to my brother. Good day, ladies." Barely giving them a chance to bid her a good day in return, she performed a perfunctory curtsy, then moved swiftly toward her horse. She felt a prickling on the back of her neck, and without turning, she knew Mr. Brandt was watching her. Furious with herself for being so aware of the man, she walked even more rapidly.

" 'Twas truly lucky for me that I chose to ride this

morning," Kirby said as he guided his horse into a position beside hers and they rode away from the gathering.

Rebecca smiled demurely. She suspected he was on horseback because he'd had one of his illicit rendezvous the night before. A horse could be easily hidden in the woods, whereas a skiff would be seen by anyone on the river.

Frustration filled her. There had to be another choice for a husband besides Mr. Garnet, Mr. Wetherly, or Mr. Loyde. But Thomas Mercer had been a jealous man, and he'd kept her isolated in his home and this small community. Also, she knew little of the art of flirting and attracting men. Being married at sixteen, she'd had little time to practice such womanly wiles. However, other women do it and I can learn, she assured herself, adding curtly, I should have gone to Jamestown long ago and spent enough time to find a suitable husband. Well, 'twas not too late. She would leave on the morrow.

"You seem in a very positive mood," Kirby observed.

"I am worried about my brother," she replied.

Reaching over, he captured her gloved hand and, drawing it toward him, placed a light kiss upon the back. "I wish you would grant me the honor of doing your worrying for you," he said solemnly. "I know I've a reputation for being a bit of a rake, but if you were to marry me, I promise I'd never stray from your bed. Your beauty haunts my dreams, and I am totally captivated by your wit and charm."

So he, too, thought Mistress Howard had been warning her that it was time to choose a husband, and he had decided it was time to vigorously further his pursuit. "You are most kind." A firm rejection formed in her mind. She knew he was lying. She had been studying him for nearly a year now, and although he tried to hide it, she was certain he did not like her independent air. He preferred women who were weak-willed and easily charmed. She had no desire to place her destiny in the hands of a man who could lie so glibly. However, prudence caused her to say, "But my concern for my brother weighs heavily on my mind. I pray you will give me some time to consider your proposal."

"I will wait a lifetime for you," he pledged solemnly.

Rebecca knew he was thinking that this was a safe vow. The colonel was certain to make her choose a husband very soon. She faked a grateful smile. "I do appreciate your patience."

Suddenly he reined his horse to a halt and dismounted.

Wondering what had brought on such an abrupt action, Rebecca also reined her horse to a stop. Her hand went instantly to rest upon the butt of the pistol that hung in a sling attached to her saddle as she scanned the woods for possible signs of danger.

"A flower of spring for a lady who is even more beautiful," he said, plucking a tiny wildflower and presenting it to her.

He was a charmer, she mused again, accepting the gift. But his charm left her cold. Behind them a horse whinnied. Drawing her pistol, she glanced over her shoulder but saw nothing.

Kirby had heard it, also. His hand rested on the hilt of his sword as he, too, peered into the woods around them.

"I didn't mean to startle you," Travis Brandt apologized, emerging into their view.

"You scared a year off my life," Rebecca reprimanded tersely, beginning to breathe once again.

"You have my apologies a hundredfold," Travis replied, performing as deep a bow as was possible on horseback.

Rebecca continued to scowl at him as she uncocked her pistol and replaced it in its holster. To her ears, the remorse in his voice did not ring true.

But there was honest concern in his words as he said, "I hope Daniel is not seriously ill."

She regarded him narrowly. He must have been listening to her conversation with Mistress Garnet and Mistress Howard. But why? He certainly had exhibited no interest in her. *You are reading more into this than you should,* she scolded herself. He was simply standing nearby and happened to overhear a bit. She scowled musingly. It did seem as if Travis Brandt was always turning up at the most unexpected moments. "Daniel has a mild fever," she replied. "I merely felt it was best if he remained at home and rested."

Travis nodded. " 'Tis always best to treat a fever with care." He turned his attention to Kirby. "May I offer my assistance? Is there a problem with one of the horses?"

"No," Kirby answered sharply, obviously furious that the mood he had been trying to create had been broken.

Travis's gaze turned back to Rebecca. There was cold amusement in his eyes. "Clearly I have intruded. My apologies again."

The hairs on the back of her neck bristled at the implication in his words. She had no desire to have the gossips add her name to the list of Kirby Wetherly's dalliances. "You have interrupted nothing," she informed him curtly.

As if to call her a liar, his eyes traveled to the flower in her hand, then returned to her face. "If you have no need of my services, I shall be on my way." After performing a second stiff, seated bow, he gave his horse a bit of heel and continued up the path.

Rebecca glared at his departing back. The man was a total bore, and she'd have a strong talk with Daniel about spending less time in his company.

"I detest those Indian ways of his that allow him to sneak up upon a person unnoticed until the last moment," Kirby muttered angrily.

Turning toward her companion, Rebecca wondered if Travis Brandt had once caught him with a different lady in a more compromising situation. For a moment the thought brought a touch of amusement, then Mr. Brandt's eyes calling her a liar came to mind. She'd not give any man reason to question her behavior. "I must be on my way," she said firmly. "Daniel is expecting me."

Looking disgruntled, Kirby mounted.

Rebecca had already kicked her horse into motion. She was determined to remain close enough behind Mr. Brandt that he would know she was present and not dallying with Kirby Wetherly in the woods.

Galloping to catch up with her, Kirby brought up his horse beside hers. "You must not allow anything Travis Brandt says or does to upset you," he said soothingly. "The man is uncouth. Clearly, all those years he spent with the Indians destroyed his manners."

Rebecca studied the straight, proudly held back of the man in front of them. "He did not spend the time with them by choice. He was a prisoner." Startled that she had defended the man, she frowned. If ever there was a man in the colonies who neither needed nor deserved her to champion him, it was Travis Brandt.

"Others have survived such incarcerations with their manners intact," Kirby pointed out curtly.

"True," she agreed.

"But then, perhaps he had no manners to begin with," Kirby added snidely. He suddenly lowered his voice, as if what he had to say next should be handled with the utmost discretion. "I have even heard rumors that he might be doing a bit of smuggling."

Rebecca had heard the same rumors and had wondered if they were true. It was not difficult for her to picture Travis Brandt as a smuggler.

"I understand Daniel spends time with the man. 'Tis my opinion you should not allow such an association," Kirby continued, his tone one of male authority. "If the rumors are true, he could be a very bad influence upon your brother."

Rebecca scowled. Here was a man who spent his time philandering with other men's wives, and he was telling her how to raise Daniel. "There are those who consider the newest Navigations Act unjust taxation. I have even heard it said that some feel smuggling among the colonies is a fair act of disobedience against an insensitive king."

"You are talking treason," Kirby warned tersely.

Rebecca flushed. She had allowed her indignation to cause her to speak imprudently. "I did not mean to defend any smuggler," she assured him quickly. "I was merely repeating some mutterings I have heard."

"In the future you must think before you speak," Kirby admonished sternly. "The governor's love of the monarchy rules his mind. I would not want to see anything happen to that pretty neck of yours."

The flush on Rebecca's face deepened. She hated being spoken to as if she were a child. But Kirby was right. She should have guarded her tongue more closely. Not wishing to discuss Travis Brandt any further, nor willing to allow Kirby to continue his pursuit of her hand, she turned the conversation to the weather and the prospects for this year's crops.

Still, she could not entirely keep her mind away from the man who rode ahead of them. She noticed him shrugging his shoulders, as if he felt a sense of discomfort, and a cynical smile tilted a corner of her mouth. There had been moments when she had felt him studying her as if she were some strange insect. Now it was his turn to feel watched.

She was not surprised when he turned off the trail fairly soon. What did surprise her was the sudden wave of disappointment that swept over her. 'Twas only because he was a distraction from my more immediate problem of deciding upon a husband, she reasoned curtly. Again the feeling of being trapped enveloped her. "I really must be getting home to Daniel," she said abruptly and kicked her horse into a fast trot.

As they approached the manor house of Green Glen, Mildred Taylor came hobbling out. Worry caused her to look even older than her fifty-one years. "Master Daniel is getting worse," she informed Rebecca anxiously. "His temperature has risen. I made some herb water and have been bathing his face with it, but 'tis doing no good."

"Can I be of service?" Kirby volunteered as Rebecca

dismounted and started toward the house without even a nod of good-bye.

Glancing over her shoulder, she saw the hesitation in his eyes that belied his words. She could not blame him. Many times a fever led to death, and no power they knew could halt it. "You are most kind to offer," she replied. "But I see no need to risk your health." Forcing herself to pause for a moment longer, she curtsied. "You were most kind to see me home."

Kirby smiled brightly, clearly thinking he had won an advantage. "I will call tomorrow." A sudden idea brought an even brighter smile. "You have merely to say the word, and I shall ride for a doctor."

Rebecca considered the offer. But the nearest doctor was a hard three days' ride away, and he might not agree to come. Even if he did, she had reason to question his ability to aid Daniel. She had her own cache of medicines and had learned how to use them from her mother. "I appreciate the offer and will send word if that becomes necessary," she replied. She curtsied once more. "Thank you again for the offer," she added, then hurried inside.

In Daniel's room she found her brother looking as pale as death. His breathing was ragged, and his skin was burning to the touch.

"I fear 'tis the same fever what passed through this winter," Mildred said anxiously, standing beside her mistress as Rebecca rested her hand on her brother's brow.

Rebecca felt the panic rising. The adults had been spared, but seven children had died. "It will not take Daniel," she said with grim determination. "We must bring down his fever. Have a tub brought up here and filled with cold water."

Mildred nodded and hurried away as fast as her arthritic legs could carry her.

Alone in the room, Rebecca fought the panic that threatened to overtake her. She again considered having Kirby ride for the doctor, but the doctor had come that

winter and had been unable to do anything to save the
children. She would practice the medicine her mother had
taught her, and if that did not work . . .   "It has to work!
It shall work!" she vowed.

Daniel moaned and began to mumble.

"You will be fine," she assured him, as much for her
sake as for his.

His mumblings continued, and she realized he was
delirious.

When the servants arrived with the tub and water, she had
them set it on the floor and leave. Then quickly she began
to undress her brother. She had always thought of him as a
sturdily built ten-year-old, but now he looked frail and
helpless.

The door of the room opened, and footsteps sounded
behind her. "We will help."

Looking up, Rebecca saw Ruth Malery, her housekeeper,
entering. Ruth's husband, Joseph, overseer of Green Glen,
was with her. "If this fever should be contagious, I would
not want your illnesses upon my conscience," she said. "I
will do this alone."

"Master Daniel is dear to us," Ruth argued, pouring the
water into the tub. A smile softened the anxiousness on her
face for a moment. "I can still remember him as a babe in
arms when you and he first came to this house."

Ruth and Joseph had not been blessed with children.
They had been at Green Glen when Rebecca arrived as a
bride and were now in their early forties. Many nights Ruth
had sat up with Rebecca nursing Daniel through the croup
or a bad teething spell, and it had been Joseph who had
taught Daniel to ride and shoot. Although taking the baby
boy into his home to raise as part of his family had been part
of the bargain Thomas Mercer had struck with Rebecca's
father for her hand in marriage, Thomas had never paid the
boy much attention.

"I've not taken the lad out into the fields and taught him
all I know about farming to have him die before he can put

his lessons to use," Joseph added, removing his coat and rolling up his shirtsleeves. Gently he lifted Daniel and laid him in the tub.

The boy let out a cry of anguish, and Rebecca's stomach knotted.

As Daniel began to shiver violently, Joseph lifted him out of the water and held him while Rebecca and Ruth dried him quickly. Daniel's skin was still scorching to the touch.

Rebecca's jaw hardened with decision. "We must dunk him once more."

Again Daniel cried out deliriously as he was submerged in the cold water.

"That is enough," Rebecca said, motioning for Joseph to lift him out. Quickly she and Ruth dried the boy and tucked him into his warm bed. Feeling his forehead, Rebecca fought back a flood of tears. "His fever is no better." Unable to bear the thought of dunking him yet again, she said, "I shall mix a brew to purge this fever from his system," then left the room for the kitchen.

All the rest of the day and that night Rebecca nursed Daniel and prayed fervently for his recovery. Ruth and Mildred took turns sitting with her in his room and aiding her as she bathed him and tried to force liquid down his throat. Periodically Rebecca slept in her chair, and each time she woke, she hoped for some sign her brother was better. But Daniel remained the same.

In the early hours before dawn, Rebecca paced the floor. She would do anything to save her brother's life. Staring out the window at the darkened landscape, she reached a decision.

Ruth was sleeping lightly in a chair beside the bed. Rebecca shook her gently to waken her. "Tell Joseph to saddle my horse," she instructed.

"There is no need for you to ride for the doctor," Ruth protested, rubbing the sleep from her eyes. "Joseph or one of the men will go."

" 'Tis not the doctor I seek," Rebecca replied. "I am going to find Oparchan."

The remaining fog of sleep was instantly gone as Ruth stared at her mistress. "The Mattaponi medicine man?"

"Yes," Rebecca replied, moving toward the door.

Ruth frowned in confusion. "I do not understand. Why would you seek him?"

"For his medicines," Rebecca answered.

Ruth shook her head, as if to say she thought her mistress was not sound of mind. "And why would he help you? There is little good feeling left between his people and ours."

"Years ago my parents saved his life. He was being mauled by a bear. My father shot the bear, then brought Oparchan to our cabin, where my mother nursed him back to health. He promised to pay back our kindness one day should we ever need it." This last was said over her shoulder as Rebecca left the room.

"Times were different then. Feelings have changed. You cannot go." Ruth was on her feet, following her mistress as Rebecca strode to her own room. "There is too much unrest. You cannot be certain which Indians, if any, are still friends. There has been too much killing on both sides."

"I have no choice." Rebecca pulled a blanket out of the chest at the foot of her bed and rolled it tightly.

"It will do Daniel no good if you get yourself killed," Ruth protested fervently.

Rebecca paused in her search for an oilcloth covering for her bedroll. "There will be no discussion. Instruct Joseph to saddle my horse," she ordered in a voice that held no room for compromise.

Shaking her head, as if to say she thought her mistress had totally lost her mind, Ruth scurried out of the room.

When her bedroll was properly secured, Rebecca left it for a moment and went to her jewelry box. From inside she extracted a necklace made of shells strung on a leather thong. Two of the shells were held together by a thin leather strap. Visible between them was a single white pearl. This talisman had been given to her mother as a sign of Oparchan's promise. She slipped it around her neck, then grabbed up the bedroll and went back to Daniel's room. "I'll not let you die," she promised him. After kissing him lightly on the cheek, she left. In the kitchen she paused long enough to pack some food, then hurried out to the stables.

Joseph was saddling a second horse when she arrived. "I am coming with you," he said in answer to the questioning look on her face.

Although Rebecca was willing to risk her own life, she was not willing to risk any others. "I will go alone."

"Neither of you should be going," Ruth said, coming down from the servant's quarters with Joseph's bedroll. "This is a foolhardy quest."

"I made my mother a promise on her deathbed that I would take care of my brother," Rebecca replied. "I must go." Her gaze fixed on Joseph. "But you will not. I am mistress here, and my orders will be followed. It is necessary for you to remain and take care of Green Glen and my brother while I am gone."

"You cannot go alone," Joseph protested as Rebecca handed him her supplies to tie to the back of her saddle. Standing resolutely, he said again, "The unrest is too great."

Rebecca took her bedroll and food back from him and quickly attached them herself. "I am going and I'm going alone," she stated with finality. "I expect you and Ruth to see to things here while I am gone." Then she mounted and urged her horse to a trot.

Two

THE sun was breaking over the horizon as Rebecca rode away from Green Glen. It had been several years since she had sought the Mattaponi encampment. She could not even be certain it was still there. Most likely the tribe had been forced to move farther north or west. She could not blame the Indians for their anger. In spite of boundary treaties the colonies continued to encroach farther and farther into the Indians' land.

She rode north along the Mattaponi River. By midmorning her body ached for a rest, but she did not stop. At noon she took only a short break to eat and allow her horse to graze and drink. She remembered the village as being an easy two days' journey from the cabin she had shared with her family. This time she hoped to accomplish it in a day.

At a spot where the river was wide but fairly shallow, she crossed to the north shore.

But as night began to close in around her, she still saw no sign of the Indian village. Admitting that she could not go on in the dark, she found a small clearing. After unsaddling her horse, she tethered it securely. Then she placed the saddle near the base of a huge old oak, wrapped her blanket around herself, and sitting with her back resting against the leather seat, ate a meager dinner. As darkness closed in around her, she wished she could build a fire. But Joseph and Ruth were right about the unrest. She didn't want to attract unfriendly Indians. Her hand went to the talisman hung around her neck. She was not certain if any Indians could be considered friendly now. Her only hope was that if she encountered any, they would honor this token of protection.

Night came full upon the world. She had never known the woods could be so dark. Only the thin crescent moon gave any light, and its narrow shafts of illumination served only to make the shadows surrounding her seem blacker. Listening for any sounds that might indicate she was not alone, she began to feel dizzy and realized she was holding her breath. Inhaling deeply, she fought the fear that threatened to spread through her by concentrating on Daniel.

"I might as well go to sleep so I can get an early start tomorrow," she muttered, hoping to find comfort in the sound of her voice. It didn't work. Coming out here on her own had been desperate. Curling up more tightly in her blanket, she rested her head on her saddle and closed her eyes. But the sounds of the night filled her senses. Her hand moved to rest on the butt of the pistol she had tucked in the hollow beneath the saddle.

Suddenly a twig snapped, and her eyes popped open. Drawing out the pistol, she sat with her back toward the tree. Only a large animal or a man would have broken a branch like that. She glanced toward her horse. But the mare was to her right, and the sound had come from the left.

"I'd feel a lot safer if you'd lower that gun, Mistress Mercer," a familiar male voice requested dryly. "I've always been leery of women with weapons."

Rebecca uncocked her pistol as Travis Brandt entered the clearing. He was the last person she expected to see, but at the moment she was willing to settle for any company.

"I heard about Daniel taking a turn for the worse," he said, unfastening the saddle on his horse. "I stopped by Green Glen this morning to see the boy, and Joseph told me where you'd gone." Lifting the saddle off of his horse, he turned to face her. "Thought I'd better come after you and try to get you back alive."

Rebecca heard the impatient reprimand in the trapper's voice, and her shoulders straightened with pride. "There was no need to risk yourself on this venture."

Travis drew a terse breath as he dropped his saddle near the base of a large oak on the opposite side of the clearing from where Rebecca sat. "I cannot abide a fool, Mistress Mercer, and you are certainly one for venturing out upon this trek."

"My brother's fate rests in my hands," she replied stiffly. "I could not sit by and watch him die without attempting to help."

"With both of your parents dead, you are the only family Daniel has. Going out and getting yourself killed is not going to help the boy," he pointed out curtly.

She glared up at him. In the darkness she could not clearly see his face, but she knew it held a reproving scowl. "I've no intention of getting myself killed."

Travis snorted impatiently. "The Indians are not only fighting us, but they are fighting among themselves. You cannot even be certain this medicine man you seek is alive, and if he is alive, he might not be able to protect you."

She knew he was right, but she could not erase Daniel's frail image from her mind. "Was my brother any better when you visited Green Glen?" she questioned, crossing her fingers that his answer would be in the affirmative.

"No," he replied gruffly.

"Then I have no choice," Rebecca said with determination.

Travis spread out his bedroll and seated himself with his back resting against his saddle. "I was afraid you would say that. Get some rest. We will leave at the first sign of light."

"To find Oparchan," she stipulated.

"To find Oparchan," he confirmed with a disgusted grunt.

If anyone could help her in her quest, it was Travis

Brandt. But she wanted no unwilling aid. "There is no reason for you to accompany me," she said with a bravery she did not feel.

"I cannot, in good conscience, allow you to go alone," he replied grimly, unwrapping a packet of food and removing some. "Now go to sleep."

Rebecca frowned at him. "There is no reason for you to feel honorbound to join me," she assured him proudly. "I do not require your companionship."

"You may not require it, but you shall have it."

" 'Tis your choice," she muttered. Although her tone was indifferent, secretly she felt a sense of relief. "Good night, Mr. Brandt," she added, lying back down and closing her eyes.

But she did not immediately go to sleep. Instead, she found herself acutely aware of her companion. When she heard him rising to check on the horses, she opened her eyes a slit. He was a well-formed man with broad shoulders and muscular legs. There was strength and assurance in his carriage that caused her to feel protected in his company. She told herself she would have felt protected in any civilized man's company. But when she pictured Mr. Garnet, Mr. Wetherly, or Mr. Loyde as her companion, her reaction was not such a secure sensation. Exhaustion has me off-balance and thinking weird thoughts, she assured herself. This time when she closed her eyes, she did sleep.

From across the small clearing, Travis watched the sleeping woman. Rebecca Mercer had been a shock. He hadn't expected Thomas Mercer's widow to be so young or so pretty. He judged her to be a coolly calculating female who had used her youth and looks to marry well above her station in life. It wasn't a sin, but he had no use for a woman like that. He'd come after her for purely practical reasons. She was the only one who could provide the answers to certain questions. Still, he could not deny the irritation he had felt when he'd come across her and Kirby Wetherly in the woods after church. Picking flowers for her, he scoffed.

He recalled the way her eyes could flash with anger, and a cynical smile curled his lips. Each of her three suitors thought they could control her once the vows were said, but it was Travis's opinion that no man was ever going to control Mistress Mercer.

The first light was just reaching the sky when Rebecca awoke. Her whole body ached. Rubbing a knotted muscle in her neck, she shifted into a sitting position. When she looked across the clearing, Travis Brandt's dark gaze greeted her. Suddenly she was acutely conscious of how she must look. Strands of her hair that had come loose from her braid blew across her face and tickled her neck. Leaves had attached themselves to her riding habit, and a night on the ground had rumpled the cloth. " 'Tis not fair to judge a woman's looks when she has spent the night in a woods," she said self-consciously when he continued to watch her in an unnerving silence.

Travis had expected her to look out of place in this wilderness, but instead, she looked as if she belonged here. "I was thinking how natural you appear in this setting," he replied evenly.

His tone made his words neither a compliment nor a condemnation, merely a statement of fact. Still his scrutiny made her uneasy. "That would be due to my gypsy heritage," she said, rising and brushing her clothing off. The words were out before she realized she had said them. Her heritage had been something she had been taught not to speak of. Mentally she groaned. It was the danger and the unnerving quality of this man's presence that had caused her to forget.

Travis's gaze narrowed. "Gypsy heritage?"

The sharpness in his voice warned her she had made a big mistake. His gaze was now most definitely cold. Obviously, he, like many others, held a strong prejudice against gypsies. "My father was of gypsy descent," she said proudly. "I am not ashamed of my heritage, Mr. Brandt."

Brandt scolded himself for showing a reaction, but this information had come as a shock. "I did not mean to sound as if you should be," he apologized, his expression becoming masked. "I was simply surprised. During all of my time here, I have never heard mention of your parentage. Considering your late husband's standing and your acceptance within the community, I assumed you were of solid English stock."

"My parents did not advertise my father's background," she replied with cool honesty. It was too late to lie her way out of this anyway. Besides, what difference did it make that this arrogant trapper should know the truth? What he thought of her did not matter. But her pride refused to allow him to think the worst of her. Catching the cynical gleam that suddenly shone in his eyes, she added with proud dignity, "However, Thomas Mercer was aware of it when he married me."

It occurred to Travis that Thomas Mercer would have been willing to overlook any shortcomings in her ancestry to possess her. Even in her current disheveled state she was a sight that could heat a man's loins. You're here on business, Travis, he reminded himself curtly, angered at the direction of his thoughts. Obviously he had been without female companionship far too long. Schooling his voice into a polite conversational tone, he said, "I met your late husband about a month before his death."

This time it was Rebecca's turn to show surprise. "You knew Thomas?"

"I met him when he was in Jamestown," he elaborated. His patience had grown thin during the past months. Besides, they might not both make it back alive. If he was to gain the information he sought, now was as good a time as any to begin. "Mr. Mercer had a brooch he had brought to a jeweler there to have its clasp repaired. The piece interested me. The workmanship was extraordinary. It was a cameo, oval in shape, nearly two inches I would say in its longest diameter, surrounded by a circlet of small diamonds crafted into an ornately worked silver frame. I attempted to purchase it from him, but he said it was a gift for his wife."

The surprise on Rebecca's face turned to confusion. "He gave me no such brooch."

"Perhaps he had it tucked away to present to you on a special occasion and died before the occasion arose," Travis suggested.

"Perhaps," she conceded. "I did not make a thorough search of his personal belongings." The truth was she had made no search at all. Her initial reaction to his death had been shock, and there had been grief that a life had been lost. But later that night guilt had assailed her as a sense of having been freed filled her. This sense of freedom, however, died with the reading of Thomas's will. She was furious that, even in death, he had not been willing to relinquish his hold upon her. Angrily she had packed his belongings away without any close scrutiny. She wanted only to get them out of her sight. Thus, today they were housed in the attic of Green Glen stored in trunks and an old wardrobe.

Travis wondered if she was telling the truth. Most likely she was, he reasoned. If she had known of the brooch, she would probably be lying in a grave beside her husband. Rising, he brushed off his clothing, then began rolling his bedroll. "If you should ever come across it and wish to sell it, I am still interested in acquiring it," he said over his shoulder.

Although his manner was nonchalant, Rebecca sensed a hidden intensity behind it. For some reason this brooch intrigued Travis Brandt greatly. "If I should ever come across it, I will remember your offer," she replied, rising, also. Mentally she made a note to conduct a search once Daniel was well. A brooch that could interest Travis Brandt so greatly piqued her curiosity.

Not willing to waste a moment of daylight, Rebecca insisted that they eat their breakfast of cheese and bread while they rode. Travis consented.

But as they headed northward along the river, he said decisively, "If we do not find this village you seek by the end of this day, we will turn back. Your brother needs you by his bedside. I know of a few herbs and roots the Indians use. If you wish, I will bring them to you, and you may try them."

She knew he was being reasonable. A person could search for weeks and not find the Indians if they did not want to be found. Grudgingly she nodded her agreement.

It was barely full dawn when they found the clearing that had once held the Indian camp. The huts were gone, and it was evident no Indians had lived there for a long time.

"If we turn back now, we can be at Green Glen by nightfall," Travis said.

Rebecca shook her head. She had come too far to turn back so quickly. "Perhaps they have moved only a short distance upstream. I must continue to search at least for the rest of the day."

Travis frowned impatiently. She was definitely the most single-minded woman he had ever encountered. He considered arguing, but the set of her jaw told him it would be useless. Shaking his head, he followed her out of the clearing.

It was around midmorning when Travis brought his horse up beside hers. "We are being watched," he said in low tones.

Rebecca glanced at him. She had seen nothing. But the certainty in his voice gave her no reason to doubt he knew what he was talking about. "By friend or foe?" she questioned in a whisper.

"Since we are still alive, there is hope it is a friend," he replied.

Rebecca reined her horse to a stop. She removed the talisman she wore around her neck, then held it above her head. "I am seeking Oparchan," she announced loudly.

There was no response.

"I have come to seek his aid. He gave his word he would

help me and my family if we should ever need it," she continued. She held the talisman even higher. "He gave me this necklace as a sign of safe passage."

Again there was no response.

Returning the talisman to her neck, she frowned with disappointment. "There is no one here."

"Have patience," Travis admonished her, catching the reins of her horse when she started to urge it forward.

"We are wasting valuable time," she argued tersely.

"Sit quietly," he ordered. "I want to determine how many are out there."

She scowled at him. "Your senses have failed you this time. We are alone here."

His eyes darkened like the sky during a thunderstorm. "Hush, woman!"

She continued to regard him with dry skepticism, but this time she did remain silent.

Suddenly a Mattaponi warrior stepped from the woods. He was Travis's size, with a regal bearing and a manner that spoke of authority. In the next instant they were surrounded by five others.

"A hunting party," Travis informed her in low tones. "And although they haven't killed us, they don't look friendly."

Rebecca didn't need him to tell her that. She read the hatred in the eyes of the Indian nearest her. He was bigger than the rest and had a long ugly scar that could have been made by a saber running across his chest.

He spoke angrily in his native tongue as he raised his bow and took aim.

The first Indian who had stepped out shouted an order, and grudgingly the bigger man lowered his weapon.

" 'Tis a good thing for us that scar-chested one is not in charge," Travis muttered.

Rebecca nodded her agreement. A cold chill ran along her spine as the big Indian continued to watch her much like a predator sizing up his prey for a later kill.

"His name is Paratough, and his feelings are those of many among us," the Indian who was obviously in charge said in Engiish. "I am Orahan, and the only reason you are still alive is because of the talisman you carry. We have lost much, but we retain our pride and our honor."

"Then you know of Oparchan?" Rebecca questioned urgently. "Will you take us to him?"

"You will surrender your weapons," Orahan ordered, ignoring her questions.

Rebecca glanced worriedly toward Travis.

"You didn't expect them to let us keep them, did you?" he said dryly as he unsheathed his knife and handed it along with his musket to the Indian who had approached his horse.

Following suit, Rebecca handed her pistol and knife to the warrior who approached her horse.

"You will dismount and follow on foot," Orahan directed. "Your horses will remain here."

While Travis tethered the horses loosely, giving them enough slack to graze, Rebecca watched a heated argument between Paratough and Orahan. As Travis rejoined her, she looked up at him worriedly, "Do you know what they were saying?" she asked in a low voice.

Travis frowned. "Paratough wants to kill the horses and butcher them for food."

Rebecca's stomach knotted. "Orahan isn't going to let him, is he?"

"Not right now, anyway," he replied as Orahan gave an order and the Indians motioned for Rebecca and Travis to follow their leader.

They moved at a rapid, steady pace. Rebecca practically had to trot to keep up with them. About two hours after leaving the horses, they entered a marshy bog. Even on this soggy, uneven ground their pace did not decrease.

Watching Rebecca's back as she walked in front of him, Travis scowled. He should never have allowed her to continue this dangerous quest. But he admired her stamina.

This forced march would have been difficult on most men. She had kept pace so far, but he worried about how much longer she could continue. Her movements were beginning to show signs of fatigue. "How are you holding up?" he asked, falling into step beside her.

That there was gentleness in the depths of his eyes that gave credence to his concern for her well-being surprised Rebecca. That the gentleness caused a warm curling sensation in her abdomen shocked her. Her legs felt as if two-ton weights were attached to them. But this was her doing, and she wouldn't complain. "I'm fine," she replied.

Travis did not look entirely convinced as he slowed for a moment to again take his place in line behind her. Mentally he cursed himself for not forcing her to return home. This had been a fool's errand. They would be lucky if they escaped alive.

For another hour Rebecca kept up the pace, then her calf muscles started to knot. She tried not to show her pain, but her legs began to move awkwardly. Each step became torture. Ahead of her she saw a large root across the path. She ordered her leg to lift over it, but the toe of her shoe struck it. Letting out a yell, she fell forward. That she was lying sprawled facedown in the dirt didn't bother her. It felt so good to be off her feet.

"Get up!" Orahan ordered with angry impatience.

Rebecca commanded herself to rise, but when she tried, the muscles in her calves knotted even tighter. "Damn!" she cursed under her breath, fighting back tears of pain. She heard the scarred Indian again arguing with Orahan and knew he was suggesting they kill her and leave her there.

Suddenly two strong hands fastened around her waist, and she was lifted to her feet. Glancing over her shoulder at her rescuer, she met Travis's cool gaze. He had the look of a man trying to control his temper. Obviously he blamed her for this mess. And he should, she reminded herself. "Thank you," she said stiffly, her words carrying an order that he could free her. But as he started to release her, her knotted muscles refused to provide any support, and her legs began to buckle beneath her. In the next instant she was lifted and tossed over his shoulder like a sack of flour.

Orahan nodded his satisfaction and again began to lead them through the marsh.

"You can't carry me all the way to the village," she hissed, flushing with humiliation.

"I've carried heavier burdens," he replied gruffly, shifting her slightly and tightening his arm across the back of her thighs even more securely. This was what he should have done this morning, he thought tersely. He should have tossed her over his shoulder and carried her back to Green Glen. Well, maybe not exactly like this, he corrected, amazed by how aware he was of her womanly form when his mind should have been entirely upon trying to get them out of this alive.

Rebecca's cheeks flushed even brighter with embarrassment as she was forced to hang on to the back of his coat for more secure balance. But the embarrassment was minor compared with the excitement that was stirring within her. Where his arm lay across her legs, she felt its heat even through the layers of her petticoats. "This is ridiculous," she muttered, uncertain if it was her humiliating position over the man's shoulder or the very womanly response to his touch that was evoking this protest.

Forcing her feet to straighten, she pulled the knots out of her calves. As the pain eased she became even more aware of the strong musculature of the shoulder she lay across. Again he shifted her slightly. This time his free hand brushed against her buttocks, and a fire ignited within her. This is crazy, she chided herself. Travis Brandt was the last man she had expected to awaken such stirrings within her. And to have them awaken at this moment was ludicrous. The blood is all rushing to my brain making me lightheaded, she reasoned. "Put me down," she ordered.

Coming to a halt, Travis gladly obeyed. He needed to keep his mind on their captors. While her body was draped over his shoulder, he'd had to expend a great deal of energy fighting the urge to run his hand up her leg to test the softness of her skin.

Orahan glanced over his shoulder and snorted at yet another delay, then resumed his steady pace.

Behind her, Rebecca could feel Travis's eyes on her back. She'd expected her disquieting reactions to the man to cease the moment she was freed from his touch, but her blood continued to race hot through her veins. Glancing over her shoulder she was met by his dark, cool gaze. With his beard and mustache he looked like a bear of a man. Returning her attention to the trail, a hot shiver shook her. His strength both stimulated and frightened her.

This is insane, she chided herself. My only thoughts should be with getting out of this alive and getting medicines back to Daniel.

To Rebecca's relief, they reached the Indian village a short while later. The huts made of woven mats covering wooden frames were arranged in a circular pattern. Several women were tending a large cooking pot on a fire in the center of the village. It did not look like the village Rebecca remembered from eleven years before. There were fewer huts, and the population was greatly reduced. But it was the atmosphere that was the greatest change. There was no friendliness in the eyes of any they passed, only suspicion and hatred. As their captors led her and Travis toward a hut at the far side of the encampment, several young children came running up and began throwing rocks and sticks at the prisoners. Orahan shouted an angry order, and the children sulked, obviously disappointed at having their fun stopped.

When they reached the hut, Orahan raised a hand, bringing the party to a halt. Then he approached Rebecca, and removed the talisman from around her neck. "Wait here," he ordered, then disappeared inside.

It seemed like forever to Rebecca before he reappeared and motioned for her and Travis to enter. Inside, she found Oparchan seated on a mat. He looked as though many more than eleven years had aged him. His bearing was proud but frail.

"You were unwise to come," he said. "The bad feelings between our people are strong. You are fortunate that Orahan is an honorable man who understands the bond of repaying a debt."

"I had to come," Rebecca replied, her voice taking on a tone of urgency. "My brother is very sick with a fever. Our medicines cannot help him."

"I will mix you a potion, then you must leave," he said, rising stiffly.

Rebecca watched the old Indian anxiously while Travis watched the door. Travis Brandt's stance was that of one preparing for a fight. Rebecca prayed he would not be forced into one.

"I am sorry for getting you into this," she apologized quietly.

"It was my choice," he replied.

But Rebecca knew he would have preferred not to be beside her. Still, he was there. Against his own best judgment he had accompanied her. She would never have pictured Travis Brandt—of all the men she knew—as her knight in shining armor.

She remembered the sarcastic amusement in his eyes on Sunday when he'd come upon her and Kirby Wetherly. She would have guessed then that she was the very last person he would choose to help. He was a very difficult man to understand.

"Make a broth of this and see that your brother drinks it," Oparchan instructed, approaching Rebecca and handing her a pouch. "It is all I can do. Now you must leave."

"Thank you," she said gratefully and secured the pouch in the leather purse hung around her waist.

"Do not come this way again," he warned her. "I will not be able to protect you a second time."

She nodded her understanding as Oparchan walked to the mat covering the doorway and lifted it aside. Orahan was waiting outside. In his native tongue the old medicine man gave an order to the younger brave. Turning back to Rebecca, he said, "Orahan will lead you back to your horses. Go quickly."

But as she and Travis followed Orahan toward the edge of camp, Paratough suddenly appeared in front of them. In his native tongue he spoke to Orahan. Orahan answered back in a tone that left no doubt this was a confrontation.

Rebecca glanced toward Travis. "What are they saying?" she asked in hushed tones.

"Paratough does not want us to leave. He says we know where their camp is, and we know their number is weak. He is afraid we will lead soldiers here to attack them."

"You must give him our word we won't tell anyone where to find them," she urged.

Travis frowned down at her. "These people have been given many a white man's word that has been broken. I don't think Paratough is in the mood for what he will probably consider an empty promise."

Rebecca watched the exchange between the two Indians worriedly. She hoped Orahan's authority and the Indians' sense of honor was strong enough to save her and Travis from Paratough.

Finally Paratough stepped aside with a grunt. But several warriors had gathered for the confrontation, and Rebecca could read in their eyes that they were not certain Orahan was right to allow her and Travis to leave. "We will do nothing that will bring your people harm," she said in firm, loud tones.

Paratough snorted with disdain.

"Come," Orahan ordered curtly.

Quickly Rebecca and Travis followed him from the encampment.

Again Orahan set a fast pace. Fear gave Rebecca's legs the strength to carry her through the bog. But as they reached solid land, she came to a halt. "I must rest for a moment," she said tiredly.

Orahan frowned at her. "It is getting late. It is best if we reach your horses and you cross to the other side of the river before dark."

There was an urgency in the Indian's voice that caused Rebecca's fear to multiply. Clearly, although he had won the argument with Paratough back at the encampment, he was not certain they were out of danger. Travis made a move toward her, and she knew he intended to carry her once again. Humiliation mingled with a wave of excited expectation. Furious with herself for this wanton reaction, she rose. "I can walk."

Travis shrugged as if to say it made no difference to him and stepped back to allow her to take again the middle position in their single-file line. In truth, he was relieved she had chosen to walk. He did not like the reactions he was having toward her. It was best to keep some distance between himself and this woman.

The men did slow their pace a little to accommodate Rebecca. As a result it was dusk by the time they reached the horses.

"There is a place where the stream is shallow enough to make an easy crossing just beyond that bend," Orahan instructed.

"I remember it," Travis replied.

"Thank you," Rebecca said gratefully.

He scowled at her. "It was foolish of you to come."

Turning his attention back to Travis, he said, "I have done what I could to assure you a safe journey home, but sleep lightly and guard your back."

"I will heed your words," Travis replied.

Orahan nodded. Then, with the fleetness of a deer, he sprinted back down the path along which they had come.

Without a word Travis lifted Rebecca into her saddle. After mounting his own horse, he led the way toward the shallow strip of river. Darkness was almost upon them by the time they reached the other side.

Instead of following the riverbank, Travis led them into

the woods. They came to a clearing as the last rays of daylight left the sky.

"I think it would be best to sleep without a fire again," he said as he dismounted.

"I agree," Rebecca replied as she, too, dismounted and began unsaddling her horse. Her arms and legs ached, but she knew the animal needed attention first.

Finally the horses were freed of their burdens and tethered. Sinking down onto the ground beside the massive trunk of a tree, Rebecca ate her bread and cheese hungrily. A cool spring breeze stirred her hair, and she gave thanks that the place where they had crossed the river had been shallow and her skirt had not gotten wet.

Travis had seated himself against the trunk of a nearby tree as he ate. In the darkness she could not see his face distinctly, but she was certain he was watching her. Her hand went up to her hair. Half of it had escaped from the braid she had bound it in. Taking out the few pins that held the braid in a coil around her head, she unwound it, and, using her fingers, combed her hair as best she could before beginning to plait it once again. Suddenly she drew a harsh breath as her calf muscle knotted and her hands sought her leg.

Immediately Travis was by her side. "What is wrong?" he demanded in a harsh whisper.

"My leg," she replied, adding through teeth clenched tight against the pain, "It will be all right in a moment."

Ignoring her assurance, he caught the hem of her skirt and pulled it back. Next he pushed her petticoats back to reveal her leg.

"What do you think you are doing?" she hissed, trying to recover herself.

"I am going to massage your leg," he replied curtly. "We cannot afford to have you suddenly unable to stand if there should be danger. Now, sit still and be quiet."

Rebecca's cheeks went scarlet with rage. "You are no gentleman!"

"And keep your voice down!" he ordered. "Indians can't track in the dark, but they can follow sound."

Rebecca glared at his dark silhouette as he began to massage her cramped calf. She told herself she should feel only indignation, but instead his touch sent a tingling trail of heat traveling upward along her leg. Her pulse began to race, and primitive urges to which she had thought she was immune began to awaken within her. She closed her eyes tightly and ordered herself not to think of him, but her mind refused to obey. An insane desire for his hands to seek an even more intimate contact shocked her and at the same time sent her blood racing hot through her veins. As he deserted the first calf and began to massage the second, she had to fight to keep her breathing regular.

Travis told himself he was merely ministering to her out of necessity. But the firm flesh of her leg taunted him. The desire to explore further was tempting. Glancing up, he saw the full-rounded mounds of her breasts. She had a body that would tempt any man. Her disheveled ebony tresses cascaded over her shoulders and down her back. Envy that Thomas Mercer had been allowed to touch her freely gnawed at him.

Rebecca trembled as his massaging became stronger. Each time his hand traveled upward toward her knee, rivulets of heated expectation raced up her leg, taunting the very core of her womanliness. It was pure torture when the expectations were not met and his hand again traveled down her leg to her ankle. Balling her hands into fists, she tried not to think of him, but his touch filled her senses. She held her breath as his hands again moved toward her knee. The fire surged up her leg, and desire ignited with an intensity that caused her to gasp.

"I am trying not to hurt you," he said with gruff apology. "But your muscles are very taut."

She tried to respond, but her vocal cords refused to work.

He looked at her then. The moonlight was dim, but he could see her eyes were closed. When her teeth closed over her bottom lip, he smiled. It had not been a gasp of pain. He knew it wasn't wise to persist, but he could not resist. Very cautiously his movements became more caressing.

Rebecca felt the change, and her heart pounded harder. When she noticed his breathing becoming irregular, a womanly satisfaction filled her. So he wasn't as disinterested in her as he wanted her to believe. Or maybe he's just interested in a warm body on a cool spring night, she chided herself. But her body didn't care what his motives were. The desire to spread her legs and encourage his touch to move higher grew with each passing moment. She had never believed any man could awaken her senses like this. There was almost an urgency about it.

We could die tonight, she heard herself reasoning. Why not give in? Only the sounds of their breathing and the horses grazing filled the night air. Silhouetted in the moonlight, she saw his shoulders stiffen with purpose. When his hands moved upward this time, they did not stop below the knee but moved slightly above it. Oh, how she wanted those strong hands to continue. Rivers of fire surged to the very core of her being. She knew that she had only to shift slightly, part her legs a little, and he would accept the invitation.

Braced against her saddle, she studied his hairy profile. She wondered how his beard would feel if he kissed her. Her tongue came out to wet suddenly dry lips. She wanted to feel his weight upon her. She wanted to feel his strength within her. Her legs started to part. But in a last flash of sanity the thought of allowing him to totally possess her brought a sudden rush of fear. It was too risky. She could not give in to this mindless lust. Her legs tightened. "I think I will be fine now, sir," she said stiffly, marveling at how calm her voice sounded while her body felt as if it were going to be consumed by a raging fire.

For a moment he considered challenging her demand for a withdrawal. He'd felt her body responding. The heat traveled from her leg up his arm. He ached to know her fully.

Rebecca held her breath as she watched him. If he did not stop, she was not certain she had the strength to refuse him. She most certainly did not have the strength to fight him. Even knowing the danger, her body throbbed with desire.

Travis took a deep breath. He needed this woman's aid. If he persisted, and she gave herself to him, she might hate him afterward. Women, he had observed, could be extremely unpredictable. Abruptly he released her and pulled her petticoats and skirt down over her. Then he rose in one fluid movement and returned to the tree where his saddle and bedroll awaited him.

A part of her was relieved, but another part was resentful that he had accepted her rejection so easily. Obviously the fire she had ignited within him had been more akin to a weak ember.

Determined to ignore her disquieting companion, Rebecca leaned back against her saddle. 'Tis the danger and the worry for my brother that is affecting my mind, she reasoned tersely. When we are back at Green Glen, my emotions will once again return to normal. Covering herself with her bedroll, she curled up on the ground and closed her eyes. But she did not immediately go to sleep. Instead, questions about the man who lay a few feet away from her again rose in her mind. So very little was known about him.

She found herself wondering why he didn't number himself among her suitors. Green Glen was a prize most any man would seek. It was rumored that he had come to the colonies to make his fortune in order to wed a woman whose family had judged him of insufficient means. Susan, Rebecca's personal maid, a pretty, slightly plump strawberry blond nineteen years of age with a healthy imagination, thought that during the time he was being held captive by the Indians, his lady had wed someone else and now he had no use for any woman. That seemed as reasonable an explanation as any, Rebecca concluded. But she could not help wondering, should this story be true, if his lady love had found a man with so enticing a touch. Just the memory of his hands upon her reawakened the fire within her. 'Tis an insanity, she chided herself. Allowing the exhaustion of the day to take hold, she dozed.

Suddenly she was awakened by an angry cry. Startled, her body jerked into a sitting position. Two dark forms were wrestling in the middle of the clearing. One was Travis, the other an Indian. There was no doubt in her mind that the Indian was Paratough. Remembering the muscular build of the savage, fear shook her. Quickly she tossed off her bedroll and rose to her feet.

Moonlight gave an eerie illumination to the clearing. Her eye caught the glistening of steel. The Indian had a knife! She picked up her pistol. But the men were moving too much for her to be certain of her aim.

Tossing the weapon aside, she moved to where Travis had left his musket. She could not fire it with any greater safety than she could the pistol, but it would make a good club.

Suddenly the men broke apart. Both were on their feet in an instant. Paratough laughed with triumph as he threw the knife at Travis. But Travis was quicker than the Indian expected. He fell and rolled and the knife missed, embedding itself in a tree.

There was pure hatred in the cry that escaped Paratough's lips as he lunged at Travis, intent on killing the trapper with his bare hands.

So intent was he on Travis that he did not notice Rebecca. Taking a step forward, she swung the musket and caught the Indian in the stomach.

As the Indian crumpled to the ground, Travis grabbed his knife. Flipping Paratough over, he placed the finely honed blade against the Indian's neck.

Rebecca held her breath, waiting for the final blow to be delivered. But instead, Travis spoke to the Indian. Unable to understand the Indian tongue, Rebecca could only watch as the two men conversed grimly.

She saw Paratough raise his hand in a sign of agreement, and Travis lifted the knife from his throat and rose. In the next instant the Indian had sprung to his feet and disappeared into the darkened woods.

"Do you think it was wise to allow him to leave?" she questioned, still holding the musket.

"He was trying to protect his people," Travis replied. "This time he believed my assurance that we meant them no harm."

She was certain any of the other men she knew would have slain the savage without a second thought. "You have a much gentler soul than your manner or appearance would suggest," she mused.

"I merely refused to kill a man unnecessarily," he replied dryly. "This way we have no body to dispose of."

Rebecca scowled at herself. She had tried to give him sensitivities he did not possess.

"Could you spare a bit of petticoat?" he asked. "That knife must have grazed my arm as it flew past."

She heard the edge of pain in his voice. Quickly, she set the musket aside and approached him. The slashed clothing was being soaked with blood. "You will have to take your shirt and coat off," she said, already working the fastenings of the coat free, then helping him remove his shirt. Her hands threatened to tremble as the broad expanse of dark-haired chest was revealed. "If you sit, I can work with your arm much easier," she directed, fighting the urge to run her hands through the crisp, curly hair and feel the hardness of his flesh beneath her palm. You're behaving as if you've never seen a man without clothing before, she mocked herself.

Without speaking, he obeyed.

After ripping off a wide strip of petticoat, she knelt beside him. The wound was not as deep as she had first suspected. Already the blood was beginning to flow more slowly.

Carefully she bound the arm securely. To her relief, the bandaging seemed to bring a complete halt to the bleeding.

"That should do until we reach Green Glen," she said stiffly.

He stretched the arm. "You have a gentle touch."

Her face was level with his. She could see him watching her, his expression unreadable. Her gaze shifted to his shoulders and down to his chest. Again she felt the fires of lust beginning to burn within her. "We should put your shirt back on before you become chilled." To her chagrin there was a shakiness in her voice.

The uneven tremor in her words was not lost on Travis. He knew he was looking for trouble, but the feel of her hands against his arm had brought his desire for her back stronger than before. As she reached for the garment, he raised the hand of his wounded arm until it came to rest lazily on her hip. With the other he cupped her chin. "There are other ways than clothing to warm a man," he said gruffly.

And a woman, she hear herself thinking wildly. But it was too dangerous. She could be risking Green Glen. But as she opened her mouth to protest, he claimed it, his hand tangling in her hair to hold her captive. His beard brushed against her cheek and her throat. It was not scratchy as she had thought it might be. Instead, there was only a mild coarseness that tantalized her skin.

She pressed her hands against his chest and ordered them to push him away. But as they flattened against the solid wall of hair-roughened muscle, heat shot up her arms, sapping them of their strength.

Travis smiled against her lips at her lack of resistance. She did desire him as much as he desired her.

Frantic, Rebecca again ordered herself to fight him. Strength returned to her arms, but as she pressed against his chest, his muscles rippled beneath her palms, and a hot surge of passion again weakened her resolve.

Teasingly Travis's mouth played over hers. Gently he

caught her bottom lip in his teeth, then released it. She trembled with delight as tiny tinglings of pleasure filled her.

Drawing a ragged breath, his desire for her grew to a strength that stunned him by its power. His hand moved from her hip upward to the small of her back. Forcing her to move with him, he laid her down.

Half pinned beneath his large bulk, she reveled in the feel of him . . . his thigh burning its imprint into her, his chest pressed against hers. But most exciting was his mouth. His tongue darted in to hers, and deep in her abdomen the center of her womanhood tightened with impatience. When his tongue entered a second time, her lips closed around it. He gave a deep-throated laugh of satisfaction, and this time he pulled it out more slowly.

When he began unfastening her riding habit, her modesty vanished and she moved to help him. Deserting her mouth, he trailed kisses to the hollow of her throat. With his tongue he greeted her breast, and she moaned with pleasure. All reason was gone. She twisted beneath him, searching for a firmer contact with him, and felt his ready maleness. Her womanly core throbbed with the need to welcome him.

"The way you have dallied in choosing a husband had led me to believe that Thomas Mercer's lovemaking was of the kind that had left you indifferent to the pleasures a man could bring you," he said gruffly, deserting the nipple that had hardened quickly under the gentle teasing of his tongue and kissing the firm roundness of her breast. "But it is clear you have missed having a man in your bed."

The mention of her late husband caused Rebecca to stiffen. Ugly memories assailed her. Her instinct for survival shouted that this could go no further. Jerking free, she rolled away from him.

"What the devil!" he demanded, finding himself suddenly alone.

Scrambling to her feet, Rebecca turned away from him and began refastening her clothing. Suddenly a hand with an iron grip closed around her arm.

With a forceful jerk Travis turned her to face him. "I don't like women who play games," he growled.

"I was not playing a game with you," she replied. The anger in his eyes frightened her, but still she stood her ground. " 'Tis you who were taking advantage of a woman in a weakened state caused by fear of savages and for her brother's life."

For a long moment his hand remained painfully tight around her arm, then with a snort of disgust, he released her. Stalking over to his bedroll, he pulled on his shirt and coat. "You best get some rest. We leave at the first light," he ordered her coldly.

Walking with stiff dignity, she returned to her bedroll. She did not have the nerve to look toward him as she lay down and covered herself. She knew she had made a fool of herself and very possibly an enemy of him. She could not understand how she could have behaved so wantonly. For so many years she had held her emotions in check. Now, suddenly, this man was capable of unleashing them with a single touch. I must not let my guard down again, she instructed herself harshly.

As Rebecca lay down on her side of the clearing, Travis sat grimly watching her. He was furious with himself. He had let lust rule his mind. But it hadn't been entirely his fault. His anger turned toward Rebecca. To tempt a man once and then turn away could be forgivable. But to do it a second time showed a meanness of character. Reminding himself that it was information he needed from the lady— and *not* her body—he dozed.

THREE

THE next morning, as they prepared for their journey, Travis treated Rebecca with polite but cool indifference.

She was determined to treat him the same. But as he swung his saddle up onto his horse, she saw him wince with pain, and a sharp shaft of sister pain ran up her own arm. 'Tis only because I feel guilty. 'Tis my fault he is here and hurt, she reasoned. Aloud she said stiffly, "You must be careful not to reopen your wound. When we reach Green Glen, I will see that it is cleaned and dressed properly."

"There is no need for you to concern yourself," he replied, keeping his attention on his work. The last thing he wanted was for her to start touching him again. Even after two nights in the wilderness, with her clothes mussed and her hair in disarray, she was a tempting sight. He tried to mask a second wince as he tightened his saddle.

Suddenly worried that he might cause damage to his arm by saddling her horse as well, she quickly threw her saddle blanket over her horse's back and then her saddle. As she tightened the cinch, she told herself that it would be safer to keep this man as an enemy. But she could not make herself completely turn her back upon him. "I owe you my life and very possibly my brother's life. You will allow me to repay you by seeing to your wound," she said with authority as she finished tying her bedroll in place and mounted.

"As you wish," he replied. He would accept her aid,

49

hoping it would give him an opportunity to learn what he needed to know. But he would keep his distance. She would not play him for a fool again.

They rode hard all day, eating their breakfast and lunch in the saddle. Night was falling by the time they saw the lights of Green Glen.

Joseph came hurrying out of the house to greet them as they rode up. "Mistress Mercer, Mr. Brandt, 'tis the answer to our prayers. You've arrived back safely."

"How is my brother?" Rebecca demanded as she dismounted.

"About the same," Joseph replied.

"Mistress Mercer, 'tis good to have you home." It was Philip James, the butler at Green Glen who spoke. Sixty years of age, lean and bent with age and the ache, he was forced to follow Joseph at a slower pace.

"We've no time to waste," Rebecca said urgently. "Rouse Mildred and have her make a broth of this." She unfastened the pouch Oparchan had given her and handed it to Joseph. As he started to obey, she added, "Also have her set an extra pan of water to boiling. Mr. Brandt has a knife wound that will need cleaning."

Joseph paused to give a hurried bow to show he had heard, then continued quickly toward the servants' quarters.

Rebecca glanced toward Travis. The sight of him brought back the embarrassing memories of the night before. She would have preferred to see that his wound was tended and immediately send him on his way, but politeness forced her to say, "Will you accept my hospitality and rest the night here before returning to your cabin?"

Travis heard the edge of hesitation in her voice. He was certain that once this night was over, Mistress Mercer would work to avoid ever speaking to him in private again. He could not lose this opportunity. He bowed deeply. "I thank you for your hospitality. A warm place to hang my hat for the night will be appreciated."

Rebecca fought not to show her surprise that he had

accepted her invitation. She had been certain he was as anxious to part company with her as she was to part company with him. "Philip, have the horses looked after and a room prepared for Mr. Brandt," she ordered. Again moving toward the house, she added over her shoulder, "I must go to Daniel."

Her pace increased with urgency, and she took the stairs two at a time. Entering Daniel's room, she found him looking thinner and paler than he had only two days earlier.

"Mistress Mercer, I'm so glad you're back," Ruth greeted Rebecca with a gasp of relief. "He's been calling for you."

Rebecca moved to the bedside and touched Daniel's heat-flushed face. "I prayed he would be better when I arrived," she said with a catch in her voice.

"Were you able to find the Mattaponi?" Ruth asked anxiously.

Rebecca nodded. "Oparchan gave me some medicine. Mildred is preparing it now. We must pray it works." Leaning down close to Daniel, she said gently, "You're going to be fine."

His eyelids flickered slightly but did not open.

Too frantic with worry to pace the floor of the bedroom until the broth arrived, Rebecca went out to the kitchen. There she found Naddie Burnes, the apprentice cook, stirring the broth while Mildred ministered to Travis's arm. Naddie, like Susan, was nineteen. But unlike Susan, she was dark-haired and dark-eyed and had a less optimistic view of the world. She felt certain that Mr. Brandt was a criminal. It was her belief that he had been sent to the colonies to be auctioned into servitude for the rest of his life or some portion thereof. Somehow he had escaped from the ship and had grown a beard and mustache so that he would not be recognized. Out of the corner of her eye she was watching him as if she expected him to rise up and slay the lot of them at any moment.

Rebecca wished she could ignore Travis, but that would

be impolite. The light from the fire played on his back, giving definition to the strong musculature, and she found herself recalling the firm, warm feel of his skin beneath her hands. Stop it! she ordered herself. "How is the wound, Mildred?" she asked, trying to concentrate on the injury and ignore the way the sight of him caused her blood to race hot through her veins.

"It will heal," the cook announced with authority. " 'Tis not as deep as the bleeding might have led you to think."

"Good." Feeling her duty done, Rebecca quickly turned her attention to the broth Naddie was stirring. "Is it ready?" she asked anxiously.

"Couldn't say," the girl answered, wrinkling her nose in an expression of distaste. "Smells right ripe to me."

Rebecca took the stirring spoon from the girl and scooped a spoonful of the broth out of the pot for a closer look.

"I would allow it to simmer for a few minutes more," Travis suggested as he pulled on his shirt.

Rebecca handed the spoon back to the girl. "Then I will," she said. "You have a greater knowledge of Indians and their ways than I." Again she found her gaze drawn to him. He looked tired, and there were lines of pain etched into his face. Her stomach knotted with sympathy for him, and the urge to place an arm around his waist to give him support was strong. In her mind's eye she saw the look of shocked horror she was certain would show itself on Naddie's face and a giggle began to build in her throat. It was nerves. This man's presence had her nearly unraveled. 'Tis not him. 'Tis fatigue and fear for Daniel, she told herself. Swallowing back the giggle, she said with cool politeness, "If you will follow me, I will show you to your room." Glancing toward Mildred, she added, "Prepare a meal for Mr. Brandt and see that it is taken to him." Shifting her attention to Naddie, she said, "Give the broth ten more minutes, then bring it to Daniel's room. Do not enter the room, simply knock, and Ruth or I will take it."

"Yes, ma'am," Naddie agreed, clearly relieved she was not to enter the sick room.

"You run a very efficient household," Travis remarked as he followed Rebecca back toward the main house.

"That is Thomas's teaching," she replied. "He was a man who insisted upon order in his life."

He had intended to make light conversation. But the swing of her hips was reminding him too strongly of how she had led him on, then drawn away. The sharp sting of having been played a fool caused him to say, "I understand you were a mere sixteen and he was better than forty when you married him. I suppose you were drawn to his *maturity*."

The sarcasm in his voice was like a slap in the face. He thought she had married Thomas Mercer for his wealth. "The marriage was arranged between Mr. Mercer and my father. My mother had died some months earlier giving birth to my brother. My father was not the kind of man who could deal with raising a family on his own. In exchange for my hand in marriage, Mr. Mercer agreed to provide a comfortable home for my brother and myself," she replied coldly, then flushed when she realized how open she had been. She had never justified herself to anyone before. Nor had she ever told the truth behind her marriage. She had known there were rumors about her using her youth to trap the wealthy planter into marriage. But she had ignored them. When subtle and some not so subtle remarks had been made about the differences in their ages, she had replied with exaggerated admiration of her husband's kindness and gentlemanly ways.

"A very practical arrangement," he mused, a cynical edge remaining in his voice.

Coming to a halt, Rebecca turned to face him. He had no right to think badly of her! "I was a good wife to Thomas Mercer, and if you have heard any differently, you have heard a lie."

Again Travis chided himself. This behavior was not

going to gain him what he needed from this woman. Besides, she was right. While he had heard a few snide remarks regarding her youth, no one had accused her of mistreating her husband or causing him grief. Looking properly chastised, he bowed deeply. "I apologize, madam, for any rudeness."

Watching him, Rebecca was not certain if he was sincere or merely mocking her. His expression was unreadable as he straightened. How could she have felt any attraction toward such a callous boor? The urge to withdraw her invitation of a night's lodging was strong. But she forced herself to remember that he had saved her life. Her head held high with dignity, she continued toward the main house in silence.

As they reached his room, her manners once again forced her to converse with him. "My husband was not as tall as you, but he was heavier," she said stiffly. "His clothing should fit you well enough. I will bring you a nightshirt and a day shirt for the morning. In the meantime I will see that your shirt and coat are mended and cleaned."

"That is most gracious of you," he replied evenly.

Again she found herself wondering if his politeness was genuine. Curtly she told herself what Travis Brandt was thinking was of no importance. Dropping a quick curtsy in answer to his bow, she left him and went to the attic. As she opened one of the trunks containing Thomas Mercer's effects, she remembered the brooch. But she had no time to search now. Daniel was a much more pressing concern. Quickly she found a nightshirt and a day shirt and carried them back to Travis Brandt's room.

When he opened the door in answer to her knock, he was bare from the waist upward. The sight of his hard, flat abdomen and the dark curly hair on his chest stirred memories that caused her legs to weaken. Furious with herself, she curtly handed him the clean clothing and took his slashed garments without a word.

Carrying them with her, she returned to Daniel's room.

Ruth looked up at her questioningly as Rebecca dropped the clothing on a chair as if it was distasteful to her touch. "Mr. Brandt's clothes are in need of mending," she explained coolly. "I will send them down with Naddie when she arrives with the broth."

Ruth watched her mistress with concern. "I do hope he was not vulgar as a companion. Joseph and I were relieved to know someone was out looking for you." Disgust showed on her face. "Mr. Kirby and Mr. Loyde both expressed grave misgivings for your safety, but neither volunteered to go after you, and Mr. Garnet did not even show his face here. He merely sent a message saying he would pray for both you and Daniel."

"Mr. Brandt was a gentleman at all times," Rebecca lied. Besides, she could not blame him for what had happened between them. It was as much her fault as his. Fairness made her add, "He even saved my life."

Ruth smiled with relief. "Then I am pleased he followed you." Concern returned to her face. "You should have a bite to eat and then rest. You look exhausted."

For the first time Rebecca remembered that she was still in her riding habit. She caught a glimpse of herself in the mirror. Her clothing and face were in dire need of a cleaning, and her hair looked as if it had not been combed in a week.

"I will tend to Daniel. You go see to your own needs," Ruth ordered in motherly tones, adding, "You don't want to frighten the boy when he does open his eyes."

Ruth was right, Rebecca conceded after another quick glance at the mirror. Besides, she was feeling grimy. A quick wash and a change of clothes would make her more fit for the night-long vigil beside Daniel's bed. "You must see that he swallows some of the broth," she instructed.

"I will be certain of it," Ruth assured her.

Rebecca's gaze traveled to the chair on which Travis Brandt's garments lay. "And instruct Naddie to see to Mr.

Brandt's clothing," she added. She wanted no reminders of the trapper in the room upon her return.

Shifting her gaze back to Daniel, she continued to stare worriedly at him for another long moment, then with a resigned sigh went to her own room. A fire was blazing in the hearth, and a warm kettle of water sat near it. Susan jumped up quickly from the chair where she had been waiting for her mistress. "You look as if you could do with a bit of washing and combing," she observed, her blue eyes sparkling with interest and her strawberry-blond curls bobbing gently below the hem of her cap. She smiled brightly, causing a dimple to appear in her slightly chubby cheek as she poured the warm water into a basin. "Been worried to death I was about you out there with those savages. 'Tis a true relief to have you home safe." Her eyes brightened even more. "When I were down fetching your water, I heard tell Mr. Brandt was wounded by one of those savages. Must have been a frightful journey."

"It was one I would not wish to make again," Rebecca admitted, beginning to work the fastenings of her clothing loose.

As she hurried to assist, Susan said in an amused voice, "Naddie was all worried Mr. Brandt would murder you in your sleep or worse." She shook her head and sent her curls bobbing again. "That girl talks like there was a black cloud hanging over her head. I told her you was lucky to have a man like Mr. Brandt as a protector." Pausing for a moment as she finished with a tie, Susan regarded Rebecca with open interest, then added with a thoughtful frown, "Though he is a mite grim for my taste. He always seems to be watching people as if he's trying to read their thoughts. Even Joseph has said the man has made him uncomfortable a time or two."

Rebecca frowned. So she wasn't the only one who had been made uneasy by Travis Brandt's inspection. However, she was in no mood to discuss the trapper. "I'm feeling hungry," she said, changing the subject. "I will finish undressing on my own. Go to the kitchen and have Mildred fix me a bite to eat."

Susan looked momentarily disgruntled. Obviously she had hoped for a bit more gossip about the man in the guest room. Then her good-natured smile returned. "Yes, ma'am," she said and, after a quick curtsy, left the room.

Alone, Rebecca finished removing her clothing and washed herself. By the time Susan returned, she was pulling on a clean shift. She allowed the girl to brush her hair and rebraid it while she ate. Then, going to her wardrobe, she chose a fresh dress.

"You should be going to bed," Susan admonished. "You look as if you are ready to drop."

"I will sleep in a chair in my brother's room," Rebecca replied in a tone that left no room for argument.

Susan shook her head but said no more as she helped her mistress finish dressing.

Ruth looked shocked when Rebecca reentered Daniel's room. "You should be resting."

"I will rest here," Rebecca replied, seating herself in a chair beside Daniel's bed. Glancing toward the bowl of broth on the table, she frowned worriedly. "Did he swallow some?"

"Some," Ruth replied. "I am letting him sleep. Then I will give him a bit more."

"You look as if you could use some rest yourself," Rebecca observed, seeing the lines of fatigue etched deeply into the housekeeper's face. "Go to your room and sleep. I will stay with my brother."

"I will stay, also," Ruth insisted.

"Go," Rebecca ordered. "Daniel needs at least one of us rested, and I cannot sleep until I have some hope he will recover."

Shaking her head at the stubbornness of her mistress, Ruth curtsied and left.

Alone in Daniel's room, Rebecca rose from her chair and sank to her knees on the floor. With her elbows resting on

the bed, she bowed her head in prayer. She felt as scared
and alone as she had the day her mother had died. She could
not lose Daniel. Fervently she prayed for his recovery.

"You should be resting," a man's voice interrupted.

Startled, she jerked around to find Travis Brandt standing
a short distance behind her, his expression unreadable.
"And you should not be in here," she countered, rising.

The grimness in his eyes deepened as he moved toward
the bed, and honest concern etched itself into his face. "I
was worried about Daniel. I wanted to see for myself how
he was faring."

"He is the same," she informed him, her voice threatening to break. Holding back the tears of fear that burned at
the back of her eyes, she moved to the table and picked up
the bowl of broth. Taking a seat on the opposite side of the
bed from where the man was standing, she slipped her arm
under Daniel's shoulders to elevate his head, then gently
coaxed a spoonful of the liquid into his mouth. To her relief
she saw his neck muscles working and knew he had
swallowed it. She expected Travis to leave. When he did
not, she glanced up toward him. Even in Thomas's ill-
fitting shirt, Travis Brandt looked like a man of authority.
She suddenly found herself wanting him to hold her, as if
being in his arms would give her strength. Mortified and
furious with herself, she said with dismissal, "I cannot
guarantee your safety if you remain."

"I am willing to take my chances," he replied, seating
himself across from her. As cold-hearted as he believed her
to be, he had to admit that her devotion to her brother was
genuine.

A heavy silence filled the room as she continued to feed
Daniel. When he had finished the entire bowl, she laid him
gently back on his pillow. The pot of broth was being kept
warm on the hearth, but she decided that she should wait
awhile before feeding him more. Setting the bowl aside, she
straightened, shifting her shoulders as she stretched.

Leaning forward, Travis laid his hand on the boy's brow. "The fever is still strong," he said with a worried frown.

Rebecca merely nodded. Leaning back in her chair, she closed her eyes. Every muscle in her body ached. She heard Travis's chair creak as he, too, sat back. She'd hoped he would leave.

For a long moment Travis studied her. He knew she didn't want him there, and he was more certain than ever that she would avoid his company entirely once he had left her house in the morning. The boy was asleep. This might be the only opportunity he would have to speak to her alone. He was not certain how to begin. Bluntly, he decided. "Have you ever considered the possibility that your late husband's death was not an accident?"

The question caused Rebecca's eyes to pop open. From across the bed Travis was studying her narrowly. She scowled at him. "Are you now going to suggest that I murdered him?" she demanded curtly.

He continued to regard her levelly. "No. I have checked. You were with Mistress Howard all that afternoon."

Rebecca's face flushed scarlet. He had actually considered it possible that she might have killed Thomas. The idea that anyone had murdered Thomas was absurd. But to have suspected her was an insult. "Perhaps I had an accomplice," she suggested cynically, her manner ridiculing him.

"I gave that some thought, also," he admitted. "But I don't believe so. The only logical accomplice would be one of your suitors with whom you were having an illicit liaison. If that were the case, you would surely have married him by now."

Rebecca drew a shaky breath. Thank goodness she had not given in to the fires his touch had ignited. "There is no one who would have done my husband harm," she said with assurance. "To even consider that his death was more than an accident is preposterous. He was riding alone. His horse was frightened and reared or it stumbled and tossed him forward. He fell into the ravine and unhappily hit his head upon a boulder."

Travis frowned as if to say he refused to believe this story. "Your husband was an expert horseman."

"Even expert horsemen have accidents," she insisted. Her jaw tensed with self-righteous indignation. "Mr. Brandt, my marriage to my husband was not easily accepted. For years I was whispered about behind my back. But I was a good wife to Thomas Mercer, and gradually people came to approve of our union. It is not fair or right of you to present this preposterous notion and again make me the brunt of unpleasant gossip."

"I have no intention of making my theory regarding your husband's death public," he assured her coolly.

Rebecca stared at him in confusion. "Then why have you presented it to me?"

"Because I have need of a few answers." In spite of his efforts to show no emotion, the blue of his eyes darkened in frustration. "I had hopes of finding those answers on my own. But during the months I've been here, I have discovered nothing."

"Because there is nothing to discover," she interjected curtly.

Travis gave an impatient snort. "Your husband died within a week of returning home from Jamestown. It is my belief that his death was due to the brooch."

Rebecca stared at him as if she was not certain he was fully sane. "The brooch you asked me about in the woods?" she questioned, finding it difficult to believe that a piece of jewelry could lead to a man's death.

Travis's expression became grim. "Yes."

Rebecca continued to frown in confusion. "Even if what you say is true, I don't know how I could help you. I have no knowledge of this brooch."

"I need to know with whom your husband met during the days following his return."

Now it was Rebecca's turn to study the trapper narrowly.

All the time she had thought he had merely found her and the rest of the community cynically amusing, he had been spying on them. She wanted to know why. "First you must tell me how the brooch could have caused my husband's death," she bargained.

He shook his head. "If my suspicions are correct, that knowledge could get you killed."

"I already know there was a brooch. Sometimes a little knowledge can be more dangerous than a lot if a person does not know why there is danger," she reasoned.

He scowled at her darkly. Rebecca Mercer was assuredly the most difficult woman he had ever had the misfortune to encounter. "This is no time for you to indulge in the idle whim of female curiosity."

Rebecca glared at him. "You suggest that my husband was murdered, and when I ask why, you accuse me of indulging in idle curiosity! Mr. Brandt, if you wish my cooperation, I demand to know why a brooch could be so important as to cost a man his life."

The scowl on Travis's face deepened further. He needed the information. He had warned her it could be dangerous. But maybe she had a point. If she understood the danger, she might be safer . . . as long as she believed there was truly a threat to anyone with knowledge of the brooch's history. Her husband had lost his life because he had treated the danger too lightly. "Eighteen years ago a lady and her maid were traveling from London to the country estate of the lady's father, the Earl of Dormott. They were stopped by a highwayman. He demanded the lady's jewels. The maid handed him a small chest, hoping he would leave without opening it. But he looked inside to discover that she had attempted to fool him. It was not the chest that held the jewels. He demanded that the correct chest be given him at once. This time the maid obeyed. He had her dump the jewels into his saddlebags, then telling her that she must pay for her earlier act of deceit, he shot her through the heart, then mounted and rode away. The maid was my mother."

In spite of the anger she felt toward him, the sadness that suddenly came into his eyes tore at Rebecca's heart. "I am sorry."

He shrugged as if to say what was done was done. "The old earl attempted to find the thief by tracing the jewels as they were sold. Each time, however, a go-between was used, and that person was found murdered shortly after the purchase was completed. Then, twelve years ago, a piece was sold here in the colonies. I begged His Lordship to allow me to come and investigate. He agreed. But the thief had again used his trick of hiring a go-between and then killing the man. I could find out nothing. But I was certain the thief had come here to begin a new life with the wealth his robberies had provided for him. I wrote His Lordship asking him to release me from his service and allow me to remain here to seek out the murderer. He consented to my wishes, and with his blessing I remained. But my luck ran bad, and I was captured by the Indians. When I was freed, I began searching, but by then the trail was cold. Then the brooch suddenly appeared."

"It was definitely one of the pieces that had been stolen?" Rebecca questioned, finding herself drawn into sympathy with his search.

"Yes." Anger glistened in Travis's eyes. "And if your husband had not been so stubborn, he would be alive today and my quest would be ended."

"Why do you say that?" she asked when his brooding pause lengthened uncomfortably.

"I arranged for one of the most respected solicitors in Jamestown to speak with your husband regarding the brooch. I would have spoken to him myself, but I have learned caution. The man I seek is treacherous. I did not want my identity known to him for fear he would elude me forever." He drew a shallow breath. "Perhaps that was a mistake. Perhaps I should have spoken directly with your husband. Perhaps I could have convinced him of the immediacy of the situation."

"My husband was not an easy man to convince of anything once his mind was set," Rebecca said.

Travis nodded in agreement. "So I surmised. Anyway, when the solicitor asked Thomas Mercer where he had gotten the jewelry, Mr. Mercer refused to tell him. Your husband explained that the person from whom he had purchased the brooch had asked him to keep his identity a secret. The seller did not want the unexpected financial reversal in which he found himself to become public knowledge. The solicitor promised not to disclose the name but insisted that it was a matter of grave importance that he find out who had sold Mr. Mercer the brooch. Your husband said he would agree to disclose the name of the seller only if he was told why the inquiry was being made and judged it to be as important as the solicitor proclaimed. When the solicitor explained, Mr. Mercer was appalled. He assured my man that the person from whom he had purchased it could not be the man he sought. Further, he said he would not tarnish the name of a friend by linking it with such deviltry. He insisted that he would speak to this friend, and when he had determined where his friend had come upon the jewel, he would write and inform us. But he did not write. Instead, he had a fatal accident."

A chill ran along Rebecca's spine. "And you think that my husband was murdered by the same man who killed your mother?"

"And he is a man your husband considered a friend," Travis added. "I believe your husband was killed because the thief had begun to feel safe and had not used a go-between this time. When your husband faced him with my story, he probably lied about having bought the jewel somewhere else. But he knew the lie wouldn't hold, so he had to murder Thomas Mercer."

The faces of the men in their community ran through Rebecca's mind as she tried to picture one as a murderer. "What you have said is very difficult to believe."

" 'Tis the truth," he growled.

The faces vanished as she once again gave him her full attention. She could not deny the honesty in his voice. "I did not say I did not believe you. I said it was difficult to believe. You are telling me that a man who has very likely supped at my table is a cold-blooded murderer."

Travis's gaze fixed on her. "Then you will tell me with whom your husband met after his return from Jamestown?"

Rebecca nodded. "I will help you as much as I can. If Thomas was murdered, I owe it to him to see that his killer is brought to justice." Pausing, she drew a tired breath. "But it has been a long time since his death. I cannot remember all that happened. However, I will allow you to look through his appointment calender." Frowning, she added, "If you cannot read, I will tell you what is in it."

At least she is being reasonable, Travis thought with relief. He had been afraid that she might prove to be as stubborn as her husband. Aloud, he said, " 'Tis most kind of you to allow me to review your husband's appointments. Also, your offer of assistance is most appreciated. However, His Lordship took pity on me being an orphan and saw that I was properly educated."

Although he spoke politely, Rebecca could have sworn that Travis Brandt was relieved he would not require her services. "Wait here," she instructed. Leaving him, she went to the study. After Thomas's death, she had determined what books and papers were of importance in the operation of Green Glen and placed all other materials belonging to her husband in the large trunk below the window. Opening it, she found his appointment book.

Walking back to Daniel's room, Rebecca had to admit that Travis Brandt's determination to seek out his mother's murderer was admirable. But that did not excuse the insults he had delivered to her this night.

Entering the room, she handed him the book. "You may keep it for as long as is necessary."

"You have my eternal gratitude," he replied politely.

His fingers touched hers as he accepted the bound

volume. To her chagrin, currents of heat rushed up her arm.
Curtly she reminded herself that he had spent months spying
on her and her neighbors. Not only that, he had actually
considered the possibility that she had murdered her husband. Determined to face the full callousness of his nature,
she said tersely, "The only reason you came after me was
because you wanted this information, wasn't it, sir?"

He met her gaze levelly. "It did occur to me that if
something should happen to you, the trail I was following
might be lost forever."

She expected to feel a wave of triumph at having been
proved right. Instead, it caused a hurtful sting. Angry with
herself, she turned toward Daniel, and another thought
came to mind. She glanced back at Travis accusingly. "You
used my brother to get information about me. While you
were pretending to be his friend, you were using him to
spy."

"I admit when I first met Daniel, that was my intention,"
he replied honestly. "However, I have come to truly care for
the boy."

The sincerity in his voice rang true. But Rebecca was in
no mood to think kindly of the trapper.

Travis saw the disdain on her face. He told himself it was
of no consequence what she thought of him. Still, he heard
himself saying gruffly, "And it was not merely for the
knowledge you might possess that caused me to come after
you. Daniel needs you, and I could not in good conscience
allow you to go off and get yourself killed on a fool-hardy
errand."

Rebecca glared at him. He was definitely the most
irritating man she had ever encountered. " 'Tis time for me
to wake Daniel and feed him again," she said with firm
authority. "And 'tis time for you to leave us."

Travis had what he had come for. He told himself it did
not matter that there was animosity between them now. In
fact, it was probably better this way, he reasoned. She was
a distraction he did not need. Bowing low, he left the room.

Concentrating on Daniel, Rebecca ladled another bowl of the broth from the pot on the hearth. Seating herself beside the bed, she again spoke to her brother as she lifted him into a semiseated position. This time his eyelids fluttered open. But his gaze was glassy. Still, it was a good sign, she told herself. He drank the broth, then went immediately back to sleep.

Ruth came in a short while later and insisted that Rebecca go to her room and sleep. Giving in to her exhaustion, Rebecca conceded.

In her room she removed only her shoes before lying down on the bed. She had no intention of actually sleeping. She wanted only to rest a few minutes, and then she would return to Daniel's bedside. But exhaustion overtook her.

The sun was peeking over the horizon when Ruth's happy voice woke her. " 'Tis Daniel," the housekeeper was saying excitedly. "His fever is broken. He's awake and demanding food."

Rebecca was up in an instant. She ran to Daniel's room and found him sitting up in bed. He was still pale, but his eyes had lost their glassiness. "You scared me nearly to death," she admonished him lovingly as she rushed over and gave him a hug. He still felt a bit warm to her touch, but it was clear the fever was leaving his body.

"I'm starving," he pleaded.

"Go fetch him some breakfast," Rebecca ordered Ruth with a laugh, giving her brother another hug. As the housekeeper left, she released him. "And you must lie down."

Obeying without an argument, he frowned thoughtfully. "I had the most curious dream. I dreamt that Travis—" Remembering his manners, he stopped and corrected himself, "Mr. Brandt was here once when I awoke."

"He was," Rebecca replied.

Daniel stared up at her in disbelief. "He was?"

"He was worried about you," Rebecca offered in explanation.

"And he's very glad to see that you are better," Travis's voice sounded from the doorway.

Rebecca was shocked by the sight of the gentle smile that spread over the trapper's face as he looked upon Daniel. It held a warmth that could melt the snow on a January day, she thought. Then he turned toward her. The smile remained, but the warmth in his eyes was gone. She felt an unexpected nudge of envy toward her brother. Don't play the fool! she chided herself.

"My clothes have been mended and returned, and your cook has fed me," he said, bowing toward her politely. "I thank you for your hospitality, and now I will be on my way."

Rebecca regarded him with matching cool politeness. She had no wish to seek his company, but he was not going to leave without telling her what he had discovered. "I will accompany you to your horse, sir."

"There is no need," he replied, bowing sharply with dismissal.

"There is a great need," she insisted firmly.

Travis had already learned from experience that arguing with Rebecca Mercer would do no good. "As you wish," he conceded, stepping aside for her to exit in front of him.

As he closed the door and joined her in the passage, she glanced around to be certain no one was near, then asked in lowered tones, "Was the information I gave you helpful?"

Frustration again appeared in his eyes. "Not immediately," he replied. "It would seem that your husband had a full week. He met with several people, and the two of you attended a dinner party at the Howards'. Thus, my list of suspects remains as it was."

As disdainful as she felt toward him, his frustration seemed like her own. "I am sorry," she said sincerely.

The sudden softness in her brown eyes caused the memories of the feel of her to tempt him. Curtly he reminded himself that Rebecca Mercer was not the kind of woman he had in mind for either a mistress or a wife. He wanted a more docile woman, one prone to obedience, who would give him no trouble. Rebecca Mercer was nothing but trouble. "Take care, Mistress Mercer," he said warningly. "As long as you do not mention this to anyone, you should be safe." Again bowing sharply, he added, "I am certain I can find my horse on my own, so I will say good day to you here."

His obvious anxiousness to be rid of her company caused Rebecca's anger to flare anew. The man was an insolent boor. "Good riddance," she muttered under her breath as she watched his departing back.

FOUR

NEWS of my safe return and my brother's signs of recovery traveled fast, Rebecca thought tiredly, forcing a smile as she entered the parlor later that day.

Mr. Loyde rose and bowed in greeting. "I was so very worried for your safety, Mistress Mercer," he said, adding with fatherly admonition, "You placed yourself in grave danger."

"I, too, was worried half to death," Kirby Wetherly interjected, brushing past Philip before the butler could announce him. Approaching Rebecca, he bowed deeply and took her hand in his. "I could not sleep for fear of your fate."

Rebecca had to fight the urge to point out that although both men proclaimed to have been concerned for her welfare, neither had sought to come to her assistance. Unbidden, Travis Brandt's image filled her mind. She reminded herself that his main purpose in coming after her was to secure information he thought she might possess. Determinedly, she vanquished the trapper's image. " 'Tis over and done with," she said, politely but firmly freeing her hand. "Daniel is improving, and for that I am grateful."

"As are we all," Mr. Loyde affirmed. An admiring smile spread over his face. "And I must say that you do not look any worse for your adventure."

"You are too kind, sir," Rebecca replied, already bored with the company of these men.

"Mr. Garnet to see you, madam," Philip announced from the doorway. Stepping aside, he allowed her third suitor to enter.

"My mother sends her deepest regards. We both prayed for your safety until our knees were quite raw," Jason proclaimed, approaching Rebecca and bowing low.

Rebecca found her eyes drawn to his bony knees and thin calves. Against her will she found herself recalling the strength in the muscular columns of Travis Brandt's legs. Heat stirred within her. Furious, she again pushed the thoughts of the trapper from her mind. "I am grateful for your prayers," she assured him.

His eyes glistened with interest as he straightened. "I understand you were attacked and Mr. Brandt was wounded."

"I would have come after you myself," Kirby interjected before Rebecca could respond. "But by the time I discovered you had gone, it was late in the day."

"I, too, did not learn until late in the day," Mr. Loyde said. "Still, I would have come after you had not one of my own children shown signs of becoming ill." He breathed a relieved sigh. "Thank goodness it was a false alarm."

Rebecca found this excuse a little hard to swallow. She had seen the tired circles under Mistress Loyde's eyes after sitting up with a sick child all night. But Mr. Loyde had never shown any signs of wear. When his wife had died, he had immediately hired a governess as well as arranged for his widowed mother-in-law to move in with him to care for his children. It was only their discipline that seemed to concern him. Still, she forced an understanding smile. She could not fault him for not wanting to come after her. It had been a dangerous adventure. "I am glad your child is well."

"Travis Brandt was, of course, the right man for the job," Jason Garnet said with an affirming nod of his head.

"He knows these woods for miles around, and he knows Indian ways much better than any of us."

"But if the rumors about him are true, he is a bit of a scoundrel," Mr. Loyde interjected. His full attention was suddenly turned to Rebecca. "I do hope he was not . . . boorish."

"He behaved as a gentleman at all times," she lied as all three men watched her closely. She felt certain Travis Brandt would say nothing of her indiscretion, and she certainly wasn't going to admit to it.

Kirby Wetherly glanced from Mr. Loyde to Mr. Garnet and smiled slyly. "I have noticed that he does not seem to exhibit an interest in the fair sex."

"You don't mean . . . ?" Jason's eyes widened with shock. "Perhaps when he was a captive of the Indians, they did something to him," he offered in sympathetic tones.

Mr. Loyde glanced toward him with sharp warning. "There is a lady present," he admonished.

Jason flushed while Kirby also gave him a reproving look.

Rebecca was shocked by the strength of her urge to defend Mr. Brandt's manhood. She most certainly had proof of it. But not only would such a defense bring questions, the man had considered her capable of killing her husband. He did not deserve her defense. Still, it irked her that these three would have the nerve to insult the one man who had risked his life for her. Even if his motives had been self-serving, she added. Aloud she said, "Mr. Brandt saved my life, and I will not have him spoken of with any disrespect in my home."

"I apologize most humbly," Kirby said, bowing deeply. "It was my relief at learning that Mr. Brandt did not try to take advantage of you that caused me to speak without thinking."

"It has been my observation that you speak without thinking quite often," Mr. Loyde remarked cuttingly.

Rebecca drew a tired breath. She had no desire to witness

a confrontation between Kirby Wetherly and Mr. Loyde over Mr. Wetherly's manners. "Gentlemen," she said before Kirby could speak. "These past few days have been an ordeal, and I am feeling greatly tired. If you will excuse me." Performing a quick curtsy as she spoke, she strode from the room, providing the men with only her departing back to bow to.

Escaping to Daniel's room, she had just begun to read to him when Philip knocked on the door. "Colonel Howard is here to see you, madam," he announced.

Rebecca groaned mentally. She would like to have sent word that she had a tremendous headache and was not receiving, but the colonel was elderly, and it would be basely impolite to put him off after he had ridden over to see her. "Tell him that I will join him momentarily," she directed. "And see that he has refreshments."

"Yes, madam," Philip replied.

Going to her room, Rebecca checked to make certain her hair and dress were both in order. Then, forcing a bright smile onto her face, she went down to the parlor.

"We've serious business to discuss, Mistress Mercer," the colonel said, setting aside the cup of tea he had been sipping and rising to greet her.

The tone of his voice caused Rebecca's smile to feel wooden. " 'Tis always a pleasure to see you, Colonel," she greeted him politely, already positive she was not going to like what he had come to say.

" 'Tis a relief to see you well and safe," he replied pointedly. Motioning her toward a chair, he added in an authoritative voice, "Please be seated."

Rebecca's stomach knotted as she obeyed. He had the look of a man who had come to issue an ultimatum.

Seating himself across from her, the colonel regarded her sternly. "As you well know, because both of your parents are deceased, it is my appointed duty not only to execute Thomas's will, but to guard over you until you have remarried. This adventure of yours has been of grave concern to me."

"I am sorry if I caused you worry," she apologized with deep remorse. "But you know how attached I am to my brother. He is all I have in this world. I could not sit idly by and allow the fever to take him when there was the slightest chance I could save him."

"Yes, I understand your attachment to your brother, but that does not excuse your behavior." The colonel shook his head to emphasize his displeasure. "We live in hostile times. 'Tis a miracle you are still alive."

"But I am alive and my brother is well on the road to recovery," she pointed out, keeping her tone subservient, and with a touch of pleading. He had a stranglehold upon her future, and she needed him on her side.

Ignoring her words, the colonel continued to regard her sternly. "And not only did you risk your life but your reputation as well. You spent two nights unchaperoned in the woods with Mr. Brandt."

Rebecca's mask of submissiveness slipped, and she glared at him with self-righteous indignation. "Mr. Brandt appointed himself my guardian. I did not seek his company."

"I understand that, also," Colonel Howard conceded. "And I have called upon Mr. Brandt and am satisfied that nothing occurred of which you should be ashamed. However, it was an unseemly adventure."

Rebecca flushed with embarrassment at the thought of the colonel confronting Travis Brandt. But to show any further anger would only do her harm. Quickly her manner again became deferential. "But it is over, and I give you my word, I will not act so rashly again in the future."

"If you had been injured, it would have rested on my conscience for the rest of my life. No. This can go on no longer. 'Tis time you chose a new husband. It is clear Thomas knew you well. You need a strong hand to guide you at all times and in all ways."

From the moment she had entered the parlor, Rebecca had known this was the pronouncement the colonel had come to make. "As you wish," she agreed resignedly. She knew it would be ridiculous to try to argue. Although the colonel had been a close friend of her husband's, he had never been a friend to her. He had never fully approved of Thomas Mercer marrying a woman so much younger. Rebecca did not think the colonel truly disliked her, but she knew he wished to be rid of the duty he felt toward her. "As soon as I have assured myself of my brother's renewed health, I shall journey to Jamestown."

The colonel stared at her in confusion. "Jamestown?"

"I will have a choice, sir," she said firmly.

"You have a choice here," he countered, his voice holding no compromise. "There are three very suitable men who have shown interest in you. I admit I'm not particularly fond of Kirby Wetherly's rumored behavior. However, he has assured me that if you should select him to be your husband, he would be completely faithful."

Rebecca looked horrified. "You have actually spoken to him?"

The colonel regarded her with self-righteous dignity. "I have spoken to all of them. Thomas placed me in the position of being your protector. It was my duty to ascertain their intentions. Each of them is ready to marry you."

Regaining her control, Rebecca forced herself to speak calmly. "My husband's will did not bind me to choosing from the available suitors within this area. It is my right to travel to Jamestown and see if I cannot find someone who would please me more."

The colonel scowled. "There is much too much turmoil in the land for you to be making such a journey. Not only are there Indians to contend with, but there is the unrest being stirred by Nathaniel Bacon. As we speak, the newly elected assembly is gathering in Jamestown, and word has come that, in spite of the fact that the governor had declared him a rebel, Mr. Bacon has been elected to represent

Henrico County." The colonel shook his head. As if speaking more to himself than her, he continued in a dour tone. "No man could have had a better start in the colony. When Mr. Bacon arrived here barely a year ago, his cousin saw that he acquired good property, and the governor even gave him a seat on the council. Who would have thought his career here would have come to this! Mind you, I find myself in agreement with the young upstart that a militia needed to be formed and the Indians terrorizing our people brought under submission once and for all times. But he should not have attempted it without a commission from the governor." The colonel rose and began to pace. "I cannot understand Sir William. There was a time when he was the champion of the people of Virginia and beloved by all. But now I can almost smell revolt in the air." He paused and, lifting his head, sniffed as if to add credence to his words.

Revolt or no revolt, Rebecca was not ready to have her plan thwarted so easily. "Surely the election of the new assembly will calm the air," she argued reasonably.

The colonel frowned impatiently at her. "Bacon has come back from his Indian campaign a popular hero. If he and the governor do not make peace, there is sure to be trouble. Even as we speak, there are rumors of a rabble army ready to unite under Bacon's leadership. Mark my words, Mistress Mercer, there is trouble brewing. These are not safe times for anyone to be traveling." He came to a halt in front of her. "You've had a suitable period of mourning. I shall give you one week to decide upon a husband. Come next Thursday you will be ready to announce a betrothal, or I will act upon the conditions set down in Thomas's will and declare this land the property of Jonathan Mercer. I have had correspondence with the man. You can expect no leniency from him. He wants no part of this New World and feels no obligation to you. He has directed me that if the property should come to him, it is to be sold down to the last peg and all profits sent to him."

Rebecca paled. One week!

The colonel performed a sharp, military bow. "In truth I would prefer to hear of your choice even more quickly. It would be a great relief to me to be able to publish the banns this Sunday."

Forcing her legs to work, Rebecca rose and curtsied. "You will hear from me," she replied.

" 'Tis for your own good," he said with a patronizing air. Then, bowing once again, he left the room.

A week! Rebecca wanted to scream that this wasn't fair. But that would do her no good. Besides, she had known this time would come. It was her own fault she had not searched out a suitable mate earlier. Sinking down into her chair, she considered her three choices. Revulsion filled her. She did not want any of them.

Momentarily she considered giving up Green Glen. She and Daniel could strike out on their own. Then her mouth formed a hard straight line. They would have practically no resources. She had a few pieces of jewelry and her clothing. That was all Thomas Mercer's will allowed her to keep if she did not wed. She and Daniel had no family they could turn to and no friends upon whom they could rely.

She gave a tired, angry sigh. She had paid dearly for Green Glen. It would remain her home.

Once that decision was firmly made, she again considered her choices. Again revulsion filled her. Rising, she paced around the room. Coming to a halt, she closed her eyes and forced herself to picture herself in each of her suitors' arms. The images left her cold.

Again sinking into her chair, she stared at the fireplace. Travis Brandt's image came into her mind. She recalled the fire his touch had spread through her body. At least the thought of sharing her bed with him did not cause a wave of nausea. But he was not interested in marrying her. In fact, he was not interested in having any prolonged association with her. His only interest was in finding his mother's murderer.

A sudden gleam shone in her eyes. But then, she didn't want a husband, either.

Her mouth formed a thoughtful frown. Maybe she could strike a bargain with the trapper. Considering their parting, this didn't seem too likely, but her options were severely limited. All the rest of that afternoon, evening, and late into the night she considered what she would say to Mr. Brandt. If she did approach him with a proposition, it would be done with dignity. She had her pride.

The next morning dawned bright. Rising, Rebecca checked on her brother. His fever was almost gone.

Going into the kitchen, she ordered Mildred to pack a basket of food. " 'Tis to be for Mr. Brandt," she explained. "A gift of gratitude for saving my life and aiding me in bringing medicine back for Daniel."

"Aye, he does deserve it." Mildred nodded cheerfully.

Naddie cast her an anxious glance and was rewarded by a scowl from the cook.

"You get that look off your face, girl," Mildred admonished her apprentice. "It's time for you to admit you was wrong about Mr. Brandt. He done a brave thing, he did."

"I suppose," Naddie conceded.

It had been a self-serving act, Rebecca corrected mentally. But then, she was counting on Mr. Brandt's self-serving nature to aid her once again.

"I'll pack a few extra corn cakes. They's his favorites," Mildred was saying as she busily filled the basket.

For a moment Rebecca wondered how Mildred would know that, then she remembered that the cook had traded baked goods to Mr. Brandt for fresh animal meat on a fairly regular basis. For the first time she realized just how much time Travis Brandt had spent at Green Glen. Spying on us, she mused dryly. The question was, was he willing to become its master . . . under her conditions?

Later, as she approached his cabin, her courage threatened to fail her. The urge to turn away grew strong.

Reminding herself of what she would be turning away to, she forced herself forward.

He was chopping wood when she arrived. His coat had been discarded and his bloused shirt hung loosely open at the neck. She remembered the hard, warm feel of his flesh below her hand, and a shiver of excitement swept over her.

Burying his ax in an old stump, he stood watching her as she dismounted. She could read nothing in his expression. He was polite enough as he bowed in greeting when she approached him, but nothing more. "I brought you a gift in appreciation for all you did for me and my brother," she said, extending the basket toward him.

"There was no need of that," he replied. He had not expected to see the mistress of Green Glen again so soon and certainly not at his cabin. In his mind's eye he remembered how enticing she had looked lying in the woods in the early morning light. She is only trouble, he growled at himself. The sooner he was rid of her, the better. Approaching her, he accepted the basket. "However, 'tis appreciated."

His cool politeness was again causing Rebecca's courage to waver. Then the faces of her three suitors played through her mind and she dismounted. "I was wondering if my husband's appointment calender has been of some help," she said, trying to ease her nerves with a bit of conversation.

"Not as yet." His jaw formed a hard line. "I explained to you that it would be best if you distanced yourself from my mission."

Rebecca's jaw formed an identically hard line. " 'Tis difficult to put it out of my mind when you tell me that you think my husband was murdered."

He gave an aggravated snort. "You are a singularly stubborn woman. Don't you understand that my request is for your safety?"

This was not going at all as she had planned! Rebecca thought frantically. It was clear he wanted her to go. Again the images of her three suitors filled her mind. Her back stiffened with pride. "I have come here to offer you a business proposition." As her words echoed in her ears, a wave of panic rushed over her. The man didn't even like her. This was insane!

He regarded her skeptically. "A business proposition?"

She was tempted to focus her attention on something behind him so she could not read the rejection on his face should he find her offer unacceptable. But instead, she forced herself to meet his gaze levelly. "Colonel Howard has decided that I must choose a husband within the week. I have no wish to be subjected to the domination of a male who would consider himself my master or, in the case of Mr. Garnet, a mother-in-law who will attempt to rule my life. I am also not interested in marrying a philanderer who will be unfaithful and make me a laughingstock within the community. Therefore, I have come to you with a proposal. If you will marry me, you will have a position in the community that will give you easier access to my former husband's friends and associates. It has also occurred to me that the information you seek could be among my husband's accounts and personal letters. These you would have free access to as well. In return I would ask that you sign a paper agreeing that when Daniel reaches the age of twenty-one, he will receive a third of the land belonging to Green Glen. Also, a third of the land including this cabin shall be placed in my name as a wedding gift. The final third containing the manor house, of course, would be yours."

For a long moment Travis could only stand and stare at her. He was shocked by how tempting the offer sounded, and it was not Green Glen that held the temptation. But Rebecca Mercer was not the kind of woman he wanted for a wife. She was cold and calculating. When he did choose to marry, he wanted a woman who would be warm and giving. " 'Tis very generous of you to allow me the manor house," he remarked dryly.

"I wish only to have a guarantee of a roof over my head

and a future for Daniel," she replied tightly. "That is not
unreasonable." Her stomach knotted as his expression
remained unreadable. He was mocking her! He was not
interested in marrying her even to further his quest for his
mother's murderer. Her chin tilted upward with pride.
"Clearly I have made a mistake. I would ask you to forget
this conversation ever took place." As an afterthought, she
added, "I will go through my husband's papers and inform
you of any information that might aid you in your search."
She finished with a sharp, "Good day, sir," and turning
away from him, she began to mount her horse.

Travis told himself to let her go. But instead, he set the
basket aside and reached her in one long stride. His hand
closed around her arm, and he forced her to turn and face
him. "If I should be found out, you and Daniel could be in
danger," he said grimly.

"You do not need to make excuses for not wanting to
marry me," she snapped. "If you are correct about my
husband's death, then my continued good health makes it
clear that the man you seek will do me and Daniel no harm
as long as he believes we know nothing. And I most
certainly do not plan to make my knowledge of the brooch
public." She tried to twist free. When he did not release her,
she glared up at him. "I will thank you to take your hand off
of me. I must find a husband, and I do not have much
time."

Travis looked down into the dark angry depths of her
eyes. He told himself he was only doing this because he
wanted to find the man responsible for his mother's death.
But he knew it was a lie. The remembered feel of her in his
arms taunted him. It was not wise, but he desired her and he
would not send her to another man's bed. "This could easily
be a mistake for both of us," he said. "But I will marry you,
Rebecca Mercer, and on your terms."

Rebecca stared at him in stunned disbelief. "You will?"

"It is a way for both of us to achieve the ends we desire,"
he replied brusquely, releasing her.

She forced a coolness into her voice she did not feel.

"Yes, it is." Her heart was pounding. Had she done the right thing? Was Travis Brandt truly the lesser of the evils that faced her? It was too late now to reconsider. Suddenly remembering another condition she had not mentioned, she said stiffly, "You would also have to give up your smuggling activities. I will not risk losing my home to the governor in payment for your misdeeds."

Travis shrugged. "You may consider my life as a smuggler ceased. It was merely a ploy, anyway. I was hoping the man I seek would try to market some of the jewels through me. However, he did not."

A sudden thought brought a worried look to Rebecca's face. "Perhaps he knows who you are and is simply biding his time until an opportunity to do away with you arrives."

Travis shook his head. "No, I think not. My solicitor never mentioned my name to your husband. I know because I was in the room pretending to be the man's law clerk. I was impressed by your husband's promise of discretion, and even if he chose to tell everything he knew, he would not have mentioned me. He barely noticed my existence."

"Thomas Mercer was not a man who paid any heed to people he considered of lower rank unless he felt they could be of use to him," Rebecca confirmed. "And he was very good at keeping secrets." An edge of bitterness had crept into her voice. Quickly she schooled it out. Returning the subject to a more immediate concern, she said in business-like tones, "The colonel expressed his wish that the marriage should take place as quickly as possible. I will inform him this afternoon of our engagement so that he may announce the banns on Sunday if that meets with your approval."

Travis had heard the bitterness in her voice when she spoke of her husband. Clearly she resented his ability to continue to rule her from the grave. In truth, Travis could not fault her for that. "I feel I should accompany you when you speak to Colonel Howard," he insisted. "It would seem more proper."

That Travis Brandt should care what was proper or improper made Rebecca want to laugh. Realizing this was due more to nervousness than to humor, she swallowed it back. "Of course," she replied.

"I will be at Green Glen in two hours to escort you to the colonel's house." Without waiting for a response, he lifted her into her saddle and, stepping back, bowed deeply.

Kicking her horse into motion, Rebecca did not look back. She had expected him to be reluctant to marry her. Still, his reluctance caused a sharp jab of pain. It was not as if she was ugly or had nothing of value to offer him. And she had been most generous in her terms. Ignoring the lingering sense of having been insulted, she wondered if he would remain in her company once his search was finished. She guessed he would not. Perhaps he would seek a special writ from the governor freeing him from their marriage, or perhaps he would simply ask her to leave and establish an independent residence elsewhere. Whatever he chose to do didn't matter, she told herself. Even if he sold what he owned of Green Glen and went back to England, Daniel would have a start in life, and she would have a place to live free of any restrictions.

Watching her ride away, Travis Brandt frowned thoughtfully. Until his quest was finished, he wanted no emotional entanglements with a woman. They could be too demanding and time-consuming. But since his expedition into the woods with Mistress Mercer, he had begun to miss female companionship in his bed. Forced to admit that it was her particular companionship he wanted, he told himself that was only because his pride had been damaged by her rejection. A cynical smile curled his lips. At least he would not have to worry about becoming emotionally attached to her. He had never liked cold-blooded, manipulative women.

Back at Green Glen, Rebecca found calling cards from Mr. Loyde, Mr. Wetherly, and Mr. Garnet. When Philip informed her that all three had adamantly promised to return that afternoon, she surmised that Colonel Howard had informed them of his dictum.

"I will receive only Mr. Brandt," she instructed the butler. "To all others, I have a sick headache." Philip had been well trained by Mr. Mercer to show no emotion, but she noticed the quick glimmer of curiosity that flashed in his eyes. She considered telling him of her intended betrothal but found herself refraining. The servants would learn soon enough. She needed time to get used to the idea first.

"Mr. Brandt will be arriving here in an hour and a half or so to ride with me to the colonel's plantation," she continued in a businesslike tone. "After which, he and I will return here, and Mr. Brandt will remain for dinner. Please inform Mildred we will have a guest, and I think it would be all right for Master Daniel to join us in the dining room this evening so long as we do not keep him at the table too long. I am going to the study. Please have Mildred prepare a luncheon tray and bring it to me."

Having issued these orders, she left Philip to guard her privacy. Grudgingly she was forced to give thanks to Thomas Mercer for seeing that she had learned to read and write. On the other hand, it was his fault she was being pushed into this arrangement. Carefully she began to draw up a paper with the conditions she had outlined to Travis Brandt. Men might make deals and bind them with a handshake, but she did not think a court would support a woman under such conditions.

When the food arrived, she was too nervous to eat more than a few bites. She finished drawing up the paper, then went up to her room to see that her hair and clothing were in proper order. Satisfied that her grooming was adequate, she went into Daniel's room to check on him. He was anxious to be out of bed, but she insisted that he remain resting for at least two more days. "You had me scared half out of my mind," she pointed out sternly.

When he did not fight her, she knew she had been right. He was obviously still weak.

Leaving his room, she wondered why she had not told him about her engagement to Travis Brandt. Again she told herself it was because she needed time to adjust to the idea herself. But this time her nerves forced her to admit this was a lie. The truth was, she believed it very possible that Mr. Brandt might have changed his mind the moment she was gone.

As she started toward the stairs, she saw Philip approaching. "Mr. Brandt is in the parlor, madam," he informed her.

Rebecca frowned anxiously. The butler's usual staid expression had remained almost fully intact earlier when she had informed him that although she would not see any of her three suitors, she would see Mr. Brandt and that the trapper would be a guest for dinner. But now it was marred by a curious and slightly apprehensive look in his eyes.

Wondering what Travis Brandt had done to so unsettle Philip, she hurried down to the parlor. Surely he would not have taken it upon himself to inform her servants that he was to be their new master before Colonel Howard had been told of her decision. Entering the study, she came to an abrupt halt as a small gasp of surprise escaped. He was clean-shaven!

"I did not think I looked so frightening without my beard and mustache," he said with an edge of self-consciousness.

"Not frightening, just different," she replied, her gaze traveling over the rugged line of his jaw. His was not a classically handsome face. The features were more angular than she would have expected and a long, thin scar marred his left cheek. But he was not unpleasant to look upon.

"I thought I would appear more presentable to the colonel," he explained, stroking his jaw. "I only grew the beard and mustache to make myself look slightly disreputable so that my charade as a smuggler might be more easily believed."

"You do look much more respectable," she admitted,

fighting down the urge to follow his lead and stroke his jaw herself. Do not allow your body to do your thinking for you, she ordered herself curtly, disturbed by the strength of her physical reactions to this man. It might have been wiser to choose someone who did not interest her so strongly. But she would not make herself turn back now. Remembering the paper in the study, she moved toward the door. "Please follow me," she requested. A few moments later, as she handed him the document in the study, she prepared herself for battle.

Travis glanced at the document. It outlined the bargain to which he had agreed. The property held no interest for him. Grudgingly he admitted it was her that he wanted. He'd been able to think of nothing but bedding her since he'd agreed to this proposal. A lust so strong is dangerous, he'd warned himself. Cynically he'd assured himself that once he'd possessed her, it would grow weaker. Probably fade quickly, he'd reasoned. Then his full concentration would return to his quest.

No man had ever given her anything without making demands. Rebecca fully expected Travis Brandt to attempt to better his end of the bargain. But to her surprise, he made no comment as he quickly read the document, then signed it.

That he had not tried to take advantage of her puzzled her. As they rode to the colonel's house, she reminded herself that Mr. Brandt had only one purpose in life, and that was to find his mother's murderer. Green Glen meant little to him, and she meant even less.

Rebecca forced a demure smile as Travis informed the colonel of their engagement.

Clearly somewhat shocked, Colonel Howard regarded Travis suspiciously. "I was not aware you were in the race for Mistress Mercer's hand."

"I am a private man," Travis replied. "I do not openly flaunt my affections or my desires."

The colonel continued to study the couple with a frown. "I have been pledged to do my duty by Mistress Mercer," he said grimly. "And while she is to be allowed to make her own choice in this matter, I feel I must be certain she is not taken advantage of. Green Glen is a prize not to be taken lightly."

He clearly implied Travis Brandt was nothing more than a fortune hunter. Rebecca felt a surge of cynical humor. It was her three suitors who had been the fortune hunters. "Colonel," she said with cool dignity, "your tone carries an unfair suggestion. Mr. Brandt has proved to be both brave and honorable in rescuing me and aiding me in gaining medicines for my brother. He has been a decent and law-abiding member of our community and has incurred not one penalty for breach of conduct."

"Yesterday you wished to travel to Jamestown in search of a husband," the colonel pointed out. "It occurs to me that you are behaving in a less than rational manner."

Sick of being treated as if she were addle-brained, Rebecca glared at him. "I am being extremely rational. I am not foolish enough to believe that any one of my suitors does not have eyes for Green Glen."

Travis found himself admiring the woman's fire. But he was wise enough to know that it would do neither one of them any good for her to continue in this angry vein. "If it would put your mind at rest," he interjected, extracting an envelope from his coat pocket, "within you will find a letter from a well-respected solicitor in London stating that I have a yearly income of two thousand pounds coming from the interest of a trust set up for me by my guardian, who wishes to remain private. Further, at any time I wish, I may draw upon the principal."

Rebecca stared at Travis in disbelief as the colonel accepted the envelope and extracted its contents.

After reading the letter, Colonel Howard returned it to Travis. His expression had changed from one of suspicion to one of interest. "This, of course, changes the entire complexion of this marriage. You have my warmest wishes."

"As I mentioned before, I am a private man. I wish my finances to be kept a matter only between us," Travis requested as he again pocketed the envelope.

"Yes, of course," the colonel agreed. Turning to Rebecca, he smiled with relief. "I am pleased this matter has been so successfully resolved."

Recovering enough to hide her confusion, Rebecca forced a returning smile. "Thank you."

"The banns will be published this Sunday. Since I wish to relinquish my guardianship as quickly as possible, I have obtained a special license. You will be married one week from today."

Rebecca gasped.

Ignoring her, Travis bowed toward the colonel. "That will suit us well."

"Yes, of course, it will," Rebecca agreed when the colonel glanced toward her for confirmation. Now that the decision was made, there was no reason to delay the wedding.

The colonel smiled with relief. "Good."

Rebecca said her good-byes with calm dignity, but as she and Travis rode back toward Green Glen, she studied him narrowly.

"You have something to say to me?" he questioned.

"You are a man of wealth," she said coolly, suspicion strong in her voice. "Yet you told me you were the son of a servant."

"My mother was a servant," he replied. "My father was the old earl of whom I have spoken. When my mother was killed, he felt he had a duty toward me. He would not claim me, but he raised me decently, and when I left his household, he provided for my future." Dryly, he added, "I did have the feeling he was glad to be rid of me. Having a bastard son around was a strain upon his marriage."

This latest revelation caused Rebecca to realize just how

little she knew of this man she had arranged to marry. "What of your mother's family?" she asked.

"They had no use for an unclaimed bastard." He smiled cynically. "Though I do believe they would have danced to a different tune if they had known His Lordship would be so generous toward me. As it is, I know very little of them nor do I want to." He laughed lightly. "I suppose that is at least one thing we have in common. You are an orphan, and for all practical purposes, so am I."

Rebecca forced a returning smile but said nothing. In truth, she admitted, they both knew very little about the other.

FIVE

At dinner that evening Daniel was ecstatic when Rebecca and Travis informed him of their engagement.

Out of the corner of her eye, Rebecca caught the flash of uneasiness that passed over Philip's face. But in the next instant it was replaced with the expression of the polite servant. She knew that by the end of the meal every member of her staff would know who their new master was to be, and she couldn't help wondering how they would react. Well, she would find out when she prepared for bed. Susan might seem a bit flighty, but she was a keen observer and she liked to talk.

Following the meal, Daniel was immediately sent back to his room to rest. "I do not want to take any chances that you might have a relapse," Rebecca explained, kissing him lightly on the cheek.

For a moment he looked as if he was going to argue, but Travis raised an eyebrow, and bowing toward the trapper, Daniel obeyed.

Rebecca saw the exchange. She told herself she should be pleased that Daniel was so ready to accept Travis's authority, but instead, it irked her. Until the wedding she was still in charge at Green Glen. "At least Daniel is pleased with our engagement," she said tightly when she and Travis were alone in the parlor.

Catching the edge of impatience in her voice, his gaze

narrowed upon her. If she had changed her mind, he would not force this marriage. He could not shake the feeling that it might prove more perilous for him than he had at first reckoned. "Does that mean you are having second thoughts?"

Yes, she answered mentally, but she had no other choice. Frustration filled her. "I have been my own mistress for a year. I do not relish again having a man to rule me," she replied with blunt honesty, then flushed when she realized she had spoken aloud her innermost thoughts.

A crooked smile tilted one corner of his mouth. "I would never make the mistake of trying to 'rule' you, Mistress Mercer."

Her nerves were too tense to deal with his cynical humor. "Do not mock me, sir!" she snapped.

Travis's gaze traveled over her. The eyes were dark with anger, and her stance was that of one ready to do battle. There was nothing docile or gentle about her. Again he questioned the sanity of entering into this engagement. But even in anger her lips looked full and inviting. Bridging the distance between them in two long strides, his hands closed around her waist. "I would never expect complete submission to my wishes from you, Mistress Mercer," he said in a low growl. "But I will expect you to show a wifely deference toward me when we are in public."

His touch sent her blood coursing hot through her veins. Her instinct for survival warned her that such a strong susceptibility to the man was dangerous. But her body seemed to have a mind of its own. Her tongue came out to moisten her suddenly dry lips. "I will, of course, behave with the proper decorum toward you," she assured him stiffly.

Travis's hands traveled slowly downward to test the roundness of her hips as a hunger to taste every part of her filled him. He disliked this craving he felt for her. It muddled his thinking. But it was too strong to resist. "It is proper, I believe, for an engaged man to kiss his bride to be," he murmured, his mouth moving toward hers.

His breath teased her sensitized skin. The frustration and anger she was feeling at again being subjected to the rule of a man faded as the fire his touch was spreading threatened to consume her. Her legs weakened, and she swayed toward him. "I suppose it is proper," she replied, marveling that she could put together a coherent sentence when all she could think about was the feel of him.

He claimed her mouth. She tasted delicious. His tongue teased her lips, and they parted willingly to allow him entry. Every muscle of his body tensed with the desire to possess her.

Rebecca's fingers fastened onto the fabric of his coat for support. She remembered the hard, hot feel of his naked flesh beneath her palms and yearned to feel it again.

His hands moved upward, awakening her body with their touch. When he cupped a breast, her breath locked in her lungs. It was insanity that she was so easily ready to surrender to him.

Lifting his head, Travis looked into her eyes. The anger was gone, replaced by a passion that matched his own. He had promised himself he would be patient, but any hold his patience had on him was broken by the open hunger he read in her eyes. "Are we in danger of being disturbed?" he questioned gruffly, his hand already moving to the fastenings of her dress.

Rebecca could barely think beyond his touch. But her instinct for survival was strong. Panic suddenly filled her, bringing her back to reality. She must not trust him so fully until their vows were said. "Yes," she lied, pushing herself gently but firmly away from him. "Besides, it would not be proper decorum."

For a moment he considered challenging her. The door could be locked to assure they would not be interrupted. But he would not take her by force. Releasing her, he watched her back away. He did not understand her withdrawal. They were to be married. He'd given his pledge. He'd even signed the agreement she'd drawn up. As the truth dawned on him, he smiled cynically to himself. She was a woman who used her body to gain what she wanted. She would not give it on a mere whim of passion. Clearly, he would have to wait until he had paid full price by marrying her. Again he found himself wondering if this price might not be too steep. Curtly he argued that if marrying her could help find his mother's killer, then it was worth it. Besides, as much as he doubted the wisdom of this marriage, he could not make himself give her to another man. "Perhaps it would be best if I leave for now," he said, bowing low.

"Perhaps," she agreed.

Standing at the front door watching him ride away, Rebecca felt a wave of regret. There was lust between them, but no love. His concerns would always be for his best interest, never for hers. But then, except for Daniel, that had always been the way with the men in her life. At least Travis Brandt had allowed her to set some of the rules.

Going upstairs, she found Susan waiting in her bedroom. "Congratulations, ma'am," the girl said, dropping a deep curtsy as Rebecca entered. "I must admit I was a mite surprised," she rattled on as she started unfastening Rebecca's dress. A slight flush came to her cheeks. "I hope you won't mind that I said I thought he was bit grim. He does look much better with his beard shaved off . . . not nearly so frightening." The flush on her face deepened as she realized what she'd said.

Rebecca smiled. Susan had a way of getting her toe in her mouth, then continuing until she worked in the entire foot. "How does the rest of the staff feel about their soon-to-be new master?" she questioned bluntly.

Susan's eyes sparkled. "Philip's a mite uneasy. He was partial to Mr. Loyde, Mr. Loyde being a settled gentleman and all. He's worried that the rumors about Mr. Brandt being a smuggler could be true and some unsavory persons might show up at our door. Naddie's a twit and encouraged

Philip's worries. But Mildred declared that Mr. Brandt behaves right gentlemanly and she thinks he's a fine choice." Susan paused for a quick gasp of air, then hurried on. "Ruth and Joseph say that Mr. Brandt did a brave thing in going after you while your other suitors spent their time talking about how worried they was about you. They also says it's your choice and that it's our duty to accept whomever you choose as the new master of Green Glen. The rest of the staff pretty much goes along with Ruth and Joseph, 'cept the smuggling business is a bit unsettling."

Rebecca breathed a sigh of relief. At least her servants were willing to be open-minded about the new master of Green Glen. She had not relished living with an undercurrent of resentment and dislike within the household. "You need not worry. Mr. Brandt has assured me that his being a smuggler was merely rumor," she informed Susan, knowing that this news would spread swiftly.

Susan breathed a sigh of relief. Then, her eyes again dancing with interest, she said, "I suppose it was right romantic being out in that wilderness with Indians stalking you and you and Mr. Brandt both having to fear for your lives."

Rebecca heard the innuendo in the maid's voice. She would not have rumors being spread about her by her own staff. "It was a terrifying experience," she said coolly. "During it, I learned to admire Mr. Brandt's courage."

Susan looked properly chastised. "Yes, ma'am. I didn't mean nothing else," she said quickly.

Rebecca frowned. There were bound to be rumors about her decision to marry Travis Brandt. It will not be the first time people have whispered behind my back, she thought philosophically as she finished undressing.

The next morning Mr. Loyde called upon her.

"I am truly sorry it was not I who won your hand," he said, solemnly. "I told myself I would accept your choice without question. But are you quite certain marrying Mr. Brandt is a wise decision? I know you must feel indebted to him, but marriage is a lifelong commitment and not something to be entered into rashly."

Rebecca was tempted to tell him that had she had a choice, she would have chosen no man. Instead, she said, "I have made my decision, and Colonel Howard has approved it. I would ask you to respect it."

Mr. Loyde bowed deeply. "Then you have my most profound best wishes. My only concern was for your happiness."

Rebecca could not fault his graciousness. Perhaps she had made a mistake. Perhaps Mr. Loyde would have been a wiser choice. But the thought of sharing his bed left her cold. She had survived a practical marriage. If she must marry again, she would wed a man whose touch did not repel her.

Mistress Garnet and Mr. Wetherly were not so gracious. Mistress Garnet called soon after Mr. Loyde's departure. She came alone.

"I wanted to speak frankly with you . . . woman to woman," she said, explaining her son's absence. Glancing toward the door to be certain it was closed, her mouth formed a reproving frown. "I cannot believe you are actually planning to marry Mr. Brandt. I know you feel obligated to him for his act of heroism, but that is no reason to enter into so unsuitable a marriage."

"I do not consider it unsuitable nor does Colonel Howard," Rebecca replied with calm dignity.

Mistress Garnet shook her head until her curls bobbed. "I've been thinking for some time now that the colonel is getting a bit senile." A beseeching expression came over her face. "And you must realize how this looks. People will think that he took advantage of you in the wilderness." She lowered her voice discreetly. "They will think he seduced you, and now you feel you must marry him to retain your honor."

Rebecca replied coldly, "He did not, and I will not have my honor questioned."

Mistress Garnet's voice took on motherly tones. "I am not questioning your honor. I am merely pointing out what others might say. I, myself, abhor gossip."

Rebecca had to fight back the urge to laugh. Mrs. Garnet was as ardent a gossip as any. Rebecca had also noticed that the woman enjoyed embellishing stories if she did not find them interesting enough. When doing this, Mistress Garnet, of course, always preceded the embellishment with an "I wonder if" or "Do you think it's possible" so she could not be accused of purposely spreading an untruth. However, once a suggestion was made, in many minds it became a real part of the story.

"And then there is the fact that he is outside the law," Kirby Wetherly interjected, entering at that moment, again without giving Philip a chance to announce him.

Rebecca swung around to face him. "He has assured me that such accusations are merely rumors."

"I am certain he has," he replied dryly. "As would I or any other man in his position."

Rebecca scowled. "You, Mr. Wetherly would likely lie about a great many things at the drop of a hat," she snapped, then frowned at herself. She should not have reacted so bluntly. But it was the truth.

"That remark is unkind, Mistress Mercer," he replied, with self-righteous indignation.

"Rebecca is obviously not thinking clearly at all these days," Mistress Garnet said sympathetically. "I have been trying to convince her that the strain she has been under caused by the worry for her brother has, perhaps, impaired her judgment."

Rebecca could hardly believe her ears. For the moment it would seem that Mistress Garnet was willing to align herself with Mr. Wetherly. "I am thinking clearly enough, she stated firmly. "However, I do have a fast-building headache. Please, excuse me. Philip will see you out."

Barely taking the time to curtsy, Rebecca strode from the room.

As she started up the stairs, she heard Mistress Garnet saying sarcastically, "Mistress Mercer is right about one thing, Mr. Wetherly. You calling Mr. Brandt a liar is very like the pot calling the kettle black."

"And you calling your son a man is very like one calling an onion a rose," he returned.

This remark was greeted by an indignant "humph" from Mistress Garnet.

At least things were back to normal between the two of them, Rebecca mused. Normally she would have found their exchange amusing. But today she was too tense. She had made the choice she found most acceptable. Still, she could not be certain it was a wise decision. "The die is cast," she told herself. "I can only pray that for once luck is on my side."

During the next few days Rebecca busied herself with getting her house in order. She packed away her mourning clothing and began to wear colors again. There was fabric Thomas had brought back from Jamestown. Time was short, but she set Ruth and Susan to making her a new dress for the wedding. There was also some fine linen from which she, herself, fashioned two new nightgowns. They were not fancy, but the newness gave her some courage for her wedding night.

Travis Brandt came to call as often as it was expected of a soon-to-be groom. But he sought no time alone with Rebecca. She told herself she was relieved and steadfastly ignored the unpleasant little nudgings she experienced when he spent more time with Daniel than he did with her. They felt like jealousy, and she refused to admit she could care so much about who received his attention.

Using the legitimate excuse that Travis would be needing clothing more suitable to his new station in life, she searched carefully through all of Thomas Mercer's clothing.

She found several items that could be altered to fit Mr. Brandt, but she did not find a brooch. A search of Thomas's toilet articles and personal pieces of jewelry proved futile also. The brooch, she was forced to conclude, was gone.

Closing the last trunk, it occurred to Rebecca that Travis might never find the man he sought. If this proved to be the case, she wondered if one day he would regret the price he had paid to further his quest. *Or perhaps it is I who shall regret the price I am paying to assure mine and Daniel's future.*

As busy as she was preparing for the wedding, doubts continued to plague her. There were moments when she considered packing what belonged to her and her brother and leaving Green Glen to Thomas Mercer's cousin. But she stayed, and on the appointed day she wed Travis Brandt in the drawing room of Green Glen manor.

All of those Thomas had considered his friends were invited, including her three former suitors. If Travis's quest was to be fulfilled, it was necessary that they remain on speaking terms with anyone who might possess knowledge that would aid him. She had wondered if the Garnets would actually attend, then chided herself for even considering the possibility they might decline. Mistress Garnet not only came but arrived early. Obviously she did not want to miss any of the action. Rebecca had the impression that Mr. Garnet was relieved that he had not been chosen. Mr. Loyde behaved graciously, as Rebecca had expected him to. Even Kirby Wetherly was at his most polite. She did, however, catch a flash of malice in his eyes when he looked at Travis and thought no one was watching. But it was quickly hidden in the next moment. By the end of the evening she noticed that he was covertly paying an undue amount of attention to the new young wife of Michael Prate, an elderly planter from down the river.

To her relief, the planter didn't notice. But Mistress Garnet did. " 'Tis my opinion that if young wives are to be kept safe from Mr. Wetherly, chastity belts will again have to become the fashion," Rebecca overheard the widow saying to Mistress Howard as the two women stood watching the dancing following the dinner. Mistress Howard, who had also noticed Mr. Wetherly casting surreptitious glances toward the young Mistress Prate, nodded her agreement. But their observations were kept between themselves.

The wedding, the dinner, and the dancing afterward all went well, Rebecca noted with a sigh of relief as the evening drew to an end. But as she bid the last of their well-wishers good-bye, her nerves were taut. Fear mingled with anticipation.

Glancing toward Travis, she was not certain what to say or what to do.

"It has been a long day," he said, breaking the sudden silence that had fallen around them. He glanced toward Philip. "Lock up," he ordered. He had paid full price. This night he would not be denied. Scooping Rebecca up in his arms, he carried her toward the stairs.

Chewing on her bottom lip, Rebecca looked up at him.

"I have behaved most properly for the past week," he informed her. "Now it is time for me to claim my reward."

"You have behaved most properly," she conceded, trying to maintain a demure manner as excitement welled within her. "You do deserve a reward."

Susan was seated in a chair outside the door of the room Travis and Rebecca would share. "Leave us, girl," he instructed. "I will aid Mistress Brandt with any unfastening that is necessary."

Rebecca was so nervous she barely noticed Susan smile widely as the maid curtsied, then hurried quickly on her way.

After entering the bedroom, Travis kicked the door closed. A fire was burning in the hearth. He carried Rebecca across the room and stood her in front of it. "I would not want you to get chilled," he said.

"You are most considerate," she replied nervously. There

was no reason to be shy with him now. Their fates were sealed together. Still, she felt a rush of fear. What if he became suddenly brutish now that she was legally his?

Tilting her head upward, he kissed her lightly on the lips, then, releasing her, he seated himself in a chair near the fire.

Rebecca frowned at him. She had not wanted him to pounce upon her, but she had expected him to show an interest in more than a mere kiss.

"Take down your hair," he requested.

Watching him watch her, she obeyed. As the long black tresses began to fall loose down her back and around her shoulders, she saw his eyes darkened to a midnight blue. A womanly power filled her. He did desire her. She had never flirted with a man before, much less played enticing games. But the pleasure she saw in his eyes as he watched urged her on. Moving slowly, because that seemed to be what pleased him most, she loosened her dress then slipped it off. Next came her petticoats. His gaze was like a caress that warmed her skin and brought a flush of pleasure.

"Now sit," he directed, rising from his chair.

Obeying, anticipation built within her as she watched him kneel in front of her.

He unlaced her shoes and slipped them from her feet. His touch seemed almost to burn as he removed her hose. Then, lifting her feet, one at a time, he kissed the tips of her toes.

It tickled and she giggled.

He smiled up at her rakishly. Then he nipped her ankles gently. Her teeth closed over her bottom lip as currents of delight traveled upward along her legs.

He rose and stood before her. After removing his coat, he tossed it on the chair that held her dress. Then, seating himself, he began to remove his shoes.

The desire to play his game fully was too strong to resist. "I will do that," she said.

Stopping, he straightened and watched her rise and approach him. As she knelt before him, he smiled. " 'Tis nice to have a wife who is willing to be of service."

She heard the huskiness in his voice and was pleased. Discarding his shoes, she removed his hose. His legs were as strong as she had imagined. Like a child exploring a new toy, she trailed her hands over his sturdy calves.

But as her exploration moved higher, he caught her by the wrists. "Your touch could entice the devil," he growled, "and I do not want to rush this." Rising, he drew her to her feet in front of him. He was determined to take his time, to enjoy this night to its fullest. But he had not counted on her arousing him so strongly and so quickly.

Her body trembled with excitement as he unfastened her corset. Freeing her of its confines, he greeted each newly exposed area of flesh with a kiss. With each new touch, he carried her further and further into a world of exotic sensations. The nipples of her breasts hardened as he playfully drew moist circles around them with his tongue, and she gasped with delight. She giggled again as he trailed kisses downward over her abdomen.

But when he gently parted her legs and kissed the inside of her thighs, it was a moan of pure passion that escaped her lips. She had never known a man could make a woman's body feel so alive. She ached to be in his arms, the length of her body pressed fully against his. But she also did not want this tantalizing awakening to end too soon.

As he sought out the very core of her womanhood, her body trembled and even her toes curled with rapture. At any moment she was certain her very being would ignite into a raging fire.

Desire coursed through her veins. "Please, now," she begged in a harsh whisper, startling herself with the sound of her own voice. She had thought herself incapable of speaking.

"Very soon," he promised, rising slowly to stand in front of her. He craved her as a starving man craves a meal. It took all of his strength not to rip the remaining clothes from his body and possess her in the next instant. But he was determined to remain in control.

As he began to finish undressing himself, she stopped him. "Let me," she said. In the far depths of her mind it occurred to her that normally this wanton behavior on her part would cause her to turn scarlet with embarrassment. But she felt no embarrassment with Travis. It was as if they were the only two people in the world. Her mind was filled with thoughts of pleasing him as much as he was pleasing her.

Forcing herself not to move too swiftly, she removed his clothing until he stood in full view in front of her. The sight of his manhood both thrilled and frightened her. "Now?" she questioned huskily, her hands seeking the feel of him.

Her featherlike touch caused him to tremble and threatened the control he was holding over himself.

"Now!" he growled, his hunger too great to contain a moment longer. Lifting her, he carried her to the bed.

Laying her down on the crisp sheets, he forced himself to wait a moment longer as he stroked her teasingly. He wanted them both to draw full pleasure.

"Please," she pleaded once again.

Smiling, he accepted the invitation of her open legs. But as he entered to claim her fully, he was shocked to meet with a barrier.

"Please, now," she begged, her body arching upward to accept him.

He would deal with this unexpected development later. Right now he was beyond thought. He had been with other women, but those times had never felt this exciting . . . this necessary. With a forceful thrust he answered her plea.

Rebecca gasped at the unexpected pain. Her need for him had been so strong she had expected only pleasure. A wave of fear swept through her. Her body recoiled.

Travis's hands closed around her hips refusing to allow her withdrawal. "The pain will pass swiftly," he promised. He did not have the will to release her. He had to bring her desire back. His fingers moved to seek the crown of her womanhood and he began to massage her.

Her fear was forgotten as an intoxicating pleasure filled her senses. She drew a shaky breath, then moaned as the fires within her were rekindled.

Even before the smile returned to her face, Travis sensed her body's return to him. Slowly he began to move within her.

Quickly she matched his rhythm. A fast learner, he mused, wanting to growl with delight.

Frantically their movements grew stronger, more demanding, their passion building to a level of mindless excitement.

Travis drove himself to the hilt within her. His hands dug into the firm flesh of her buttocks as he held her tightly against him. The thought that he might die of this pleasure brought a low, throaty laugh from down deep.

She squirmed as if wanting even more of him. More slowly, with purpose, he began to move with her again.

Rebecca was gasping for every breath now. Her hands raked over his shoulders, and she drew his head toward hers. She wanted the taste of his mouth. She had never believed mating could feel like this. She had thought that in the end it was something a woman endured . . . not something a woman could crave as if it was life-sustaining.

She bit back a scream as her body reached its pinnacle, every fiber of her being exploding with savage pleasure. She felt Travis tremble, then let out a deep satisfied growl as he joined her in this moment of ecstasy.

Even satiated they continued to cling together, both gasping for breath. Finally, as their breathing became more regular, Travis lifted himself from her and, finding the comforter, covered them both.

Rebecca lay staring up at the canopy with a soft smile on her face. In her wildest dreams she had never imagined a wedding night could be this enjoyable.

Travis lay beside her. He could not deny that she was the most exciting woman he had even been with. But she was also the most devious. He waited until his breathing was regular once again and he was in full control of his body. Then, levering himself on an elbow so that he could look down upon her face, he said grimly, "You were a virgin."

The anger in his eyes and the accusation in his voice chilled Rebecca to the bone. The feeling of enchantment that had possessed her vanished as her body stiffened defensively.

"Now I understand your hesitancy in the woods and in the parlor," he continued in a low growl. "Your marriage to Thomas Mercer was never consummated. In many eyes that would make your marriage to him invalid. You could have lost everything if you had been found out. So you were forced to wait until you and I were legally bound . . . until you felt my fate was securely enough tied to yours that I would say nothing."

Rebecca's chin lifted with pride. "I admit that I felt my hold on Green Glen was tenuous. But that my marriage was not consummated was not my fault."

Travis smiled sarcastically. "I find it hard to believe that Thomas Mercer married you but did not try to bed you."

Rebecca glared at him. "He tried, but he was impotent." Ugly memories assailed her, and tossing the coverings aside, she left the bed. Grabbing an afghan from a chair, she wrapped it around herself as she stood in front of the fire. This was the first time she had spoken aloud of Thomas's inability. Now that she had made this admission, the words began to flow in an angry, bitter stream. "My father and Mr. Mercer arranged the marriage. My father was not the kind of man to raise a family on his own, and he had no desire to remarry. Thomas Mercer desired to have a woman of his own but could not. He thought that my youth and beauty would breathe life into his loins. It did not. At first he tried mightily. When he could not consummate our marriage, his frustration led him to beat me. He always hit me where the bruises would not show when I was clothed. Until they faded, he would play the ardent husband and insist on aiding me in dressing and undressing so that my maid would see nothing. The day after each beating, he would be appalled by his actions and make it up to me with a gift or some other kindness." Turning, she scowled at the man in the bed. "Although I was never truly his wife, I feel I paid fully for Green Glen."

Travis studied the woman before him. He had gravely misjudged her. She had been brutally misused. If Thomas Mercer were alive, he would thrash him to within an inch of his life. "No man should treat a woman thusly," he said gruffly.

Rebecca's shoulders straightened. "I do not require your pity, sir," she said proudly. " 'Tis over and done with and best forgotten."

The fire gave her skin a soft pink glow and the memory of the warm, enticing feel of her filled Travis's mind. The knowledge that he had been the first man to possess her caused a rush of exultation. Leaving the bed, he moved toward her. "It is not pity that I am feeling," he said huskily.

Rebecca wished she had more resistance to him. At every turn he had believed the worst of her. But already her body was hungering for his touch. You are his wife, she told herself, her pride seeking a reason to give in to him. He has the right to claim you. And you, she added to herself, have the right to enjoy what pleasure he brings you. Letting the afghan fall, she stood waiting for him.

SIX

THE next morning Rebecca awoke alone. Frowning with disappointment, she lay staring at Travis's side of the bed. After their night of lovemaking she had expected him to be there to greet her. Obviously his lust for her had been satisfactorily quenched, she thought dryly, and willed herself not to care that he was absent.

Hearing a slight scraping sound, she turned. He was dressed and standing at the window looking out. The sun was fully up. Well, no one could blame her for sleeping late. He had been a most enthusiastic lover and had quite worn her out.

"Good morning," he said evenly, turning to face her. It had been difficult forcing himself out of her bed this morning. It had been even more difficult standing there watching her awaken. When she'd arched her back in a sort of catlike stretch, he had almost shed his clothing and rejoined her. But he was here on a mission. That must come first. And, although he now knew she had been badly mistreated by Thomas Mercer, she had also shown herself to be a woman who knew what she wanted and was willing to strike a bargain to gain it. It was best not to crave such a woman too strongly, he warned himself. If a better offer came along, she would surely take it.

"Good morning," Rebecca replied in matching tones,

determined to show the same indifference to him that he was showing to her.

"I would like to begin going through your late husband's papers this morning," he said, returning his attention to the view beyond the window. She looked much too inviting lying there, her bare shoulders exposed.

"We should have breakfast together first," she replied stiffly. "It would seem most peculiar to the servants and Daniel if you were to completely ignore me this morning."

"We would not want to arouse anyone's curiosity," he conceded. "I will wait for you in the parlor while you complete your toilet and dress."

Rebecca rang for Susan as he left the room. She felt insulted that he could so easily leave her. Well, she would be as immune to him as he was to her! Tossing off the covers, she began to prepare herself for the day.

Summer was soon to arrive, and already the weather was showing signs of becoming oppressively hot, she thought as she descended the stairs a short while later. Travis was waiting for her, and together they entered the breakfast room.

"Where is Daniel this morning, Philip?" she asked as Travis, insisting on playing the part of the attentive new husband, took Philip's role and held her chair while she seated herself.

"He has gone with Joseph to inspect the crops, madam," the butler replied.

Rebecca suspected Ruth had arranged for Joseph to occupy Daniel to allow Rebecca and Travis time alone. But at the moment Rebecca would have preferred the company of her young brother. Once she and Travis gave their breakfast orders, they would have to make conversation. It would not look natural to the servants if they ate in silence. Daniel would have solved this problem with a flood of talk about anything that came into his mind. Now she would have to think of something to say.

She knew it would sound mundane, but she was forced to

comment on the weather when nothing better came to mind. "I'm afraid this summer might be oppressively hot."

"It would seem that way," Travis replied politely.

"But it should be good for the crops as long as we get enough rain," she persisted, wondering how much a person could say about the weather without sounding like a complete fool.

"I've noticed your crops are doing very well," he replied, "Joseph is a good man."

"Yes," she agreed, trying to think of what should come next. Normally she had no trouble making small talk when it was necessary, but Travis Brandt was not the kind of man it was easy to make small talk with. In spite of her determination to remain indifferent toward him, she found herself remembering how tantalizing his touch could be. Furious with herself, she turned her mind to less intimate thoughts. "What do you think of this latest news of Bacon?"

"It would seem that all is in order once again," he replied. "The colonel has it on good authority that Mr. Bacon has been forgiven by the governor. He has even been returned to his seat on the council."

Rebecca studied him. "You do not sound as convincing as your words."

Travis shrugged. " 'Tis the reforms Bacon has presented to the assembly. Many are directed against the purse strings of the governor and his friends. And even if 'tis true that it is Lawrence and Drummond who are guiding him and who actually drew up the paper, Bacon is willing to use his popularity to try to get the reforms passed into law."

Rebecca had heard talk of these laws at the wedding. "They seem fair and just," she said.

"Fair and just and have the hearts of the majority of the assembly," Travis conceded. "But the governor is very likely to see them otherwise. He does not like his authority threatened."

She had often wondered if Travis Brandt paid any heed to

what was happening around him. He rarely offered an opinion in public unless it was solicited from him. Rebecca found it interesting that he understood the affairs of government so clearly. "So you think there will be trouble."

Travis shrugged. "'Tis difficult to predict. But with profits down, people are complaining more and more of the taxes being levied by the governor and his appointees to support their rule here in Virginia. And the Indians are still a threat."

Rebecca could not fault his assessment of the situation. Frowning, she added regretfully, "'Tis a shame we could not live in peace with the red man."

Travis shrugged. "Greed and peace do not walk hand in hand. The Indians were certain to stop allowing themselves to be pushed farther and farther off of their native lands. And once their wrath is unleashed, they are a vicious foe."

Rebecca saw the shadow that passed over Travis's face. "Was your time with the savages difficult?" she asked, unable to ignore her curiosity about this man who was now her husband.

His jaw tensed. "My first master was a kind man. When he died, I became the property of his daughter. Her husband was not so kind." A bitter smile curled his lips. "He thought he could beat me into docile subservience."

Rebecca's gaze narrowed. "Only a fool would think that," she mused, then flushed when she realized she had spoken aloud.

"He died for his folly," he replied, then fell silent.

Watching him covertly as she finished her breakfast, it occurred to Rebecca that Travis Brandt had endured much in pursuit of the man who had murdered his mother. And she could not help wondering if he viewed their marriage as another distasteful but necessary path he must follow. The thought stung. "Mr. Brandt and I will be spending the majority of the day in the study," she informed Philip as she put her teacup aside and prepared to rise. Directing her attention toward Travis, she added for Philip's benefit,

" 'Twould be best if you acquainted yourself with the running of Green Glen as quickly as possible." Out of the corner of her eye she caught the look of approval that passed over Philip's face. It irked her that although she had done an excellent job in administering to the running of the estate for better than a year, her butler was relieved that the management was passing back into the hands of a man. It was that male attitude of superiority that had placed her in this situation in the first place, she reminded herself.

"You're right," Travis agreed, rising and helping her with her chair as he continued his role of the attentive husband.

As soon as they were sequestered in the study, Rebecca found the key she kept pushed to the back of the desk's large bottom drawer and unlocked the large trunk that occupied a far corner of the room. "My late husband's personal correspondence is in here," she said as she lifted the lid. Crossing to the bookshelves, she ran her hand along two shelves of leather-bound volumes. "These are Thomas's journals. He began keeping them twenty years ago." Reminding herself that he was now master of Green Glen, she added, "Or would you wish to begin with the books regarding Green Glen?"

"My first interest is to find the man I seek," he replied, moving to the shelf of journals.

She clamped her teeth on the inside of her bottom lip as the sudden urge to ask him what he planned to do once his quest was ended swept over her. That was his concern, not hers. She had struck a bargain for hers and Daniel's future. What Travis Brandt's future held for him was his business, not hers. If he should disappear from her life for good once his task was completed, she would not care. She told herself that her enjoyment of his lovemaking was simply because it was a new experience. But as she watched him choosing a journal, she found herself wanting to repeat it. The sooner his task was completed the better, she decided. Every instinct warned her that forming any sort of attachment to this man would only cause her trouble. "Do you have any physical description of the man you seek?" she questioned.

"Very little. He wore a mask that covered the majority of his face. His hair is brown and his eyes a dark color, most likely brown." A frown of frustration wrinkled his brow. "The witnesses were badly shaken, and their descriptions conflicted. He remained upon his horse. Some said he was short-legged, some said he was long-legged. His height was judged anywhere from five and a half feet to over six feet tall. His age could have been anywhere from sixteen to the late twenties."

Rebecca shook her head. "That is not much to go upon."

"The only other prerequisite is that he would have appeared in the colonies over eleven years ago," Travis added. "But not more than fifteen."

"That would include several of the planters in this area," she said, quickly going over the histories of her neighbors.

"As well as some of the servants, overseers, and so on," Travis confirmed, his frown deepening with each word. "Let us hope your late husband's journals can be of some help." Pulling out the last volume, he seated himself at the desk.

"I will go through his papers," Rebecca said. She pulled over a footstool and seated herself beside the trunk.

Pausing, Travis looked toward her. "It might be best if you do not concern yourself with this," he said. "I do not wish to place either you or your brother in danger."

"Until this man is caught, whoever knows him is in danger," she replied. "He is a cold-blooded murderer."

He nodded. "Perhaps you are right."

Rebecca was just beginning to read the first letter when Travis rose from the desk and replaced the journal on the shelf. "Do you know where your husband kept the journal on which he was currently working?" he asked.

"It should have been the one you had," she replied.

"That one ended a year before his death," he informed her tersely.

Rising, she walked over to the bookshelf. "I have not bothered these books since his death." Quickly she scanned the rest of the shelves. There were no other volumes. "He was a very ordered man. The journal should have been the last in the line," she said firmly.

"Perhaps it is shoved into one of the desk drawers," he suggested, already on his way across the room.

"No. I went through all of the drawers. If I had found his journal, I would have put it on the shelf," she assured him.

Travis regarded her grimly. "Then it would seem someone has taken it . . . someone with access to your home."

A cold chill ran along Rebecca's spine.

"Who knew your husband kept a journal?" he questioned.

"All of his acquaintances," she replied. "If a question arose about the weather or the crops in any particular year, he would insist upon consulting his journals to determine the answer. They were a great source of pride to him."

"Who had access to this room?" he asked sharply.

Rebecca felt a sinking sensation in her stomach. "Any of the servants and anyone who called upon me during the winter months." Seeing the angry frustration in his eyes, she nervously explained, "This room was kept heated at all times. I spent a portion of each day here keeping my accounts. Also, I went through Thomas's ledgers to learn as much about running this place as I could. And I used this room for Daniel's lessons. Because it was already warm, I would often have guests shown in here."

"He is ahead of me again," Travis growled. Pacing to the window, he gazed out, his stance rigid.

Watching him, Rebecca felt his frustration as if it were her own. "I am sorry," she said stiffly.

"You did not know," he replied, continuing to stare out the window. "Perhaps if I had made myself known to you sooner, I would have my answer."

The desire to go to him and place her arms around him was strong. I must keep my situation here in the proper perspective, she warned herself curtly. "But first you had to decide if it was I who murdered my husband," she muttered dryly, reminding herself of what he had thought of her.

"Yes," he admitted, "I had to decide if you were a part of it."

At least he was honest, she told herself. Still, it stung. Forcing her mind to their current problem, an old memory nagged at her. He would not like to hear it, but it would save them from another fruitless search. "When I was going through the ledgers, there was a page missing," she said. "It confused me at the time. Thomas was a man who kept meticulous records. I could not understand why there should be anything missing."

He turned back toward her, his jaw set in a determined line. "No one who could be the man I seek has moved from this area since your husband's death. At least I know he is still here. Can you make me a list of all the people who have entered this room?"

"I cannot guarantee it will be entirely accurate, but I will try," she replied.

"And I will start through the papers in the trunk," he said. "But I have little hope I will find anything."

Seating herself at the desk, Rebecca compiled her list. The most frequent visitors were her three suitors. But there had been others. Two of the smaller landholders had both called to offer her bids on pieces of her acreage, and another had wanted to purchase some livestock. Colonel Howard had come by and so had Reverend James.

After handing Travis the list, Rebecca pulled another footstool near the trunk and began going through the papers while he went over it.

"'Tis my guess it was someone who was here frequently very soon after your husband's death. He would not have wanted to give you a chance to look at the journal," he muttered.

After pausing a moment, she said thoughtfully, "That would eliminate the two smaller landholders and Gus

Murdock. They came by at least six months later, and Mr. Murdock came by only once toward the end of the winter hoping to purchase some livestock. His had not fared so well."

Travis nodded and scratched their names from the list. The room was warm, and looking across at her, his attention was caught by a moist curl that had escaped from her tight chignon. Slowly his gaze traveled to her cheeks, which were slightly flushed by the heat, then downward to the steady rise and fall of her breasts. He remembered how silky her skin had felt, and his hands hungered to touch her once again.

Rebecca was aware he was looking at her. Lifting her head, she saw the desire in his eyes. So he was not as immune to her as he wished her to think he was. This knowledge brought a rush of pleasure.

She is my wife, Travis told himself, as if he needed justification to put his task aside for the moment. But even without justification, he could not have resisted the demand of his loins. She was too tempting. Laying the list aside, he knelt in front of her. As if to refresh his memory, he ran his hand along the cord of her neck, testing the smoothness of her skin. When he felt her pulse quicken, he smiled and kissed her lightly.

She wanted to be indifferent, to let him feel the rejection she had felt this morning when he had left her bed so easily, but instead her mouth was soft and yielding. He is your husband, it is his right to claim you when he wishes, she reasoned when her body refused to turn coolly away from him.

Suddenly it was Travis who was turning away. Anger ignited within her as he rose and moved toward the door. He was rejecting her again. Then the anger vanished as quickly as it had flared when he turned the key in the lock, thus ensuring their privacy. "I would not want us to be disturbed," he said huskily as he returned and, placing his hands around her waist, lifted her to her feet.

"We would not want to shock Philip," she agreed, her blood already racing through her veins in anticipation of what was promised in his midnight-blue eyes.

His hunger mounting, Travis began to undress her.

Rebecca knew it was wanton, but her desire, too, was strong. Not waiting for him to finish, she began undressing him.

"You look much more comfortable," he said huskily as he discarded the last of her clothing.

"Comfort is not the feeling you are evoking," she murmured, nipping his shoulder as his hands stroked her hips. His patience grew thin. He sought a deeper intimacy and smiled at the warm wetness that told of her willing readiness. His wife was most certainly a very passionate woman.

He drew her up hard against him, and Rebecca reveled in the feel of his rough-haired chest against her softer skin. But it was his manhood that thrilled her most. As if her body had a mind of its own, she moved against him with blatant invitation.

A low, pleased growl issued from deep within him. Accepting the invitation, he lay her on the floor and claimed her.

Rebecca had hoped her pleasure would not be as great today as it had during the night. She had hoped that the newness of this lovemaking would wear thin and she would not crave him so passionately. But instead, her body seemed even more alive. Fire raged through her, and she had to bite her bottom lip to keep from screaming with delight as he brought her to the pinnacle of passion.

Travis trembled as he joined her at this height of pleasure. But even as his body relaxed, he did not want to release her. Holding on to her, he rolled over onto his back, carrying her with him, until she lay upon him. Slowly his hands moved possessively along her back to her buttocks, massaging her passion-flushed flesh. It is only a physical attraction, he assured himself. But it was an attraction like none he had ever felt before.

Rebecca's tongue darted out to taste a salty trail of perspiration at the hollow of his neck. The rise and fall of his chest beneath her was exciting. She laid her head upon his shoulder and let her hands roam along the length of him as the desire to spend the day thusly spread through her.

Suddenly, through the open window, she heard the sound of Daniel's voice floating in to them. For a moment it did not completely register. Then she realized that he and Joseph had returned from their morning inspection. Her body stiffened. "Daniel will come looking for us," she said with a mild flush of panic. "And Joseph will want to make a report on the crops."

Reluctantly Travis released her. Dressing swiftly, he watched her as she pulled on her garments. Even before she was fully dressed, he wanted to undress her again. This is a dangerous insanity, he warned himself. Still, he found himself impatient for the night to come, when he would once again have her to himself undisturbed.

Tossing him a disgruntled glance because of the ease with which he had dressed himself, she said urgently, "You will have to help with the fastenings."

It took all of his strength to make himself refasten her.

"You'd best go meet Daniel," she said, freeing her hair so she could rewind it.

"Maybe I had better," he agreed, fighting down the urge to tangle his fingers in the thick ebony tresses. This craving he felt for her could easily lead to trouble. He must work on his control, he commanded himself.

As he left, Rebecca sank down on a chair and finished refastening her hair. She could not believe how wantonly she had behaved. Making love in the middle of the morning in the study . . . people would be scandalized. But it had felt so right, so necessary. "The excitement will soon wear thin," she assured herself. But her heart was still pounding, and when she thought of Travis, a fire ignited within her. "Soon," she said more firmly. "It will grow dull soon."

By the time Travis returned with Daniel, she had closed the trunk and was sitting at the desk with the current ledger as if she had been going over the accounts of Green Glen with her new husband.

Daniel ran across the room toward her. "Travis says that if you'll agree, we can go fishing and have a picnic. Please, Sis, say yes."

Rebecca smiled. It was good to see him looking so healthy again. " 'Tis too nice a day to remain inside," she agreed. "Go tell Mildred to pack us a basket."

Letting out a happy yelp, Daniel turned and ran from the room.

As soon as he was gone, Rebecca's expression became apologetic. "I know Daniel probably harangued you into this. He can be very persistent when he sets his mind to something. I'm sorry you feel forced to spend the afternoon with us when I know you would rather be going through Thomas's papers."

"The papers will be there tomorrow," he replied, adding grimly, "Though I doubt they will do me any good."

"I am sorry," she apologized again, wondering if he was already regretting having entered into this bargain with her.

He shrugged. " 'Tis not your fault." In truth he had been glad when Daniel had suggested plans for the afternoon. Some fresh air might help clear this insatiable passion he was feeling for his new bride.

"Mildred is packing us a meal," Daniel informed them excitedly, rushing back into the room.

"Then we must get our fishing supplies together while your sister changes into her riding clothes," Travis directed, moving toward the door.

Happily Daniel jogged after the man.

On the surface they seemed like a real family, Rebecca thought, watching the two departing backs. She suddenly found herself wishing it were so. But Travis had married her only to discover the murderer of his mother. He felt no bond. You will only be disappointed if you allow yourself to wish for that which will never be, she warned herself.

But up in her room she took a little extra time with her wardrobe. There were arranged marriages where the husband and wife had learned to care for one another, she found herself thinking. And physically she and Travis were very compatible. If he could learn to care for her, she did not think it would be difficult to learn to care for him. He was, perhaps, a bit rough around the edges, but he had some admirable qualities. She refused to admit that she was already learning to care for him, assuring herself that the extent of what she was feeling at the moment was a purely physical attraction.

When she joined Travis and Daniel a little while later, they had the basket of food, their fishing equipment, and the horses ready and waiting.

"You were slow," Daniel admonished as Travis lifted her into the saddle.

The feel of his hands sent a surge of warmth through her. She saw the flash of desire in his eyes, and the warmth became a heat. When he moved away to see to Daniel and their supplies, she felt deserted. Be careful, she again warned herself curtly. 'Tis not wise to want too much.

They found a spot near the river. It was shady, and a breeze was blowing gently over the water, cooling the air around them. As they ate, Daniel and Travis bantered back and forth about another fishing trip they had been on. Travis had been teaching Daniel to fish with a net like the Indians used, and they had thrown their catch up on the bank. But before they could get to it, a mother bear with her cubs had claimed it, and Daniel and Travis had been forced to stand very still in the cold water until the bears had moved on.

"But this time we will have Rebecca to guard us," Daniel was saying. "She is an excellent shot."

"Your sister is a good companion to have at one's side in times of trouble," Travis agreed, his gaze shifting to her as he remembered her aid in fighting Paratough. Unexpectedly he found himself recalling how deliciously inviting she had looked after a night in the woods, and it suddenly occurred to him that a docile woman might bore him.

That he was willing to admit she had been of assistance to him caused Rebecca's cheeks to flush with pleasure. It was nice to know he held some good thoughts of her.

Daniel smiled broadly. "We make a nice family, don't we?"

"Certainly the best I have had in a long time," Travis admitted. He had been alone for so long, he thought it had become a way of life with him. But he liked being here with Rebecca and Daniel.

Rebecca saw the shadow that passed over his face. She wanted to reach out and stroke his cheek and tell him that he could be a part of their family for as long as he wished. But prudence held her back. He might be thinking only of the loss of his mother, and she would not make a fool of herself by reading more into his words than was meant to be read.

Putting aside all thoughts of futures, she lay back and let the sun warm her while Daniel and Travis continued to talk.

Travis tried to ignore her. He wanted to clear her from his mind. But instead, his gaze went to her. The innocent rise and fall of her breasts caused a heat to stir within him. "Come along, Daniel," he ordered, grabbing up the net and heading for the cold water. "We promised Mildred fresh fish for dinner."

Rebecca smiled lazily as Travis sat down at the edge of the cold stream and pulled his boots off. Tonight she would pull them off for him again. He seemed to enjoy her undressing him. Careful, her inner voice warned. But there can be no harm in enjoying the companionship of a man, especially if that man is one's husband, she reasoned. She just mustn't begin to believe it could last.

The rest of the afternoon passed pleasantly, and the night even more pleasantly.

The next morning Rebecca and Travis returned to sorting

through the trunk of papers but found nothing. She read the disappointment in his face, and again found herself wondering if he was beginning to regret having married her for nought.

"I will have to find another way to ferret him out," he muttered, frowning in concentration. Then a small smile began to play at the corners of his mouth. "In the meantime, it will not be so disagreeable being the master of Green Glen."

She looked up to find him watching her with those midnight-blue eyes of his. It would seem that he did not yet regret his decision. Excitement stirred within her. He does not even need to touch you to cause your blood to run hot, she chided herself. 'Tis a fool's weakness.

"Come along," he said, standing and offering her his hand. " 'Tis time you gave me a tour of my domain. We shall start with the livestock and then the crops."

Rebecca fought back a rush of disappointment. She had hoped they would start with their bedroom. You are becoming totally wanton! she scolded herself.

"Would you like some help in changing into your riding habit?" he asked as they moved toward the door.

Pausing, she looked up at him and saw the question in his eyes. He was letting her choose, and a part of her demanded that she show some resistance. But instead, she heard herself saying, "If you are offering your assistance, 'tis always welcome."

He played with a curl dangling near her ear. "You are certain you are not tiring of my company? I would not want to feel I am making too great a demand upon you."

His fingers brushing her ear and neck were creating havoc with her senses. "You are my husband, 'tis your right," she replied.

His smile became a frown. "I would not want you to think me a bore."

Rebecca sensed his withdrawal. He had taken her remark to mean she was simply allowing him his privileges. Damn, she cursed mentally. She had never been any good at playing games with men! A coolness was descending over his features. Say something, she ordered herself. "I have not found you boring thus far." Her nervousness made the words come out with a coquettish air, and his smile began to return.

"But you will tell me if you do," he requested.

The warmth that had returned to his eyes was causing her legs to weaken. "I will tell you."

He bent and kissed her shoulder. "Then shall we continue upstairs so that I may assist you with your clothing?"

His breath teased her neck as he lifted his head, and the hunger for his more intimate attentions became unbearable. She wanted to dash toward the bedroom. But instead, she forced herself to move with the proper sedate decorum.

A little later as they lay together, their passion spent and a warm summer breeze blowing through the window, cooling their bodies, she wished she did find him even just a bit boring. She had been so certain the newness would wear off and her body would not crave his so greatly. But that had not happened. The excitement was still strong.

But even more dangerous, she could not stop herself from wondering if he felt anything more for her than mere lust. During their lovemaking he told her of how much her body pleased him, but he never spoke of caring. 'Tis only lust, she told herself, refusing to allow herself any fantasies. They would only lead to disappointment. And, she told herself sternly, it was merely lust that she felt for him as well.

SEVEN

"THINK lust and nothing more!" Rebecca ordered herself under her breath.

June had turned to July. Outside the sun shone brightly and hot breezes stirred the trees. The news from Jamestown had been disturbing earlier in the month. Mr. Bacon had left and returned with a small army to demand that the governor issue him the commission he'd been impatiently awaiting so that he could end the Indian threat once and for all. Even though the reforms he and his friends had proposed had been passed during his absence, he was not appeased. He had demanded that two of the governor's close friends, a Mr. Edward Hill and a Mr. John Stith, both of whom had badly abused their power, be removed from office and never allowed to serve again. He further demanded that a letter recanting his position as a traitor be sent to the king and that the governor make a public apology. With Mr. Bacon's army of battle-trained frontiersmen behind him, the governor had been persuaded to accept these conditions. But everyone knew Sir William could be pushed only so far. Then news came that the Indians had murdered eight settlers on the upper Chickahominy. The governor had started to send all the assembly home and form a militia. But Bacon had been quicker. He had demanded that he be placed in charge of the Indian war and had left Jamestown for Gloucester to recruit more men.

When Rebecca had heard this latest news, she had said a prayer that the feeling of unrest within the colony would now fade. Reforms had been set in motion, and the Indian threat was now being dealt with.

She'd had enough unrest in her life as it was, she thought as she stood by the window watching Travis and Daniel riding off for their morning inspection of the crops. Daniel was talking adamantly, and Travis was laughing.

She loved the sound of his laughter. Not "loved," she corrected herself sharply . . . "enjoyed."

Travis Brandt had been a surprise. She had expected him to be single-minded, restrained, even reticent, and above all grimly serious. But during the past weeks he'd shown a side of himself she had never believed existed. The most surprising thing was that he had a sense of humor. Even more, those blue eyes of his had an infectious way of dancing with amusement that caused joy to spread through her.

"When his quest is done, 'tis likely he will no longer want to remain at Green Glen," she warned herself. " 'Tis best not to learn to enjoy his company too greatly." But that was easier said than done.

And there was Daniel to consider. Her brother had grown even more attached to Travis since the marriage. He looked upon him almost as a father.

"Daniel must someday learn that those you care about will leave," she muttered to herself. A sudden wave of melancholy washed over her. Giving her shoulders a sharp shrug, as if that would shake it off, she left the window and returned to her sewing.

She had been working quietly for a little less than an hour when Philip appeared at the door. "Madam," he said, bowing stiffly.

Rebecca looked up from her needlework. Not only had his voice sounded anxious, but there was a readable uneasiness on his face. Immediately her guard was up. It took a great deal to unsettle her butler. "What is it, Philip?" she asked, keeping her voice calm.

"There is a man to see Mr. Brandt." Philip's nose crinkled in distaste. "A rather unfortunate-looking person, if I may say so."

Rebecca's anxiousness was immediately replaced with curiosity. Was it someone who had information for Travis, or was it someone from his past? Either way this guest could prove interesting. "Then you must show him in, Philip," she ordered.

"Really, madam." His expression became one of fatherly protectiveness. "I am not so certain it is wise of you to meet with this man alone."

"I am certain I shall be safe in my own home," she assured him, more determined than ever to meet this stranger. "Please, show him in."

For a moment it appeared as if Philip were going to launch a new protest. However, being a well-trained servant, his expression returned to its normal staid look, and he bowed. "Yes, madam." But as he started to carry out her order, he turned back and took a small silver bell from the mantel. Placing it upon the table beside her, he said, "Should you feel the need for any assistance, you've only to ring, madam," and with a final bow, he went to invite their caller to join her.

Rebecca reminded herself of what curiosity had done to the cat, but she could not hold her desire to learn about Travis in check. He is growing much too important to you, she warned herself. At that moment Philip returned, and Rebecca rose to greet her guest.

"Mr. Gyles Woods to see you, madam," her butler announced in his most formal and formidable tones.

"Mr. Woods." Rebecca curtsied as her visitor entered. She could immediately see what had caused Philip's concern. The man's appearance was that of a ruffian. Very likely Philip assumed he was one of the smugglers with whom it was rumored Travis had associated. Her caller wore heavy boots that came up to his knees, and his coat was amateurishly patched in several places, as if he had done it himself. Like Travis, he wore his own hair. It was blond and pulled back into a ponytail at the nape of his neck. He wore a sword in a sheath that hung at his waist from a wide leather strap that came over one shoulder and crossed his chest. His breeches, what she could see of them between the coat and the boots, were also well worn.

"Mistress Brandt," he replied, bowing deeply. "'Tis a pleasure to meet you. Had I known Travis had married, I would have come sooner to see his bride."

His smile was enticing, and Rebecca found herself returning it. She noted that his eyes were also blue, but of a lighter shade than her husband's, and they were filled with a curiosity that matched her own. If he was a rogue, he was a most charming one, she decided. "Philip, have a tray of food and some fresh tea prepared and brought to our guest," she ordered.

Mr. Woods bowed again. "You are most gracious. The truth is I've been traveling and haven't had a decent meal in days."

"Then you must make certain Mildred fills the tray," Rebecca instructed Philip. "And tell her that we shall have a guest for the noon meal." Standing at the door, Philip continued to hesitate. Frowning at him, Rebecca gave a wave of her hand. "And hurry. We would not want Mr. Brandt to return and discover we have not cared properly for his caller."

Philip hesitated for a moment longer, then, bowing low, hurried away.

"I am afraid my disreputable appearance has upset your butler," Gyles said, glancing toward the servant's departing back. "But I assure you I am quite safe."

Rebecca smiled politely. She would wait to determine that. "Won't you be seated."

Gyles glanced at the chair with the needlepoint seat she had indicated. With his hand he gave his coat a slap, and a small cloud of dust floated away from him. "Might be best if I just stand," he said with an edge of self-consciousness.

She could not fault his manners. "Bring the chair from near the window," she directed.

Looking over his shoulder he saw the simple unupholstered piece of furniture and smiled brightly. "Thank you, madam." After positioning the chair so that it was a few feet in front of Rebecca's, he lowered himself into it like a man grateful to have a place to sit.

"Philip informs me that you have business with my husband," she said, continuing to study him thoughtfully. He was not as young as she had first thought. Her first impression was that he was no older than eighteen or nineteen, but now she realized that he was closer to thirty than he was to twenty.

"Not business exactly. I was passing by on my way to join Mr. Bacon's army. I'd heard Travis was living around here and thought I'd look him up," he explained.

"Then you are an old friend of my husband's?" For Travis's sake she had hoped this man might bring news that would help her husband find the man he sought. But his being an old friend of Travis's made her visitor of more interest to her.

Gyles nodded. "He saved my life."

She knew it was not polite to indulge her curiosity, but she could not resist the opportunity to discover anything she could about Travis Brandt. "Please, tell me about it," she encouraged.

A sudden shadow of sadness clouded the man's face. Immediately Rebecca regretted her curiosity. "But not if 'tis painful," she added quickly.

Gyles shrugged as if trying to cast off the sudden melancholia that had shown on his face. " 'Twas nearly four years ago. My wife and I had set up a homestead on the southern side of the Potomac near the frontier. It was almost the end of harvest time when she told me she was pregnant. She was afraid of having the baby alone in the wilderness and begged me to take her to her mother. Her parents have a place up in Pennsylvania." A wistful smile played across his face. "I could never deny that woman anything." The smile faded, and a grimness came over his features. "We were just beyond the northern Maryland border when the party we were with was attacked by Indians. My wife was killed, and I was taken prisoner. Travis was being held by the same band of savages and had been with them for several years." Gyles's gaze wandered to the empty hearth. "I learned later that when Travis had been attacked, he had fought hard and was nearly killed. An old Indian by the name of Nagahaw had stepped forth and claimed Travis as his slave, saving Travis from being slain on the spot. Nagahaw had seen that Travis was nursed back to health, and in return Travis had pledged to serve him. I've no love for the Indians, but from what Travis told me, Nagahaw treated him well. The old Indian taught Travis the Indian way of trapping and hunting. But when Nagahaw died, Nagahaw's daughter inherited Travis, and her husband was a brute of a man. When they brought me into camp, Travis was barely skin and bones. He was being worked like a beast, nearly starved to death, and bound at night so that he could not escape. As for me, I didn't care whether I lived or died. All I could think about was my dead wife and our unborn child."

"Really, if this is too painful for you, please do not continue," Rebecca interrupted, angry with herself for having let her curiosity get the best of her. The news of Travis's past interested her greatly, but she did not want to make this man suffer any more than he already had.

Gyles smiled a crooked smile. " 'Tis about time I learned to talk about it." He drew a deep breath. "Anyway, that night I was brought out by the campfire and tormented. They didn't do any real damage. One old woman threw hot coals at me. But it was their laughter . . . it drove me crazy . . . literally. They were sitting around eating and celebrating murdering my wife and child. They had me bound to a stake, and I remember fighting my bonds until blood was running down my hands. I wanted to get free and kill as many of them as I could before they killed me and my soul was freed to join my wife." Gyles stopped abruptly. "I'm sorry, I shouldn't have been so blunt."

" 'Tis all right," Rebecca assured him, finding herself wishing that Travis could feel just half as much for her as Gyles had felt for his wife.

"Anyway, Travis had been plotting his escape carefully. He had already convinced his master that he was near death so that his bonds were not being as securely tied as was normal. That night he waited until all of the Indians were asleep, then freed himself. I guess he realized that they'd kill me pretty soon. I sure wasn't going to make any of them a decent slave. At great risk to himself, he cut me free." Gyles frowned self-consciously. "He could have made his escape easily on his own. As it was, I almost cost us both our lives. All I wanted was revenge. I started to make a dive for the nearest Indian to strangle him with my bare hands. But Travis knocked me over the head and carried me out of camp. He tossed me in the bottom of a canoe and paddled upstream all night." The crooked smile returned to Gyles's face. "I can still remember the ache in my neck when I came to. Travis, he just handed me an oar and ordered me to paddle. One look at him and I obeyed. He looked as crazy as I felt. There was this wild gleam in his eyes as if he were escaping from Hades and nothing was going to stop him."

Rebecca could picture Travis, half starved, dressed in rags, with that determined, single-minded look on his face. "Travis is a good man to have on your side when you're in danger," she said, remembering her own experience.

Gyles nodded. "And he'd planned his escape well. The Indians were leaving the next day for their winter camping grounds. He figured they wouldn't want to take the time to come after us. He was right, except for his master. That was one nasty Indian. It was almost as if he harbored a personal grudge against Travis. Maybe he did. From what Travis told me later, it was likely the savage resented his father-in-law's friendly treatment of Travis. Anyway, he came after us. I remember it was around dusk. We had left the canoe and been trekking across land for a full day. The savage came out of the woods yelling and dived at Travis with his knife. He had double Travis's weight. I was sure Travis was a goner. But the next thing I know, Travis was on top. They fought like a couple of wild men. I tried to help, but they was moving too fast. Then it was all over. Travis had been cut a couple of times, but it was the Indian who was dead, his own knife buried in that evil heart of his. After that, Travis kept me with him for the winter. He taught me to trap and hunt. At first I refused even to talk. I was feeling guilty that I was still alive and my Emily was dead. But Travis, he talked to me anyway, made me eat, kept me alive. It took awhile, but I finally came around. Emily was a good and loving woman. She wouldn't have wanted me to give up on life." Gyles smiled. "Travis and I trapped and traded together for another year. Then he got a message and went to Jamestown. A little after that he told me he was going to come up here and settle. I decided it was time for me to go back to my old homestead, and I ain't seen him since."

"I'm sure he'll be pleased to see you again," Rebecca said, still picturing Travis forcing this man back to health.

"Gyles!" Travis strode into the room, a smile of welcome on his face.

Gyles greeted Travis with a hug. Then, stepping back, he looked Travis up and down. "Never thought a rough-edged sword like you could land yourself so marvelous a wife," he said jovially.

Travis's gaze traveled to Rebecca. "She has come as quite a surprise to me, also," he admitted.

There was a warmth in his eyes that caused Rebecca's toes to curl. He appeared both pleased and proud to call her his wife. Joy filled her and she smiled.

"And to what do I owe this visit?" Travis asked, his attention returning to Gyles. "I thought you would be tending your fields."

Gyles's smile became a frown. "I'm on my way to join Mr. Bacon. I'll not sit idly by and allow those savages to murder other men's wives and children."

Travis nodded his understanding.

"I thought perhaps you might want to join me," Gyles finished.

Rebecca's heart missed a beat as a sudden wave of fear swept over her. The thought of Travis leaving was difficult enough. The thought of him getting killed fighting Indians was more than she wanted to bear.

"I think not," Travis replied. "We are near the frontier. There is always the possibility that my sword will be needed here to defend my wife and home. Besides, from what I hear, Mr. Bacon has gathered a stout number of men from Gloucester alone."

Gyles nodded in agreement. "Aye." His hand went to his sword. "But another hand won't do any harm."

Travis patted his friend on the back. "He should be glad of having yours."

Rebecca was breathing again. Travis was not going to leave. You should not care so much, she warned herself again. But this time the warning was barely heard.

Gyles stayed the night and left the next day. Travis sent a pack mule with him, laden with food to contribute to Bacon's campaign.

"From what I hears tell," Joseph said, standing beside Travis as Gyles rode away, "they's some people getting a mite angry with Mr. Bacon. Heard he was demanding arms and food like he was king. Just taking them from the people."

Travis had heard the same mutterings. "But they also want the Indian threat ended," he said in a reasoning voice. "They can't have it both ways."

"Suppose you're right," Joseph conceded, but he didn't

look convinced. "One thing that does puzzle me, though . . . heard tell that Mr. Bacon had Major Lawrence Smith and Major Thomas Hawkins arrested just 'cause they was gathering men to fight. Both are fine gentlemen and done a good job in the past protecting the settlers along the Rappahannock."

Travis shrugged. "It would seem that Mr. Bacon prefers to be in total command."

"Guess it would work better if all the men was together and not in separate militias," Joseph conceded. "But I still don't understand why he had to arrest Major Smith and Major Hawkins."

Travis, too, had an uneasy feeling. The sense of rebellion in the air was growing stronger. Any fool could see that Bacon was challenging Sir William's power, and Sir William was not a man to sit by idly and allow that to happen. He just hoped Gyles did not get caught in the middle. "We've got crops to see to, Joseph," he said aloud.

Rebecca had been watching from an upstairs window, afraid that at any moment Travis might change his mind and leave with Gyles. She did not breathe a sigh of relief until he and Joseph had headed back to the stables.

Going down to the kitchen, she ordered Travis's favorite meal to be served that evening, and when he returned from his inspection of the crops, she brought him a cool drink herself.

Travis was surprised by this personal service. He was also more pleased than he wished to be. But it was not just Rebecca's added attention that unsettled him. Gyles's visit had caused him some consternation. Travis had assured himself that he had chosen to remain at Green Glen because his suspects were nearby and he had spent too many years searching to leave them to disappear on him. But his honesty had forced him to admit that his real concern lay with Rebecca and Daniel. Their safety had grown to mean a great deal to him. "I must admit I did not expect such service from the mistress of Green Glen," he remarked, watching her closely as he took a drink of the water.

Suddenly worried he would guess how much he was growing to mean to her, Rebecca curtsied to avoid his steady gaze. "I am most grateful to you, sir, for considering my brother's and my safety."

" 'Tis a husband's duty," he replied noncommittally.

Rebecca's stomach knotted. She had hoped for more than a sense of duty on his part. Straightening, she faced him levelly. "Then I will thank your sense of duty," she said stiffly and turned to go.

He told himself to let her leave, but he didn't want her to. "Rebecca," he said sternly. "Does not a man's sense of duty deserve some sort of reward?"

Had she not thanked him? It stung that he thought of her only as a duty. Turning to face him, she was determined to keep a distance between them. But the hint of mischief in the blue depths of his eyes destroyed her willingness to remain aloof. "And what reward do you have in mind, sir?" she questioned, already knowing the answer and her body already beginning to respond.

"A kiss might do," he replied. Approaching her, he tilted her chin upward and kissed her lightly.

She had never played lovers' games, but with Travis the skill seemed to come naturally. "Is that all you require?" she asked coyly as he lifted his head away.

He wanted to claim her instantly, but that would rush the enjoyment he saw promised in the dark depths of her gypsy eyes. "What else would you offer?"

"I could massage your shoulders for you, sir," she suggested with mock innocence.

He seated himself in a low-backed chair that would give her free access. "Then proceed."

She would make him care, she told herself. "It would be best done with your shirt removed," she said. "And for that we need a bit of privacy." Going to the door, she locked it.

Watching her, he had to fight down his impatience.

Satisfied they would not be disturbed, Rebecca returned to him and removed his coat, then his shirt. Walking around to the back of his chair, she began to knead the muscles of his shoulders.

It occurred to Travis that no man could feel as good as he did at that moment. Remembering he had almost allowed Rebecca to go to another caused his stomach to tighten.

The hard warm feel of him beneath her hands sent Rebecca's blood racing hot through her veins. Unable to keep up the pretense of a massage for long, her hands moved downward, and leaning forward, she kissed his shoulder. Leisurely her fingers combed through the dark curly hairs covering his chest as she trailed kisses to his neck. When her hands moved lower over his flat abdomen, she felt his muscles tighten, and beneath her mouth, the pulse in his throat throbbed. Smiling to herself with womanly satisfaction, she leaned farther forward and let her hands roam until they found his maleness.

Her touch was making it impossible for him to control his patience. Capturing her by the wrists, he lifted her hands from him and rose. Backing her against a wall, he stooped quickly and lifted her skirts. "I am not certain I can wait to undress you," he warned, his finger seeking her womanly port. He smiled at the moist warmth that greeted him. She was as ready for him as he was for her.

Rebecca's legs ached to have him between them. Deftly her hands sought the fastening on his breeches. His readiness pleased her as she freed him from the confines of his clothing.

Travis could wait no longer. "Wrap your legs around me," he ordered her gruffly as he lifted her.

Rebecca obeyed and in the next instant found herself seated upon him, the depth of their union exciting her beyond the bounds of mere pleasure.

Travis buried his face in her bosom as he moved within her. Never had a woman smelled so sweet.

Rebecca felt wanton, but it was an exhilarating sort of wantonness. She tightened her legs around him for a firmer hold. It had never occurred to her that having her husband take her when she was fully clothed could feel this delectably exquisite.

"You do know how to reward a man," he growled against her heat-flushed skin.

" 'Tis my pleasure," she assured him, her voice coming in gasps as her body peaked and her legs tightened around him even more. Trembling with the pleasure he had brought her, she felt him join her in this moment of ecstasy and wanted to laugh with delight.

"You have a body well worth a man's life to protect," he breathed, continuing to hold her to him.

"You, too, have a body worth protecting," she replied, slowly letting her legs slip downward until her toes touched the ground.

Laughing, he gave her bottom a pat, then released her and began to fasten his own clothing. But as she started to move away, he caught her and, cuddling a breast in his hand, kissed it through the fabric of her dress.

Even with the cloth barrier between his lips and her skin, she felt the warmth of his mouth. He owned her body. She could not deny that. But did she dare allow him to own her heart? *Are you certain that choice is yours?* her inner voice questioned. That was an answer she did not have.

Travis moved away from his wife. *His wife.* He repeated the words to himself. He liked the sound of them. His wife, his home. The thought of Rebecca pregnant with his child stirred his blood. Perhaps it was time to have more in his life than this quest. He looked at her as she smoothed down her skirt. Another woman might have protested such unrefined lovemaking. But his gypsy had loved it. Yes, he would be very certain to guard her body well.

But it was not just her body that pleased him, he admitted later that evening as they sat on the porch watching the sunset over the river. She was good company. She didn't chatter as some women did, and she could manage a jest as well as any man. His jaw suddenly tensed. The desire to find the man he sought and end his quest was stronger than it had ever been. But this time revenge was not his only motive. He wanted to finish with the past so that he could devote himself to his new life . . . with Rebecca here at Green Glen.

"I have decided to exclude Myles Johnson from my list," he announced, "unless you can give me reason not to. I was reading Thomas's journals the other day and discovered he harbored a deep resentment toward the man. I doubt if he would have referred to him as a friend."

Rebecca nodded. "You're right. Thomas took Mr. Johnson to court over the ownership of a few acres of land on the south side of our property. For years they had been considered a part of Mr. Johnson's holdings, but then one day Thomas got it into his head that they were actually his. The court ruled against my husband." Rebecca's mouth formed a hard straight line. "Thomas did not like it when things did not go his way."

Travis reached over and touched her cheek. Again he found himself wishing he could thrash Thomas Mercer. Never had he felt so protective toward a woman.

The warmth of his touch erased the chill the memories of Thomas had brought. Turning toward Travis, Rebecca smiled. He did seem to enjoy being here with her. Perhaps he would not be so anxious as she had thought to leave Green Glen once his quest was finished.

EIGHT

JULY turned to August. Mistress Garnet's warning that the omens signaled a great upheaval proved true. Mr. Bacon had used threats and intimidation to acquire supplies from the planters for his second campaign against the Indians. Some had filed complaints against him. The governor had seized the opportunity and issued a warrant for Bacon's arrest. But Mr. Bacon had proved to be too popular. After all, he was ridding the colony of the Indian threat. Even more, it was their friends and relatives who fought with Bacon, and the colonists who had remained at home could not turn against them.

Hearing of the governor's warrant for his arrest, Mr. Bacon had turned his forces upon the governor. Sir William, without an army to match Mr. Bacon's, was forced to flee to the eastern shores. Now it was Nathaniel Bacon who was in control of nearly all of Virginia, and the loyalties of the colonists were being sorely tried.

Rebecca looked down the long table toward Travis. Tonight they were giving their first formal dinner party since the wedding. He appeared in all ways the master of Green Glen. His clothing, his manners, and his bearing were that of a man of substance who held a firm hand over his home and lands.

It had not been the most perfect weather for a dinner party. The days had been sweltering. But tonight luck was

135

with them. A cooling breeze was blowing in from the river.
Travis had narrowed his list greatly. To her shock, her three
former suitors seemed the most likely suspects. And tonight
all three were present along with Colonel and Mistress
Howard, Mistress Garnet, Mistress Hansone who was Mr.
Loyde's mother-in-law, and Mistress and Mr. Prate.

Rebecca's gaze left Travis and traveled around the table.
It was still difficult for her to believe any of the three men
was the one Travis sought. The thought that she had almost
married a cold-blooded murderer caused a chill to run along
her spine.

"Bacon would never have amassed the support he now
has among our more prominent citizens if it had not been for
the governor's selfish stupidity," Colonel Howard was
saying.

Rebecca knew he was referring to the incident at Tindal's
Point on the York River. Early in August, Bacon had invited
the prominent men of Virginia to meet with him. Seventy
had gathered at the residence of Captain Otho Thrope. They
had agreed that the reforms Bacon wished to institute were
to the advantage of all of Virginia, and they were also in
agreement that Sir William had become a despot and was
best removed. But they had not been ready to swear an oath
agreeing to fight the king's troops. That, they had pointed
out, would be treason. It was at this point that news reached
them that Sir William had sailed to the fort at Tindal's Point
and taken all of its arms and munitions, leaving the people
there defenseless against attacks by the Indians. Infuriated
that Sir William could be so selfish and uncaring of the
people he had ruled for so long, all had taken the oath to
follow Bacon wherever he might lead.

"Ridding Virginia of Sir William and his despot rule is
one thing," the colonel continued. "But treason is quite
another."

"Does that mean you plan to sail to the eastern shore and
join the forces Sir William is raising to retake Virginia?"
Mr. Loyde asked.

The colonel shook his head. "I'll not leave my lands and home to be confiscated by Bacon and his men. I've worked too hard to build my life here."

"But if you stay, they may be confiscated by Sir William and you yourself declared a traitor and hanged," Mr. Wetherly pointed out, adding with a mildly mischievous air, as if he found this whole discussion a jest, "I understand Sir William is in a hanging mood."

From the looks exchanged around the table, it was clear to Rebecca that none of the others found anything amusing about it. Nor should they, she thought. Either way, they could lose all they had struggled to build—and possibly their lives as well.

"He's right," Mr. Loyde conceded grimly. "We are caught. 'Tis not the king with whom we have a grievance, but Mr. Bacon has made it so."

"Careful," Colonel Howard interjected, a cynical edge entering his voice. "If word should get out that any of us have questionable loyalties toward Mr. Bacon, we will have his men knocking on our doors and throwing us all into jail."

"Or forcing us to take an oath," Mr. Loyde added. "I've heard that he is so worried about the hearts of the men in Westmoreland County he has sent orders that they are to take an oath swearing allegiance to him and declaring that the governor and council have acted illegally. He is even demanding that they agree to arm against any forces sent by His Majesty until such time as Mr. Bacon can present his grievances to the king." Mr. Loyde's expression grew grimmer. "And the name of any man not taking the oath is to be sent back to Mr. Bacon."

"'Tis this being caught in the middle I do not like," Mr. Prate muttered.

"But surely you cannot disagree with Mr. Bacon's reforms," Mistress Garnet insisted.

Mr. Prate scoffed. "I have it on good authority that those reforms were drawn up by Lawrence. Further, everyone knows Bacon was not even present in his seat when the assembly voted the majority of them in."

Mistress Garnet glared at the planter indignantly. " 'Twas Bacon's wish that those reforms be put into law and his popularity that forced the assembly to vote for them. Not only that, you must agree that Mr. Bacon is taking action where action is needed. Too many times, Sir William has allowed himself to be lulled into inaction by promises of peace made by those savages who lurk in our midst. Mr. Bacon is willing to rid us of them once and for all. Many's the night I've gone to bed and wondered if I would wake the next morning or be killed as I slept."

"And should Bacon gain a secure seat of power, how can you be so certain he will rule any more fairly than Sir William?" the colonel argued. "I have it on good authority that he was sent here by his family because he'd gotten himself into money difficulties in England. Even more, I've heard that he has long harbored a grudge against the governor for financial reasons. He wanted a bit of the fur trade Sir William held a monopoly over until this last assembly. And, too, he resented Sir William giving the choicest land to his close friends."

"As do we all," Kirby Wetherly interjected dryly.

"What is your position on this, Brandt?" the colonel demanded, suddenly turning everyone's attention toward Travis.

"I applaud the reforms Bacon supported, but I am not certain I am ready for a new Cromwell," Travis replied. "And as the colonel has pointed out, we cannot be certain of the man's character."

"Cromwell." The colonel shook his head in a gesture of regret. " 'Tis a shame how times change. Before Cromwell, Sir William was a good man . . . a man of the people. The beheading of his king changed him greatly."

Mr. Loyde frowned thoughtfully. " 'Tis a difficult choice. Do we want King Bacon or King Charles?"

"If the king sends troops—and surely he will," the

colonel said with finality, " 'twill be a bloody choice either way."

Mistress Garnet's gaze traveled around the table. " 'Tis as I've been saying," she declared in a voice that seemed to predict doom. "The omens of the past year cannot be discounted."

Kirby Wetherly drank down another glass of wine. Then, leveling his gaze upon Travis, he said with honied cynicism, "It must be difficult for you to have all of this"—he waved an arm to indicate their surroundings—"threatened now that you have paid the price of marriage to become master of Green Glen."

Rebecca caught the brief moment of malicious amusement in Mistress Garnet's eyes before the woman lowered them and faked concentration on her food. Their other guests, however, appeared shocked or appalled. She wondered if this was due to Mr. Wetherly's blatant suggestion that Travis had married her only for Green Glen or their embarrassment that he should have stated so openly what was the general consensus of the community. Her gaze traveled to Travis.

He was regarding Mr. Wetherly with an indulgent smile. "Unlike you, Mr. Wetherly, I do not find marriage to be so great a price to pay."

No price was too great to find the man who had murdered his mother, Rebecca added mentally, forcing herself to read the truth of his words and not put more into them. Covertly, her gaze scanned the assemblage as she wondered if they believed the implication in Travis's words and voice that he was finding marriage to her agreeable. Then it dawned on her that she didn't care what they thought. She'd been forced to make a choice and she was pleased with the one she had made.

Colonel Howard rewarded Travis with a look that said "well spoken." Then giving Wetherly a cutting glance, he said sharply, "You're drinking too much, Wetherly." This reprimand delivered, he turned the conversation to talk of the crops. Those, at least, were growing well.

Following the meal, all adjourned to the drawing room. Jeremia Brown, a young indentured servant at Green Glen, was awaiting them with his violin tuned. He had provided the music following Travis and Rebecca's wedding and was again to provide music for their guests. The furniture had been moved back so that those who wished to could dance.

"You are looking very lovely tonight," Mistress Howard addressed Rebecca. "It would seem you find your marriage suitable. I know it has taken a great weight off of my husband's shoulders."

"And placed it upon mine," Travis said, joining them at that moment.

Rebecca frowned up at him, embarrassed that he should present her as a nuisance. "You will have Mistress Howard thinking you consider me a burden."

"A burden I am more than willing to carry," he replied, smiling down at her warmly. What shocked him was how deeply he meant those words.

Rebecca flushed with pleasure under his gaze, and a twinkle glistened in Mistress Howard's eyes. "It would seem this marriage has worked out quite well."

"Quite well, indeed," Travis assured her. Offering Rebecca his hand, he said, "I have come to claim the first dance."

"'Tis your privilege, O lord and master," she replied with playful subservience.

He laughed as he led her onto the dance floor while Mistress Howard watched approvingly.

"I have other privileges that interest me more," he whispered in her ear as they began to move to the music.

Rebecca forced a reproving smile that belied the way her blood was suddenly rushing hotly through her veins. "You are a most lustful man," she reprimanded mockingly, enjoying the way they bantered so easily together.

"I hope that is not a hint that you wish me to change," he countered.

" 'Tis not," she assured him.

Again he laughed lightly, then concentrated on the dance.

As the evening progressed and Rebecca danced with each of her male guests, she had the most tremendous urge to mention the brooch and study their reactions. It had grown very important to her to help Travis find the man he sought because it meant so much to him. But prudence held her tongue. She did not want to put the killer on his guard.

" 'Twould seem that your marriage agrees with you," Mr. Wetherly was saying as she danced with him. It was getting late, and he had waited until nearly the last tune to approach her.

"Yes, it does," she confirmed.

His gaze traveled beyond her momentarily, and she caught sight of Andrea Prate over her shoulder. "Does Mr. Brandt guard you as well as Mr. Prate guards his young wife?" he asked dryly.

Rebecca recalled the covert interest he had shown toward the fair Andrea at the wedding. It was obvious his attempts to gain access to Mistress Prate had been thwarted. "He has no need to guard me," she replied.

Kirby smiled warmly down at her. "I am, of course, happy for you, but 'tis my loss." A mischievous gleam sparkled in his eyes. "However, should he ever begin to bore you, I would be most pleased to give you of my time."

Rebecca frowned. "That, Mr. Wetherly, was a most improper remark."

At that moment the music stopped. "I most humbly apologize," he said in a low voice. Still holding her hand, he bowed and kissed the back of her lace glove.

"I believe the last dance is mine," Travis said, coming up behind them. There was a look of disapproval in his eyes as they rested on Rebecca's hand still being held by Wetherly.

" 'Tis with regret that I relinquish your lovely bride to

you," Kirby said gallantly, releasing her and taking a step back. "You are a truly lucky man, Brandt."

"I believe so," Travis replied with cool politeness, claiming Rebecca and leading her onto the dance floor. As they moved away from Wetherly, he leaned toward her and demanded in a harsh whisper, "What was the man saying to you?" Suddenly embarrassed that he both felt and sounded like a jealous fool, Travis quickly schooled his face into an expression of less emotion.

Startled and pleased by the strong edge of what sounded like jealousy in his voice, Rebecca glanced up at him, but his expression was merely one of impatience. You wanted him to be jealous, she chided herself, and you read more into his words than was there. " 'Twas unimportant," she replied.

Travis told himself to drop the subject. But he could not banish from his mind the picture of Wetherly kissing the back of his wife's hand. "His attentions can ruin a woman's reputation."

Rebecca's back stiffened at the reprimand in his voice. "You do not need to warn me of a risk to my reputation," she replied curtly. "I suspect that his attentions toward me were merely a ploy to weaken Mr. Prate's guard over his young wife."

"Most likely," Travis conceded, casting a glance toward Mistress Prate. Still, he did not like Wetherly being anywhere near Rebecca. Dryly he added, "The man has the morals of a mongrel dog. One day he will get himself shot by an enraged husband."

"Most likely," Rebecca agreed, feeling mildly insulted that Travis could so easily brush off Mr. Wetherly's attentions toward her.

To her relief, their guests began to leave soon after the last tune was played. The dinner party had gone well, but it had been tiring.

As she and Travis stood at the door waving good-bye to the last of their guests, he said musingly, "Mr. Prate took me aside and suggested that in the future I might want to exclude Mr. Wetherly from our guest list."

Rebecca glanced up at him. "And what did you tell him?"

"I told him I was not worried about Wetherly," he replied with forced indifference. The truth was he would gladly have excluded Mr. Wetherly if he did not feel it necessary to keep an eye on the man. Almost more to himself than to her, he added, "It would be imprudent of me to exclude him. Although I doubt very much it is so, I cannot yet be certain he is not the man I seek."

Rebecca wondered if Travis would feel the same if he knew the truth of what Kirby Wetherly had said to her. Probably, he would, she decided. His quest was more important to him than she. This truth hurt sharply. And with that hurt, another truth forced its way upon her. She was falling in love with her husband. She could deny that no longer.

"I must make a few notations," he said as they entered the house.

"Did you discover something useful?" she asked, attempting to guide her mind away from the folly of her emotions.

"Probably not," he replied. "They are mostly dates of when members of the community were traveling and where they traveled." A tired smile curled his lips. "I probably know more about the movements of certain male members of our community than the worst gossip."

Rebecca forced a returning smile. Watching him walk toward the study, she felt torn. For his sake, she wanted his quest to end soon. But she knew that once it was over, it was likely he would leave and she did not want to lose him. Foolish girl, she chided herself. A restlessness threatened to overwhelm her.

Stepping out onto the back porch, she gazed up at the night sky. It was clear. A crescent moon shone brightly among the stars.

"A night for lovers," a man's voice suddenly broke into her thoughts.

Startled, Rebecca frowned as Mr. Wetherly suddenly appeared from behind the shrubbery and climbed the short flight of stairs from the lawn to the porch. "You scared me," she admonished.

"My most humblest of apologies," he replied, bowing low in front of her, his voice a silky caress. "Frightening you is the last thing I wish to do."

His manner was quite forward, and the frown on her face deepened. "You should not be here."

"I could not resist," he replied, moving closer until he stood within inches of her. "I was hoping you might appear alone."

She could smell the alcohol on his breath. "You are drunk," she said, taking a step backward to put more distance between them.

"Drunk with your beauty," he amended.

"I want you to go," she ordered sternly. How she could have ever considered this man suitable for a husband, she did not know. He was a lecherous boor.

"Aren't you the least bit interested in what you missed by marrying Brandt?" he coaxed. "I've been told by many that I'm a most expert lover."

"Your expertise in other men's bedrooms does not interest me," she assured him. Her expression one of disgust, she started to move toward the house.

But his hands closed around her upper arms, holding her captive in front of him. "With one little kiss I am certain I can prove my prowess," he murmured.

She twisted her head as his mouth descended toward hers and prepared to kick him hard.

"What the devil . . . ?" Travis's angry voice suddenly sounded from the doorway.

Releasing Rebecca abruptly, Wetherly took a step back. His expression became one of accusation. "I thought you told me you had gotten rid of your husband."

Stunned that he should be trying to make it look as if she had invited his attentions, she glared at him. "I said no such thing!"

He glanced toward Travis. "You cannot blame me if you cannot keep your wife satisfied," he said, then with the speed of a jackrabbit, he leapt from the porch. In the next moment he mounted his horse and rode off into the night.

"It would seem that Mr. Prate is much more observant than I," Travis remarked, studying Rebecca coldly. He felt like a fool. Still, if he could have gotten his hands upon Mr. Wetherly, he would have beaten the man to within an inch of his life.

"Mr. Wetherly lied," she snapped. "I made no arrangements to meet him. I came out here to look at the night sky, and he suddenly appeared."

"And so you decided to share a little kiss," he snarled. "I did not realize you had grown so quickly bored of my lovemaking." Turning on his heels, he stalked back into the house.

For a long moment Rebecca stood frozen. He believed Kirby Wetherly. Her skin flushed scarlet with indignation. How dare he! Striding after him, she caught up with him as he entered their bedroom. She closed the door behind her, barely able to stop herself from slamming it, and stood glaring at him. "I was attempting to get away from him when he grabbed me and tried to kiss me."

The blue of his eyes reminded her of the sky before a storm. "He had best stay away from you in the future," he said warningly. "You are my wife. I'll not allow any other man to touch you."

She stood watching him in amazement. Recalling the look in his eyes when he had claimed her from Wetherly on the dance floor, she heard herself saying, "You are jealous."

His jaw twitched in anger. He had not meant to be so open, but seeing her with Wetherly had weakened his control. His expression grew grim. "I'll not be made a fool of," he growled.

There was a possessiveness mingled with his anger that caused a thrill of womanly delight to race through her. He was not as immune to her as he would have her believe. She met his gaze. "I have never been bored by your lovemaking."

Travis drew a deep breath. He was behaving like a jealous idiot. He had no reason to doubt her version of what had happened between herself and Wetherly, and he most certainly did not want to doubt her last words. The hint of a pleased smile played at one corner of his mouth. "I am glad to hear that."

She read the desire in his eyes, and an answering fire began to burn within her.

"You are the most tempting woman I have ever known. I should not be surprised that Wetherly has persisted in his pursuit of you."

The desire in his eyes grew warmer, and she moved toward him. " 'Tis not his pursuit that interests me," she said, beginning to unfasten his coat.

His hands trailed along the smooth skin of her shoulders to her neck. With his thumbs beneath her chin, he tilted her face upward and kissed her with hungry possessiveness. "If he should ever come near you again, I will teach him a sound lesson about staying away from other men's wives," he promised gruffly against her lips.

Reaching up, she stroked the hard line of his jaw. His manner gave strong proof that he did not plan to leave her once his quest was finished. It would seem there would be a future for them after all. Trailing kisses down to the hollow of his neck, she again began to work the fastening of his clothing lose.

"All evening I have wanted to get you alone." He tossed his shirt aside and began helping her out of her dress.

She raked her fingers lightly down his chest and felt his

sharp intake of breath. "You're trying my patience," he warned.

She laughed and, reaching upward, loosened her hair and let it cascade down over her shoulders and back as he slowly rolled her hose down, then slipped them from her feet. Still kneeling in front of her, he trailed his hands up over her calves and thighs to the roundness of her hips.

She bit her bottom lip as a moan of pleasure issued from deep within her. His touch became more erotic, and she trembled with delight. "You are tempting *my* patience."

Rising, his eyes burned into her. He had thought that he would grow used to her, not crave her body so much. But each time he wanted her as strongly as the time before. Deftly he relieved her of the rest of her clothing and carried her to the bed. Seeing her lying there, her skin soft and inviting, her dark tresses spread in wild abandon over the linen pillowcase, he wanted her as powerfully as a man who had been lost on the desert would want water. It was as if possessing her was not merely a pleasure to seek but a necessity. Quickly shedding the remainder of his clothing, he went into her waiting arms.

As she welcomed him, Rebecca felt a wonderment and happiness she had never known before. She was not merely a warm body to him, someone to satisfy his lust and provide a means to further his quest. He wanted *her*!

A thrill rushed through her as she felt the added forcefulness in his lovemaking. It was as if he was intent on proving to her that she belonged to him. Her body arched harder against his as her way of telling him he was the only one she craved.

He trailed kisses over her face and down the line of her neck. "You're mine, Rebecca."

"Yes," she replied breathlessly, closing her eyes and letting herself become lost in the sensual delight of their union.

"Open your eyes," he demanded. "I would not want you to forget whom you are with."

Obeying, she looked up at him. "I know who I am with," she assured him, then gasped with pleasure as his movements brought her to new heights.

Her hands moved over the strong musculature of his shoulders, and she raised her head to allow herself to lightly run the tip of her tongue over his sweat-soaked skin. When he groaned with pleasure, she smiled and raked her fingers along his back.

His groan grew into a growl, and she bit back a scream of ecstasy as the fires of passion consumed them fully.

Later, as she lay in his arms, she felt a security that had long eluded her. He had not spoken of love, but he did desire her. It was a beginning.

For a long while she was satisfied to lay snuggled in his arms, thinking only of this moment. Then Kirby Wetherly again came into her mind. Leaning up on an elbow, she looked down into his face. "Are you asleep?" she asked gently.

Travis opened his eyes. "No," he replied, acutely aware of the way her hair lay softly upon his chest and the warmth of her body alongside his.

"I was wondering if perhaps Mr. Wetherly might truly be the man you seek," she said with a thoughtful frown. "What he tried to do tonight showed a definite meanness of character."

"He is gravely disappointed in having lost Green Glen," Travis reasoned. His hand moved possessively along the curve of her hip, and he added huskily, "If he knew of all the pleasures he had missed as master of this estate, he would have behaved even more grievously."

Rebecca frowned down at him. "I'm serious."

"So am I," he replied, forcing himself to stop thinking of how inviting she looked and felt. "I have made a study of the man I seek. He is much cleverer than Wetherly. He would never allow his lust for women to place him in so scandalous or so dangerous a position as Wetherly has at times placed himself. I still marvel at the fact that Wetherly has not been injured by an irate husband." Travis shook his head slowly. "No, the man I am looking for would present an honorable and dignified face to his fellow men."

"I suppose you are right," she conceded.

He combed her hair back over her shoulder and sought the firm feel of her breast in his hand. "And I think 'tis time to put Wetherly out of your mind for the remainder of this night," he said.

Leaning forward, she kissed him as he rekindled the fires of desire. "Yes," she replied.

NINE

Two days later Rebecca was humming as she sat sewing. Life was going well for her. She had not been this happy since before her mother's death. Travis was an attentive husband and a truly exciting lover. He had still not yet confessed that his feelings toward her were growing, as were hers toward him. But his actions were those of a man falling in love. Yesterday he had brought her a small bouquet of wildflowers upon his return from an inspection of the crops. The memory of the warmth that had been in his eyes when he had given them to her brought a flush to her cheeks, and she smiled as she glanced at the violets sitting in a bowl of water on the table beside her.

And Daniel was fond of Travis, and Travis was fond of him. They made a very pleasant family, she and Daniel and Travis, she mused happily.

There was, of course, the political turmoil that hung over them. Mr. Bacon had gone into Dragon Swamp to pursue the Indians whilst Sir William attempted to build up his forces across the Chesapeake on the eastern shore. But Mr. Bacon had control of the water. There had been no warships protecting the Virginia shore, but under Mr. Bacon's orders, Giles Bland and Captain William Carver had captured two merchant vessels and equipped them with cannons. They had, however, allowed Captain Eveling's ship to evade their capture and it was said that the captain had sailed to

England with letters from Sir William to the king declaring Bacon a traitor and requesting the king to send men to put down the rebellion.

Rebecca breathed deeply of the warm summer air and shoved the worries of what might happen when the king's men arrived to the back of her mind. Today was too beautiful and too peaceful to think of the dangers that lay ahead. There were always dangers in this wild land.

"Mr. Loyde to see you, madam," Philip's formal tones broke into her thoughts.

Setting aside her sewing, she rose. She continued to find it difficult to picture this man as a murderer. He seemed much too civilized. But then, Mr. Garnet seemed much too much of a weakling for the part. No, Travis might place Mr. Wetherly last on his list, but he would remain the first suspect on hers. " 'Tis pleasant to see you," she said, curtsying toward her guest. Straightening, she glanced toward Philip. "Arrange for a tray of tea to be brought to us."

"Yes, madam," he replied.

As Philip departed, Rebecca seated herself and indicated the chair across from her to Mr. Loyde. " 'Tis a most beautiful day."

"Yes," he agreed. His expression became solemn as he, too, seated himself. "I was out riding and thought that perhaps I should stop by in case you have not heard what has happened."

The seriousness of his manner caused the peacefulness she had been feeling to vanish. "What has happened?" she demanded when he paused as if uncertain whether he should go on.

"I am not a man who likes to spread gossip," he said, defensively, "but Wetherly has numbered himself among your friends." He shook his head. "You were very lucky, Rebecca, to have avoided choosing him for a husband."

"What is this about Wetherly?" Travis questioned from

the doorway. "Has he finally been caught in another man's bed?"

Loyde rose to meet his host. "Not that, although I am amazed he has avoided such a fate for so many years," he replied.

"What has he done, then?" Rebecca asked as the men seated themselves.

"He was never much of a farmer," Mr. Loyde noted with a reproving frown. "Now it seems that he was also a gambler. He has not paid his taxes and was in such arrears, the sheriff has confiscated his land." Again Mr. Loyde shook his head. " 'Tis always been preached that if a man does not live rightly, evil will befall him. Mr. Wetherly took no heed of the Lord's word. Perhaps now he will change his ways."

Rebecca now realized the full extent of Mr. Wetherly's unsavory nature. He had hoped to marry her and attain Green Glen's wealth to bail himself out of the financial dilemma he'd created. Clearly his little scene on the porch following the dinner party had been a malicious attempt to punish her for rejecting him. "I doubt very much that he will change," she said stiffly. She saw Travis's jaw tense and knew he was recalling the scene, also.

"What is Wetherly planning to do now?" Travis questioned.

"He has already left to join Bacon's army," Mr. Loyde replied. " 'Twill be a relief to many a husband and father if he never returns."

"I suppose it will," Travis agreed with an indifferent shrug.

Philip arrived with the tea tray, and Travis turned the conversation toward the weather and the crops. As the men talked, Rebecca grew uneasy. This latest news about Wetherly might have changed Travis's mind about the man not being the one he sought. Truly Mr. Wetherly had a very weak moral fiber. Fear that Travis might feel compelled to follow him began to fill her.

To Rebecca, the remainder of Mr. Loyde's visit seemed interminable. Finally he left. But as she stood on the front porch waving good-bye, she suddenly didn't know what to say to Travis. She didn't want him to leave. Yet she would not stand in his way. He had hunted too long and suffered too much for her to attempt to thwart his quest.

"Will you be going after Mr. Wetherly?" she forced herself to ask.

"I may have misjudged him," he replied, gazing down the road, his jaw set in a grim line. "He would seem to be most certainly cut from the same cloth as the man I seek."

Rebecca felt her heart sinking. He was going to go after Kirby Wetherly.

"I cannot allow Wetherly to escape me should he be the one I seek." Turning on his heels, he strode into the house.

Rebecca followed him up to their room and watched as he began to pack his bedroll. "How long will you be gone?" she asked, trying to sound unconcerned.

The frown on his face deepened. "I cannot be certain. If anyone should ask, say that I had to go south on business."

Rebecca drew a shaky breath. She had never spoken to him of her growing feelings toward him. Now she admitted that was because she was not certain how he felt about her. But she could not let him leave thinking his movements did not matter to her. "I will miss you," she admitted softly.

He stopped his packing and turned to face her. For all of his life he had walked alone, never fully accepted by his mother's class and ignored as one would ignore a disagreeable blemish by his father's class. But here at Green Glen with this woman he had found a sense of belonging. Leaving her for even a day was difficult. "I will miss you, also," he confessed. Reaching her in one long stride, he drew her into his arms and kissed her soundly.

Her legs felt weak when he released her, and the urge to cling to him and demand that he remain was strong. But she forced herself to release him and step back.

His kiss had promised that he would return, she told

herself a little later, standing on the front porch as he rode away. But as she watched him disappearing from her sight, an emptiness filled her. She had always experienced a sense of relief when Thomas had left on a journey. Those were the times when she was the most comfortable at Green Glen. But now it suddenly seemed as if a very important portion of her existence was missing.

"He'll be back soon," Daniel said assuringly, reminding her that he was standing beside her. "He said 'twas only a short business trip."

"I hope so," she replied from the very depths of her heart. Travis Brandt had grown to mean more to her than she had ever thought any man could.

As she turned to go back into the house, she continued to cling to the memory of his kiss. His admission that he would miss her caused her hopes to grow even stronger that he was learning to care for her.

The sound of a wooden flute suddenly filled the air, stirring old memories of her childhood. Startled, she stopped and looked down at her brother.

Daniel finished the short little tune, then, holding up the flute so she could have a better view of it, he said enthusiastically, "Isn't it grand?"

" 'Tis very nice," she replied, her gaze never leaving the instrument. "Where did you get it?"

"From an old trader." Daniel gazed admiringly at the carved flute. "It was two days ago when Joseph and I were down by the river fishing. This old man came along and asked if I would trade one of my fish for one of his wares. I told him he could have the fish for free, but he insisted on giving me this."

"And where did you learn that tune?" she asked, keeping her voice level.

"He taught it to me." Daniel's smile brightened even further. "He asked me if I had a sister. I told him I did, and he said I should play this tune for you if you ever needed a bit of cheering up. He wagered you would like it."

"He was right," she replied. Tears burned at the back of her eyes as she recalled watching her father and mother dance to that cheerful tune. Her mother would beg to rest, and then it would be Rebecca's turn to dance with her father. Their cabin had been filled with laughter and the warm glow of love. "What did the trader look like?" she asked, forcing her voice to sound casual.

Daniel shrugged. "He was old. His hair was almost all gray, and he had a beard and mustache like Travis used to have." He shrugged again. "He just looked sort of ordinary." He glanced up at her quizzically. "Why?"

"'Tis unimportant," she replied levelly. "I've work to do," she added. "You run along."

Again playing the tune, Daniel skipped toward the back of the house while Rebecca went into the study.

Standing looking out the window as her brother continued toward the barn, a mixture of emotions filled Rebecca. "Perhaps 'tis best that Travis is to be gone for a while," she muttered.

That night she lay restlessly in her bed. Maybe the flute and the tune had been a mere coincidence, she reasoned as the minutes dragged on into hours. Midnight came and went. She had almost convinced herself that she was letting her imagination run away with her when she heard the faint hooting of an owl. She ran to the window. Outside the night sky was clear. The owl hooted again.

Leaning out the window, she gave the coo of the mourning dove. The owl hooted once again, then fell silent.

Rebecca dressed quickly. Moving silently so as not to awaken any others in the household, she went downstairs and out the back door. She ran across the open lawn and entered the woods. Just within the shelter of the trees, she saw him. It was too dark to make out his features. His posture looked like that of an old man, and he'd grown a beard.

"Reba, my little girl," he said gruffly, holding his arms out to her.

Tears filled her eyes. "Father," she choked out as she ran to him. "I knew it had to be you when Daniel showed me his flute and played me the tune."

"It has not been easy keeping my word all these years and staying away from you and my son," he said, holding her. "When I heard that Thomas Mercer had died, I began the journey back. But I was far north, and the news reached me only a very few months ago." He held her more tightly. "And I do not travel as swiftly as I once did."

She could feel him sobbing lightly, and her own tears trailed down her cheeks.

"I've not come back to disrupt your life," he assured her. "'Tis why I waited until your husband was gone. I just wanted to see you once again and see how Daniel had grown. You've done a fine job with him."

"'Tis good to see you once again," she said, stepping back for a better look. A slender shaft of moonlight was the only illumination. She could see that his clothing was well worn and in need of mending. His dark hair was now heavily streaked with gray, and the silvery light emphasized the age lines in his face. It tore at her that he looked so far beyond his forty-nine years. "I've long wondered if you were still living or dead."

"I don't want to cause you any trouble," he said. "Now that I've seen you and know you're doing well, I'll be leaving at first light."

She recalled Travis's reaction when she'd mentioned her parentage. She could not be certain he would welcome her father's return. Still, she was not ready to lose Hadrian Riley again so quickly. "Please stay a few days," she urged. "The cabin is empty. Go there. I'll come to see you tomorrow."

"One day," he agreed. "Now, you best be getting back inside."

She caught his hand. "Promise me you'll go to the cabin."

"I'll go to the cabin," he assured her. " 'Twill be nice to spend a night in a place filled with such fond memories."

Giving him a final hug, Rebecca hurried back to the house. But before she drifted off to sleep, she thought of a plan that would enable her father to remain.

The next morning she ate a hurried breakfast, then packed a basket of food. "Yesterday when I was out for a walk," she informed Joseph, "I met an elderly trapper. He's a bit worse for wear having traveled from the northern colonies, but he seemed pleasant enough. I gave him the use of the cabin for now until he is stronger. It seemed the only charitable thing to do."

"Would it be the same man what gave Daniel the flute for the fish?" Joseph asked.

" 'Tis the same," she confirmed, watching Joseph closely. He had known her father, and she had to know if he had recognized him.

But Joseph showed no signs of recognition. He merely nodded and said, "He seemed right nice enough. He were polite and insisted on paying for his food."

Rebecca breathed a relieved sigh. So far her plan was working well.

When she reached the cabin, she found Hadrian waiting for her. In the light of day he looked even older than he had the night before. There was very little of the original dark color left in his hair. His face was drawn and haggard, and he looked as if he hadn't eaten well in years. His tall, once muscular frame was now as thin as a willow branch. His nose was no longer straight but crooked with a lump across the bridge, clear evidence it had been badly broken. Only his dark eyes remained the same, sparkling with ebony light as he took the basket from her and watched her dismount.

"You've grown even more beautiful," he said. "Life has been good to you."

She had not told her father of Thomas Mercer's treatment of her. As agreed in the bargain he'd struck with Thomas,

Hadrian's fake death had been arranged very quickly following the wedding. There had been no opportunity to confide in him. Besides, what could he have done? Thomas Mercer was a respected and wealthy man with powerful friends. She gave a mental shrug. It did not matter now, she told herself. All had worked out well.

"You seem very pleased with your new husband," Hadrian was saying as they walked toward the cabin. He suddenly frowned. "But 'twas unfair of Mercer to put such a binder upon you." Worry entered his eyes. "He did treat you well, did he not? He promised me he would be most kind and generous."

'Twas a little late to be asking that question, Rebecca suddenly found herself thinking acidly. Quickly she pushed the small amount of lingering bitterness from her mind. Telling her father the truth now would do no good. "He treated me as well as many husbands treat their wives," she replied.

Coming to a halt, Hadrian turned to look down at her anxiously. "I kept track as best I could. The gossip was that you were a reasonably happy couple."

"Thomas was most kind and generous the majority of the time," she replied honestly. She could not fault her father. He had done what he thought was best. It would be unfair to burden him with guilt now. "But like us all, he was not perfect. However, I do not wish to discuss him. I want you to tell me about your life since you left us."

" 'Tis been mostly a gypsy existence," he replied.

As they sat at the table her family had once shared, eating the food she'd brought, he told her of his travels to the north. "Journeyed beyond the western frontier with some friendly Indians," he said. "Nearly got killed when they ran into a pack of their foes. Decided I wanted a bit more quiet company, so I went to Pennsylvania."

Rebecca listened to his tales, glibly told. Suddenly his expression turned serious. "But there was never a day that went by that I didn't think of you and Daniel." Reaching toward her, he took her hand in his. "But I'll not regret my decision. You and he have the life your mother would have wanted for you." He gave her hand a squeeze and rose. "And now I best be on my way."

Rebecca was on her feet in the next instant. She could not let him walk out of her life again. "No. There is no reason why you can't stay."

His eyes brightened. "Are you certain your new husband will not mind having a gypsy for a father-in-law?"

"I cannot be so certain of that," she admitted, "but he need not know you are my father. Joseph did not recognize you. I doubt that anyone would after all this time."

"I have changed a bit," he admitted, frowning down at himself. "A bit worse for the wear."

"A bit," she conceded. She took his hand in hers. "I've told the people at Green Glen that you're an itinerant trader in need of a place to rest and that I'm allowing you to use the cabin. My husband is a good-hearted man—he'll not object."

A wistfulness entered Hadrian's eyes. "I would like to remain—at least for a while."

Rebecca smiled brightly. " 'Tis settled then. You're staying."

Smiling also, he hugged her. "You've grown into a fine daughter."

When he released her, she said thoughtfully, "You'll need a name."

"Miller is a good solid one and easy to remember," he replied. "Paul Miller from London many years past."

"Paul Miller it is," she agreed.

That afternoon Rebecca informed Mildred that she'd taken pity on the old trader. "He's getting on in years and has no family," she informed her cook. " 'Tis an unhappy thing to grow old alone. I'll be taking him a bit of food on my daily rides."

"'Tis a good soul you have, ma'am," Mildred replied. "Perhaps a bit too generous at times," she cautioned.

On the second day Rebecca took Daniel with her. "I thought you could show Mr. Miller the best fishing holes," she'd suggested, and Daniel had readily agreed.

During the next days both she and Daniel spent time with their father. For her it was renewing an old attachment, while for Daniel it was building a new one.

Hadrian had never been one to live off charity, even his daughter's. He insisted on bringing fresh-killed game to her kitchen in exchange for the baked goods. And when he'd learned that one of her horses had a leg wound that wouldn't heal, he went to see the animal.

Watching him clean the wound and apply a special salve he made himself, Rebecca recalled how good he'd always been with animals.

"You've got a fine touch with the beasts," Joseph said approvingly the next day when Hadrian came to inspect the wound and discovered that it was already beginning to heal. To Rebecca, he added, "'Tis good to have a man nearby who knows about animals."

Rebecca breathed a sigh of relief. Joseph's acceptance of her father would make Hadrian's being here a great deal easier.

But it wasn't Joseph who really worried her. She was not certain how to deal with Travis when he returned. She did not like lying to him, but she was not convinced it was wise to tell him that her father had returned from the grave. "Maybe 'tis better to leave things as they are," she muttered to herself as she wandered through the hedge maze one warm sunny day.

Travis had been gone for over a week, and she missed him terribly.

"And what 'things' are troubling that pretty little head of yours?" a man's voice demanded from behind her.

She'd been so intent on her own thoughts she had not heard anyone approaching. But at the sound of his voice, she whirled around. "Travis!" she gasped and rushed into his arms.

His two days' growth of beard was rough against her face, but it only thrilled her as he kissed her soundly.

" 'Tis nice to be greeted so welcomingly," he said, releasing her reluctantly.

She flushed at her openness. So much for behaving demurely, she chided herself. But she did not care. Being in his arms was all that mattered to her. She looked up into the blue depths of his eyes. "I'm so very pleased you're home."

They darkened with desire. "I'm very pleased to be home." The word *home* echoed in his mind, and for the first time he realized that he had begun to think of Green Glen as his home. But it wasn't the place, it was Rebecca who made it so.

"Where is Daniel?" he asked as she accompanied him back to the house.

The time for her decision had arrived. "I've allowed an elderly trader to use the cabin. He and Daniel are fishing this afternoon." She hated lying to him, but fear held her back. She should have told Travis before the wedding that there was the possibility her father was still alive. He might have thought twice before marrying her if he'd known there was a gypsy father-in-law who might come into their lives. She was not prepared to face the rejection in his eyes.

They had reached the door of their bedroom. "Then we shall not be disturbed," he said with a smile, opening the door and allowing her to enter ahead of him.

A tub had been set up by the fire. It was partially filled with cool water and two kettles of steaming hot water were waiting on the hearth.

"I've ordered a bath," he explained, beginning to discard his clothing. He paused to kiss her lightly. "I was hoping you would be willing to scrub my back."

" 'Twould be my pleasure," she replied, wishing he had more in mind than a bath.

Travis kissed her neck, then nipped lightly on her

earlobe. "But I would not want you to get your pretty dress wet."

Currents of excitement raced along her shoulders. "No, we would not want that," she agreed. His warm breath was creating havoc with her senses. She ordered herself to behave with some decorum, but the effort to move with reserve was so trying her fingers trembled as she began to unfasten her clothing.

Discarding her dress, she saw him watching her, and the hunger in his eyes dissolved what control she still maintained. Her hands no longer moved with reserve. Instead, she watched him watching her as she quickly discarded the remainder of her clothing. Her body flamed beneath his gaze.

"I have missed you," he growled as she cast aside the last of her garments.

"And I you," she replied honestly.

Smiling, he discarded his clothing while she watched. It took all of her control not to help him. She had never thought a man could look so inviting.

When he had finished and moved toward her, she could hold herself back no longer and rushed into his arms.

"I do not think I can be patient," he warned her as he carried her to the bed.

She had sensed his readiness, and the core of her womanliness ached with the desire to welcome him. "There is no need of it," she breathed against his neck. Her tongue darted out to taste the saltiness of his skin as he laid her down and claimed her. Her mind whirled as her senses took control. It was as if she was whole once more, and she wanted to scream with pleasure.

He tasted the hardened nipple of one breast and then the other as he possessed her more fiercely. "At night I dreamed of you," he murmured huskily. "But my dreams could not match the reality of being with you. No other woman could ever feel this good."

She smiled happily and ran her hands along his back to

the curve of his hips. "You please me, too," she confessed, delighting in the firm feel of him.

" 'Tis a pleasure to serve you." He gave a deep-throated laugh as his breathing became ragged.

Colors swirled in her mind, and the rest of the world vanished. It was as if she and he were all that existed. Her body became lost in the sensation. Every fiber of her being tingled with excitement and joy. When she thought she could stand no more . . . when she thought she might die of the ecstasy, her breath suddenly locked in her lungs, and together they reached a fulfillment so intense it left them both gasping for breath.

Slowly releasing her and easing himself off of her, Travis kissed her lightly, beginning with her mouth, then moving downward over her stomach and along her leg.

She giggled when he reached her toes.

Playfully he nipped her ankle. "And now for my bath," he said.

"I'll wash you," she replied, unwilling to allow him to get too far away from her.

A smile curled his mouth. "First, I'll wash you," he said. He moved to the fire. "The water in the kettles is no longer steaming hot," he cautioned as he poured them into the tub. "But 'tis a hot day outside." He lifted her and stood her in the water, and then began to lather her body.

The remaining embers of passion within her maintained a heated glow as he made her bath feel more like a lover's game than a washing. Beneath the heat of his touch, she took no notice that the water was merely lukewarm. When he rinsed her, she breathed a regretful sigh that it was over.

Then it was her turn to wash him. As she soaped his back, a knot of pain formed in her stomach at the sight of his scars. It was as if the pain he had suffered from the beatings was her pain. Caressingly she moved to his chest.

"I'd better finish," he said huskily, "or we'll be spending the rest of the day in this room."

She smiled shyly, pleased with his lust for her.

Taking the rag from her, he kissed her lightly on the mouth. " 'Tis nice to come home to you, Rebecca," he said softly.

She flushed with pleasure. The gentle look in his eyes made her heart soar.

"When I'm finished, we'll go looking for Daniel," he said as he soaped himself. "And I should like to meet this new tenant we have."

Again apprehension filled Rebecca. She wasn't ready for Travis to meet her father. The lie she was telling taunted her. It was harmless. In fact, it actually served a good purpose, she reasoned. It would cause less strife. Still, she did not like lying to this man she had grown to love. Besides, she was not certain her father would play his part well enough to deceive Travis. She had begun to dress, and now she hurried with the fastenings. "You've done enough riding for today. I shall send Joseph for Daniel. Meanwhile, you and I can have a quiet tea, and you can tell me about your journey."

Stepping out of the water, he stopped her as she finished fastening her dress and started toward the door. "Don't send for Daniel. He will come home in his own good time." He smiled down at her. "And I would enjoy having a quiet tea with my wife."

Rebecca's heart leapt at the open caring she read in his eyes. "I would like that, too. I'll have it set up in the drawing room."

He breathed a sigh of regret. "I would rather spend the rest of the day with you right here," he confessed with playful wistfulness. "But I do feel the need for a bit of sustenance."

"I can have the tea brought up here," she volunteered, not caring if this sounded brazen.

The blue of his eyes deepened to the color of midnight. "That is an invitation I will not refuse."

Smiling softly, she arranged the screen to shield him from

the door and rang for the tea. Impatiently she waited for it to arrive while he finished his bath and dried himself.

He looked at her and she saw her own eagerness mirrored in his eyes. When the tea came, she poured them each a cup.

He quickly ate one of the butter scones and drank his tea down. "That should sustain me for a while," he announced, rising from his chair and lifting her from hers.

"I hope so," she teased as he quickly discarded her clothing once again. "I would not want you to grow weak from hunger at an important moment."

Laughing, he picked her up and carried her to the bed. "I can guarantee I will not."

Watching him toss off his clothing, she smiled and welcomed him with open arms.

The tea was cool when they finally returned to it. But neither minded. They sat in the bed propped up by pillows with the tea tray between them.

"Now you must tell me about your trip," Rebecca insisted as she ate a seed cake.

Swallowing down the last of the scones, he frowned. "I have arranged for Gyles to keep an eye on Wetherly and let me know of his movements. At the present time he has done as he said he would and enlisted with Bacon." Yawning, he set aside the tray. "And now I have need of sleep. You have exhausted me more than even a two-day ride could." Laughing, he added, "But it has been much more enjoyable." Then, after kissing her lightly, he lay down.

Rebecca waited until he was fully asleep, then slipped from the bed, dressed, and went downstairs to check on dinner and wait for Daniel. It was Hadrian's routine to bring the boy all the way to the door, and she needed to talk to her father. This afternoon had been one of the most wonderful of her life, and she would do nothing to risk losing Travis. She needed to assure herself that Hadrian would keep their secret. He must let nothing slip. Travis was a clever man and one adept at watching other people.

Nervously she paced the study until she saw her father and brother coming across the back lawn. Before they could reach the house, she went out to meet them and sent Daniel up to the kitchen with his catch.

"I must speak to you," she informed Hadrian in a lowered voice. "My husband has returned."

"Perhaps 'tis time I traveled on," he suggested.

Rebecca studied his aged face. He did not look as if he had many years left. She could not let him go. "I do not want you to leave."

"But I do not want to cause any trouble," he countered.

Rebecca felt a prickling on the back of her neck. Glancing over her shoulder, she saw Travis watching them from the bedroom window. "We cannot talk now."

Her father followed her line of vision. Taking off his hat, he bowed to the master of Green Glen. "A formidable-looking man, your husband," he mused. His gaze returned to his daughter, and there was concern in his eyes. "He does treat you well, does he not?" he demanded.

"He treats me very well," she assured him.

He did not look convinced. "I'll come back tonight and hoot twice," he whispered, bowing low in front of her as a peasant would to a lady of breeding. "We can decide then what shall be done."

He's going to overact his part, Rebecca fretted, anxiously watching as her father accompanied his bow with a wide sweeping gesture of his hat much in the fashion of the cavaliers. "Hurry and go," she ordered under her breath, not wanting Travis to have time to join them.

"Tonight," he repeated, clearly intent on speaking to her to reassure himself she was being well treated.

"Tonight, if I can get away," she confirmed.

Bowing once again, he strode across the lawn and into the woods.

TEN

LATE that night Rebecca lay in bed listening. Travis's breathing was gentle and regular. Lying on her side, she watched him sleep. The urge to reach out and tenderly caress his face was strong, but she did not want to wake him.

Suddenly she heard the hooting of an owl, and her body stiffened. It hooted again.

As quietly as possible, she slipped out of bed and grabbed a long cloak out of her closet. Wrapping it around herself, she hurried downstairs. As she descended the porch steps to the lawn, she saw her father in the shadows.

"I want your word that your husband treats you well," he said sternly when she joined him.

"He treats me very well," she assured him again. "And he knows of my parentage, but I am not so certain 'tis wise to tell him you have come back to life."

Hadrian cocked a cynical eyebrow. "So you think he, too, would object to having a gypsy for a father-in-law?"

Rebecca shrugged. She did not like to think Travis would be so prejudiced, but she was not willing to take the chance. "I cannot be certain."

He held up his hand. "Do not worry, I'll not give myself away. I did not come here to cause you trouble."

"You must be very careful," she cautioned. "He is a very clever man and one that sees more than most."

"Perhaps I should leave," he repeated his suggestion from that afternoon.

"No, please stay," she pleaded. "But you must not act too friendly toward me."

"Except when we're alone," he stipulated. Smiling broadly, he reached into his pocket and pulled out a wooden whistle. "I carved this for you," he said, handing it to her. "You had one as a child and loved it so."

Taking the new whistle from him, she fingered it lovingly. "I remember." She also remembered the old one. She had broken it in a fit of anger toward her father after Thomas had beaten her the first time. "Just whistle whenever you need me, and I'll be there," her father had said when he'd given it to her. But he hadn't been there to stop Thomas from brutalizing her. Later she'd regretted her act of destruction. She'd picked up the pieces and kept them. 'Twas not his fault; Thomas Mercer had not been the man he had portrayed himself as. "Thank you," she said, giving her father a hug. "Now I best be getting back inside."

"Good evening, ma'am," he said, slipping into his role of a stranger and bowing regally.

"A simple doff of your hat will do in the future," she directed, adding anxiously, "You must not behave too extremely."

"A simple doff it will be, then," he agreed, and giving her a final little kiss on the cheek, he hurried away into the shadows.

Smiling down at the whistle in her hand as she mounted the steps to the porch, Rebecca became lost in the happier memories of her childhood. She had learned to whistle a little tune, and her parents would whirl around the cabin in a graceful dance while she tooted it. In her mind's eye she could still picture her mother laughing merrily and a much younger version of her father laughing with her.

"I believe we need to have a little talk."

Rebecca gasped, her body suddenly frozen in fear. She

had just stepped into the drawing room, and Travis stood towering in front of her.

"I thought there was something peculiar in your behavior and the behavior of our new tenant this afternoon," he continued dryly. "But I did not expect to find you in his arms."

She heard the accusation in his voice, and her body stiffened defensively. " 'Twas not as you are thinking."

"I should hope not. With your appetite for mating, you could bring about the death of a man that age quite quickly," he noted sarcastically.

She glared up at him. "I did not realize being my husband was such a strain upon your person."

" 'Tis no strain upon *my* person," he assured her. The anger in his eyes grew more intense. "I want an explanation, Rebecca."

Glancing around at the darkened drawing room, it occurred to her that a servant might have heard them and be coming to investigate. " 'Twould be best if we had this talk where we cannot be overheard," she said tightly.

Issuing a guttural growl of impatience, he took her by the arm and roughly guided her through the house and up to their room. He shoved her through the door and kicked it closed. "Now, Rebecca, I will have an explanation."

She knew another lie would only lead to more trouble. "Mr. Miller is in reality my father, Hadrian Riley."

"Your father?" His eyes bore into her as if beginning to truly see her for the first time. "I was under the impression that your father was dead."

"When Thomas Mercer asked for my hand in marriage, I insisted that he be told the truth about my parentage," she explained tersely. "He accepted me anyway. Perhaps he thought my gypsy blood could cure his impotence. But, as I have said before, he was also a man who concerned himself greatly with his image. He feared my father's lineage might become public knowledge, so as part of the bargain they cut, he demanded that my father stage his own death and disappear from mine and my brother's lives. The drowning worked well because it was reasonable that the body would be washed downstream and into the bay and never found."

He sneered. "And your father agreed and left you at the mercy of a man who beat you?"

Rebecca glared. "He thought he had arranged a good life for my brother and myself . . . one my mother would have wanted for us. He did not know of the beatings. Everything was arranged too quickly. There was no time for me to tell him." She flushed self-consciously. "Besides, at the time I was young and inexperienced. I thought that perhaps my husband's problem was my fault."

Travis studied her in a brooding silence for a long moment. He had been foolish enough to begin to trust her. "I suppose you felt that a bit of honesty toward me was unimportant."

She could feel a barrier building between them as if it had a physical presence. "When we married I did not know if he was dead or alive," she explained, hoping to stop the barrier from becoming even more solid. "I had not heard from him for over ten years. I had thought perhaps he would reappear after Thomas died, but it had been a year and he had not. I assumed he would not."

"And so you decided not to mention the possibility," he said acidly, his sense of having been betrayed growing stronger with each moment.

"Yes," she admitted curtly. "I saw no reason to explain further the bargain my father had struck with Thomas Mercer."

"That part I could forgive," he said with a scowl, his anger showing fully. "But you were going to continue the lie."

Her shoulders straightened with pride. "I did not know if you would be any more amenable to having a gypsy for a father-in-law than was Thomas. My father is old. These past ten years have aged him greatly, and I did not want him sent away again."

Travis chided himself for having begun to care for her. It was as he had first thought . . . she would do what was necessary to have things her way. He would not again make the mistake of thinking he could trust her. His gaze narrowed further upon her. "It occurs to me that you might have an even stronger motive for keeping your father's identity a secret."

Rebecca frowned in confusion. "And what would that be?"

"Daniel once mentioned to me that although he had been born here in Virginia, you had spent several years in England," he replied. His gaze grew colder. "When did you and your family come to Virginia, Rebecca?"

Rebecca felt a sinking sensation in the pit of her stomach as she realized where the trail of his thoughts lay. "We came here fourteen years ago. But my father is not the man you seek. He could never kill a woman—or anyone—in cold blood."

"Spoken like a loyal daughter," he sneered.

"I was wrong not to tell you about the possibility of my father being alive. I was even more wrong not to tell you this afternoon that he had come back," she admitted shakily. "But you're mistaken if you think I kept this secret because I thought he could be the man you seek."

The urge to believe her was strong. Don't play the fool again, he ordered himself. He scowled at her. "My first impression of you was correct. You are a cold, deceitful, conniving woman who will do whatever she must to gain the ends she seeks."

Rebecca's chin trembled. Hot tears burned in her eyes. How could she have cared for a man who thought so little of her? She met his anger with her own. "Believe what you will!"

He turned away from her. That he could have married the daughter of the man who had murdered his mother was a hard blow. That he had begun to care for a woman who practiced trickery and deceit was even worse. Striding across the room to put distance between them, he stood gazing out at the night. "We shall go on as before," he said sourly. "We have a bargain. You shall behave as the proper wife until I have found the man I seek. We shall also expose your father for who he truly is."

Rebecca stared at his back. "What do you mean?" she demanded.

He glanced toward her, looking as though he found the sight of her disgusting. "We shall let it be known that he is Hadrian Riley returned from the dead." His tone became even more cynical. "Do you have any idea what he has been doing these past ten years?"

"He told me he had gone north and west beyond the current settled land with some Indians he befriended. They got into a skirmish with another tribe, and he came back. After that he traveled from place to place as a trader," she replied coldly.

He turned his back toward her once again. Her father was the perfect suspect. Gypsies were not well known for their honesty. And, he told himself, his wife was proof this was not just a prejudicial assumption. Immediately Hadrian Riley went to the top of his list. "We shall tell people that he was washed ashore far downstream and was rescued by friendly Indians. He'd sustained a blow to the head and could not remember who he was. He stayed with the Indians for several years, then traveled the colonies as a trader. Recently he'd nearly drowned again. The incident sparked a memory, and he remembered his life here. He came back, but in disguise because he did not want to shock anyone. He merely wanted to see his son and daughter again. We will say that you recognized him and he revealed himself. He will be welcomed in our home and can remain at the cabin for as long as he wishes."

"You are doing this so that you can keep a closer eye on him," she muttered, realizing the reason behind his plan.

He shrugged. "If he is innocent, you have nothing to fear."

"Aren't you worried that I might warn him about you?" she questioned sarcastically.

"That thought has occurred to me. But unlike your former husband, I shall be guarding my back closely."

"You'll not have to guard it against my father," she snarled. Again her shoulders straightened with pride. "He is not the man you seek. He couldn't have sold the brooch to Thomas, because he's not been near Green Glen for the past ten years."

"Can you honestly swear to that?" he asked in a patronizing manner.

Rebecca glared at him. In her heart she knew her father had not been near Green Glen, but she could not swear to it. "Thomas would not have gone to any lengths to protect my father as he did the man who sold him the brooch," she countered, taking another tactic.

"He might not have liked your father, but he was related to him by marriage. The scandal would have touched all of you."

Rebecca clamped her lips tightly together. It was no use trying to dissuade him. He had an answer to each of her attempts to defend her father.

" 'Tis late," he said, breaking the heavy silence filling the room. "And I have need of some sleep."

Rebecca's gaze traveled to the bed they shared. "Things will not be exactly as they were," she said tersely. "I will be your wife but in name only. I'll not allow a man who thinks so little of me and my family to use my body for his base gratification."

"As you wish," he replied with a shrug of indifference.

Rebecca felt as if she had been slapped. Her eyes traveled to the hearth, where the tub had been set, and she remembered their lovemaking during the afternoon. It had meant nothing to him but a bit of physical pleasure. She scowled at herself for allowing the truth to hurt. You hoped for too much, she chided herself. But she could not bear the thought of lying beside him. "I'll sleep in one of the chairs," she muttered.

He crossed the room in one long stride. "You'll sleep in our bed," he growled. After stripping her of her cloak, he lifted her and tossed her onto the mattress. "You've no need to fear me," he assured her coldly. "I'll not touch you."

Unwilling to allow him to know how much his words cut, she gave him a haughty look and crawled under the covers. But she could not sleep. She heard him undressing and felt the bed move when he climbed in on his side. A hard knot formed in her stomach. "I will need to speak to my father and tell him of the story you have devised." She kept her back turned toward him. "Then I will speak to Daniel. After that you may tell the world that Mr. Miller is in reality Hadrian Riley."

"And what will you tell Daniel?" he asked acidly. "The truth or the lie we have concocted?"

"I will tell him the truth," she replied with self-righteous indignation.

"That should be a unique experience for you," he returned dryly.

Her chin trembled. Damn him! she cursed under her breath. She would care no more for Travis Brandt.

Travis lay on his side of the bed. There could be no future for him and Rebecca. It angered him that he had even begun to think of one. He had warned himself many a time that she was not to be trusted. He should have heeded his own warning!

The next morning after breakfast Rebecca and Travis rode out to the cabin. During breakfast Rebecca had behaved the part of the dutiful wife as she had agreed to in their bargain. But during the ride to her father's cabin, she'd neither spoken nor glanced toward Travis as she continued to build a wall around her emotions he could never again penetrate.

Hadrian was chopping wood when they approached. After setting aside his ax, he bowed. "Mistress Brandt, Mr. Brandt, welcome."

"My husband knows the truth," Rebecca said with forced cheerfulness as she dismounted. "He has decided that you should present yourself as my father." Quickly and concisely, she outlined the lie Travis had devised. "I will, of course, tell Daniel the truth, but there is no need to publicly rake up the past."

"And what if it becomes known that I am of gypsy blood? Would it not be best to allow Hadrian Riley to remain dead?" Hadrian suggested with a worried frown. His gaze fixed on Travis. "I would not wish to cause you any embarrassment."

"I am not worried about your heritage becoming exposed," Travis assured him. "I learned long ago to turn a deaf ear to gossip. 'Tis only a man's moral fiber that concerns me."

"However, I think it would be best if we continue to keep our heritage a private matter," Rebecca insisted. "There is no need to present more fodder to the gossip mongers than they can find for themselves." Rebecca knew this would only strengthen Travis's belief that she was a dealer in dishonesties, but she had no wish to become the center of malicious talk once again.

Hadrian nodded his understanding, then his gaze shifted back to Travis. "You honestly want to claim me as your father-in-law?"

"It is what is right," Travis replied. His manner one of polite deference, he added, "I want you to feel free to come to our home and visit whenever you please. This cabin belongs to Rebecca. She has informed me that she wishes you to consider it your home. This is my wish also."

Hadrian smiled broadly and bowed low in gratitude. "My thanks. I'm an old man, and 'tis a delight to be with my children." Straightening, he indicated the cabin with a sweep of his arm. "Won't you come in and rest a spell?"

"Another time," Rebecca replied. Her nerves were still too taut from her confrontation with Travis the night before to maintain this pleasant facade much longer. "I want to tell Daniel so that you may quickly assume your proper place in our lives."

"You cannot know how much this means to me." Hadrian gave his daughter a tight hug. Releasing her, he turned to Travis. "My daughter was speaking the truth when she said you were a good-hearted man."

Rebecca's face hurt from the continued effort it took to keep smiling. She had been very wrong about Travis Brandt.

Travis accepted the compliment with a half bow. Foolhearted is what she thought I was, he mused to himself. Well, he would play the part of her clown no longer.

"You put on a very good act for your father," he said when he and Rebecca were well out of earshot of the cabin. "You are a truly accomplished liar."

She turned to glare at him. "I was merely keeping our bargain. I assumed that everyone, my father included, is supposed to believe we have a happy union."

He smiled cynically. "You do not fool me. I know that as soon as you are able, you will warn him of me."

"I have no need to warn him. He is not the man you seek." Her stomach once again churning with anger that she could have cared for this man, she kicked her horse into a gallop.

Riding behind her, Travis found himself again wanting to believe her. Don't play the fool, he again ordered himself.

Immediately upon arriving back at Green Glen, they sought out Daniel, and Rebecca explained to him the bargain their father had struck with Thomas Mercer.

"But how could he just leave us like that?" Daniel demanded.

"He wanted us to have a good and prosperous life," she offered in her father's defense. "One he could not give us. But he missed us terribly. When he heard Thomas had died, he considered the bargain finished and came back. But he did not want to shock us by his reappearance. Also, he was not certain he would be welcomed. But Travis has accepted him, and we are now free to claim him. However, Travis and I feel 'tis best not to mention the bargain Father struck with Mr. Mercer. It will only cause gossip." Carefully she outlined the lie Travis had devised to explain Hadrian's absence.

When she had finished, Daniel turned toward Travis, his expression solemn. "I thank you." Returning his attention to Rebecca, he said, "I knew there was something about Mr. Miller that was special. But having a father is going to take a little getting used to."

"Why don't you ride over and visit with him," she suggested. "I'm sure he's anxious to know if you forgive him for leaving us as he did."

After giving her a quick hug, Daniel raced from the room.

Her back stiff with pride, Rebecca turned to Travis. "And now you may spread your story."

"You're such an excellent liar, perhaps you should do it," he replied dryly.

Her jaw twitched with her effort to control the anger and pain churning within her. "I'm sure you can handle it just as well as I," she snapped, and brushing past him, she went upstairs.

With her hand on the door of their bedroom, she came to a halt. That room now housed only bitter memories. Her mouth set in a grim line, she lifted her hand from the knob and crossed the wide hall to the guest room. The window seat that had been her sanctuary during those difficult years of her marriage to Thomas beckoned to her. Releasing the curtains, she let them fall until they masked it. Then lifting them aside, she climbed onto the window seat and allowed the curtains to hide her presence. Wrapping her arms around her knees, she sat with her back against the wall.

The tears she had refused to allow release the night before

began to trickle down her cheeks. "It would seem I am to have no luck with husbands," she muttered as she thought of how eagerly she had awaited Travis's return. Furious with herself for crying over a man who considered her less than an insect, she brushed away her tears. She had survived her marriage to Thomas Mercer. She would survive this arrangement with Travis Brandt. But as soon as he found the man he sought, she would seek a separation. A bitter smile curled her mouth. She would probably not have to seek it. He would probably demand it. Well, good riddance!

Exhausted from the turmoil of emotions brewing within her, she laid her head upon her knees and dozed.

She awoke to her name being spoken sharply. Lifting her head, she saw Travis staring down at her angrily.

"I have invited your father to partake of the noonday meal with us," he informed her curtly. He did not tell her of the sudden panic he had experienced when he had first gone looking for her and had not found her. I was merely worried that by her disappearance my quest would be hampered, he assured himself, refusing to admit to the relief he had felt when he found her hidden in this cubbyhole.

"I shall join you momentarily," she said in dismissal.

Without a word he bowed stiffly and left.

Going downstairs a few minutes later, Rebecca found her father and Daniel with Travis in the sitting room. As soon as she arrived, the meal was announced, and they adjourned to the dining room.

"Where in England did you live before coming to the colonies?" Travis asked Hadrian as the first course was set in front of them.

"We lived a vagabond existence, traveling all over," he replied, adding quickly for the sake of the servants in the room, "I was a trader there." He smiled at Rebecca. "You must remember a bit of those days. Though I'm afraid your mother grew tired of never having a permanent home."

Rebecca nodded. "I remember." She glanced toward

Travis—she knew what he was trying to do. He was trying to place her father near the scene of his mother's murder.

"Guess there wasn't an inch of England I didn't travel during my youth," Hadrian mused reminiscently.

Inwardly Rebecca cringed. Glancing toward Travis, she saw the polite mask on his face.

"I understand you came to the colonies about fourteen years ago?" Travis persisted.

"Right you are." Hadrian nodded. "My wife wanted to settle down. We thought this would be a good place for a new start." A wistfulness entered his eyes. "She'd tried my way of life, but she wanted a more settled existence for our children."

" 'Tis understandable," Travis conceded.

During the rest of the meal, he attempted to extract more exact information as to her father's whereabouts during the past eighteen years. But Hadrian remained vague about his travels in England, explaining that they had moved so constantly it was difficult to remember.

By the time the meal was over, Rebecca's nerves were on a razor's edge.

Pleading a headache, she sent her brother and father off for the afternoon without her. It was clear to her that Travis was growing to believe more and more that her father was the man he sought. She was pacing the drawing room floor, trying to think of some way to find the true highwayman, when Mr. Loyde was announced.

"I heard of your father's miraculous reappearance," he said. "It must have been a shock to you."

"A pleasant one," she replied.

"I, myself, am glad of his return," Mr. Loyde continued, seating himself. "He was a right good hand with animals. There's been many a time I've had to destroy a beast, and in my heart I knew Hadrian Riley could have saved it."

"Hadrian Riley could have saved what?" Travis asked, entering the room at that moment.

"I was just remarking what an excellent healing touch her father had with animals," Mr. Loyde replied.

"I've been hearing the same from Joseph," Travis confirmed, seating himself and ringing for Philip. "You will have some tea?" he offered.

"Yes, thank you," Mr. Loyde accepted.

Philip arrived at that moment, and Travis ordered tea.

"So you knew Hadrian before his assumed death?" Travis said in a questioning voice.

"For a short while," Mr. Loyde replied. "Perhaps a year or so. I hired him to help clear some of my land when I first arrived. Cheerful fellow."

The tea arrived and Rebecca poured, rewarding Travis with a covert "you'll discover nothing bad about my father" look as she handed him his cup.

"But as pleased as I am for Mistress Brandt that her father has returned," Mr. Loyde was saying, " 'tis news of the rebellion I have come to share. 'Twould seem that Sir William has regained control of the water. He has captured Mr. Bacon's fleet through the stupidity of Captain Carver."

"That would give Sir William the advantage," Travis acknowledged.

"If you ask me, 'tis for the best." Mr. Loyde frowned anxiously. "I do not trust Mr. Bacon to be any less greedy than Sir William and his friends."

"The business with the Occaneechees does disturb me," Travis admitted, " 'Tis a shame Sir William has changed so greatly. He once was a man all of Virginia looked to with respect."

Mr. Loyde nodded with agreement. "Some say 'tis the onset of senility. He is, after all, in his seventies. But there are others who say 'tis the Lady Francis who has encouraged the change. She is quite beautiful and much younger than he. And, she is intent upon living in the most aristocratic style even in this wilderness."

"The choice of the wrong woman for a wife can bring about a man's downfall," Travis conceded grimly.

Rebecca knew the jab was meant for her. Glancing toward him, she smiled as if to tell him his opinion meant nothing to her. But in truth it was like a knife through her heart.

As the men continued to talk, she turned her mind to her earlier deliberations. There had to be a way to discover the identity of the true highwayman. Perhaps the jeweler in Jamestown knew more than he had admitted, or perhaps he had information he did not realize he had. Either way, he was a start, and right now she would settle for the smallest glimmer of a clue. The sooner the identity of the highwayman was discovered, the sooner she could put Travis Brandt out of her life.

And she would do it on her own. She would find out who the man was and throw the truth into Travis Brandt's self-righteous face!

Again pleading a headache, Rebecca left the two men to finish their tea alone. She needed to talk to her father. For once luck was with her. As she left the house, she saw him and Daniel coming across the lawn.

"You're welcome to stay for dinner," she offered Hadrian, meeting them halfway.

"I would not want to overstay my welcome so quickly," he replied, refusing the invitation.

Rebecca did not argue. She was in no mood to sit quietly while Travis pried into her father's life once again. "You take your part of the catch up to the kitchen," she told Daniel. As the boy raced away, she slipped her arm through her father's. "I'll walk with you a ways."

Hadrian studied her with a frown. "You look like you've got something important on your mind," he observed as they strolled toward the woods.

Glancing back toward the house, Rebecca saw Travis watching them from the sitting room window. He was too far away for her to read his expression, but she knew it would be one of cynicism and distrust. Her resolve stiffened even more. "I have something I must do. It involves my

going away for a short while, and I want your word that
you'll watch over Daniel while I'm gone." It had occurred
to her that the journey she was planning was dangerous.
Under the circumstances, she doubted that Travis would
want the responsibility for the boy should anything happen
to her, and she did not want Daniel left all alone in the
world.

"I'll not desert either of you again," he promised
solemnly. "Now tell me about this 'something' you must
do."

She shook her head. "That I cannot do. I can only ask
you to trust me."

He gave her hand a reassuring pat. "If ever there was a
person I would trust, 'twould be you."

Rebecca experienced a twist of pain. If Travis only felt
that way, their life could be so very different. She swallowed back the lump of regret that had formed in her throat.
He didn't and he never would. And I shall not care, she
ordered herself curtly. Aloud she said, "I must be getting
back." She gave her father a hug, then hurried back toward
the house before he could ask more questions.

"Did you have a pleasant chat with your father?" Travis
asked, meeting her at the door.

"Very," she replied coolly. It was evident that he thought
she had told her father of his quest. But to deny this would
be futile. He would believe nothing she said.

Brushing past him, she went into the study. There she
composed a note informing him that she had gone to
Jamestown to speak with the jeweler. In the note she
suggested that he tell the others she had received a message
from an ill friend in need of help, and being afraid he would
not allow her to go on such a journey at this time, had gone
off on her own so he could not stop her. Finding Daniel, she
told him that she was planning a surprise for Travis and that
he must give the note to Travis at dinner the following
evening. "But you must say nothing about it before then,"
she cautioned.

"Promise," he replied.

She knew how much he loved surprises. Watching him smiling brightly as he went off to hide the note, she trusted him to keep his word.

Next she removed her bedroll from the bedroom and placed it in a trunk in the hall where she could find it quickly. Going to the kitchen, she informed Mildred that she planned a day of visiting on the morrow and wished to have a basket laden with food prepared to give as gifts. "Cheeses, breads, and a few seed cakes," she stipulated.

Finally she found Travis. He was in the sitting room reading. "I'm planning to go visiting tomorrow," she informed him. "I'll be gone the major portion of the day." She had not expected him to raise any objections. When he responded with an indifferent nod, she guessed he was glad to be rid of her presence for a full day. He should rejoice heartily when he discovers I will be gone much longer, she thought. Curtsying low in exaggerated homage, she added icily, "Good evening, sir," then she exited the room.

As the door closed behind her, Travis snapped the book he had been holding shut. Had he not told himself a hundred times to stand clear of Rebecca Mercer? But he had not heeded his own warning.

He had spent the majority of his life alone. But with her he had begun to feel a sense of belonging. Now he was alone again—only this time it was different. This time there was a void as deep as the one he had felt following his mother's death. "Damn her!" he cursed under his breath.

ELEVEN

IMMEDIATELY after leaving Travis, Rebecca went to bed. But sleep didn't come easily. She was anxious to be on her way. She was even more anxious to be away from him, she admitted a little later when he entered the room and joined her in the bed. As angry as she was with him and as determined as she was to ignore him, she was aware of his nearness. Keeping her back toward him and as much distance as possible between them, she finally dozed only to awaken snuggled up against him.

She left the bed and went to stand by the window looking out at the night. Even the night breeze was warm. Her hair was damp with perspiration, and she worked it into a long braid to get it up off of her neck and shoulders.

"Are you planning another midnight rendezvous with your father?" Travis's voice suddenly broke the stillness of the room. "Or is it with someone else tonight?" Bitterness entered his tone. "Perhaps I judged Wetherly too harshly."

Glancing toward the bed, she saw him lying there propped up on an elbow watching her. His implication that she was so wanton and deceitful she would seek out other men cut deeply. She wanted to scream at him that she could be trusted, but the words remained locked in her throat. It would do no good. " 'Tis too hot to sleep," she said simply and turned away from him to again look out the window.

Travis continued to watch her. The wind blew her shift

against her body, accenting its soft curves. She could very easily be the daughter of the man who had murdered his mother. She was a willing liar . . . a woman who knew what she wanted and would use any means to get it. And yet he desired her. Even more, the thought of her in another man's arms brought a surge of jealousy. He rose from the bed and approached her. "You will remember at all times that you are my wife," he ordered in a low voice.

She turned to face him, meeting his gaze with level dignity. "I have never forgotten."

His fingers came up to trace the line of her jaw. "And when you feel the need of a man's company in your bed, it will be mine." There was a threat in the warning.

In spite of her determination to remain cold toward him, his touch sparked a fire within her. "How could any woman refuse so romantic an offer," she spat back.

He ordered himself to go back to bed, but his body did not respond. Instead, his hands moved to her neck and then to her shoulders. She was his wife, he told himself. It was his right to satisfy his lust.

Rebecca commanded herself to push him away. 'Twas only her body that interested him. But then that had been their original agreement, she reminded herself.

"You would be much cooler without that shift," he said huskily when she did not resist his touch.

"I am fine," she assured him, determined not to give in to the desire he so easily aroused within her.

"Do not try to be coy with me, Rebecca. I know your body." His fingers rested on the traitorous pulse throbbing in her neck. "We do not have to like each other to satisfy our needs."

Behind the cold anger in his eyes, she saw the heat of awakened passion. Her pride told her to reject him. But her flesh was weak. 'Tis a perilous journey upon which I am embarking tomorrow, she reasoned. 'Twould be foolish not to allow myself this moment of physical pleasure.

Travis had knelt before her. Placing his hands below the

hem of her shift, he trailed them along the curves of her body as he rose, carrying the shift upward on his arms.

Any remaining resistance vanished as he lifted the shift from her and kissed the hollow of her neck. He was right, she told herself. She would think only of the excitement and not the man who brought it.

When she offered no resistance, he carried her to the bed.

His touch stroked the fires of her passion until they burned with a white heat. In response she greeted his possession with willing hunger. Like two dancers who moved together to the same music, their bodies responded each to the other, reaching for the ecstasy their joining could bring. Their flesh glistened with perspiration from their exertion, but neither noticed as they allowed themselves to be lost in the exhilaration of their mating. And, as they had so many times before, each brought the other to the pinnacle of pleasure. But when their bodies had been satisfied, and he turned his back toward her and slept, she had to fight down the most tremendous urge to cry. There had been a different feel to their lovemaking this time. Before there had been a playfulness, a gentleness, a sense of mutual sharing. This time there had been nothing more than pure animal lust. She told herself she was not being fair. She had wanted to share his body as badly as he had wanted to share hers. Still, she could not shake the sensation of having been used.

Promising herself she would never again give in to him, she finally slept. But only for a short while.

She was up and dressed before the first hint of dawn. Quietly she slipped out of the bedroom, then retrieved her bedroll and saddlebags from the chest. In the stone pantry built onto the kitchen she found the basket ready and waiting.

Out in the stables she saddled her horse and tied on the bedroll and saddle bags. Then she rode away from Green Glen without a backward glance.

All day she rode hard. The sun was sinking in the sky when she stopped for a light dinner. Watching the red and pink sunset, she wondered if Daniel had given Travis her note. "He will probably be relieved to be rid of me for a few days instead of only a few hours," she muttered. Her appetite suddenly gone, she remounted and continued southward. She rode well into the night until exhaustion finally forced her to rest. Dragon Swamp, where Mr. Bacon and his men were pursuing the Indians, was to the northeast. But it was uncertain if the Indians still remained within the confines of the swamp. Unable to be sure that she was well out of the path of any marauding bands of warriors, Rebecca chose not to light a fire. She ate a little and slept and was back in her saddle by the first rays of dawn.

On her third day out a heavy downpour forced her to seek shelter in the cabin of a freeholder. The man of the house was with Bacon's army, but his wife and three children were kind enough to welcome her into their home.

"'Tis Sir William's own fault the hearts of the people have turned against him," the woman said as she dished up a plate of rabbit stew for Rebecca. "Him making peace treaties which those savages ignore the next day and letting those friends of his levy taxes to fill their own purses." She shook her head. "My man and I are barely able to keep body and soul together, and even while we tend the fields, we have to keep an eye out for Indians coming to kill us. Mr. Bacon, now, he cares about us common folk."

Rebecca held her tongue. Like Travis, she was not so certain Bacon would prove any more benevolent than Sir William once he had a firmly established seat of power. But she did understand the woman's frustration. "Times are rough," she agreed noncommittally.

The woman nodded. "And once the king has heard Mr. Bacon's case, I'm certain he'll do the fair thing and grant a pardon. 'Tis only right that we protect ourselves against the savages, and 'tis not fair for Sir William to allow such taxes as have been levied upon us."

Remembering that she owed her brother's life to Oparchan, Rebecca had to fight down the urge to point out that it had been the white man who had provoked this latest surge of Indian uprisings. But to lay blame would not change the situation. Now that the Indians were on the warpath, the colonists had to protect themselves or die. "'Tis a shame we could not live in peace," she said sadly.

"I never trusted those savages," the woman replied. Seating herself across from Rebecca, she frowned worriedly. "And you shouldn't be traveling alone. 'Tis much too dangerous. Not only is there the savages to fear, but Sir William is gathering an army to face Mr. Bacon, and there is no telling where he might land. These are very unsettled times."

Rebecca's jaw hardened. "I've no choice." Neither Indians nor Mr. Bacon's army nor Sir William was going to stop her. "I must complete my journey," she stated firmly.

While Rebecca spent the rainy night in the shelter of the cabin, Travis was spending it in a quickly put together lean-to not many hours behind. "Headstrong, stubborn women were surely put on this earth only as a curse on men!" he muttered under his breath. Why couldn't Rebecca Mercer have been a docile, gentle creature who behaved rightly and properly? His jaw set in an angry line, he closed his eyes and leaned his head back against the trunk of the huge old oak he had chosen to back his shelter. Exhausted, he slept.

A low guttural command brought him sharply awake. Forming a single line across the entrance of his lean-to were four large forms. Indians. Probably a small band that had escaped from Bacon's militia. He reached for his knife only to discover it was gone.

The largest of the party half entered the lean-to and pulled Travis's arm. Travis's muscles readied for action. If he was going to die, it was going to be quick. No long hours of torture for him. When the Indian gave another tug on his arm, he used the savage's strength and his own to practically vault out of the lean-to and into his captors.

He sent two sprawling. But he, too, lost his balance. Run, he ordered himself. As he started to spring to his feet, a blow that felt as if a boulder had fallen on his head struck him. Blackness engulfed him as he sank back to the ground. When he awoke, he found himself bound and lying in the rain outside the lean-to. The smell of fresh meat cooking reached his nostrils. Lifting his head, he could make out the shape of his horse lying on the ground. The Indians had slain the animal for food. Inside the lean-to, they were roasting pieces of it over a fire while they discussed his fate.

Two wanted to spend the night slowly torturing him to death. But the other two pointed out that they had far to go before they would be safe. It would be best to rest this night and use him as a slave. When they had no further use for him, they could put him to death, they argued. Relenting, the two who wanted to end his life that night settled for some sleep before dawn.

Lying facedown on the wet ground, Travis cursed Rebecca and the day he had aligned himself with her. She was nothing but trouble.

Rebecca reached Jamestown to find it overflowing with soldiers. Seven hundred of Bacon's troops were stationed there. Finding a room looked as if it would be an impossibility. But she didn't care. She would happily sleep in the open as long as she was able to discover information that would prove her father's innocence and point a finger at the true murderer.

Ignoring her exhaustion and soreness, she went directly to the jeweler's shop.

A man who looked to be in his early thirties rose from behind his desk, where he had been working on a clock, and bowed in greeting.

"My husband brought in a brooch about a year ago," she began to explain.

"I've only had this place for barely six months," the man

interrupted politely. " 'Twould have been Mr. Sparner who worked on the piece your husband brought in. But if there is a problem, I'll be more than happy to fix it."

Rebecca felt her heart sink. But she was not ready to give up hope. "Thank you, but I really must speak to Mr. Sparner. Would you happen to know where I can find him."

The man looked at her with sympathetic apology. "Mr. Sparner died this past winter of a bad chill."

Rebecca felt suddenly light-headed. She had come all this way to discover that the man who she had hoped would provide her with a clue was dead.

Moving quickly, the jeweler caught her arm. "You best sit a bit, miss," he said, helping her into a chair. "I'm sorry for breaking the news to you like that."

Her was watching her with a puzzled expression, as if he didn't understand why a stranger's death should cause such a reaction. " 'Tis the heat," she said quickly, fanning herself. " 'Tis so oppressive this September."

The puzzlement vanished. " 'Tis," he agreed.

Rebecca tried to think. This long journey could not be for nothing! Maybe Mr. Sparner had a wife whom he might have told something about Thomas. "Did Mr. Sparner leave any family? I should like to send them a note of condolence. He worked on several pieces for my husband, and we were always very pleased."

"He did leave a widow," the man replied. He gave Rebecca the address.

After thanking him for his kindness, she left.

"Let us hope Mr. Sparner was the kind of husband who spoke with his wife rather than ignored her," she muttered to her horse as she guided him through town.

The home belonging to the widow was on the western edge of town. It was a narrow two-story structure with an herb garden to one side and a vegetable garden to the other. An elderly woman was on her hands and knees carefully weeding the herb garden. She was thin and taller than average. Her hair was fully gray and pulled into a bun at the nape of her neck. She moved a bit slowly, as if the aches of old age were catching up with her, but her brown eyes were sharp as she rose and watched Rebecca.

"Mistress Sparner?" Rebecca inquired politely as she dismounted. She gave a quick brush to her dress, and a light cloud of dust flew. Frowning, she realized how disreputable she must look. "I've ridden a great distance in the past few days," she said, hoping to explain her disheveled appearance.

"You do look it," the woman replied, her gaze traveling critically over her caller.

Rebecca read the hostility in the woman's eyes. This was not going well. She thought of Mistress Garnet's dire prediction not to discount the omens. Perhaps they had been a warning of the turmoil that was now tearing the colony apart, but to Rebecca, it felt as if all the bad luck they had signaled had fallen upon her shoulders. Again she found herself wondering if it would have been best if she had simply given up Green Glen and taken Daniel and gone to another colony to begin a new life. I may yet be doing just that, she mused. If Travis chose to remain at Green Glen, she would not live anywhere in the vicinity. She had already made herself that promise. When this quest was finished, she never wanted to see him again. "I was greatly grieved to hear of your husband's death," she said sincerely. "I had come to Jamestown for the sole purpose of speaking with him."

"You're not one of the wives of one of Bacon's men?" the woman demanded curtly.

"No," Rebecca assured her.

The anger vanished from the woman's face. "You look like you could use some rest and a spot of tea. Come inside." She waved for Rebecca to precede her into the house.

"I apologize for sounding so sharp outside," she said as she started a kettle of water heating. "But I thought you might be a wife looking for a place to stay while you visited your husband." Suddenly looking worried that she might have said something offensive that could get her into trouble, she added quickly, "I've no love for the governor, but I don't think it's fair for Bacon's men to come to my house and take my husband's weapons and ammunition without nary a writ saying they was to pay for them. And they took a fourth of my food as well!" Indignation shown on her face. "I ask you, miss, if Mr. Bacon is supposed to be so strong for the rights of the people, should he be letting his men take things without nary a please or a thank-you? Especially from an old widow."

Rebecca nodded sympathetically. It would seem that the price of war was causing Bacon's popularity to wane among many.

Mistress Sparner breathed a deep sigh. "Forgive me, child," she said. "But it has been a difficult year. I was tempted to sail for England right after my husband died, but the thought of the voyage gave me pause. Now I am caught in the midst of a rebellion I have no stomach for. I'm not saying I don't appreciate Mr. Bacon going after the Indians to stop their murderous ways, but treason is another matter." She gave a large shrug of her shoulders as if trying to shake off a sense of foreboding. "Enough of an old woman's complaining." Smiling, she indicated with a wave of her arm for Rebecca to be seated on one of benches at the table. Seating herself, she studied her guest with open curiosity. "You said you have ridden a great distance to speak with my husband."

"I am Rebecca Brandt." Her married name left a bitter taste in her mouth. Quickly she added, "I was Rebecca Mercer. My first husband, Thomas Mercer, brought a brooch to your husband to have the clasp repaired. That was nearly a year and a half ago now. Mr. Mercer died shortly after returning home from that trip. It was only recently that I learned of the brooch and that it has a mystery behind it. I was hoping my late husband might have said something to your husband that could help clear it up."

"This all sounds very intriguing." Mistress Sparner studied Rebecca with interest. "What is this mystery you wish to uncover?"

"I am sworn to secrecy," Rebecca explained solemnly. "I cannot divulge the mystery. What I have need to know is if Mr. Mercer gave your husband any hint of where he had gotten the brooch."

Mistress Sparner frowned thoughtfully. "'Twas a long time ago." A wistfulness entered her eyes. "Each evening George and I would sit at this very table, and he'd tell me of his day." Her brow knitted in concentration. "I believe I do remember something about a brooch. It were a regular customer of my husband's what brung it in," She nodded. "Yes, I do believe the name was Mercer. I remember my husband was right upset. A local solicitor, Mr. Wartan, had asked George to keep an eye out for such a piece among others. They was supposed to have belonged to an English nobleman. But it was all supposed to be a big secret. My husband was supposed to say nothing to the customer. Mr. Wartan said the man might be dangerous. George had known Mr. Mercer for many years and knew him to be a true gentleman, but he kept his word and went to the solicitor. It turned out that the piece was one of the ones the solicitor was looking for. But Mr. Mercer wasn't the man he was looking for. In fact, according to my George, Mr. Mercer was right upset. Not at George, but at what the solicitor told him."

"Yes, he was," Rebecca confirmed. "The problem is, he died before he revealed the name of the person from whom he had purchased the piece."

"Oh, my, I'm so sorry, my dear." Reaching across the table, she patted Rebecca's hand. "Widowhood is a terrible thing. I've been so lonely since George passed away." Tears filled her eyes. She patted Rebecca's hand again. "'Tis good that you've remarried. You're young. You need a husband. For me, it would never be the same with any other man."

" 'Tis never the same," Rebecca replied. The pain simply comes in different forms, she added to herself. She found herself envying Mistress Sparner. Bitterly she recalled the hopes she'd had that she and Travis might have such a relationship as Mr. and Mrs. Sparner had had.

"You must stay with me a few days and rest," Mistress Sparner was saying. "I would greatly love the company, and this will give me time to try to remember anything my husband might have told me that could help."

"Thank you," Rebecca replied. She did feel the need for a rest. Besides, she was not eager to return to Green Glen with no information. The truth was, she was not eager to return to Green Glen under any circumstances as long as Travis was still there.

Mistress Sparner smiled brightly as she rose to make the tea.

It had been late in the day when Rebecca reached Jamestown. There was no time to call upon any of the other acquaintances she guessed her late husband would have visited. Instead, she wrote notes asking if she might call upon them the next day, and paid a boy to deliver the messages and wait for the responses.

The replies were in the affirmative.

The next morning Mistress Sparner bid Rebecca good luck as she rode off to pay her first call. It was to a Mr. Vaughn. He was a business associate of her husband's, and she doubted that Thomas would have spoken to him of the brooch, but she did not want to overlook the slightest possibility. Being extremely discrete, she inquired if her husband had mentioned anything about a brooch. Mr. Vaughn's answer was in the negative. She was disappointed but told herself this was to be expected.

She made three more calls only to receive the same response. But she refused to be defeated. Tomorrow she was to call upon a Mr. Kelso. He was the person she thought most likely to have been her husband's confidant. He was an elderly gentleman with holdings in the far reaches of Virginia. Because of his age and his rheumatism he remained in his home in Jamestown, allowing overseers to run his plantations. His family and that of the Mercers' had been friends in England, and he and Thomas had often shared news of home. Thomas also considered the man's advice valuable and had sought it on many an occasion.

That night at dinner Mistress Sparner was sympathetic. "Tomorrow you are sure to learn something," she said encouragingly.

"Have you been able to remember anything?" Rebecca asked, hopefully.

Mistress Sparner wrinkled her brow in concentration. "I've been thinking hard. I wanted to get it right." She paused for a moment and closed her eyes as if trying to see a picture in her mind.

"Then you have remembered something?" Rebecca demanded anxiously.

Mistress Sparner opened her eyes. "I cannot recall my husband's exact words. But he said Mr. Mercer was quite upset about the brooch. He said Mr. Mercer kept muttering about scandal and how he had no interest in being brought into it."

Rebecca felt her heart sinking. This would only give Travis more reason to suspect her father. "I appreciate your aid," she forced herself to say, adding coaxingly, "Please try to remember whatever you can."

Again Mistress Sparner closed her eyes. Opening them a minute later, she shook her head. "That's all I can remember for now."

Rebecca thanked her and hoped that Mr. Kelso would be more helpful. Her appointment with him was the next afternoon. She was busily putting the ingredients for a stew in the kettle the next morning when Mistress Sparner came rushing into the kitchen.

"Sir William is here!" the woman gasped out, holding her chest as if she'd been running.

Worried the widow was going to collapse, Rebecca

helped her to a chair. "What is that about Sir William?" she asked as Mrs. Sparner's breathing became more regular.

"He's come to take back Jamestown," the woman said in calmer tones. "His ships are in the harbor, and he's sent word to Bacon's men that they may either surrender to him and be granted mercy or fight him and be declared traitors and hanged."

Rebecca had no desire to be caught in the middle of a battle. She could not in good conscience allow Mistress Sparner to remain, either. The widow had been kind to her, and Rebecca was determined to repay that kindness. "We must leave as soon as I've spoken with Mr. Kelso. You will come to Green Glen."

Mistress Sparner shook her head. "I'll not leave my home."

"You cannot stay," Rebecca argued, stunned that the widow was even considering this possibility.

"I've survived heat, cold, Indians, even the hurricane of 1665. I'll not leave my home," the elderly woman repeated even more firmly.

Rebecca breathed a heavy sigh. She'd think of some way to get the widow to go with her. But first she must speak with Mr. Kelso.

A knock on the door interrupted her thoughts. It was a message from Mr. Kelso.

"Bad news?" Mistress Sparner questioned.

"Mr. Kelso apologizes, but says he must concern himself with Sir William's arrival and cannot see me today," Rebecca replied with a sinking heart. Mr. Kelso had been her final hope. She could not leave without speaking with him.

"Perhaps you should leave and return at a more peaceful time," Mistress Sparner suggested. "I've got reason to remain. You've not."

"You are wrong," Rebecca replied. "We will both stay for now."

That afternoon Rebecca walked to the harbor and peered

out at the flotilla of ships. In addition to the *Rebecca* and the *Adam and Eve*, both of these larger vessels now outfitted with cannon, she counted three smaller ships and sixteen sloops. None were warships but their number was impressive, and there was no question but that Sir William controlled the seas.

Upon the faces of Bacon's soldiers she did not see the looks of resolute rebels.

"We've no chance against all of England," she heard one saying. "Besides, I never signed on to be declared a traitor to the crown. All I wanted was to be free of the Indians and Sir William's rule."

That night she and Mistress Sparner watched covertly from the windows as Bacon's men quietly deserted the town. The next day, September 7, 1676, Sir William entered Jamestown victorious with nary a shot fired.

"You see we came out unscathed," Mistress Sparner said triumphantly as they sat eating their dinner that night.

Rebecca did not look so convinced. Jamestown was not only the seat of government of the colony, but the only town in all of Virginia. Surely Bacon would not allow the governor to keep it without a fight. She sent a message to Mr. Kelso begging for an audience that evening but was informed that he was much too busy.

While Rebecca anxiously paced Mistress Sparner's sitting room, Travis concentrated on finding a way to escape from his captors. They had been slowed on their escape to Carolina because of a wound one of their number had received in the leg during their last skirmish with Bacon's men. It had gotten infected. They had drained it and seared it, but Travis had seen the red streaks spreading from the wound and knew their medicines would do no good. The Indian had become unable to walk, and it had fallen upon Travis to be the pack mule and carry the man upon his back. The Indian's hands were bound together, and his arms, which now formed a loop, were slipped over Travis's head.

Travis was ordered to lift the man's legs in a piggyback fashion, and then his own hands were tied together to prevent him from releasing his load.

Even the breeze was hot, and the Indian was heavy. The others prodded at Travis with their weapons when he did not move fast enough to please them. They had chosen not to feed him or provide him with fresh water during the trek. His arms and legs ached from the weight of his burden. Exhaustion and hunger threatened to numb his mind. He told himself he had lived through worse. But at the moment he could not remember when.

He had been carrying the man for two days. It was midafternoon, and he guessed they were drawing close to the James River when he heard the death rattle in the Indian's throat. His captors' tempers had grown short during the hot trek. He considered it likely that when they discovered their comrade had died, they would have no further reason to keep their human pack mule alive either. Saying nothing, he continued through the rest of the afternoon.

His only chance would be when they momentarily untied him to remove the body. He hoped that the discovery of their comrade's death might cause them to lower their guard briefly. Even if they did not, he would have to try an escape.

They reached the shores of the James River at dusk. The Indian loosening Travis's bonds looked up into the unseeing eyes of his dead comrade. He let out a grunt of sorrow, and the others quickly gathered as Travis's bonds were freed. Carefully they lifted their dead comrade from Travis's back. As they turned to lay him down upon the ground, Travis made a dash into the underbrush. That his legs actually carried him vaguely surprised him.

Letting out angry yelps, his captors raced after him. The river was his only chance. He dived into it and let the swift current carry him downstream. An arrow hit the water near him, but he barely noticed. The current was either a great deal stronger than he had thought, or he was a great deal weaker. Either way it was a struggle to keep his head above the choppy water. The cold chilled him, and his mind threatened to become hazy. He could not last long this way. In the dim shadows he spotted a log floating a few feet from him. In one last desperate attempt to survive, he fought his way across the current to reach it. Wrapping his arms around it, he used it to keep him afloat.

But he knew he could not hold on forever. He scanned the shore for signs of civilization. As the last of the light was fading from the sky, he spotted a small wharf and made his way toward it. He did not have the strength to climb onto the wooden extension. Instead, he was forced to use it to pull himself hand over hand until he reached the shore. Saying a silent prayer that he had found a friendly landing, he crawled up onto the muddy land and collapsed.

It was three days before Rebecca was granted her audience with Mr. Kelso. But finally she found herself being led into his sitting room, where the elderly gentleman waited. He did not rise to greet her. "I must apologize," he said, from his seated position, "but my old legs have given way to rheumatism." He patted a bony knee covered, even on this hot day, with an afghan.

" 'Tis I who should be apologizing for troubling you about so trivial a matter when we are in the midst of a war," she replied.

"No, no. I was greatly grieved to hear of Thomas's death," he said solicitously as she seated herself and tea was served. "But I understand you have remarried."

"It was Thomas's wish that I do so," she replied with an edge of defensiveness. It would not do if Mr. Kelso thought she had betrayed her husband's memory by remarrying. She wanted the man's cooperation.

He nodded his head. "Yes. Yes, I know. Thomas was a thoughtful man. He discussed the terms of his will with me.

Even in death he was determined to look after your best interests."

Not mine, she thought acidly. Outwardly she looked properly respectful. "His death came as a shock," she said. "Just recently I've had another shock. It appears that when he was in Jamestown last, he had in his possession a brooch. It seems there is a mystery behind this particular piece of jewelry, and for his sake I feel it my duty to discover the truth."

"And what is this mystery?" Mr. Kelso prompted.

"That I am not free to divulge," she replied apologetically. "But I was wondering if he might have mentioned the brooch to you."

The elderly gentleman frowned in concentration, then his eyes glimmered. "I do believe he did mention a brooch. He was quite agitated. Yes. Yes. He called quite unexpectedly the afternoon of the day before he left. He was quite concerned. He said something about helping an acquaintance and finding himself caught up in a scandal." Mr. Kelso shook his head. "Thomas hated even the breath of scandal. The Mercers were always ones to care about their good name."

"What you say is true," Rebecca agreed, fighting to keep any hint of bitterness out of her voice.

"In fact, I hope you won't mind my being so blunt, but I was quite surprised when he married you. You were so much younger than he." Mr. Kelso offered her another tea cake. "But he did assure me that your lineage, although from common stock, was pure and quite acceptable. Thomas did so want sturdy children."

Rebecca wondered what this elderly gentleman would say if he knew he had the daughter of a gypsy seated in his drawing room. She guessed he would be appalled. "I know it was a great disappointment to my husband that we had no offspring."

"Yes. Yes." Mr. Kelso nodded. "But you must not blame

yourself. The Mercers always seemed to have a bit of trouble breeding."

Rebecca wondered if Mr. Kelso either knew or guessed her husband's problem. But that was of no concern to her now. The only information that interested her was that which could lead her to the man Travis sought. "Do you remember anything else he might have said regarding the procurement of the brooch?" she coaxed, turning the conversation back to the piece of jewelry.

"It was quite a long time ago." The elderly gentleman pursed his lips as he sat quietly in thought for a long moment. Then he shook his head in a gesture of regret. "I recall asking him if he wished to ease his mind by confiding in me. But he said he could not. He had given his word, and he considered his silence a matter of honor."

And so he went to his grave with the secret, Rebecca mused as she left the house a little while later. Now, because of Thomas Mercer, she was married to a man who thought her to be an incorrigible liar and the daughter of a murderer. Men! If she never had anything to do with another one, she would die a happy woman!

Frustrated and angry, she returned to Mistress Sparner's home. But as she entered the house, she came to an abrupt halt.

" 'Tis about time you returned." It was Travis, his large bulk filling the doorway of the sitting room. He looked tired, thinner, and his clothing was torn and dirty. And behind his mask of politeness, she saw the anger in his eyes.

TWELVE

ALTHOUGH he was relieved to find Rebecca well, Travis had to fight down the urge to take her over his knees and spank her heartily.

"Mr. Brandt was telling me of his capture by Indians. 'Tis why he was not here sooner," Mistress Sparner said, studying Travis as if she was not certain he was completely safe to have around.

He probably growled at her, Rebecca thought. Charm was not one of Travis's strong points. But as hurt and angry as she was feeling toward him, she had no wish to see him harmed. "You were captured by Indians?" Her gaze traveled over him searchingly. "Were you injured?"

Travis had to admit that her show of concern seemed genuine. Do not be fooled by her again, he ordered himself. "'Tis unimportant," he replied coolly. "Following you has always proved to be a hazardous task."

The censure in his voice irked her. "I did not ask for your assistance," she snapped, then realizing Mistress Sparner was watching with great interest, she added in gentler tones for the widow's sake, "But 'tis good to see you."

Startled by this last remark, Travis eyed her cynically.

Before he could publicly question the honesty of her words, she approached him and placed a light kiss upon his cheek, saying pointedly, "I would not want Mistress Sparner to think I am an ungrateful wife."

Suddenly reminded that they had an audience, Travis forced a smile. His wife was a marvelous actress. Well, he could match her. "Come have some tea," he said. "And tell me what you have been doing to occupy your time."

Mistress Sparner fidgeted uneasily. "She's been visiting friends," she said hurriedly.

Looking past Travis's shoulder, Rebecca saw the concern on the widow's face and realized that Mistress Sparner did not know of Travis's involvement in the mystery. *And my making the journey alone must have convinced her that I had no wish for him to know of my inquiries.* She rewarded Mistress Sparner with a grateful smile. " 'Tis all right. He knows why I came."

Relief shone on the widow's face. "Then come sit down and have some tea and tell us of your interview with Mr. Kelso," she ordered, already returning to the table to pour a cup for Rebecca.

As she seated herself, Rebecca could not hide her disappointment and frustration. "He was of no help."

"I am sorry, my dear." Mistress Sparner patted Rebecca's hand sympathetically.

"Does that finish your inquiries?" Travis questioned.

Rebecca nodded. "They have proved futile," she admitted grudgingly.

"Then I would suggest we leave within the hour." It was an order.

"And you must come with us," Rebecca again pleaded with Mistress Sparner. "It could prove dangerous to remain."

The woman shook her head vehemently. "I'll not leave my home."

A knocking on the back door interrupted Rebecca's second plea.

It was the young lad she had hired to deliver her letters.

"Thought I should let you know, mistresses," he said with breathless excitement, "Mr. Bacon and his men have arrived. They are just beyond the palisades." Having said what he'd come to say, he waved and hurried off to the next house.

"I came by boat," Travis said as the two women stood watching the boy's disappearing back. "We must leave now."

Rebecca took Mistress Sparner's hand in hers. "Now you must see the necessity of coming with us."

"I'll not leave my home," the widow repeated firmly.

"Rebecca is right," Travis interjected impatiently. "It could be dangerous for you if you should stay."

Mistress Sparner shook her head and reseated herself at her table. "I wish you Godspeed," she said as she poured herself another cup of tea.

Travis did not like leaving the widow, but he could see she was seated firmly. Cut from the same cloth as his wife. Why did it seem to be his fate to come against hard-headed, independent women? "I wish you would change your mind," he urged. When the widow's jaw hardened even further, he knew it was futile. "Gather your belongings," he ordered Rebecca.

For a moment she hesitated. Then, giving Mistress Sparner a quick hug, she hurried up to her room.

Half an hour later she and Travis were heading toward the wharf. The heavy silence between them was setting her nerves on edge. "What kind of boat do you have?" she asked.

"A rowboat," he replied grimly.

His tone told her that he found this whole adventure distasteful. She hated the thought that he had felt forced to place himself in danger because of her. "And how did you come by it?"

"The planter who gave me food and shelter after my escape sold it to me. When we get home—*if we get home*," he amended dryly, "I owe him a horse."

He was acting as if she was a cross he had to bear. Rebecca glanced up at him hostilely. "You could have remained at Green Glen."

"If I had not come, your father would have come," he growled. "And I did not want to risk losing my primary suspect."

Rebecca scowled at the ground. Down deep she had been hoping he'd come because of a concern for her. Fool! she chided herself.

"And where might you be going, sir?"

Rebecca looked up to find herself and Travis facing a troop of Sir William's soldiers.

"I was taking my wife home," Travis replied easily.

"And what might be your name, sir?" the commander of the small troop questioned.

Rebecca experienced a sinking sensation in the pit of her stomach.

"Travis Brandt."

"And where might you reside, sir?" the commander demanded.

"Green Glen," Travis answered.

"And where might that be?" the commander persisted.

"On the northern reaches of the Mattapony," came Travis's reply.

"Sorry, sir." The man's shoulders straightened with authority. "Sir William is calling every able-bodied man into service. Those what won't fight beside him are to be declared traitors to the crown and hanged."

"I am no traitor to the crown," Travis declared. Then he spread his hands in a gesture of helplessness. "But as you can see, I've no weapon."

"You'll be issued one," came the sharp reply. "You may see your wife to a place of safety, then report to the courthouse."

Knowing he had no alternative, Travis nodded his consent and the troop marched off.

Fear for Travis caused a hard knot to form in Rebecca's stomach. Because of her he would be forced into battle. "I am truly sorry to have drawn you into this," she said in low tones as they retraced their steps to Mistress Sparner's home.

"My sympathies go to anyone you ever intend to draw into trouble," he mused grimly. "They will surely be lost."

The next few days were nervous ones. The mood of those in Jamestown was one of anxious expectation.

The governor did not immediately attack, even though he had a well-fortified position and outnumbered Bacon's men three to one. Some said he was hoping Bacon would simply surrender in the face of such odds. Others said that the governor could not be certain of the loyalty of his soldiers. Many had entered the service for the promised plunder of Bacon's followers. Others, such as Travis, were there so they would not be branded traitors to the crown and hanged.

On the second day of the siege it became clear that Bacon had come to fight.

"The governor has ordered his ships in as close to shore as possible," Travis informed the ladies when he returned for the noon meal.

"What—?" Rebecca began to ask what Sir William planned when the sound of cannon fire shook the house. Rushing to the window, she saw dirt and dust being spewed upward from beyond the palisades and had her answer. Sir William was using the guns aboard his ships to bombard Mr. Bacon's position. Suddenly a volley of musket fire rattled the plates on the table. Squinting to see through the smoke that followed, Rebecca could see a line of the governor's men on the ramparts firing down at Mr. Bacon's encampment.

"Obviously Sir William is hoping to scare Mr. Bacon into surrendering without a face to face confrontation," Travis muttered, his voice barely audible above the rounds of cannon and musket fire.

A sudden thought caused Rebecca to study her husband worriedly. "Do you think Mr. Wood is with Mr. Bacon?"

The frown on Travis's face deepened. "I cannot be certain."

Rebecca hated herself for causing Travis to be caught in this. She could see that he believed it was very likely Gyles was among those beyond the palisades, and she knew he did not want to be pitted against his friend. "You must attempt an escape," she encouraged. "You cannot fight against your friend for a cause in which you do not believe."

Travis scowled down at her. "I cannot escape with you and Mistress Sparner, and I will not leave either of you unprotected." He shrugged. "Besides, the governor now knows my name. To escape would only have me branded a traitor and sought out and hanged."

Rebecca could not fault the accusatory anger she saw in his eyes. Because of her he was trapped in the midst of a war he had no heart for. And for nought! She'd discovered nothing here in Jamestown. Mentally she kicked herself for going upon this foolhardy errand.

"One strong sally and Bacon would be defeated," Travis muttered as the volleys continued. "His fortifications are weak."

But there was no sally that day. After Travis left to rejoin his troop, Rebecca kept a sharp eye out for any signs that the governor was forming his men near the gates. None came. But all afternoon the cannon and musket volleys continued until she thought her head would split from the sound of it.

"If the governor's ploy was to frighten Mr. Bacon into a surrender, he has been disappointed," Travis said at breakfast the next day. "Even during the cannon fire, we could see his men continuing to strengthen their fortifications."

"Surely the governor will send his forces out now," Mistress Sparner declared. Suddenly realizing what this meant to Travis, she studied him worriedly. "Perhaps you are wrong. Perhaps Mr. Bacon will see the folly of opposing the governor and surrender."

"Mr. Bacon has nothing to lose," Travis replied. "The

governor would like nothing better than to hang him at the first opportunity. I doubt very much that he will give up without a fight."

When the dawn came up fully, Travis's prediction proved to be true.

"I just couldn't believe my ears," Mistress Sparner said as she and Rebecca stood by the windows watching the soldiers standing idly upon the palisades. "But the men say it's true." Mistress Sparner pursed her mouth in abject disapproval. "Mr. Bacon has proved he is not a gentleman!"

Rebecca, too, found this latest development to be singularly ungentlemanly.

"Sending his men out to the surrounding plantations to bring back the wives of some of Sir William's staunch supporters." Mistress Sparner shook her head until her gray curls bobbed. "And making the women stand upon the ramparts as shields while he and his men enlarge their fortification." Mistress Sparner drew a deep angry breath. "I've heard they have Elizabeth Page, the wife of Colonel John Page, Angelica Bray, the wife of Colonel James Bray, Anna Ballard, the wife of Colonel Thomas Ballard, Francis Thrope, the wife of Captain Otho Thrope, *and* . . ." Mistress Sparner emphasized the *and* with a whole breath. "And Elizabeth Bacon, the wife of Mr. Bacon's very own cousin, Nathaniel Bacon, Sr." Mistress Sparner shook her head again. "Can you imagine that? The man has no honor. Mistress Bacon is not a young chicken anymore, and didn't she and her husband welcome Mr. Bacon to Virginia with open arms? They even saw he got a decent piece of land and a nice home." Mistress Sparner's mouth pursed even tighter. "'Tis my belief it's unlikely he'll prove to be the hero, or the savior of the common folk, as some would like to believe."

"'Tis difficult to find a real hero these days." Rebecca was tempted to add that it had been her experience that most men had selfish motives for their actions. But such a cynical observation might reveal too much to her hostess.

"Your Mr. Brandt seems like a fine man," Mistress Sparner was saying, bringing their conversation to a more personal vein. "When he first arrived, I thought him a bit gruff. But 'tis understandable. No doubt he's a mite jealous about you wanting to clear up a mystery involving your first husband. Men don't generally like their wives fussing over other men."

Rebecca found herself wishing that were the problem between her and Travis. In the next instant she berated herself for the wish. She would not allow herself to harbor any such feelings for a man who thought so little of her. She was determined not to care even the smallest amount for him. Still, she did not want to see him going into battle. "I am sorry to have gotten him into this mess," she said worriedly.

The next few days were anxious ones for Rebecca. She did not doubt that once Bacon was satisfied with his fortifications, he would mount some sort of attack. She wondered if perhaps he was only awaiting reinforcements. But there were no rumors of large numbers of men coming to aid him.

"Joining him to fight the Indians was one thing," Mistress Sparner reasoned as they sat eating dinner one night. "But to declare against the crown is quite another."

Travis said very little. He sensed a battle in the air and hoped that Gyles had gone home and not followed Bacon to confront the governor.

That night, as Rebecca lay on her side of the bed, she knew he was not asleep. In private they kept their distance from one another and spoke only when it was necessary. She would have preferred to keep it that way. But she could not. He was in this mess because of her. "I am truly sorry to have gotten you into this," she said stiffly.

"It has occurred to me that I should suggest to Sir William that he offer you to Mr. Bacon," he replied. "With your propensity for finding trouble, you could lead Mr. Bacon to ruin within the month."

Rebecca's jaw tensed. She had been trying to apologize. Obviously he wanted nothing from her, not even a momentary kindness. Well, that suited her just fine. Had she not promised herself that there would no longer be any closeness of any kind between them? Turning her back toward him, she feigned sleep until it finally came.

The next day, as Rebecca helped Mistress Sparner weed the garden, she sensed an increased restlessness in the air. "There seems to be added activity upon the street," she said as she straightened and stretched her knotted back muscles.

"They is grouping for an attack," the young boy who had delivered messages informed her. He had arrived a few minutes earlier and was standing by the fence watching the men in the street.

Fear so strong it caused her to tremble swept over Rebecca. "Are you certain?" she demanded.

"I heard some soldiers talking," he replied. "They's been getting ready nearly all day." He pulled a note from his pocket. "Mr. Brandt asked me to give this to you."

Rebecca took the note with a shaky hand. Inside was a blunt note from Travis cautioning her and Mistress Sparner to seek a place of shelter and safety.

Travis was going off to be shot at, perhaps killed, and it was all her fault! "Travis says you must seek shelter," Rebecca ordered Mistress Sparner.

Mistress Sparner straightened and, shading her eyes, looked at the soldiers mulling in the street. "I suppose the root cellar would be the most secure place," she said, motioning for Rebecca to follow her.

Leading Rebecca around the house, she lifted the heavy wooden trapdoor that opened into the hollowed-out hole in the ground. " 'Tis a bit small, but we should fit." Closing the lid, she seated herself on a rock nearby. "However, I'll wait out here until the shooting starts."

Rebecca's gaze traveled toward the palisades. It was

foolish, but she had to see Travis one last time. She had to make him understand that she was truly sorry for having gotten him into this. "If I am not back when the battle begins, you go inside," she ordered Mistress Sparner.

"And where will you be?" the widow asked anxiously, grabbing Rebecca's arm as Rebecca started back around the house.

"I must see Travis," Rebecca replied.

"You cannot find him among all those men," Mistress Sparner reasoned. "And he would not want you taking the risk."

"I must." Giving Mistress Sparner's hand a reassuring squeeze, Rebecca freed herself and moved toward the street. She was not certain what she would say to Travis. She only knew that she had to see him.

"You best be staying inside," an officer ordered her as she made her way out onto the street.

"I must be getting home," she lied, implying her home was on the other side of town.

"You best hurry," he ordered.

Nodding, she moved away, but the moment his back was toward her, she changed direction and headed toward the palisades. The front lines of soldiers were being gathered together in a hurried manner. She scanned their ranks for Travis. Suddenly she spied him and a chill of fear shook her. He was in the second row. Suddenly the gates were swung open, and the men marched forward. Not even realizing her legs were moving, she started after them.

A strong arm caught her and pulled her to the side. " 'Tis no place for a woman," a young soldier told her. "Stand aside. This is a man's duty."

"Please, I must . . ." she insisted. Travis was already beyond the gate, and a panic like none she had ever felt filled her.

"You'll likely get your man killed if you distract him," an older soldier cautioned. In a tone that held no compromise, he added, "You best be getting home."

Rebecca stopped her pursuit. Travis was beyond her reach now. But she did not go home. Instead, she stood frozen, watching the men march through the gate and out onto the field of battle. Fervently she prayed that Travis would return unharmed. Feeling dizzy, she realized she had been holding her breath. Forcing herself to think beyond her fear, she took several deep breaths.

It occurred to her that she should go back and join Mistress Sparner in the root cellar, but her legs refused to carry her there. She had to know what was happening. Ignoring the protests and shouted orders that she should return to her quarters, she made her way to the ramparts.

"You should not be here, miss," a young soldier, his musket at the ready, said as she peered over the top of the fortification.

Rebecca gave no response. Below, the governor's forces were marching toward Bacon's encampment. Some men were on horseback while others were on foot. Still, the men in each line marched shoulder to shoulder with hardly a space between them. It was an impressive sight.

She knew where Travis was and kept her gaze steadfastly on his position. But the trees and underbrush on either side of the roadway obscured her vision at times. "They must be nearly to Bacon's fort," she muttered worriedly as the line of men continued with no shot being fired.

"That they be," the young soldier beside her replied nervously.

Rebecca peered harder. "Maybe he has decided to surrender without a fight."

But as the last word issued from her mouth, Bacon's forces suddenly opened fire. Smoke filled the air, and a multitude of muskets and cannon fired all at once with a deafening sound.

"I would not have wanted to be on the front line," the young soldier said grimly.

The bile rose in Rebecca's throat. Frantically she tried to see through the smoke as a return volley was fired.

"Poor bastards," an older soldier standing on the other side of the younger man said. "Sir William placed the men he least trusted to stand by him at the front of the line. They're to be a shield for his more seasoned troops." He shook his head as if the men on the front line were in a hopeless position. "They've no experience in battle, and they're to face Bacon's trained Indian fighters."

Rebecca's hands tightened into fists. Travis had to come out of this alive! She peered harder over the ramparts, but the smoke from the musket fire obscured her view. Suddenly loud shouting and yelling could he heard above the sounds of battle.

"They must not have liked being used as a shield," the young soldier observed.

It was then that Rebecca, too, saw what was happening. The front ranks had broken. They were running back toward the fort, forcing the troops behind to turn back, also, or be trampled. Behind them upon the field of battle lay the bodies of the dead and those who were wounded too badly to run for safety.

Below her it was mass confusion as the men crowded back inside the palisades.

Frantically she searched the faces for Travis. He was not the kind of man to turn heel and run, but his heart had not been in this fight. Please, she prayed silently, let him come back.

But she had not seen him by the time the last of the troops rushed through the gates, and the gates were swung closed. Telling herself that she had merely missed him in the confusion, she spent the next two hours searching. But he was not there.

Rebecca raced back to the ramparts and looked out upon the field of battle. The smoke had cleared, and now she could plainly see bodies lying upon the road and in the marshy fields on either side. Cries for help floated up to the palisades. "We must go out and bring them in," she insisted frantically, rushing down from her perch to the gate.

" 'Tis too dangerous to go out there now," the guard in charge of the heavy wooden gate informed her, refusing to open it and allow her to pass. "We will go under the cover of darkness."

In her mind's eye she saw Travis slowly bleeding to death. "It might be too late if you wait until dark."

"Anyone who goes out now will be shot," he replied matter-of-factly.

"Surely they will not shoot a woman," she reasoned.

The guard's jaw set in a firm line. "I have my orders, ma'am."

Rebecca glared up at him. Arguing, she could see, would do no good.

As she made her way back to Mistress Sparner's home, Travis's image filled her mind. He had every right to be angry with her. She had tried to deceive him about her father. But only because she had not wanted to risk their union. Her deception, however, had backfired, and he had turned against her. Now because of her he might well be dead. At the very least he was lying wounded, in need of help. She remembered the sound of his laughter and the playful look that would come upon his face when he was jesting with her. Tears burned at the back of her eyes.

She had to find him. "He has to be alive!" she muttered to herself.

"Travis did not return," she blurted out when the widow came out to meet her.

Mistress Sparner's eyes filled with tears. "I'm so sorry, my dear."

Rebecca wanted to cry, but crying would do no good. As they moved toward the house, she said, "I must go in search of him. I'll not believe he's dead, but he may be lying wounded in need of immediate help." Her chin trembled.

Mistress Sparner looked at her worriedly. "You cannot go out onto the battlefield."

"I must," Rebecca insisted. "The guard at the palisade

would not let me pass that way. I came to you hoping you might be able to suggest another way."

Mistress Sparner looked uncertain. " 'Tis very dangerous. If he is already dead, you cannot be of any help to him."

The knot in Rebecca's stomach tightened until she felt nauseated. "I will not believe that he is dead. With your aid or without it, I must go in search of him."

Still looking dubious, Mistress Sparner nodded her consent. "I think it's a fool's errand, but I will help."

A fool's errand was an apt description, Rebecca mused. As hard as she'd tried not to, she still cared for Travis Brandt. There was no denying the way she felt. Aloud, she said, "Thank you."

"My husband kept a small rowboat for fishing purposes. If you know how to row, you could make your way along the isthmus." The widow's mouth suddenly formed a hard line. "I had best come with you."

"No." Rebecca refused firmly. " 'Tis my fault Travis was forced to fight with the governor's troops. I'll not have anyone else placed in danger because of me."

Mistress Sparner argued as she led Rebecca to the small dock near the back of her house, where the boat was moored. But Rebecca held firm. "Then you may need this," she said, handing Rebecca a large hunting knife. " 'Tis the only weapon Bacon's men left me."

Rebecca thanked the woman again as she accepted the sheathed knife and tied it around her waist. Rowing away from town, she prayed no one would notice. Even if they did, she was a mere woman and would be of no concern to the men who made war, she reasoned. It was slow rowing against the tide. But eventually she left the palisades behind. The shore was lined by a marsh bog. It took some maneuvering to dock her craft near solid ground. After making certain it was properly moored, she made her way toward the battlefield. Bodies lay scattered over the ground. From where she stood, she could see the faces of the men on guard at Bacon's camp. There was a determined look on their grim countenances.

Her gaze shifted to the battlefield, to the area she guessed Travis would have been. Her heart began to pound with renewed panic. He was there, lying facedown, not moving. Maybe 'tis someone else who resembles him in size and color and clothing, she thought hopefully. But she knew it was not. It was Travis with a large, dark stain making an ominous circle on the back of his coat. Forgetting her own safety, she ran to him.

"Travis, please be alive," she prayed aloud as she reached him and fell to her knees beside him.

Gently she turned him over. There was blood on the front of his coat as well. The musket ball had caught him in the shoulder and passed through. He had lost a great deal of blood, but at least the ball would not have to be dug out. Her hand rested on his chest, and she could feel him breathing shallowly. He was still alive!

Pulling her gaze away from the blood-stained coat, she looked upon his face. His complexion was ghostly pale. It was then that she saw the shot that had felled him. The hair on the right sight of his head was soaked with blood. With trembling fingers, she gently combed the thick black mass aside.

Travis groaned as if even this light touch caused him great pain.

Tears welled in her eyes. The ball had not penetrated the skull, but it had left a long, deep gash. There was swelling, and the side of his face was already turning blue, signaling the beginning of heavy bruising.

"I've always thought you were a hardheaded, thick-skulled man," she muttered. "Please prove it now."

His eyes flickered momentarily. "Ruth?" he murmured questioningly.

A cold chill passed through Rebecca's heart. Ruth? Who was Ruth? He had lied to her. He had left someone behind in England. Here she was risking her life for him, and he was dreaming of another woman. It was truly a fool's errand, she chided herself, recalling Mistress Sparner's remark. But it did not matter that he loved someone else. All that mattered now was that she get him to safety and pray his wounds would heal.

"Well, well, what have we here?" A familiar male voice broke the silence around her.

Glancing up, she saw Kirby Wetherly looking down upon her. He had changed greatly since she had last seen him. His dapper image was gone. His face was unshaven and his clothing was in need of mending and a good cleaning. But it was his manner that had changed the most. There was no rakish gleam in his eyes. Instead, there was bitterness. And his flirtatious smile had been replaced by a cynical sneer. "Mr. Wetherly," she greeted him in level tones, her hand moving to the hilt of the knife. If she was to die, it would not be without a fight.

But Kirby's eyes were sharp and his movements lithe. "Unless you want another hole in this husband of yours, you'll hand me that knife right now."

The threat in his voice was real. For a moment she hesitated. But he had a musket and a sword. He could kill Travis and wound her before she could act. She handed him the knife.

Maliciousness entered his eyes, and he lowered his musket until the barrel rested against Travis's head.

"You can't shoot a man in cold blood!" Rebecca hissed, starting to make a dive for Wetherly's legs.

Suddenly the musket was against her breasts. " 'Tis war, Mistress Brandt," he said coldly.

"You find a couple of prisoners, Kirby?" another familiar male voice suddenly interrupted.

Glancing over her shoulder, Rebecca breathed a sigh of relief. It was Gyles. She started to give a word of welcome, but he cut her short. "Looks to me like the gent's in pretty bad shape."

She had caught the glint of warning in his eyes and

remembered that Mr. Wetherly would not know Gyles Woods was a friend of Travis's. And under the circumstances it would be best to keep that a secret.

" 'Tis a couple of old neighbors of mine," Kirby replied. "Mistress Rebecca Brandt and Mr. Travis Brandt." He lowered the musket, but the murderous gleam remained in his eyes.

"We should be getting back to cover," Gyles suggested strongly. "The guards on the palisades can see us."

Kirby fastened a hand around Rebecca's arm and jerked her to her feet. "They'll not fire for fear of hitting her."

"Let's just get them and get back to safety," Gyles insisted, bending to pick up Travis. "I'll need your help," he said as he pulled Travis into a sitting position.

"No reason to take him back," Kirby replied with a shrug. "He's as good as dead."

"He is not!" Rebecca fought to free herself. She could not leave Travis behind. He was not dead now, but left without aid, he might be by the time darkness fell and the governor's men ventured out to retrieve the bodies.

Kirby jerked her hard and captured her free arm to hold her pinned in front of him. "You're not at Green Glen, Mistress Rebecca," he informed her curtly. His cynical smile returned. "You are not in charge here. I am."

"If this man is master of Green Glen, then he is a man of wealth," Gyles said in a speculative tone. "Could be he might make a very valuable prisoner."

Gyles was appealing to Wetherly's greed. It was a good ploy, Rebecca decided. And she had another. Wetherly had proved he was a man who looked after himself first of all. Stopping her struggle, her voice took on a pleading quality as she faced Mr. Wetherly. "Someday you may need a friend. Mr. Bacon's position is tenuous at best. He may defeat the governor, but he will have to face the king's forces."

"And Mr. Bacon ain't been in the best of health lately,"

Gyles interjected. "Don't know if the men will hold together under a different leader."

Rebecca held her breath as Kirby stood silent for a long moment. "You could be right," he admitted finally. Releasing Rebecca, he shoved her toward the Bacon encampment. "You walk ahead. I'll help Gyles with Brandt."

Rebecca hurriedly obeyed. The men had each taken one of Travis's arms and hoisted it around their shoulders. They were dragging him suspended between them, and she was worried they would cause him to bleed even more freely.

"Let them bury their own dead!" one soldier yelled at Kirby disgruntledly as they crossed the outer fortifications.

"He ain't dead yet," Kirby growled back. "If he dies, we can just throw him back."

"Looks to me like that could be any minute," another tired-looking soldier sitting leaning against the base of a tree observed as they passed him. "You should have saved yourself the trouble."

"Looks like a corpse already," another muttered.

Rebecca closed her mind to their comments. She had to keep Travis alive.

Kirby and Gyles dragged Travis to the base of a large old oak within the perimeter of the encampment. "I'm going to go inform an officer of our prisoners," Kirby said as they laid Travis down none to gently. "You keep an eye on them," he snarled. "And since it was your idea to bring him, when Brandt dies, you can drag him back out yourself."

"He is not going to die," Rebecca insisted.

Kirby rewarded her with an indulgent glance, then hurried off.

Falling to her knees, Rebecca opened Travis's coat. Fresh blood was soaking into his shirt. "Best get the coat off," Gyles said, helping her by lifting Travis's limp body into a sitting position. Moving quickly, she removed the garment and laid it down so that Gyles could lay Travis upon it.

Then she lifted Travis's shirt. Her face paled at the sight of the free-flowing blood.

"That'll help clean it," Gyles stated matter-of-factly, drawing out his knife and placing the blade in a fire nearby.

Rebecca scowled up at him impatiently. "A lot of good a clean wound will do him if he bleeds to death."

Picking up his knife, Gyles pressed the red-hot steel against the wound. The smell of burning flesh filled Rebecca's nostrils, and her stomach churned. But the cauterization stopped the bleeding.

"You got something clean we can put on that while we turn him over and take care of the other side?" Gyles asked as he returned the knife to the fire.

Swallowing back her nausea, Rebecca ripped a strip from her petticoat.

"Hold it over the wound whilst I turn him," Gyles instructed.

Rebecca obeyed and watched as he cauterized the other side of the wound.

"Now I'll fetch some boiled water, and you can clean him up," Gyles said, starting to rise.

"You're wasting your time," Kirby snapped, coming up behind them. " 'Tis the head wound that's going to kill him." Reaching down, he captured Rebecca by the arm. "Besides, Mr. Bacon wishes to speak to Mistress Brandt."

"Leave me a bit of petticoat," Gyles requested as Kirby jerked Rebecca to her feet.

" 'Tis a waste of a good bandage." Kirby started to drag Rebecca away.

Rebecca's shoulder squared for a fight. Refusing to budge, she glared up at Kirby. "If you want my cooperation for your commander, you will allow me to do this for my husband."

For a moment he looked as if he was going to refuse, but then he released her. "Go ahead. It's a waste of time, but if I should ever need a favor some day, I don't want you saying I didn't live up to my part of the bargain."

Quickly, before he could change his mind, Rebecca ripped off a large piece of petticoat. Barely giving her time to hand it to Gyles, Kirby again grabbed her by the arm and began half dragging her toward a tent set up in the middle of the camp.

A youngish man was seated outside the tent with several other men. He looked tired and drawn. His complexion was that of a man who was not well. His clothing was in need of a cleaning, and she was certain she saw a louse crawl out upon his shoulder, then quickly duck beneath the collar. But there was a gleam of determination in his eyes that overshadowed all else. And it was clear he was in command.

"Mr. Bacon, may I present Mistress Brandt," Mr. Wetherly said with a bow of deference toward his commander.

"Mistress Brandt." Bacon rose and bowed in cavalier fashion.

He had a charm about him, Rebecca admitted. But she was in no mood to be charmed.

"I wish you to tell me of what is happening within Jamestown at this moment," Mr. Bacon ordered in firm but kind tones.

"I can tell you very little you could not guess for yourself," she replied. "The troops are regrouping." She looked at him pleadingly. "The truth is I paid little attention. My only concern was finding my husband," She clenched her jaw in an effort to hide her anxiousness. "What will you do with us?"

"You will be sent home, and your husband will be sent to prison," he replied matter-of-factly.

Panic swept over Rebecca. "He is gravely wounded. He will die if you send him to prison."

"'Tis a moot point. He will die before the night is out," Kirby interjected.

Rebecca glared at him. "He will not die!"

Scowling impatiently at this diversion, Bacon held up his

hand, putting an end to their dispute. "I wish to know how badly the governor's forces were hurt," he demanded, his gaze leveled on Rebecca. "If you give me this information, I will consider being lenient upon your husband."

"I do not know," she insisted. "You can count the dead as well as I. There were many wounded, but Sir William's main force was driven back before it could engage in battle. I should be the one to suffer, not my husband," she begged. "He was only in this battle because of me. I had come to Jamestown on an urgent matter, and he followed. We were in the town when Sir William arrived, and Mr. Brandt was forced into the governor's service."

"That may be," Mr. Bacon conceded. "But Mr. Wetherly has informed me that your husband is not in sympathy with me."

"He has no wish to disassociate himself from his mother country," she replied stiffly. Hitting upon a new ploy, she added, "He is not certain you would be any more lenient a ruler than is King Charles. But you could sway him to your side, should you show mercy and allow me to take him home."

The impatience on Bacon's face deepened. "I shall consider what you have said." His attention shifted to Wetherly. "In the meantime, Mr. Wetherly, the prisoners shall be your responsibility." He waved his hand in dismissal and turned his attention to a plumpish gentleman seated to his left.

Remembering her manners and hoping to gain some quarter, Rebecca curtsied low as if she were in the presence of royalty. Then quickly she followed Wetherly back to where Travis lay beside the tree.

His shoulder was bandaged and his clothing put back on. Gyles had also bandaged the wound to his head, but Rebecca could see that the bruising was spreading to Travis's eye. "Has he shown any signs of awakening?" she asked urgently, seating herself and lifting Travis's head into her lap.

"No, ma'am," Gyles answered. "But give him time. That ball delivered a hard blow."

Rebecca looked worriedly from Travis's head wound to his shoulder. "Were you able to obtain any medicine to ward off an infection?" she asked hopefully.

Gyles could not bring himself to tell her that the camp surgeon refused to waste his supplies on a prisoner in so bad a condition. "We're short on medicine," he said instead. "So I made him a poultice I learned from my wife."

"Thank you," she replied, praying that his wife's medicine would work.

"Since you seem to enjoy watching over the dying so much," Wetherly snipped at the other man, "you can stay here and guard the prisoners."

As soon as Wetherly was out of earshot, Rebecca turned to Gyles. " 'Tis lucky for Travis you showed up when you did."

Gyles frowned. "I thought he had no heart for either side of this struggle."

"He hasn't. 'Tis my fault he ended up in Jamestown and was pressed into the service of the governor," she replied. Determination glittered in her eyes. "Now I must keep him alive."

Gyles smiled warmly. "He confessed to me that he was enjoying married life, though any blind man could see the two of you were well suited to each other. 'Tis my guess thoughts of you will keep him alive."

Thoughts of me might keep him alive, Rebecca thought dryly. But only because he might want to extract a bit of revenge for my getting him into this. She forced a smile for Gyles but said nothing.

"Travis has a right hard head," he continued in encouraging tones. "Why, once when we was out of ammunition and hungry, he picked a fight with a stag. Head-butted that deer senseless, so we could slaughter him for food."

Rebecca rewarded this story with a skeptical glance.

Gyles winked, then added, "He'll make it through this."

But Rebecca saw the doubt in the man's eyes, and her arms tightened protectively around Travis.

All that night and through the next day she sat with him. She bathed his lips with water, hoping he might swallow a few drops, but to no avail. "Damn it, Travis, wake up," she growled as the day lengthened into another night.

All day long Mr. Bacon had fired his cannon at Jamestown. The noise alone should have aroused the dead. Around her the soldiers moved restlessly, waiting for another sally by Sir William. A battle would offer the perfect cover for her and Travis to escape. But Travis had to be conscious and able to move with only her assistance. Gyles would be required to be at his post.

Tired from trying to will Travis to live, she leaned her head against the tree and dozed.

A low moan woke her. It was dark and only the light of the campfire gave any illumination. Travis was moving his head. Hope grew within her. Gently she stroked the line of his jaw.

Opening his eyes, he squinted as he tried to focus on her face.

"Here, try to drink," she coaxed, holding a cup of water to his mouth and raising her legs to lift his head higher.

He obeyed, then closing his eyes, he fell back into the state that bordered between sleep and unconsciousness. But now at least she had hope. Leaning back against the tree, she slept again.

When she opened her eyes the next morning, she discovered Travis watching her. He had not shifted his position. His head was still lying in her lap. For a moment she felt a surge of pleasure that he had not moved away from her. Then he closed his eyes and slept again, and she realized that he had not moved because he did not have the strength. She found herself wondering who Ruth was and envying the woman Travis had called out to when he thought he was dying. With the envy came another thought. During their bouts of lovemaking had he pretended Rebecca was this love he had left behind? The thought stung painfully.

She breathed a shaky sigh. The sooner she could discover the identity of the man Travis sought and thus free herself from this husband who cared nothing for her, the better it would be. But right now her main concern must be to get him back to Green Glen alive.

He woke again a couple of hours later. "How do you feel?" she asked as she gave him another sip of water.

"Like a limp fish with a dragon's headache," he replied.

"So you've decided to rejoin the living after all," Gyles said, joining them with a mug of stew in hand.

"Gyles?" Travis frowned in confusion.

"We are in Bacon's camp," Rebecca explained hurriedly. "And you must not act as if you know Mr. Woods."

Travis closed his eyes as his face contorted in a spasm of pain. Opening them, he regarded Rebecca suspiciously. "What happened?"

"You got shot and this wife of yours decided to save you," Gyles answered for Rebecca. "Right brave woman . . . a mite stubborn . . . but you'd of died if it hadn't been for her."

Travis lifted his head slightly to peer around, then dropped his head back onto her lap, as if the effort had cost him what energy he had. "You should not have risked yourself," he said gruffly, watching her narrowly.

Pride would not allow her to let him guess how much she cared. "I could not let you die before I had proved my father's innocence," she replied.

Gyles frowned in confusion as his gaze shifted from one to the other.

"So he has awakened," Kirby Wetherly interrupted, approaching them at that moment. "Well, well, it may be that you will prove valuable after all, Brandt." Again ordering Gyles to keep an eye on the prisoners, he went off toward the earthworks on the outer perimeter.

"What did he mean by my being of value to him?" Brandt demanded.

"Gyles convinced him that Mr. Bacon's campaign might not be a success, and he might need a friend," Rebecca replied.

Travis smiled up at her cynically. "A friend?"

Rebecca's back stiffened with pride at the insinuation in his voice. Glancing toward Gyles, she said tersely, "Give me your bedroll. I'm sure my husband would prefer it to my lap for a pillow." Suddenly realizing it was within her reach, she snatched it up before Gyles could act and quickly placed it under Travis's head.

"I don't know what's going on between the two of you," Gyles said, frowning down at Travis as Rebecca shifted away and sat staring at the battlements. "But your wife risked her life to save yours, and so far I ain't heard you say thank you."

"He has no reason to thank me," Rebecca snapped. "I was merely repaying a debt."

Looking from one to the other, Gyles scratched his head, then smiled rakishly. "My wife used to say the best part of an argument was the making up."

Travis rewarded him with a sour look.

Seeing it, Rebecca cast Travis a haughty glare. "Some men have understanding souls, and then there are others who are so self-righteous that only they are perfect enough to please themselves."

Travis's gaze narrowed on her. "And some women consider honesty a virtue whilst others lie as glibly as a bird sings, and one cannot tell truth from fiction as it issues from their mouths."

His words hurt her. But Rebecca would not give him the satisfaction of knowing that. Tossing him a second haughty glare, she seated herself so that her back was toward him.

"An old trapper I met in the mountains once told me there was two things a man should keep his nose out of," Gyles said. "One was the den of a mother bear with cubs, and the other was a dispute between a married couple. But if I was forced to stick my nose into one or the other, he said I'd have a better chance against the mother bear." Sitting down, he leaned against the trunk of a tree and began to whittle. "Looks like he was right."

THIRTEEN

DURING the next couple of days, Travis slept and ate, concentrating all of his energy on rebuilding his strength. On the morning of the nineteenth of September, Rebecca noticed a great deal more movement in the camp.

"We're going into Jamestown," Gyles informed her. "Seems there's been some activity. Word is going around that the governor has gone and taken his troops with him."

Rebecca stared at him in shock. "Sir William deserted Jamestown?"

Gyles nodded. "Lookout says the harbor is empty."

"Come on." It was Kirby Wetherly. Reaching them, he jerked Rebecca to her feet. "You help Brandt," he ordered Gyles. "We're getting ready to move into Jamestown."

In spite of his anger toward her, the sight of another man touching Rebecca had Travis on his feet in an instant. The quickness of his movements caused an almost blinding dizziness. Grabbing hold of Kirby's arm, as much for support as in anger, he swung the man around. "Let go of my wife!" he ordered threateningly.

"You're in no position to be giving any orders," Kirby sneered back, jabbing at the wound in Travis's shoulder with two fingers.

Rebecca saw Travis grimace with pain. Even worse was the paleness of his complexion when matched with the bruising that covered a third of his face. His defense of her was admirable, but she had risked too much to save his life to have him throw it away now. "I do not need you to protect me," she addressed him coolly. Besides, she reasoned, he had only come to her aid because he thought it his duty.

"Don't cause no trouble," Gyles warned his friend.

Scowling, Travis released Kirby's arm. "Seems my wife doesn't mind you handling her," he growled.

Rebecca lifted her chin. She had been trying to protect him. Travis wasn't ready to fight an able-bodied man. He was still weak and none too steady on his feet. But he did not see it that way. He was determined to think the worst of her. So be it! she fumed.

They fell into the rear of the line making its way into Jamestown. After only a couple of steps Travis was forced to use Gyles as a crutch to keep pace with Kirby. As they entered the town they were greeted by an eerie sight. It was empty of all save Bacon and his men. Every house, every business had been deserted.

"Every last one of them done left with the governor," Gyles muttered.

All except one, I'll wager, Rebecca said to herself.

Word spread through the ranks that Bacon was furious. His soldiers began to search the homes and businesses for anything of value that might have been left behind.

"You keep an eye on the prisoners," Kirby ordered Gyles as he went to join the other scavengers.

"We must check on Mistress Sparner," Rebecca whispered as soon as Kirby was out of ear shot.

"Who's Mistress Sparner?" Gyles demanded uncertainly.

"A very stubborn widow," Rebecca replied.

"She's right," Travis agreed gruffly. "We'd better check on her before she gets herself hurt."

Moving away from the main force, they made their way down a side street to the widow's home. "Mistress Sparner," Rebecca called out as they entered the house.

The widow rushed out of her kitchen to greet them. "I've

been so worried about you!" Suddenly spotting Gyles, she froze.

"He's a friend," Rebecca assured her quickly. In a reprimanding voice, she added, "You should have left."

The widow's back straightened until she stood as stiff as a ramrod. "I've told you before, I'll not leave my home. I was just getting ready to fix a bit of dinner."

Gyles fidgeted nervously. "We've got to get Mistress and Mr. Brandt hid. And Mr. Bacon's right angry. It might be best if all three of you hid until I find out what's going to happen."

"My husband had a hiding hole built into the house in case of an Indian attack. 'Twill be a might tight, but we should fit," Mistress Sparner offered. Scowling, she added, "But I don't like the idea of having to hide from my own countrymen. Surely they won't harm an old widow."

" 'Tis war, mistress. I cannot guarantee your treatment," Gyles replied honestly. " 'Tis always best to exercise a bit of caution until you see how the land lays."

"What will you tell Wetherly?" Travis demanded. "I'll not let you place yourself in danger because of me."

"I'll tell him you was only acting as weak as you was. As soon as he was gone, you asked me to take you onto a quiet side street so you could sit down, and then you attacked me and escaped. You can hide here until I figure a way to get you out of town."

"I left Mistress Sparner's rowboat in the marsh on the west side of the battlefield, not far from where you found me," Rebecca said. "Perhaps we could get it."

"Perhaps. But in the meantime, you best get into hiding," Gyles advised as the sound of approaching men was heard from the street.

Quickly Mistress Sparner led them into the drawing room. Reaching down, just inside the fireplace, she touched a lever, and a side panel swung open. Rebecca entered first. Next came Travis, followed by Mistress Sparner. There was a bench along one wall.

"I told my husband I couldn't stand for hours and insisted that he provide me with a way of sitting," Mistress Sparner explained as she closed the panel and sat down.

Rebecca's knees pressed against the opposite wall while Travis was forced to sit slightly sideways.

"Snug as peas in a pod," Mistress Sparner whispered.

A little too snug, Rebecca decided. Travis's shoulder and back were pressed hard against her, and in spite of her efforts to be immune to him, she was acutely aware of the contact. He shifted his shoulders as if he found her nearness distasteful. Determined to make him believe she was indifferent to his presence, she gave a small shrug in response.

From within the house they heard voices. "This one left in a hurry. Left all their silver behind," one man was saying.

" 'Twill be a nice donation to our cause," another added.

"They've no right!" Mistress Sparner hissed.

Travis's hand closed around her arm when she started to rise. " 'Twill do you no good to go out there," he said in a low commanding voice. "They will most likely confiscate your silver anyway and take us prisoner in the bargain."

Mistress Sparner breathed a frustrated sigh but settled back down.

They heard Gyles's voice and heard him leaving with the others.

When she was certain they were again alone, Rebecca leaned forward to allow herself to speak around Travis "You must come with us back to Green Glen," she said in a whisper just in case she was mistaken about their being alone.

"But this is my home," the widow replied. There were tears mingled with anger in her voice. "No Englishman has a right to run another Englishman from his home."

Reaching across Travis, Rebecca found the woman's hand and gave it a squeeze. "Someday you will be able to return."

"I won't leave," the widow said again firmly.

"You can consider your stay at Green Glen a small vacation," Travis said encouragingly. "Not a desertion of your home."

" 'Tis all I have," Mistress Sparner replied with a quiet sob.

"But the price you might have to pay for staying might prove to be too dear," Rebecca continued. She knew how dear a price a person could be forced to pay to retain one's home. Attempting to keep Green Glen had cost her much more than she had ever imagined.

"You would be wise to listen to my wife," Travis said dryly. "She understands the practical aspects of survival." He felt Rebecca straighten. He shouldn't have been quite so cynical, he admitted. She had risked her life to come out onto the battlefield to save him. But he did not trust her motives. Most certainly she had a practical reason for her action, he told himself, angered by the way his body warmed at the closeness of her. A bittersweet smile played across his face. There had been a time when he had imagined himself, Rebecca, and their children living out their lives in love and laughter at Green Glen. Angrily he pushed the images from his mind.

Leaning her head against the wall, Rebecca closed her eyes. His words had cut deeply. She tried to think of being anywhere but here with Travis. She pictured the river and thought of going fishing with Daniel. Against her will, Travis's image impinged, and she found herself remembering a day spent on the riverbank with him and her brother. She and Travis were sitting upon a blanket enjoying a picnic lunch with Daniel. Her brother was telling another of his wild stories and Travis was laughing. His laughter had warmed her, and she felt so full of happiness she thought she might burst. Stop it! she ordered herself curtly.

She shifted and he glanced toward her. His breath played against her hair, sending warm currents along the cords of her neck. Determined to ignore him, she again closed her eyes. But this time her mind wandered to their bedroom. He had been so very good at making love. Her chin trembled, and she frowned as she forced herself to remember their last night together in that bed. It would never again be as it was before that night, and she could not bear the way she had felt used. There was no future for them, and it was best if she forgot the past.

They had been closeted in the cubbyhole for nearly two hours when Gyles returned.

"Do not let anyone see you through the windows," he cautioned as they came out into the drawing room.

"Did Wetherly believe your story?" Travis asked worriedly.

"Yes, and Mr. Bacon has lost interest in you. When told you had managed to get away, he took almost no notice. He is furious that the governor has escaped, but even more, he is in a rage because the townspeople are gone. He had expected them to remain and greet us as heroes saving them from Sir William's rule. Any sign that he is not well supported among the citizenry is causing his temper to flare." Gyles shrugged. "Guess I can't blame him. He did risk his life to go after the Indians." His frown deepened. "Anyways, when I told him I felt responsible for your escape and was going to go hunting for you, he told me not to bother. If you was hidden in Jamestown, you would be flushed out." Gyles glanced toward the widow apologetically. "He's planning to burn all of Jamestown as soon as it gets dark. He wants the governor to see the flames and know what's happened."

Mistress Sparner stared at the man in horror. "Burn Jamestown? But why? 'Tis the only town in all of the colony!"

Gyles frowned thoughtfully. "Word has come that Colonel Brent has a thousand men marching toward Jamestown at this minute to challenge us. We've no navy, which means if we stay here, we'd be trapped. So we have to leave. I guess Mr. Bacon doesn't want to leave Jamestown for the governor to reclaim. Or maybe he's just mad because the townsfolk didn't stay behind to welcome him. I'm not privy to the reasons for his decisions."

Travis frowned in confusion. "I thought Brent was one of Bacon's men."

"He were once," Gyles replied. "There's a lot like me what signed up to fight the Indians. But we sure didn't expect to be fighting all of England." Gyles shook his head, as if he didn't fully understand how this confrontation had grown into a rebellion.

"Come with us," Travis encouraged. "I can find Wetherly when this is all over."

Gyles shook his head. "I gave Mr. Bacon my oath. I'll not go back on my word."

"A man who would burn my house for no good reason does not deserve anyone's loyalty," Mistress Sparner muttered.

"'Tis war," Rebecca said, placing a comforting arm around the woman's shoulders. "Now you *must* come with us."

Mistress Sparner nodded glumly. "I've a sister in the upper reaches of Hanover County. 'Tis on your way. I'll ask your company for the journey."

"You shall have it," Rebecca assured her.

Gyles glanced toward the window as a group of men passed by outside. "Keep still and don't get caught," he cautioned. After handing Travis a pistol and a knife, he headed toward the door. "Take care. I'm going to fetch that rowboat. Escape by water is your only way to safety."

"I'll go see if those scavengers left us any food," Mistress Sparner said as soon as Gyles was gone. "And I guess I'd better get to my packing."

"You won't be able to take too much," Travis cautioned.

"What I can't take, I'll put in the root cellar and hope for the best," she replied.

Rebecca frowned worriedly as her gaze rested on Travis. He was looking paler than he had a little while ago. There were lines of pain around his eyes that told her his head was hurting and a drawn look that told her this day had tired him greatly. Fear for him spread over her. "You must rest," she said stiffly.

He frowned at her. "I'll keep guard."

She wanted to scream at him for his stubbornness. But venting her frustrations would do no good. Instead, she approached him and held out her hands for the weapons. "You look as if you might faint at any moment. I suspect your head is pounding and you're still weak from the loss of blood. You will do yourself and the rest of us no good if you should collapse. Now, give me those weapons and go get some rest," she ordered grimly.

For a moment Travis considered arguing with her. But he knew she was right. His head was pounding, and he was feeling weak. He would need all the strength he could muster to make it to the water on his own. Grudgingly he surrendered the pistol and knife to her.

Glancing toward the stairs, he knew he could not make it to one of the bedrooms. Not really caring where he laid his head, he stretched out on the floor near the hearth.

Rebecca told herself he deserved nothing better than the hard wood beneath him. But in the next instant she was on her way up the stairs. With Mistress Sparner's aid, she moved the bulky feather mattress from the bed she and Travis had shared to the drawing room downstairs. "You can lie on this," she told him curtly as she unrolled the bedding beside him.

When he started to rise, a groan of pain issued from deep within him. Immediately Rebecca was beside him, helping him to move from the hard surface to the softer one. His coat and blood-stained shirt were covered with mud and dirt. But because he had lost everything when he was captured by the Indians, he had no others. Worried that his wound would get infected, she turned to Mistress Sparner. "His clothing is filthy and I have not the time to clean it.

Would you have anything to spare that he might be able to wear?"

"I've a coat and shirt that belonged to my husband," Mistress Sparner offered, already moving toward the stairs. "It might be a bit big—Mr. Sparner was a well-rounded man—but it would be better than the one Mr. Brandt wears now." They reached her bedroom. Mrs. Sparner's gaze scanned the bottles that had been scattered over the floor when one of the soldiers had opened her medicine box and dumped it out looking for valuables. "And here's an ointment you might want to spread on his wound to help it heal."

Rebecca accepted the coat, shirt, and ointment gratefully. Although the poultice Gyles had made seemed to have worked quite well, the wound was still fresh enough that the danger of infection remained strong.

"And he might be more comfortable with these," Mistress Sparner added, shoving a pillow and a cloak into Rebecca's arms. "Those men took all of my blankets. Now you run along whilst I pack us a few things for our journey."

Rebecca returned to the drawing room and knelt beside Travis. He was already asleep, and she hated waking him, but it was necessary. Gently shaking him, she said, "We must change your shirt and coat, and I've an ointment for your wound."

Looking as if he was in a fog, he sat up for her while she helped him out of his coat and then his shirt. Unwrapping his wound she was relieved to see that although it still looked like an ugly gaping hole, the skin was pink and the swelling was minimal. He flinched when she applied the ointment, and the urge to circle her arms around him and hold him to her was strong. Furious with herself for this weakness, she finished quickly. After redressing the wound, she helped Travis into the fresh shirt and coat. Then, after helping him lie back down, she placed the pillow under his head and covered him with the cloak.

Trying not to think of the pain in his head and shoulder,

Travis found her gentle touch reminding him of the inviting feel of her body. "If a man did not know of your devious ways, he could fool himself into believing you really cared."

Hot tears burned at the back of her eyes. The urge to tell him that she did care was strong. But he would not believe her, and her pride would not allow her to beg him to do so. "Rest," she said sharply, and she went to watch out the window for any soldiers who might return.

To her relief they seemed to be content to leave Mistress Sparner's home alone now they had stripped it of what they considered valuable.

"I found a bit of cheese and bread they missed," Mistress Sparner said, rejoining Rebecca in the drawing room.

Rebecca nodded. Dusk was closing in, and the main body of troops was moving toward the palisade gates. She glanced at Travis. He was sleeping.

"I have moved what things I hope to salvage to the kitchen. Now, I think the time has come for me to store them in the root cellar," Mistress Sparner said, breaking the uneasy silence that hung over the room. "If we're lucky, they didn't find the cellar, and there'll be a bit more food left."

"I'll whistle like a whippoorwill if I see anyone coming," Rebecca said.

Mistress Sparner nodded and headed toward the kitchen.

Her nerves taut with worry, Rebecca watched the street. Night had fallen fully now. An eerie stillness hung over the town. Suddenly a huge spout of flame shot up into the air. Bacon's men had begun to burn the town!

Forgetting her vigil, she hurried to Travis. " 'Tis time to be on our way," she said, shaking him gently.

He groaned as he opened his eyes and looked up at her.

"They've begun to burn the town. We have to make our way to the water and hope Gyles is there," she explained quickly.

As Travis rose to his feet, Rebecca could see on his face

the effort this movement was costing him. She frowned worriedly, thinking of the long journey they had ahead of them. He will make it, she told herself firmly. She would see that he did.

Mistress Sparner rushed into the room. "They're coming this way with their torches."

Rebecca slung her saddlebags over her shoulder. Then, acting as a human crutch, she slipped under Travis's arm on his uninjured side. "We'd best be going."

Mistress Sparner had found a sheath for the knife Gyles had left, and Rebecca had spent some time modifying it so that she could secure it around her leg. If they were caught, she wanted a weapon where her captors would not immediately find it. The pistol she carried in her free hand.

"I can walk unassisted," Travis said, straightening away from her. It was clear he did not like having to lean upon her for aid.

"You don't have your balance back completely yet. If you should stumble in the dark, you'll fall flat on your face and get us all caught," Rebecca replied, keeping her arm around his waist. She glared up at him, adding dryly, "You'll have to forgo your male pride this one time."

He scowled down at her but made no more protests.

With Mistress Sparner carrying the sack filled with what food she could find and her satchel, the trio quietly left the house.

As they made their way toward the riverbank, a figure suddenly emerged from a grove of trees.

Rebecca froze, cocked the pistol, and held it at the ready.

"Don't fire!" a familiar male voice called out in tones barely loud enough for them to hear.

Rebecca breathed a sigh of relief. It was Gyles. He took Travis on his shoulder, and then they hurried toward the cover of the trees and underbrush lining the river.

Only when they were safely hidden did Mistress Sparner look back. "Oh!" she cried out softly as tears began to run down her cheeks. Rebecca looked, too, and saw the widow's house now engulfed in flames.

"You've no time to linger," Gyles said urgently. "The boat is here." Quickly he led them to the rowboat. " 'Tis my advice you row up the James for a ways and make a wide circle to the west to get home." He glanced anxiously over his shoulder. "I will wait to give you a quick shove off, then I must hurry to rejoin my companions."

"Thank you," Rebecca said.

"You've got a sanctuary at Green Glen if ever you should need it," Travis assured him.

"That will depend on you getting back there safely," Gyles replied, helping Travis to the boat. "Luck be with you."

"Luck be with you," Travis replied, then climbed into the boat and seated himself between the oars.

Rebecca stared at him. "That blow to your head knocked whatever sense you did have out of it," she observed. "You'll be seating yourself somewhere else, and I'll be doing the rowing. I'm not taking a chance on you reopening that wound in your shoulder or fainting and falling out of the boat."

"I have never fainted, nor will I ever faint," he replied.

"We've no time to argue," Rebecca growled.

"Rebecca's right," Mistress Sparner interjected. "Besides, I'm a right good rower, if I do say so myself. I can break her for a spell when it's necessary."

Travis moved his arm in a rowing motion. The pain caused flashes of red at the back of his eyes. "You win," he conceded grudgingly.

Quickly Rebecca and Mistress Sparner stowed their belongings and the food in the bottom of the boat and climbed aboard. Gyles pushed them off, then he was gone.

"He'll need as much luck as we if he stands to face the king's soldiers," Mistress Sparner said, staring into the woods worriedly. " 'Tis a sad time for all of us."

Rebecca heard the tears in the widow's voice. Already

the flames of Jamestown were glowing red on the water. Smoke bellowed toward them. Coughing, and with her eyes stinging from the acrid fumes, she began to row upstream.

Against the night sky the entire town was engulfed in flames. It was an impressive sight.

" 'Tis wanton destruction," Mistress Sparner said with a sob. "He'd no reason to burn a poor widow's house."

" 'Tis war," Rebecca repeated, but she could not help but agree with the woman.

"For a man who is ruler of all of Virginia save the eastern shore, he does not treat his subjects well," the widow continued. "I thought he was supposed to be a man of the people."

"It has been my experience," Rebecca said pointedly, "that men wait to expose their faults and selfishnesses until they have what they want or until they are frustrated in achieving what they want. Then they will strike out at whatever is most convenient."

"Men," Travis interjected, "are mere babes in the woods where deviousness and selfishness are concerned—when compared to women."

Rebecca gave him a hostile glare while Mistress Sparner turned to look at her fellow companions. But she said nothing, and a heavy silence descended among them.

Rebecca rowed near the shore with Mistress Sparner giving her directions every once in a while to keep them from going aground. Forced to face Travis, she tried to concentrate only on her rowing. He had such little regard for her, why should she care about him at all? But despite her attempt to ignore him, she was aware of his every movement. When he wavered slightly, panic filled her. It was obvious he was having trouble staying awake. If he fell asleep, he could easily fall out of the boat.

"Make a pillow with my saddlebags and lie down in the bottom of the boat," she ordered him.

" 'Tis no need for that," he growled back.

"There will be a great need for you to be strong when we

start over land," she snapped, furious with his stubbornness.

Travis drew a tired sigh. "You're right," he admitted.

It was a tight fit. He was cramped in the bottom of the boat. Even in a half-sitting position it was necessary for him to put his legs under the rower's bench. As Rebecca's ankles brushed against Travis's, a fire spread through him.

The moonlight glistened on her ebony hair. It was tightly bound into a single braid and wrapped around her head, but in his mind's eye he saw it loose and flowing around her shoulders. The remembered feel of her in his arms taunted him. She was still his wife. He could claim her body when he was again strong enough.

A deep, bittersweet regret filled him. It was not only her body he had grown to desire. She possessed a fierce loyalty toward those she loved. He had seen it when she had gone seeking the help of Oparchan for Daniel, and she'd shown it again when she'd come to Jamestown to attempt to aid her father. There had been a time when he had envisioned that loyalty directed toward him. But now there would never be anything between them but distrust and anger. Closing his eyes, he ordered himself not to think of what he had hoped would be.

Rebecca rowed until she thought her arms would break. Only then did she relinquish her seat to Mistress Sparner. Alternating frequently after that, they rowed well into the night. Finally, when neither could row farther, they put in to shore.

Too afraid to build a fire, they sat in the dark and ate cheese and bread. After their meager meal Travis insisted on keeping guard while the women slept, and neither argued with him.

Rebecca woke with the breaking of dawn. Sharp jabs of pain shot up her arms as she started to shift herself into a sitting position, and an uncontrolled gasp of pain escaped her.

"Are you all right?" Travis asked gruffly.

The honest concern in his voice shook her, and she looked at him. The bruising on his face as well as the primitive conditions under which they had lived these past few days had prevented him from shaving. His beard was growing back, giving him a rough appearance. It reminded her of their first trek together, and she recalled how soothing his touch could be on sore muscles. His presence alone had given her strength. She wished that just for a moment he would hold her with the tenderness he had shown when they were first married. Angry with her train of thought, she lowered her gaze to the ground. "I'm fine," she replied, rubbing her arm. "Just a little stiff from last night."

"Aye, me, too," Mistress Sparner said, sitting up and rubbing her own arms. " 'Twas a good bit of rowing we done."

Avoiding even glancing toward Travis, Rebecca rose. "I'll have a look around." Before anyone could protest, she marched off into the woods. But she had gone barely twenty feet when a hand closed around her arm, bringing her to a halt.

"You should not go wandering off alone and unprotected," Travis said gruffly.

"And you should not be wandering at all," she replied. His touch was causing heat to run along her arm. Afraid he might see her weakness for him, she jerked free.

Her obvious distaste for his touch annoyed him. Curtly he told himself he should not care. Caring how she felt toward him was not in keeping with his reason for being here. He had come after her not only because it was dangerous for her to be off on her own, but also because he wanted to speak with her alone. What surprised him was the difficulty he was having making himself say what he had come to say. There was a finality about it that he had assured himself would please him, but instead he found a cold lump forming in his stomach. "I'm feeling much stronger today," he said, for want of something to say.

She had to admit that the side of his face that was not

bruised did have more natural color. "I'm glad," she replied. "I would not want you to have died because of me."

There was a softness behind the defensiveness in her eyes that threatened his determination. Angered by this weakness and his hesitation, he ordered himself to say what he had come to say. Breaking this bond with her should come easily, he told himself. She is not the kind of woman you wish to spend the remainder of your days with. "Whatever your reason was for coming to my rescue, I owe you my life. I am in your debt," he said with stiff formality. "When this is over and I have found the man I seek, I will leave Virginia so that you may live your life as you see fit. Also, I will have papers drawn up to make Green Glen yours to do with as you please."

Bile rose in her throat. He disliked her so much, he could not bear the thought of being indebted to her even if it had been her fault his life had been put at risk. Even more distasteful was his notion that she would take Green Glen as payment for coming to his aid. "I want nothing from you but the bargain we agreed upon. The manor house and your acreage is yours. I want no part of it ever. When your quest is done, I wish only the cabin for myself, my father, and Daniel, and Daniel's land for him when he reaches his majority." Turning, she started back to camp, then reaching a decision, came to an abrupt halt. She would not allow her body to be used to satisfy a man who disliked her so greatly. "If you insist upon repaying this debt you feel you owe me, then you will grant me my own room upon our return to Green Glen. And you will respect my privacy."

Travis's jaw tightened. He had never forced himself upon a woman who did not desire his companionship. Besides, it was folly to crave her. This arrangement would be the best. "As you wish," he replied coolly.

Rebecca experienced a sharp jab of insult that he had not even attempted to try to assert his husbandly prerogatives. No doubt any warm body would accommodate him. She had been foolish to think it was truly her he craved. No doubt he had imagined her to be his beloved Ruth when he'd made love to her. She'd been a complete fool to think he was learning to care for her. Well, she would be his fool no longer. "Thank you," she said with quiet dignity and walked back to their camp.

Again she and Mistress Sparner rowed upstream. The going was slow but steady. Near midafternoon they spotted a cabin. Three small children were playing near the front door, and a man was chopping wood nearby. Hoping to get a bearing on their location, they landed.

"Would you know what was causing the red glow in the sky last night?" the frontiersman asked with concern, walking to meet them as they approached the cabin.

" 'Twas Jamestown burning," Mistress Sparner replied. "Mr. Bacon done burned my house."

Rebecca could hear the woman's ire rising, and she laid a restraining hand on her arm. There was no way of telling which side the man favored, and they did not need to make any enemies.

The frontiersman breathed a heavy sigh. "I'm sorry about your loss, ma'am," he said with honest sincerity. "But he must've had good reason."

" 'Tis war," Rebecca said, for what seemed like the hundredth time.

"Aye," The man agreed. But his attention was not on Rebecca. His gaze rested on Travis, and a sudden suspicion entered his eyes. "You look as if you've done a bit of battle yourself in the past few days."

" 'Twas in the wrong place at the wrong time," Travis replied noncommittally. "Now my only concern is to get these ladies to a place of safety."

The man nodded his acceptance of Travis's explanation, but the concern lingered on his face. "I hear tell that Colonel Brent is traveling to confront Mr. Bacon with a large force."

"Aye, so we heard, also," Travis confirmed.

The frontiersman's wife had joined them, and she placed a hand on her husband's arm, as if she feared he might suddenly leave.

Patting the hand reassuringly, he said, "I fought with Mr. Bacon against the Indians. But now my duty lies with my family. We've need to put in stores for the winter." He placed a protective arm around his wife's shoulders. "Got five mouths to feed and one on the way." Suddenly remembering his manners, he added, "You're welcome to stay for dinner and spend the night. I've done well with my hunting. There's a right good meal cooking."

They agreed readily.

While Travis went to help the man with the rest of his chores, the women followed his wife into the cabin.

Regarding Rebecca and Mistress Sparner nervously, the frontiersman's wife said, "We've no argument with the king. But 'twasn't right of the governor to leave us all to be massacred in our beds just to protect his fur trade with the Indians."

"No, 'twasn't," Rebecca agreed wholeheartedly while Mistress Sparner nodded her agreement.

The woman visibly relaxed, and the rest of the afternoon passed peacefully.

But as they sat eating dinner, Rebecca found her gaze constantly shifting to the children. Remembering a time when she had looked forward to bearing Travis's offspring, she felt a sudden surge of bitter regret wash over her. She tried to push from her mind the thoughts of what she had hoped would be their future, but they lingered to taunt her as she watched the children laughing and playing and as she saw the proud glow of motherhood on the face of the frontiersman's wife.

When the meal was finished and the dishes cleaned, Rebecca's need to escape grew too strong to suppress. Wandering down to the riverbank, she sat watching the moonlight reflecting on the water.

"You'd best come in and get some rest," Travis's voice

broke into her thoughts. "I've traded the boat for a few extra supplies. Tomorrow we'll start overland."

Rebecca did not look up at him but continued to stare at the light that seemed to dance upon the water. "I suppose 'tis a good thing our marriage has not produced a child," she said grimly, speaking aloud what she had been telling herself for the past half an hour.

"Yes," he agreed tersely.

She had known this would be his response. But a part of her had hoped he would voice some regret. Foolish woman! she chided herself. Rising stiffly, she circled around, never once looking at him as she made her way back to the house.

One of the children's pallets had been laid upon the floor for her while the child lay on the rough wooden planks that made up the flooring. Kneeling, she touched the little girl's cheek. "You sleep upon the pallet," she said gently. "The floor will suit me fine."

The child looked up at her dubiously with large dark eyes.

"Please," Rebecca said. Smiling, she lifted the small girl and placed her upon the pallet.

Travis had followed her and did the same for the child whose pallet he had been given.

Hot tears burned at the back of Rebecca's eyes as she listened to the gentleness in his voice when he spoke with the child. She had once hoped to hear him speaking that way to their children. But he could never have truly loved a gypsy brat anyway, she told herself and steeled her heart against any further thoughts of Travis Brandt.

The trek to Mistress Sparner's sister's home was long. Because Travis was still weak and Mistress Sparner was not young, they could not travel swiftly. But they met with no incidents and reached their destination tired and dirty but unharmed.

They were greeted by a tall, slender woman who looked to be a few years younger than Mistress Sparner but resembled the widow closely in facial features. "I've been so worried about you," their hostess proclaimed as she threw her arms around Mistress Sparner and hugged her tightly.

That night at dinner she informed her guests that Colonel Brent's men had all disbursed and gone home when it came time for them to face Mr. Bacon. "They refused to fight the man who had rid Virginia of the Indian menace. Now Mr. Bacon's gone on to Gloucester to recruit more men."

"Then he should be well out of our way," Travis observed.

During the meal and into the evening, Mistress Sparner and her sister tried to convince Rebecca and Travis to remain several days and rest, but Travis was feeling much better and was eager to get home. Although Rebecca was not in a hurry to return to Green Glen, she was eager to see Daniel and her father once again. So after accepting Mistress Sparner's sister's hospitality for only two nights, she and Travis prepared to resume their journey.

"I'll not pretend to understand your relationship with Mr. Brandt," Mistress Sparner said, taking Rebecca aside. "But I do hope you can work out whatever is standing between you. You have both grown quite dear to me."

Rebecca gave the woman a hug. "We have too much between us, I am afraid," she replied honestly.

Mistress Sparner took Rebecca's hand in hers. "You cannot hide the truth from me. I know how much you care for him. A woman who did not care would not have been worried when he went off to battle nor would she risk herself to save him the way you did. My George used to say if the heart desires it, there is always a way to overcome those troubles that lie in the way."

"I cared once," Rebecca confessed, adding with a determined set of her jaw, "but there is nothing left of that caring." Feeling a prickling on the back of her neck, she turned to find Travis watching from a short distance away. The shuttered expression on his face gave no hint whether or not he had heard what had been said. Telling herself it did not matter, she gave Mistress Sparner a final hug before the two of them joined him so that Mistress Sparner could wish him a farewell also.

Travis had heard the exchange. As he and Rebecca again resumed their journey toward Green Glen, her confession that she had cared for him haunted him. But then he reminded himself that when she had been forced to choose, her loyalty had remained with her father. If she had cared, it had been a shallow caring.

They spoke only when necessary during the following days, and it was with a sense of relief that Rebecca began to recognize the countryside and knew they were nearly home. Not your home, she reminded herself harshly. Travis's home and your living quarters until he finishes his quest.

Still, tears of joy filled her eyes when Daniel and her father rushed out to greet them.

FOURTEEN

TRAVIS had remained true to his word, Rebecca mused as she sat in a tub washing off the grime of the long journey. He'd made an excuse about his wounds causing him to sleep restlessly. Claiming he did not want to disturb her rest, he'd arranged for her to have a private room. She'd chosen the guest room with the window seat that had so long been her sanctuary.

Expecting to feel relief at the loss of his constant company, she instead found herself remembering the bath they had once shared. "Idiot!" she cursed herself aloud and quickly finished with her bathing.

That night, as she lay in bed, tears of frustration threatened to fill her eyes. She had lived a life of pretext with Thomas; now she must live a lie again. But this time it was different. It was much more difficult to play the part of the dutiful, adoring wife knowing how much Travis disliked her.

There must be a faster way to discover the man he seeks than just waiting for the man to reveal himself once again, she thought. And I will find it.

As if in answer to a prayer, Colonel Howard came to call the next afternoon. "I am glad you are back safely," he addressed Rebecca pointedly. To Travis, he said, "And I am equally glad she is now your responsibility."

Rebecca wanted to say that she was no man's responsibility but held her tongue. She wanted the colonel's cooperation and would not gain that by antagonizing him.

"I just received news from Gloucester," the colonel said as they sat down and Philip brought in the tea. "Seems Bacon wanted the men there to swear a new oath of allegiance to him. But they refused. Said they were willing to fight the Indians but not the king. Seems that got Bacon's temper up. He arrested the Reverend James Wadding, claiming the reverend was discouraging the people from siding with him. Said the reverend should stick to preaching the Bible and stay out of politics. And the reverend wasn't the only one he arrested for speaking his mind. He's been holding court over anyone he thinks doesn't support him." The colonel scowled, and added, "He actually had a man by the name of James Wilkenson executed for desertion. After that he called the men of Gloucester together again. This time they took the oath."

Travis's hand went up to rub his head where his wound had left a scar. "A coerced army can be unreliable in battle."

The colonel nodded. "'Tis a restless time with men's loyalties shifting like the leaves in a brisk wind."

"Sometimes 'tis difficult to know where one's loyalties should lie," Travis replied.

Rebecca glanced toward him. She would prove that her loyalties were not misplaced. She forced a naive innocence into her voice. "I was wondering, Colonel Howard, if my husband ever mentioned a brooch to you at any time before he died." She caught the momentary shock that appeared on Travis's face before he masked it. Ignoring the cautionary look in his eyes, she continued. "Whilst I was in Jamestown, I heard a most extraordinary story from the wife of a jeweler there. It seems my husband had had a brooch repaired as a gift for me. It was a cameo, encased in silver with a ringlet of diamonds. But I received no such gift nor was there a piece of jewelry such as she described anywhere among Thomas's belongings."

The colonel frowned thoughtfully, then shook his head. "I can recall no such piece of adornment mentioned to me. Perhaps the woman was mistaken about the name of her husband's client."

"I don't believe she was. Thomas had done business with the man before and was known to him." Rebecca shrugged as if she had been asking out of mere curiosity. " 'Tis not important, but 'tis a mystery. I thought you might know something since he did go to visit you soon after his return. I thought perhaps the jeweler might have been mistaken about whose wife the gift was for and Thomas had had the brooch repaired for you to give to Mistress Howard."

Again the colonel shook his head. "He performed no errand of that kind for me. Perhaps he had it with him when he had his accident. It could have fallen from his pocket and been lost in the brush."

"That is probably what happened," Rebecca agreed. Her mouth formed a thoughtful pout. "He did seem to be quite preoccupied those few days following his return. He probably even forgot he had the brooch."

The colonel nodded. "Now that you mention it, I, too, noticed that he did not quite seem himself." The creases in his brow deepened. "Actually, it was almost a state of agitation. I recall he paced my study the day he came to see me. I asked if there was something he wished to discuss with me, but he said he could not."

"It worried me that there seemed to be something on his mind," Rebecca mused innocently. "But when I asked him about it, he simply told me it was nothing for me to concern myself with. I assumed it was a business matter that had not gone as he hoped it would."

The colonel shrugged. "It could explain his accident. He could have been so preoccupied with whatever was on his mind, he was not paying attention to his horse."

"That would explain a great deal," Rebecca agreed.

"How much time do you estimate there will be before the

king's forces arrive to aid the governor?" Travis interjected sharply, changing the subject.

"That's hard to say," the colonel replied, his mind quickly back to military matters. "Not till after the winter. Eveling's ship must reach England, there will need be time to organize a party of troops, and the winter storms must be taken into consideration."

Having taken the colonel's mind from Thomas Mercer, Travis then switched the conversation to crops.

Rebecca, meanwhile, remained quietly in the background for the rest of the visit. She was disappointed by the colonel's response. If her husband would have spoken to anyone, she was certain it would have been Colonel Howard.

She wished now she had mentioned the brooch to Kirby Wetherly when she'd had the opportunity. She would like to have studied his reaction. He was still at the top of her list. Mr. Wetherly had certainly shown a very dark side of himself on their past few encounters.

"Rebecca." Travis's sharp tone brought her mind back to the men in the room. "The colonel is preparing to leave," he said in a milder voice once he had her attention.

Rebecca rose and curtsied, then bade Colonel Howard good day. As Travis accompanied their guest to his horse, she sat back down, poured herself a second cup of tea, and pondered who she would next approach about the brooch.

"What the devil did you think you were doing!?" Travis demanded, storming back into the sitting room and kicking the door shut with the heel of his boot.

"Trying to discover the identity of this man you are seeking so we can end this charade."

Stalking across the room, his face white with rage, he caught her by the upper arms and lifted her from her chair. "You could get yourself killed the same as your late husband," he growled.

"I am a wife innocently inquiring about a piece of jewelry. No one will suspect I know anything of the history of the brooch," she replied. Glancing at his hands holding her captive, she added curtly, "You are hurting me. I'll thank you to let go."

He released her so abruptly she collapsed back into her chair. Then he walked to the window and stood with his back toward her. "You do not realize what a dangerous game you are playing."

"I am perfectly aware of how dangerous it is," she assured him. "And if my actions should prove to be fatal, I will at least have the satisfaction of knowing my death will not go unavenged."

Whirling around, he glowered at her. "This is not a jesting matter, Rebecca!"

"No, 'tis not," she agreed solemnly. "But you have waited for better than a year now for some clue, and nary a one has shown itself."

"Except for your father's return from the grave," he said pointedly.

Rebecca rose to face him. "My father has nothing to do with your quest." She walked over to the wall and pulled the cord to signal for Philip.

"I forbid you to continue with this inquiry," Travis said, his gaze narrowing warningly. "I'll not have your blood on my hands."

Rebecca regarded him coolly. "You'll not tell me what I can or cannot do."

A knock signaled Philip's arrival. "Enter," Rebecca responded. "You may take the tea tray away and tell Joseph I wish to speak with him."

Travis watched in grim silence as Philip gathered the cups on the tray, bowed, and left. "And what do you want of Joseph?" he demanded the moment the door closed behind the butler.

"I have thought a great deal about this situation," she replied in a reasoning tone. "My late husband was quite conscious of his position in society. To him servants were nothing more important than a piece of furniture. Therefore, he might have let something slip in front of one of them that he would have guarded against with someone he considered of his own level."

"You can be the most infuriating woman!" Travis snarled. "That fiery gypsy blood of yours is clouding your mind." He strode toward her.

Before Rebecca could act, she found herself being tossed upon his shoulder like a sack of flour. At that moment a knock sounded on the door. "Enter," she ordered, adding in a threatening whisper, "Put me down!"

Ignoring her, Travis turned to greet Joseph. "You will not be needed after all," he said with dismissal. Striding past the overseer, he headed toward the stairs.

Rebecca flushed with embarrassment as she saw Joseph watching their progress, first with a shocked expression, then with a grin of amusement as he misinterpreted Travis's intentions.

"How dare you!" she seethed. "You've humiliated me in front of the servants."

Travis carried her into her room. There, he dumped her unceremoniously upon her bed. "I am trying to save your life."

"I do not see how my life can be in danger simply because I am making inquiries about a brooch," she retorted, scooting off the bed. Standing, she straightened her dress, then lifted her head to face him with cool dignity. "It was part of the bargain that your marriage to me would aid you in finding the man you seek. I am merely living up to that part of our agreement."

"It was not agreed that you would be placed in danger." He raked a hand through his hair in an agitated manner.

"If my father is the man you seek, as you are so determined to believe, then I shall be in no danger," she pointed out coldly.

"There is," he admitted grudgingly, "the possibility that I am mistaken."

Her eyes rounded in mock shock. "Am I to believe my

ears? Mr. Travis Brandt has actually admitted that he could be in error?"

Travis's jaw twitched as he attempted to control his anger. "I have never claimed to be perfect."

"But you expected me to be," she snapped. Suddenly realizing how far she had gone toward exposing her frustration, she clamped her mouth shut before she could say more.

Travis regarded her coldly. "I expected you to be honest with me. But you have chosen where your loyalties lie."

A protest formed, but the words lumped in her throat. He had not believed her the first time she had tried to explain. He would not believe her now, and she would not lower herself to beg him to understand. Besides, I do not care what he thinks of me, she assured herself. I care nothing for him any longer. Her mouth formed a hard straight line, signaling that she had nothing more to say, and she strode to the window and stood staring out.

"I want your word that you will speak to no one else about the brooch," Travis demanded.

Rebecca held her silence. She was going to get to the bottom of this matter once and for all. Then she would be free of Travis Brandt.

"What of Daniel? Who will care for him if something should happen to you?" he demanded, attempting to reason with her.

"He will have our father." She turned to glare at him cynically. "There was a time when I thought that perhaps you would show him some consideration. You professed to care for him, and I believed you were sincere. But now it occurs to me that your alliances are very easily destroyed."

"I will always consider it my duty to see that both you and Daniel are provided for."

"I want nothing but the cabin and land that was agreed upon."

"And I want nothing more than to see that you remain alive to possess them," he replied impatiently. "Therefore, you will remain in your room until 'tis time for dinner and consider the folly of your ways."

"You can't be serious! You cannot imprison me in my room. I am not a child."

"You are behaving as one. Therefore, you will be treated as one." Turning on his heels, he left the room, taking the key with him.

Rebecca's cheeks flared scarlet when she heard the key being turned in the lock. She'd never been so humiliated! She stalked over to the window seat and sat gazing out. Mr. Travis Brandt had gone too far. He was not her master. No man would ever be her master.

Downstairs Travis paced in the study. He'd seen the fire in Rebecca's eyes and knew that locking her in her room would do no good. "It will, in fact, probably only provoke her into even less prudent action," he muttered.

He did not like admitting how deeply it had cut him that she had chosen a loyalty to her father over him. It was as he should have expected, he chided himself. Still, the peril was his fault, even though it was she who insisted upon being involved, and he would see that no harm came to her.

At last he went back up to her room, unlocked the door, and entered.

Rebecca acknowledged his entrance with a cool glance, then returned her attention to the view beyond the window.

He closed the door, crossed the room, and stood looking grimly down upon her. "It is clear you have chosen a course for yourself. I would beg you again to reconsider."

"I have already set sail. There can be no turning back now."

"If you were to speak of the brooch to no one else, it might be assumed you had put it out of your mind," he countered.

Turning back toward him, she raised a cynical eyebrow. "I have long been under the impression that men considered women's curiosity to be unquenchable."

"You are determined to go through with this, are you not?"

"Yes, I am."

"Then I shall lay down some rules, and you will abide by them," he ordered. "The first and most important one is that you will not leave this house without me. Also, you will give no indication that you know any of the true history of the brooch."

Having Travis for a constant companion caused her stomach to knot. She had taken this course because she felt the need to rid herself of him. "The second rule I shall abide by," she replied. "But surely you cannot be serious about accompanying my every step."

"I am most serious," he assured her. The grimness of his face increased. "If you will not abide by my rules, then I shall have to change the game. I shall have to reveal my reasons for being here."

Fear for him caused a cold chill to shake her. "You cannot! The man you seek will surely find some way to kill you."

He saw the fear in her eyes and wondered if it was for him or for her father. "I will guard my back."

He did not love her. He did not even trust her, but she could not bear the thought of him dead. "There will be no need," she replied. "I will abide by your rules."

He stood regarding her coolly. "And who will you approach next?"

She read the challenge on his face. "I will speak to my father."

"I will have our horses saddled."

Rebecca watched him leave. She wished he had stayed in England and married his beloved Ruth and never come into her life. But he was there, and until the man he sought was found, he would remain. She hastily changed into her riding habit.

Hadrian came out to greet them. " 'Tis good to see the two of you looking more like your old selves," he said. He helped Rebecca dismount, then gave her a hug before he bowed toward Travis. Turning back toward Rebecca, he regarded her with fatherly concern. "But you do still look a bit tired."

"'Twas a long journey," she replied.

He nodded. "And a dangerous one to undertake alone." There was strong reprimand in his voice. "You should not have gone with times being as they were. You're right lucky to have a husband who would go after you. He's a brave man."

Rebecca had heard all of this upon her arrival back at Green Glen. She'd been tempted to reveal to her father that Travis had come to her rescue only because of his sense of duty, but she'd held her tongue. She did not, however, want to listen to this glorification of Travis Brandt once again. Especially when Travis was there for the specific reason of proving that her father was a cold-blooded murderer.

"I was going to come myself, but Mr. Brandt insisted that he should go alone and I should remain to look after Daniel. I would only have slowed him down anyway," Hadrian was saying.

"You told me all of this when we returned," Rebecca reminded him, fighting to keep the impatience out of her voice.

"Yes, I know." He drew a grateful breath. "I'm just so relieved to see you back safely. I guess I keep rattling on." Taking her arm, he ushered her toward the cabin. "Come inside and sit for a while. You were too tired when you arrived back to tell me of your adventures. Now you must relate to me everything that happened."

Inside the cabin a fire was burning to ward off the fall chill in the air. Memories of her childhood again swept over her, and in her mind's eye she saw her mother sitting near the fire, smiling up at her father. There had been love in Alison Riley's eyes and a returning love in Hadrian's that would have warmed the cabin in the dead of winter with no fire. Rebecca glanced toward Travis. She had thought she had a chance of finding that same kind of love with him, but she had been greatly mistaken. Pushing such thoughts from her mind, she seated herself. "I was wondering, Father," she said in a carefully schooled casual voice, "if you ever communicated with Mr. Mercer during the years of my marriage to him."

A sadness came over his features. "I wanted to. But I had given my word that I would remain away, and I did not want to cause you trouble in your marriage." He took her hands in his. "I hope you've not been thinking all these years that I deserted you. I only did what I thought was best for you and Daniel. But there wasn't a day go by that I didn't think of you."

"Then you had no communication at all with Mr. Mercer," she persisted.

He looked up at her sheepishly. "Well, there was a time about three years ago. I found myself nearby. I couldn't help but cross the river just for a peek. Came across Mr. Mercer on the path. He were with Joseph. Joseph didn't recognize me, but Mr. Mercer did. He sent Joseph ahead and warned me that if I should ever show my face here again, he'd be sending Daniel out on his own . . . maybe sell his services to one of the local landholders and make the boy work as a servant. I begged him to just let me see the two of you from a distance, but he refused."

Rebecca could visualize Thomas astride his horse ordering her father to be on his way. "You had no choice," she said gently. "He would have done as he threatened." Thomas had been a man who enjoyed ruling those over whom he had control. 'Twas his way of proving his manhood. Glancing toward Travis, she again recalled her husband's will and cursed Thomas Mercer under her breath.

Hadrian kissed her hands. "Aye. And I didn't want to risk your future."

Rebecca glanced toward Travis and saw the skepticism in his eyes. This was an exercise in futility. He was not going to believe anything her father said. Still, she had to go through the motions of the game. "When I was in Jamestown, I encountered a mystery."

Hadrian's eyes glistened with interest. "A mystery?"

"It concerns a brooch. I chanced to meet the wife of the jeweler Thomas always commissioned when he needed a bit of fine work done. It seems that he'd taken a brooch to be repaired with him on his last trip. 'Twas supposed to be a gift for me. But after his death the brooch was not found among his belongings, and I knew nothing of its existence."

Hadrian frowned musingly. "I've always thought those servants of yours were an honest lot. But I suppose one of them might have pinched it."

"I suppose," she conceded. Since her father could not be told the true story behind the brooch, this was the most reasonable explanation for him. "I do hate to think any of them would do such a thing though."

Hadrian nodded. "'Tis a terrible thing to have to live among those you distrust."

Rebecca saw Travis's jaw tighten ever so slightly. She knew he was mentally agreeing with her father and that he would be relieved when this was over and he was rid of her. Well, she would be glad to be rid of him. "'Tis a terrible thing," she agreed.

Hadrian lit his pipe. After taking a couple of puffs, he said sagely, "I'll keep me eyes and ears open. If you do have a thief amongst you, you'd best find out."

"We intend to," Travis assured him.

A little later, as they rode back toward the house, Rebecca could not maintain her silence. "You're not even willing to give him the benefit of the doubt, are you? You're determined that he is the man you seek."

"He admitted to having been here without your knowledge," Travis pointed out.

"But he did not stay nor was he ever here before or after that," she retorted.

"We have only his word for that," Travis countered. "He might have felt he had to admit to that one time because

Joseph saw him and might someday remember if asked the right question."

"If my father's such a cold-blooded murderer, then surely he would simply have killed Joseph rather than take the chance of being exposed," she snapped and kicked her horse into a fast trot.

Catching up with her, Travis captured her reins and brought her horse to a stop. "I am not as certain as you seem to think that your father is the man I seek. But he is one of the suspects, and I'll not overlook him," he said gruffly.

Rebecca stared up at him. "But you have constantly spoken against him."

For a long moment he regarded her in silence, then said, "It is your reaction that interests me. Tell me honestly, Rebecca, if you should discover that he is the man I seek, will you expose him or protect him from the justice he deserves?"

"My father is not the man you seek," she stated firmly.

The blue of his eyes turned cold like the sky before a winter storm. "But what if he is?" he demanded.

She faced him levelly. "He is not!" Her jaw trembled slightly as she added, "I cannot even consider that possibility."

A cold smile tilted the corners of his mouth. "It is as I thought. You would continue to stand beside him. You would lie to protect him. But then, lying to achieve whatever ends you seek is second nature to you."

Without thinking, Rebecca raised her hand to slap him, but Travis caught her by the wrist. His grip was painful as she tried to twist free. Giving up, she met his angry gaze with equal fury. "It must have irked you greatly to have been forced to stoop so low as to marry someone of my lineage to find your mother's killer."

"What irks me is that I cannot trust my wife." Releasing her abruptly, he kicked his horse into action.

Pacing her horse a short distance behind, Rebecca studied his strong broad back. She remembered the firm feel of him beneath her hands, and her body began to ache for his touch. The urge to catch up to him and tell him that he could trust her was strong. 'Twould be a fool's errand, she chided herself, watching his shoulders straighten even more as if he felt her watching him and her gaze annoyed him. Reminding herself of the Ruth to whom he had called out, the barrier she wished to keep between herself and Travis Brandt remained strong.

It was too late when they returned home to call upon any others that day. But that night, lying alone in her bed, she contemplated her next move. Mr. Loyde, she decided, would receive her next visit. She found him an unlikely candidate for a murderer. But it had suddenly occurred to her that it was possible that whoever had offered the brooch to her husband might also have offered it to Mr. Loyde. After saying a silent prayer that tomorrow would provide the necessary clue to end this hunt, she fell into a restless sleep.

The next morning dawned clear and bright. There was a slight crispness in the air that gave the taste of autumn. As had grown to be their custom, Rebecca and Travis spoke little during their ride to the Loyde plantation.

As the butler opened the door and admitted them, they could hear the sound of children's laughter coming from the drawing room. Adult male laughter mingled with it. Mr. Loyde was playing with his children. Rebecca had never pictured him as a man who spent much time with his offspring. And she'd rarely heard him laugh. Now it occurred to her that what she had thought of as coldness had been merely reserve. He would have been a more practical choice for a husband than Travis and perhaps not nearly so difficult to live with as she had thought. But when she tried to picture herself as mistress here with Mr. Loyde by her side, her stomach soured. He would probably have been as good in bed as Travis Brandt, she told herself hotly. When she couldn't make herself believe this, she added that time spent in the bedroom was not the most important portion of a marriage. As the butler left them to announce their arrival, she said quietly, "It would seem that Mr. Loyde has a much gentler side that he does not normally expose."

Glancing down at her, Travis found himself suddenly wondering if she was thinking that Mr. Loyde would have been a much better choice for a husband. The thought brought a rush of jealousy. Furious that he should care whom she preferred, he told himself to put it out of his mind. But instead, he heard himself saying, "And he would, most likely, have been easier to fool. 'Tis too bad for you that you made the wrong choice in husbands."

Rebecca's chin threatened to tremble. Clearly, he was wishing she had chosen Mr. Loyde. Her shoulders straightened. "Yes, 'tis," she replied.

Her confirmation cut like a knife. What had you expected her to say? he questioned himself cynically. Hadn't she made it clear when she had come to him with her proposal of marriage that she considered the union nothing more than a practical solution to her problem? He did, however, find himself recalling that she had admitted she found him more appealing than her other suitors. "Obviously, you have decided that one man's bed is as good as any other's," he said sarcastically.

Rebecca glowered at him. Did he really expect her to admit that his bed was the only one that continued to appeal to her? "Obviously," she replied.

The urge to take her home that moment and prove to her that no man could satisfy her body as well as he was close to overwhelming. No! Travis ordered himself. It would only prove torture for him. As hard as he tried to put her from his mind, he still lay awake at night wanting her in his bed. But he would not indulge this weakness.

A sudden hush fell over the house. The butler had announced their arrival, and the laughter had ceased in a breath. Almost immediately the children filed out, each pausing to politely bow or curtsy as they passed Rebecca and Travis on their way toward the stairs. Daniel, too, would have had some difficulty fitting into this household, she decided as the children continued upstairs, each walking sedately in a line. As often as she had spoken to him about slowing his pace within the house, he still insisted upon running nearly everywhere.

" 'Tis a pleasure to see you," Mr. Loyde greeted them as they joined him in the drawing room.

Mistress Hansone was doing needlepoint near the fire. Upon seeing her guests, she rose and curtsied. "You are looking fit and well after your long journey," she said, studying Rebecca with open curiosity. " 'Twas a most dangerous trek, especially with the colony in the midst of a civil war."

" 'Twas unwise," Rebecca admitted.

Stunned that his wife had admitted to her folly, Travis could not entirely hide his surprise.

Seeing his slightly raised eyebrow, Rebecca shrugged. "And I am sure my husband will not allow me to forget my foolishness for a very long time."

Mistress Hansone nodded. Leaning toward Rebecca, her manner became womanly conspiratorial. "Men do seem to enjoy reminding us of our shortcomings," she replied in lowered tones with a sympathetic smile.

Out of the corner of her eye Rebecca glanced toward Travis. "Some more than others," she returned in matching lowered tones.

Travis, who had been standing close enough to hear the exchange, was tempted to point out that some women had more serious shortcomings than others, but he held his tongue. It would not do for their host and hostess to believe he and Rebecca were not reasonably happy together. Bowing toward his wife, he captured her hand and, lifting it to his lips, kissed the back of it. "But I am most pleased to have you back safely."

Shaken by this sudden show of open caring, she looked hard into his face. Fool! she thought when she saw that the warmth in his voice was not matched in his eyes. They were instead cold and calculating. His action had been purely for Mr. Loyde's and Mistress Hansone's benefit!

"Have you news of Bacon?" Mr. Loyde questioned, changing the direction of the conversation.

Mistress Hansone shook her head sadly. " 'Tis not right that neighbor should fight against neighbor and friend against friend in a war of succession when in truth 'tis only Sir William and not the king whom many hold a grievance against."

Mr. Loyde cast her an impatient glance. "As I have tried to explain to you, 'tis Mr. Bacon's life and the lives of his followers that are at stake. If Sir William should capture them before the king has heard their case and, as they hope will happen, rule to pardon them or, at least, grant them leniency, Sir William will surely hang the lot of them for treason."

Mistress Hansone shook her head again. " 'Tis a sad muddle."

"And one we can all find ourselves caught in the midst of," Travis said grimly.

Remembering the day she found him near death on the battlefield, Rebecca shuddered. "Actually, 'twas not news of the war that brought us here," she said. " 'Tis about a brooch." She studied Mr. Loyde's face but saw only curiosity. " 'Tis a very fine cameo set in skillfully worked silver with a border of diamonds forming a frame."

"My daughter wrote me about a cameo brooch," Mistress Hansone spoke up suddenly. Her cheeks flushed as all attentions shifted to her. "Oh," she breathed worriedly, meeting her son-in-law's gaze. "She told me it was supposed to be a surprise. I suppose I should not have mentioned it."

Mr. Loyde smiled encouragingly. "Please, tell us."

Mistress Hansone looked like a child who had been caught with her hand in the cookie jar. "She told me I was not to say anything." Her face flushed even further. "She told me that she had surprised you in your study one day and seen you with a box that looked like a jeweler's box. You had quickly pushed it into a drawer of your desk and pretended it was of no importance." Mistress Hansone glanced defensively toward Rebecca and Travis. "My daughter was not normally a snoopy person. She wrote that she did not know what prompted her to return later and peek into the box. Anyway, inside was this lovely cameo brooch. She quickly hid it again." Her gaze shifted back to Mr. Loyde. "She assumed it was to be a gift for her, and she did not want to spoil your surprise by letting you know she had seen it."

Rebecca noticed Travis's body stiffen as Mistress Hansone told her story. Her own heart was beating at a rapid rate. Had they found the man they were seeking? It did not seem likely, but then, none of the suspects excepting Mr. Wetherly seemed likely to her.

"She was quite right." Mr. Loyde rose from his chair and crossed to a table on the far side of the room.

Rebecca noticed Travis's hand going to rest on the hilt of his sword, and her posture became one of readiness.

After unlocking the drawer of the table with a tiny gold key he had extracted from his pocket, Mr. Loyde took out a small box. Carrying it back to the assembled group, he opened it. Inside was a cameo brooch, but it was much smaller than the one Travis sought. It also had no diamonds, and the silver frame in which it was encased was quite plain. "It was to have been for her birthday," he said, a sadness coming to his face that tore at Rebecca's heart. He sighed deeply. "I wish now I had given it to her sooner. I was just so certain she would get well." His voice broke slightly as he closed the box and returned it to the drawer. "Now I shall keep it to give to our daughter on her wedding day."

Mistress Hansone nodded. " 'Tis a wonderful thought. My Amanda would have wished it."

"I did not mean to bring up a subject that would cause you grief," Rebecca apologized.

"Do not trouble yourself," he said reassuringly as he returned to his chair. He smiled gently. "Now you must tell us about the brooch that interests you."

Rebecca felt a wave of futility wash over her. Mr. Loyde was not the man she sought. Still, he might know something, she told herself for encouragement. "'Tis a mystery."

"A mystery?" Mr. Loyde queried, glancing toward Travis.

Travis's posture was again relaxed. He gave a nonchalant shrug. "'Tis Rebecca's mystery," he said, as if he found the whole business boring.

"And how may I help with this mystery?" Mr. Loyde asked, returning his attention to Rebecca.

She quickly repeated the same story she had used with her father and Colonel Howard, explaining that she had discovered the existence of the brooch quite by accident when in Jamestown but had found no such piece among her husband's belongings.

When she finished, Mr. Loyde frowned thoughtfully. "'Tis a most interesting occurrence." His frown sharpened. "But perhaps not so much of a mystery. 'Tis my guess one of your servants has it tucked neatly away."

Rebecca fought back a bout of frustration. This was getting them nowhere. Making a snap decision, she persisted. "I was given the impression that my husband had purchased the brooch from an acquaintance." She saw Travis stiffen but ignored him. He wanted to discover the identity of the man who had murdered his mother, and she wanted to be free from him. It was worth the risk. "My coming here is not merely a whim to satisfy my curiosity," she explained hurriedly. "Whilst I have a fairly accurate description of the brooch, 'tis a description that came second hand. And it has occurred to me that there is always a chance there could be another brooch almost identical to the one that was supposedly in my husband's possession. If I should discover a servant in the possession of such a brooch, I would want to be certain it is the one my husband had and not simply one that is similar. 'Twould be most horrendous to accuse someone of a crime they did not commit." She regarded him pleadingly. "Would you know of anyone who might have sold the brooch to my late husband?"

Mr. Loyde sat in silent thought for a moment. Finally, in a confidential tone, he said, "I would not want to be accused of gossiping. But I do recall hearing Mr. Garnet complaining about the price he was getting for his crops, and he mentioned that he might have to offer some of the family jewels for sale to remain solvent."

"I think it would be most prudent to drop this matter," Travis spoke up, his manner that of one whose indulgence was growing thin. "If one of the servants has taken it, they will have surely secured it so well by now we will never find it. And it would be most impolite to approach Mr. Garnet on this subject."

Rebecca saw his ploy. They must not act as if they would pursue this to the death, because death might be what awaited them. "I suppose you are right," she conceded.

Travis changed the subject to the crops and the prices they could expect. While the men talked, Rebecca tried picturing Mr. Garnet as the highwayman. It was the most improbable of all images. On the other hand, he might be an excellent actor, she reasoned. If so, his disguise was perfect. Who would ever believe someone who behaved so effeminately could be a cold-blooded murderer?

"We will call upon the Garnets this afternoon," she informed Travis as they rode away from the Loyde plantation.

"I should have kept you locked in your room. You almost went too far with Loyde. If the man I seek should begin to believe that you can determine who he is, he will surely kill you."

"Unless he is my father," she interjected dryly.

Travis regarded her grimly. "I do not believe the man I

seek has a heart. He has left a trail of blood to cover his identity. 'Tis my belief he would kill even his own child to protect himself."

"Then he is most assuredly not my father," she tossed back.

It took all of Rebecca's control not to bolt down her food at the noonday meal. While she was still having a bit of trouble picturing Mr. Garnet as the highwayman, she was not having a bit of trouble visualizing Mistress Garnet in the role of a murderer's accomplice. A part of her felt a bit guilty at this harsh judgment of the woman. But another part hoped that this afternoon's inquiry might lead to the end of Travis's quest.

As they rode toward the Garnet plantation, Travis drew up beside Rebecca. "I want your word that you will behave with more discretion that you showed this morning," he demanded.

"I behaved with the utmost discretion this morning," she replied. "My inquiry followed a most reasonable path. I said nothing that should warn the highwayman that I know of the history of the brooch."

"That you know of the brooch at all could be seen as a threat to him," he argued. "That you are making inquiries could cause him to feel you must be stopped."

Rebecca glanced toward him. It was proving to be much more difficult than she had thought it would be to forget the tender feelings she had begun to feel for him. Each time he voiced any concern for her, she experienced a rush of hope. But it was always dashed by the coldness in his eyes. Curtly she reminded herself that his heart had always belonged to someone else. "I trust you to guard my back. I know you are as anxious to be rid of me as I am to be rid of you. If my placing myself in a position of danger will bring a quicker end to this arrangement, then it is well worth the risk." She urged her horse into a gallop to signal an end to this discussion.

Travis watched her riding ahead of him. The temptation

to catch her, take her home, and lock her in her room was great. But he knew it would do no good. Never had he met so hardheaded a woman. Galloping, he joined her as they reached the manor house.

Luck was with them. Both Mistress Garnet and her son were home. Again, Rebecca repeated the story of discovering that her late husband had taken a brooch to Jamestown to have it repaired for her. "But you see, the mystery is that he never gave it to me nor was it among his possessions after his death," she finished, frowning perplexedly. "I suppose 'tis possible one of the servants stole it. But I do hate to believe that."

A malicious gleam sparkled in Mistress Garnet's eyes, then was quickly replaced by a look of sympathetic concern. "I know I probably shouldn't be saying this," she said hesitantly. Her mouth formed a reproving pout. "But men do have their weaknesses. You don't think it's possible that Mr. Mercer could have . . ." She paused, as if what she had to say was too indelicate to actually speak the words.

"Please go on," Rebecca urged.

"Well, I hate mentioning this," Mistress Garnet continued with the same hesitancy. "But I suppose you must consider all the possibilities." Again she paused.

"Please, do go on," Rebecca coaxed. It had suddenly dawned on her what Mistress Garnet was leading up to, and she wanted to know if the woman had the nerve to actually put it into words.

"Men being men," Mistress Garnet said, the reproving look on her face becoming even stronger, "there is always the possibility that Mr. Mercer had a mistress to whom he gave the brooch."

"Mother, really!" Jason stared at his mother in shocked disbelief. "That is a most unkind suggestion."

It was preposterous, Rebecca knew. She was also fairly certain Mistress Garnet didn't believe for one moment that Thomas had had a mistress. The woman had merely brought up the possibility in a selfish effort to cause

Rebecca hurt and perhaps even a touch of humiliation. However, Mistress Garnet's subtle insults were not important. The information Rebecca had come to gather was. "I suppose you could be right," she replied with a heavy sigh. Suddenly thinking of Travis, she found herself adding, "Men can be most deceiving when it comes to their true feelings."

She noticed the corner of Travis's mouth twitch as if he had to fight to keep from adding his own thoughts. None of which would be flattering to me, she mused. Well, she did not care what he thought!

Mistress Garnet nodded. She was attempting to keep a totally solemn expression, but Rebecca saw the triumphant gleam that flashed in the woman's eyes. Clearly, Mistress Garnet was pleased with herself for being able to deliver this blow to the woman who had rejected her son.

"I am certain Mr. Mercer was a most loyal husband," Jason interjected curtly.

Rebecca caught the glance he shot his mother, and to her surprise, she noticed a slight recoil on Mistress Garnet's part.

"I'm sure my son is right," Mistress Garnet said hastily.

Jason was not quite so meek as she had thought, Rebecca realized. Nor was he as much under his mother's thumb. "I did have a purpose in telling you of this mystery," she said, letting the suggestion that Thomas could have had a mistress drop. "'Tis because I have reason to believe the brooch was bought by my husband from an acquaintance." Again she launched into the story of how she had only a second-hand description of the brooch and did not want to accuse any of her servants of theft when they might have a brooch that legitimately belonged to them. "So I was wondering if you might know of someone from whom my husband may have purchased the brooch," she finished.

"No, I'm afraid not," Jason replied. "I, myself, came close to having to sell a bit of the family silver, but luckily we managed to get by and hold on to it."

"We got a price for our crop we did not expect to receive," Mistress Garnet interjected quickly.

Rebecca could have sworn she saw a flash of panic in the woman's eyes. She was about to ask to whom they had sold their crop when Travis suddenly announced that it was time for them to be leaving.

"You certainly got us out of there swiftly," she admonished as they rode toward home. "Didn't you notice how nervous Mistress Garnet behaved when her son mentioned that they had not had to sell the family silver?"

"I noticed—and I noticed you noticing," he replied with a scowl.

"What's wrong? Did it suddenly look as if Jason Garnet might be the man you are seeking instead of my father and you didn't want to believe it?" she demanded.

"I know how Garnet got his money. He did a bit of smuggling."

Rebecca stared at him in shock. "Jason Garnet, a smuggler? I don't believe it." She continued to regard him skeptically. "How do you know?"

"I kept a close eye on that sort of activity in case any of the jewelry showed up that way."

"You knew he had done a bit of smuggling, and yet you were still ready to put my father at the head of your list of suspects," she seethed.

"A great many people are doing a bit of smuggling," he replied with a shrug. "A large majority of the populace does not even consider it a true crime."

She recalled saying the same thing to Kirby Wetherly in Travis's defense. The memory caused a bitter taste in her mouth. She had been quick to champion Travis that day. Yet, he, even then, had been ready to believe the worst of her. In her mind's eye she saw him regarding her cynically as she sat with the wildflower in her hand. Both his tone and manner had suggested that he thought she was one of Mr. Wetherly's dalliances.

She'd been right about him in the first place. He was an

arrogant, bullheaded boor and not worth her consideration. The sooner he was out of her life, the better.

She wondered if he would merely leave or seek a legal separation. Considering the way he felt about her, he might even prevail upon the earl to plead with the king and grant him a divorce. 'Twas rare such a thing happened. But she did not care. She would endure any humiliation to be rid of him.

FIFTEEN

THAT night Rebecca was too restless to sleep. She paced the floor of her room. Mr. Wetherly still seemed to her to be the most likely suspect. That Travis did not position him at the top of his list irked her greatly. Had not the man shown a true blackness of character!

Her stomach growled, reminding her that she'd eaten very little all day. Sharing a table with Travis greatly affected her appetite. She thought of the cold meat left over from dinner and her mouth began to water. "I cannot figure this out on an empty stomach." She found her heavy cloak, flung it on, and went downstairs. The wind whipped around her as she left the main house and made her way toward the kitchen.

Suddenly a shadow flickered in the corner of her eye. In the next instant a cloth was wrapped around her throat and pulled tightly. She tried to gasp for breath, but the cloth was closing her windpipe. Frantically she struggled, kicking backward at her assailant while trying to pull at the cloth. But her attacker was much bigger and stronger than she was. His attack had taken her by surprise, and now he had an overwhelming advantage.

She clawed at the hands holding the strangling cloth, but they were protected by heavy gloves, making her attempts to harm her attacker insignificant. Darkness began to close in over her mind. Just when she was certain she was on her way to meet her Maker, the cloth around her neck suddenly slackened, and she felt herself dropping to the ground. She was vaguely aware of two large forms locked in combat above her. Gasping for breath, she pulled at the cloth still wrapped around her neck. Too weak to rise, she managed to turn herself toward the battle. She recognized Travis. The man he fought wore a heavy cloak masking his clothes and a full hood over his head with only holes for his eyes, giving no chance for identification. Travis let out a sharp groan as the cloaked man suddenly landed a solid blow to his head. Momentarily dazed, Travis staggered back.

Suddenly the moonlight caught the blade of a large hunting knife. Fear for Travis shook Rebecca. But it was her the assailant suddenly turned toward. She rolled as the knife whizzed past her and buried itself in the dirt where she had lain only a moment earlier.

The cloaked man issued a snort of disgust. Then his attention again turned to Travis. Picking up a piece of firewood from the stack near the kitchen, he swung at Travis. Still slightly dazed, Travis swerved, but a little too slowly. The blow missed his head but caught him on the shoulder.

Before Travis could again regain his balance, the cloaked attacker took off running toward the woods. Travis started after him. Suddenly the man came to a halt. He turned with a pistol in his hand.

Cold panic washed over Rebecca. She screamed as he fired and Travis dropped to the ground. Staggering to her feet, she rushed to Travis's side as their assailant ran into the woods.

He had shifted himself into a sitting position and was brushing off his shirt.

"Where are you hurt?" she demanded, falling to her knees in front of him, her gaze raking over him as she tried to see his wound in the faint light provided by the moon.

"I'm not," he replied, adding in disgust, "I managed to duck his shot, but he got away."

"What's going on?" Joseph and Philip demanded in unison, rushing from the servants' quarters, muskets in hand.

Still sitting, Travis scowled at Rebecca. "What were you doing out here at this time of night?"

Rebecca rubbed her throat in an attempt to ease the lingering soreness. "I was on my way to the kitchen for a bite to eat."

"I thought I told you that you were not to go anywhere without me," he growled in a lowered voice for her ears only.

"I didn't think that meant walking from the house to the kitchen," she whispered back in her defense.

Travis's scowl deepened. "It was a lucky thing I was awake and heard you leave and decided to see where you were going."

"Are you injured?" Joseph asked, worried, reaching them a few paces ahead of Philip.

"Only a few bruises," Travis replied, easing himself to his feet and offering Rebecca his hand.

Refusing his help, she rose from her kneeling position on her own.

"What happened, sir?" Philip demanded anxiously.

"Mistress Brandt was in search of a midnight meal when she was attacked by a prowler," Travis answered as he walked over to where Rebecca had first fallen and pulled the knife from the ground. " 'Tis my guess he was a scavenger looking for food and was surprised by my wife's appearance."

The warning glance Travis gave her caused Rebecca to swallow back her protest that he was mistaken. Instead, she quietly retrieved the cloth that had been wrapped around her neck while Travis sent the two men back to their beds.

When they were once again alone, he turned to Rebecca. A part of him wanted to grab her by the arms and shake her, he was so furious with her for placing herself in this danger, while another part wanted to crush her to him and hold her until the panic he still felt for her was gone. But neither would be for the best. Shaking her would do no good. She was too hardheaded. And holding her would only bring about his downfall. 'Twas best to keep his distance. "Are you still hungry?" he asked coolly.

She was about to say no when her stomach growled. "Yes," she admitted grudgingly.

Escorting her into the kitchen, he lighted the lamp, then seated himself on the bench at the long table and examined the knife used by her would-be murderer as she brought out the meat and a loaf of bread. "It has an Indian's mark upon it," he said after a few moments. "But that was no Indian who attacked you."

Pausing in the middle of slicing a piece of meat, she glared at him. "You know as well as I that it was the man you seek. Were you able to discern anything about him that might identify him?"

"No." Anger mingled with frustration in his voice. "But you're right, I'm certain he was the man. However"—his manner took on the sharp command of one who expected to be obeyed—"you will give no hint that you even suspect the attack was because of the brooch. You will go along with my story that it was a scavenger looking for food. With any luck our prey will think you are honestly innocent in your inquiries about the brooch and leave you in peace."

Rebecca had to admit that she hoped he was right. She had not expected the man they sought to act so swiftly nor so viciously. Her hand went again to her throat. "I will say nothing," she promised, buttering herself a slice of bread.

As she sat down and began to eat, he picked up the cloth that had been wrapped around her neck. It was several strips of course linen braided together to form a sturdy rope. A knot formed in the pit of his stomach as he remembered coming out of the house and seeing her being attacked. I would feel the same for anyone, he assured himself.

Rebecca's throat hurt as she swallowed, and after only a

couple of bites, she put her plate aside and began to return the food to the larder.

Travis scowled. She had risked her life for a bit of food and now she was not eating. "I thought you were hungry."

He made her feel like an unwanted nuisance. "My throat hurts," she replied defensively. She was about to add that she had not requested his company but bit back the words. It would be a childish thing to say under the circumstances.

Renewed anxiousness for her swept over him. Rising from the table, he approached her. "Let me see," he ordered gruffly.

Rebecca had no desire to be inspected by him. " 'Tis unnecessary." Ignoring his command, she continued into the larder.

He was waiting with the cloth and knife in hand when she returned. "Then 'tis time to return to bed." He blew out the lamp, but as he moved to the door, he came to an abrupt halt. The argument he had been having with himself for the past few minutes came to an end. "You will be returning to my room this night and for every night until I am certain you are safe."

The last thing she wanted was to share a bed with him once again. "That is unnecessary," she protested.

He would have preferred to concede to her protest, but he could not. The image of her being strangled was too vivid. In spite of the anger and frustration she caused him to feel, he could not bear the thought of her being harmed. " 'Twas you who began this," he pointed out curtly. "Now it is my duty to protect you. Until this man is caught, you will be my constant companion."

His constant companion! Rebecca glared at him. "You cannot be serious!"

"I am deadly serious," he assured her, holding up the cloth and knife.

In the dim light provided by the moon, she could not see his face clearly, but his voice told her that he would give no quarter. Cursing mentally, she preceded him out the door and back to the house.

But upstairs she balked at the thought of reentering the bedroom they had once shared.

Renewed anger swept over Travis as he saw her hesitation. "You have no need to fear me," he said dryly. "I've no interest in forcing myself upon a woman who does not want me to hold her."

The problem was, she admitted a little later as she lay as far away from him as the bed would permit, she did want him to hold her. The shock of the attack was beginning to wear off, and the realization of what would have happened if he hadn't followed her was causing a delayed terror to spread through her. Against her will she wished his strong arms were around her. Furious with this weakness, she told herself that she needed no man to protect her. Closing her eyes, she willed herself to sleep.

But her sleep was a restless one with dreams of a hooded man stalking her. She ran until she thought she would drop. But he was still there. He placed the cloth around her neck and began to tighten it. She fought, but he seemed to be winning.

Travis lay watching Rebecca tossing and turning. Just to touch her was dangerous. He had always thought of himself as a strong-willed man until she had come into his life. Against his better judgment he had married her. When she had betrayed him, he had ordered himself to care for her no longer. But still, he continually found himself remembering her laughter and the unexpected happiness her company had brought into his life. Such thoughts will only lead you into trouble, he warned himself. But he could not stop himself as he moved toward her. Her nightmares were his fault, he reasoned. He would not be so callous as to not offer her some comfort.

A gentle warmth spread through Rebecca as she was drawn into a protective cocoon of strong arms while a soothing voice assured her that all would be well. The hooded man vanished in a wisp of smoke. Relaxing, she snuggled closer into the offered sanctuary.

The next morning Rebecca awoke slowly. She was warm and filled with a sense of security. The desire to linger in the foggy mist between sleep and wakefulness was strong. She moved her head to snuggle it farther into her pillow. Crisp hairs rubbed against her cheek, sending a current of delight flowing through her. A sound not unlike a purr came from deep in her throat as her hand moved upward over a warm, hard, muscular surface. Pleasure mingled with excitement. Her legs were intertwined with sturdy muscular columns that offered them a warm haven.

Don't give in to this, Travis ordered himself. He had been lying awake for nearly an hour now holding her. Dawn was breaking outside, and he told himself to leave the bed and go about his day. But she had been sleeping so peacefully, he had not been able to bring himself to disturb her rest. That was a lie, he admitted. He had wanted to hold her. It was stupid and he'd called himself a fool a hundred times in just the last few minutes. Now she was waking, and her movements were nearly bringing his control to the snapping point. She was his wife. It was his right to bed her. Cynically he recalled how certain he had been that his craving for her would fade.

Rebecca moaned softly as the embers of desire began to smolder within her. Stretching, she shifted her weight until she lay half upon the long form beside her.

Travis ached to possess her, and she was inviting him. Granted, she was more asleep than awake, But her invitation was too tempting to resist. Freeing her leg, he gently worked her nightgown upward. Again a moan of delight escaped from her. Travis stroked her calf, then worked his hand to the inside of her thigh. He sought the heart of her womanhood and smiled at the heated readiness that greeted him.

Beneath her leg Rebecca felt the hardening of male lust, and pleasure surged through her. No dream had ever felt this good. Her breathing quickened, and every sense began to come to full life. Her muscles tightened, and her body arched toward the promised pleasure. It felt so real. "Travis, please," she murmured pleadingly.

"If you wish," he growled back, pleased that she knew who was going to take her body where it craved to go.

The sound of his voice brought a shock of reality. Rebecca's eyes opened. He had felt so real because he was real, and her traitorous body was inviting him to do with it as he pleased. How could she be so wanton? He did not want her . . . he wanted his Ruth. To him she was merely a warm body to satisfy his lust. "No," she snarled, stiffening and pushing at him in an effort to gain her freedom.

For a moment he considered demanding his right. She could not deny that her body had been more than willing to surrender to him. But he had never taken a woman against her will, and he would not do so now. Releasing her, he watched with cold cynicism as she scooted across the bed. "I was merely offering you the comfort you sought."

Rebecca's cheeks flamed with embarrassment and self-directed anger. "I asked for no comfort from you," she retorted.

"You were sleeping so restlessly neither of us was going to get any rest. So I offered you my shoulder for the night." His gaze narrowed upon her. " 'Twas you who invited more."

She glared at him with self-righteous indignation. "I was asleep, and you took advantage of me."

He shrugged. "Not completely." After a moment's pause he added, "You cannot expect a man to disregard so open an invitation."

Rebecca drew a shaky breath. He was right. Cursing her traitorous body, she admitted that she had held on to the dream because she had wanted it to be real. Even now the vestiges of desire lingered within her. But clearly, although he had been willing to satisfy her, his lust was easily forgotten. Humiliated by her display of weakness, she moved even closer to the edge of the bed. Afraid it might happen again, she said stiffly, "I see no reason why I cannot sleep in my own bed. I shall lock the door and be perfectly safe."

Travis wanted to concede to this wish. It was taking monumental control not to pull her into his arms and claim his husbandly prerogative. But as his gaze shifted to her neck and he saw the bruising, he knew he could not. This danger she was in was his fault, and he would not take any chances with her safety. "You will remain in my bed," he ordered. "This day you will move your things back into this room."

Rebecca glowered at him, but the set of his jaw told her that arguing would do no good. "I will attempt not to disturb your sleep again," she said, adding sarcastically, "but if I should, please do not offer me any comfort."

"You have my word," he replied, promising himself he would not again tempt himself.

It was so easy for him. Hurt mingled with her anger. She had to get away from him.

Travis, too, would have preferred to end this private session. But there were questions he needed to ask, and he didn't want to worry about the servants overhearing. As she started to toss off the covers, he captured her by the wrist. "Now that you are less frightened," he said coolly, "I would like for you to try to remember if there was anything familiar about the man who attacked you. Did he speak?"

To her dismay, every fiber of her being was aware of the contact. "No, he did not speak, and I can think of nothing familiar," she replied, attempting to jerk free from his touch.

His grip on her wrist tightened. "Think," he demanded. "Your life may depend upon it."

She took a deep breath. He was right. It was stupid to allow her body's reaction to him to place her in more danger. "Release me," she ordered, and he obeyed. Lying back, Rebecca closed her eyes and forced herself to remember. "I am certain he did not speak." She closed her eyes more tightly. "He was strong." A cold sweat broke out on her brow as fear again gripped her. "I tried to claw at his hands, but he wore gloves."

Travis read the pain on her face and frowned at his callousness in insisting that she relive the attack. It was for her own safety, he reasoned. Still, he did not enjoy causing her this anguish. " 'Tis over," he soothed gruffly, combing a wayward strand of hair from her cheek. "Do not think of it again."

His touch left a trail of fire. Quickly she tossed off the covers and left his bed.

Travis, too, rose. "You will wait for me to accompany you to your room," he ordered, pulling on his shirt.

Rebecca glanced toward him, and other early-morning memories assailed her . . . memories of playfulness as they dressed that had led to passion. Damn, she cursed herself. "There is no need. I will ring for Susan."

Travis had to admit that he was not certain he was strong enough to stand by and watch her dress. There had been too many times when he had ended up helping her undress. Ringing for Susan was a welcome solution. "You will wait for her here whilst I inspect your room."

"I am sure my room is quite safe," she retorted, wanting desperately to escape his company. She had ordered herself to turn away from him but had instead been watching him dress, and the desire to turn his dressing into undressing was causing a hard twisting pain in her abdomen. You are a lustful wench, she chided herself, but that did not quell the desire welling within her. He loves another and thinks nothing good of you, she reminded herself, and a coolness spread through her.

"You will wait here," he ordered again, her stubbornness weighing on his nerves. When he had finished pulling on his boots, he stalked out of the room. Keeping Rebecca under his guard was not going to be easy. "You knew from the beginning she would be difficult," he muttered to himself as he entered her room. "You let lust rule your mind; now you must pay the penalty." Satisfied that her room was secure, he opened the door to find Susan and Rebecca waiting outside.

"I cannot believe Mistress Rebecca's bad luck this night," Susan shook her head sympathetically. "First she was attacked by a scavenger and then discovers a mouse in her bedroom. I do hate those little hairy things." Susan crinkled her nose with disgust at the thought of the rodent. "I hopes you found him, sir, and have sent him on his way."

Rebecca gave Travis an "I had to tell her something" look in response to his raised eyebrow.

"The culprit is gone for now," he assured the maid. Then, still not trusting Rebecca to obey his command, he added, "You will see that your mistress's belongings are returned to our room this day. My wounds have healed, and I would not want her again bothered in the night by any creatures other than myself."

Susan's cheeks pinkened at the suggestiveness in his tone. "Yes, sir," she replied, curtsying low.

I will think of him as nothing more than a piece of furniture, Rebecca ordered herself.

"I've never believed in husbands and wives having different beds," Susan rattled on as she helped Rebecca dress. "All that running from one bedroom to the other in the dead of winter could give a person the chills or consumption or some such thing. Then they'd die and all because they wasn't sharing the same bed." She shook her head at the tragedy of it all.

"You have a truly romantic mind." Rebecca was continually amazed at the paths her maid's thoughts could take.

Suddenly worried that she'd overstepped her bounds, Susan's cheeks pinkened again. "'Course, however a person sleeps most comfortably is important, too." Clearly deciding that a change of subject would be prudent, she said, "Mildred were right shaken when she heard what happened last night. She made Joseph go in and make certain no one was lurking in the kitchen before she'd go in this morning." Her gaze shifted to Rebecca's neck, and fear showed in her eyes. " 'Course, I can't blame her for being careful."

A knock suddenly sounded on the door, and Daniel rushed in. "I heard what happened," he said, studying Rebecca worriedly. "I wish I had been there. I'd have taught that scavenger a lesson."

Rebecca gave him a hug. "I'm sure you would have."

"Travis is having Joseph arrange for someone to be on guard at night from now on," the boy continued excitedly. "He says with all the unrest in the colony, there is no telling what might happen. Do you think we might see some of the war all the way up here?"

Rebecca drew a worried breath. "I should hope not," she said, recalling the bodies scattered over the battlefield outside of Jamestown.

Suddenly renewed anxiousness shone in his eyes. "We must go and check on father. He is alone and the scavenger might have attacked him."

"Our father knows how to protect himself," she assured him. "But if you wish, we can ride out to check on him after breakfast."

"I've already eaten." The worry remained on his face. "Really, Rebecca we must go."

"You win," she conceded. She hadn't wanted to face Travis over the breakfast table anyway. "Have our horses saddled."

She was changing into her riding habit when another knock sounded on the door. It was sharp and followed immediately by Travis's entrance. "Daniel informs me that the two of you are going to visit your father. I thought I had made it clear I wanted you to rest today. You had quite a scare last night."

Rebecca saw his jaw twitch and knew he was holding a tight rein on his temper because of Susan's presence. "He is worried about our father. I could not stop him from going and could not allow him to go alone."

"Then I shall come along, too. I'll not take any chances on your being harmed once again."

He had said he intended to be her constant companion, but she had not truly believed him. Rebecca followed him out into the hall. "There is really no need. I will be with Daniel and in broad daylight."

He bent toward her so that Susan could not overhear. "Are you willing to risk Daniel's life as well as your own if you are wrong?" he questioned grimly.

A shaft of fear shot through Rebecca. "No."

"Then I shall come along." In a louder, more congenial tone he added, "A morning ride will do me good."

"It must be nice to have someone so protective of you," Susan cooed as she helped Rebecca finish fastening her riding habit.

If Travis loved her, Rebecca would have agreed that it was wonderful. But she felt like a nuisance he was forced to put up with, and the thought of spending every minute of every day under his watchful eye left a sour taste in her mouth.

At least Daniel was not in the mood for a slow, lazy ride that would have required conversation, she mused as they trotted toward the cabin. When they drew closer, Daniel could control himself no longer and nudged his horse into a gallop. Rebecca followed suit with Travis close behind her.

"My, my, what a hurry you're in this lovely fall morning," Hadrian greeted them with a laugh.

"We were worried about you," Daniel said breathlessly, jumping from his horse and running to give his father a hug.

"Worried about me?" Hadrian looked questioningly toward Rebecca and Travis.

"Rebecca was attacked last night by a scavenger seeking food," Travis elaborated.

Rebecca followed his line of vision, her gaze falling on her father's hands. They were bandaged. She did not care what Travis thought, she knew her father would never have tried to kill her. Dismounting, she approached him. "You have injured your hands," she said solicitously.

"Scratched them on some thorns when I was clearing away a bit of underbrush," he explained. A self-conscious smile tilted one corner of his mouth. "Thought that if I was going to stay, I should put in a bit of a garden next year, some corn and such."

"You're welcome to whatever stores we have at Green Glen," Travis offered politely.

Hadrian bowed low. "I thank you for your generosity." Smiling at Rebecca, he added, " 'Tis a fine husband you've chosen for yourself."

She wondered how strongly he would praise Travis if he knew Travis suspected him of being a murderer. Forcing a returning smile, she requested to see the land he was clearing.

" 'Tis not much yet," he said, leading them to the side of the cabin. "I only began late yesterday."

Rebecca looked at the small area that had been cleared and knew it could have been done that morning. Glancing toward Travis, she saw by the look in his eyes that he'd had the same thought.

She and Travis lingered for only a few moments more, then said their good-byes. They left Daniel to help his father finish clearing the land and rode back toward Green Glen.

Rebecca waited until they were well out of earshot of the cabin, then said to Travis with firm confidence, "My father is not the man you seek. He would never have tried to harm me. Also, the man who attacked me wore heavy gloves. I could not have scratched his hands."

"I believe your faith may be sorely misplaced," he replied. "However, I admire your loyalty."

Rebecca's gaze narrowed in disbelief. "There is actually something you admire about me?" she inquired cynically.

His lips curled into a bitter smile. "There are a great many things a man could admire about you." Against his own intentions, he heard himself adding, " 'Tis my regret that you are not a bit more trustworthy."

Rebecca met his gaze levelly. She had lied to him only once and never to harm him. If he had cared for her, she would have stood by him to the death. "I am as trustworthy as any woman you will find."

He shrugged. "That may be so," he conceded.

As a renewed silence fell between them, Rebecca found herself wondering if he was thinking of his Ruth. She had asked him before they had wed if he had a love waiting for him at home, and he'd said he had none. Obviously, Susan had been right. His Ruth had married someone else. A surge of jealousy rushed through her. He would probably have forgiven his precious Ruth anything. "I am sorry you lost your Ruth," she said stiffly, unable to hide her knowledge of the other woman any longer.

Catching the reins of her horse, Travis brought them to an abrupt halt. "How did you know about Ruth? Only someone who was aware of my life on the earl's estate would know of her."

Rebecca heard the accusation in his voice and read the suspicion in his eyes. " 'Twas not my father who told me of her, if that is what you are thinking," she snapped.

Travis's gaze narrowed threateningly. "Then how did you know of her?"

"You called out to her when you were delirious," she replied frostily, furious that she had allowed jealousy to rule her tongue.

Releasing her reins, Travis's gaze shifted away from Rebecca, and a gentleness came into his eyes. "Ruth was a good and honest woman."

Rebecca's stomach knotted. She told herself to say no more, but instead she heard herself saying snidely, " 'Tis a shame she is not the one riding with you this day. But I suppose she was too fragile a flower to accompany you on your quest."

The scowl on Travis's face deepened. "Ruth died before I left England."

The knot in Rebecca's stomach tightened, but this time there was sympathy mingled with the jealousy. "I am sorry," she said honestly, hating herself for having persisted until she had brought back memories that were clearly painful to him.

"She lived a long life," he replied philosophically, urging his horse into motion.

Rebecca frowned in confusion at his departing back. Giving her horse a nudge, she caught up with him. "What do you mean, she lived a long life? You were no more than eighteen or nineteen when you came here."

This time it was Travis's turn to look confused. "What has my age to do with this?"

Rebecca flushed and wished she had held her curiosity in check. But it was too late now. Travis expected an answer. "I simply did not picture you engaged to an older woman," she replied, barely above a mutter.

Travis frowned impatiently. "I was not engaged to Ruth. She was an elderly servant on my father's estate. After my mother's death she took me under her wing and provided me with the only real kindness I had." Long-suppressed resentment he thought he had put behind him burned in his eyes. "The others I learned not to trust. They all had their devious reasons for befriending me. When those reasons were met, they turned against me." His gaze narrowed accusingly upon Rebecca as he added pointedly, " 'Twas only Ruth who never betrayed my trust."

Rebecca studied his cold, proud profile. There was no hint that forgiveness played any part in his character. "There are very few paragons in this world. I suppose I should be honored to know you and of your Ruth," she said with biting sarcasm. "You must consider the rest of us poor wretched souls who make mistakes once in a while to be less than dirt under your feet. And you must be extremely pleased with yourself for your self-righteous perfection."

Suddenly very weary of his company, she kicked her horse into a trot.

What I feel is very alone, Travis said to himself.

"I've chores to see to around the plantation," Travis informed Rebecca as they ate their noonday meal. He had dismissed the servants, and they were serving themselves. "You will remain within the house."

Rebecca was tempted to argue with him. But she recalled the darkening bruises on her throat and recognized her irritation as childish pride. "If that is what you wish."

Travis paused to stare at her. "I cannot believe this. You have actually agreed without an argument."

He sounded so disconcerted, Rebecca couldn't help smiling. It pleased her to have caught him off-guard. "I've often heard it said that 'tis a wife's duty to obey her husband," she replied with exaggerated deference.

Travis regarded her with suspicion. He had been prepared to use his most authoritative manner, perhaps even a threat or two. But she was acquiescing without a single protest. "I want your word that you will remain here and behave yourself."

His suspicion of her every move cut deeply. "Pray tell me, sir," she demanded dryly, "what good will the word of a liar be?"

For a long moment his gaze rested on her. She was a most frustrating woman. "You have a point," he conceded coldly and returned to eating his food.

Rebecca glared at him. What had she hoped? Had she thought that perhaps he would show some indication that he was willing to give her a chance to prove she could be trusted? Idiot! she chided herself. "Perhaps 'tis you who should be giving the Sunday sermons," she spit out. "You, who are above reproach."

Travis set aside his utensils. "I do not claim to be a paragon, Rebecca. I am simply a foolish man who once let himself believe he could trust you. I'll not make that mistake again." He rose, shoving his chair back, and strode from the room.

She bit back a scream of frustration. "I must discover the identity of this man he seeks and rid myself of Travis Brandt!" she seethed under her breath.

But she had said she would remain in the house, and she would show him that she could be trusted. However, it was not easy to remain so confined. She paced through the rooms trying to think of some ploy that would expose the murderer.

Mr. Wetherly could no longer remain at the top of her list. He was with Bacon and would not even know of her inquiries into the brooch. Again she was forced to reconsider all of the others.

She was about ready to actually let out a true scream of frustration when Philip announced the arrival of Mr. Loyde.

"I heard of your terrifying experience and came quickly to assure myself that you were unharmed," he said with much gallantry as she joined him in the sitting room.

"You are too kind," she replied, her gaze going to his hands as he removed his riding gloves. There were no signs of her struggle. Her practical side knew it was futile to hope she could have inflicted a tell-tale injury upon her attacker. Still, she could not stop herself from making the inspection. "I've instructed Philip to bring tea. You will stay and visit for a while, will you not?" Hoping she looked and sounded like a muddleheaded female, she added, "I could so use the company. I'm still feeling rather shaken."

He smiled with patronizing reassurance. "I'm sure you're quite safe. I noticed that Travis has posted a guard."

"Yes." Rebecca's hand went to her throat. "But I still find myself looking over my shoulder at every little sound."

" 'Tis merely a bit of nerves," Mr. Loyde sympathized, his manner indicating that he understood the weaker mind of a female could be easily unsettled. "But if it pleases you, of course I shall remain for some tea."

Rebecca smiled gratefully. "You are most kind."

Philip arrived with a tray laden with tea, cakes, bread, and jam. Rebecca poured, allowing her hand to shake slightly, encouraging Mr. Loyde's assessment that her nerves were quite fragile.

"Were you able to ascertain any information about your attacker?" he asked politely as he accepted his cup.

Rebecca caused herself to tremble. "I was unable to gain anything. I was struggling for my life and totally terrified. My mind was a near blank except for panic." What galled her was that this was true. She had always thought of herself as a person who was much more in control. But her chance to expose the true murderer had come, and she had failed miserably.

Reaching across the tea tray, Mr. Loyde patted her hand in a fatherly fashion. "Now, now, 'tis understandable."

Rebecca breathed a heavy sigh. "I don't wish to dwell upon it. What I wish is to forget." She smiled her sweetest smile. "Let us speak on something totally different." She closed her eyes for a moment, as if in thought, then opening them said brightly, "Let us speak of England. I was born there. I remember London when we were preparing to sail. It was so full of people." She crinkled her nose. "But I have to admit I do not remember the smell with any great favor."

Mr. Loyde laughed. "Nor do I," he admitted.

"Tell me about your life in England," she encouraged. "I do so wish to take my mind away from Virginia and all of our troubles."

Mr. Loyde took a bite of buttered bread. Leaning back in his chair, he chewed and swallowed it. "My memories are not the fondest," he admitted at last. "My father was a merchant. We would have lived well enough if my mother had not been prolific. There were ten of us in all by the time she finished laying. Almost as soon as we could toddle, my father began apprenticing us boys out. I was sent to a cobbler. 'Twas not a bad position. The man was a fine craftsman, and members of the court would come to him for their footwear."

Rebecca forced a childishly enthusiastic smile. "That must have been quite exciting."

Mr. Loyde took another bite of bread. "Not truly," he confessed. "I was kept in the back of the shop the major portion of the time."

Rebecca regarded him with interest. He'd had contact with the court, even if it had been in a slight way. It was possible he knew what ladies traveled with what jewels. "But if you were raised in the city, how did you gain your knowledge of farming?"

"I developed a congestion of the lungs." He smiled mischievously. "My master was forced to send me into the country to a small village where his younger son had set up shop. 'Twas there I discovered I preferred the open sky over my head. From the locals I picked up a bit of knowledge of farming. It pleased me more than working in a shop. One day I read a pamphlet about the colonies. 'Twas a place where a man could own his own land, it said. I decided then and there that was for me. I had a small bit of money my father had given me when he sent me away. I saved and did odd jobs on the side until I had enough for passage. You know the rest. Luck was with me. I met and married my fair Amanda and found a place for myself here that pleases me greatly."

Rebecca did know the rest. Amanda had been the daughter of a wealthy landholder. Her father had hoped for a marriage of more substance, but Amanda had fallen head over heels in love with Mr. Loyde. Her father had tried to discourage the match but had failed. He had insisted upon a long engagement to satisfy himself of Mr. Loyde's loyalty to his daughter. But that winter he had caught a chill and died, leaving her alone and heir to his estate. Within a month she and Mr. Loyde had married.

"What was the name of the village you were sent to?" she asked. Stories could be checked, and if he was lying, that could label him the murderer. Of course, it would take months, perhaps even a year to find out.

Mr. Loyde shrugged. " 'Twas a small place of no consequence." He smiled warmly. "Now you must tell me of your life in England."

There was no polite way to persist in her inquiry. Another time, she promised herself. "There is little to tell." The truth was there was little she could tell without divulging her heritage.

"I believe Mr. Mercer once mentioned that your father had been an itinerant trader but had tired of living an unsettled life and came here as I did because he wished to own his own land."

" 'Tis true," she replied. 'Twas a good thing Travis was not present, she thought. She could visualize the look in his eyes as if her glib lying only confirmed his opinion of her.

Mr. Loyde again smiled warmly. " 'Tis a miracle he has come back to you and Daniel."

"Yes, 'tis," she agreed. But she did not want to talk about her father or his miraculous reappearance. She wanted to know about Mr. Loyde. She was about to make another attempt to discover the name of the village in which he had resided when a knock sounded on the door and Philip announced the arrival of the Garnets. She would have to continue her questioning of Mr. Loyde another day.

"I'm so pleased to see you well," Mistress Garnet gushed as she entered. She gave Rebecca a hug.

Rebecca was stunned by the woman's unexpected show of warmth. But as Mistress Garnet released her, Rebecca saw the woman's gaze fixed on the scarf she had wound loosely around her neck to hide her bruising. She realized that Mistress Garnet's attention had been nothing more than an act to get a closer look at the injury.

"I had heard you were injured most nastily," Mistress Garnet said, confirming Rebecca's assessment.

" 'Tis only a bit of bruising," Rebecca assured her.

Jason bowed deeply. "We are so pleased to hear that. I am afraid we are living in the most dreadful of times."

"Yes," Rebecca agreed, trying not to be too obvious as

she watched him remove his gloves. His hands, too, showed no signs of a struggle. 'Twas to be expected, she reminded herself. Still, she could not halt the wave of frustration that washed over her.

"I've just had news from Gloucester," Mr. Garnet was saying in a worried tone. "I suppose I thought Sir William deserved it when Bacon took over the governor's estate at Green Spring. Fortunes of war and all that. But now it seems Bacon turned his men loose to plunder the homes of anyone thought to be a Berkeley supporter. But some didn't stop there. They began taking whatever they wanted from whomever they wanted."

Mr. Loyde looked appalled. " 'Tis a disgrace." Indignation etched itself into his features. "They'll be in for a fight should they attempt to confiscate any of my property."

"Mr. Bacon has ordered his men to cease such activities," Mr. Garnet assured him. "His position depends upon his popularity, and it was gravely threatened. Still, I'm afraid many a man may have lost more than his pocketbook could stand."

Listening to the exchange, Rebecca was struck by the irony of it all. Both men were equally indignant toward the behavior of Bacon's men, and yet one of her guests could very easily be a thief and murderer himself. And discussing Mr. Bacon wasn't going to help her discover the truth. "We were speaking of England," Rebecca interjected, adding with a wistful smile, "I do so want to take my mind away from the trouble surrounding us, if only for a brief while." Turning her attention toward Mistress Garnet, she said, "I believe I once heard mention that you lived in the northern reaches."

"Yes, quite so." Mistress Garnet smiled reminiscently. "My husband's family was quite well off." The smile turned to a frown. "But he was the youngest son of five. Even though it was he who knew the most about working the land, it would be his eldest brother, Eldon, who would inherit." Her face wrinkled into an expression of disgust.

"And Eldon Garnet was a spendthrift and a drunk. When he was finished, there would be nothing left." Her shoulders straightened with pride. "Mr. Garnet determined that there was no future for us in England nor for our son. When his father died, he used the few hundred pounds that had been left to him to bring us to the New World and build a life for us here. Mr. Garnet did not expect, however, to have to fight Indians nor to be killed by one of the savages. We were told they were mostly friendly and that those who were not were controlled by the militia." She shook her head. "In truth, Virginia was not at all as described in the brochures used to lure us here." A look of triumph shown in her eyes. "But we have survived, Jason and I."

A sudden thought struck Rebecca. It could have been Samuel Garnet who had killed Travis's mother. Now Jason and Mistress Garnet were trying to hide the source of their wealth. That seemed more probable to her than picturing Jason as the highwayman. Still, someone had tried to kill her, and with Samuel Garnet dead, that left Jason to perform the dirty deed. Again she recalled Travis mentioning that Jason had involved himself with smugglers.

Rebecca smiled sympathetically. She'd heard this story before. What she wanted to know was exactly where the Garnets had resided in the north. But as she started to frame the question, a familiar male voice interrupted.

"Well, 'tis pleasant to see my wife being so well entertained."

Rebecca glanced toward the door to see Travis striding into the room.

"We were gravely worried about her," Mr. Loyde spoke up, rising to greet Travis.

Rebecca noticed Travis's gaze quickly scan the men's hands to discover as she had that they showed no signs of a struggle. She smiled up at her husband with a smile that did not reach her eyes. "We were reminiscing about England in an effort to take my mind off the unpleasantries happening in Virginia at the moment." She turned her attention toward the widow Garnet. "I was just going to ask Mistress Garnet if the north of England was as beautiful as it is said to be."

"Yes, 'tis nice," the woman replied.

"I do appreciate all of you coming to visit," Travis cut in before Rebecca could pursue her line of questioning. "But my wife had a harrowing experience, and I think she should rest quietly the remainder of the day."

"Quite right," Mr. Loyde agreed, standing quickly to take his leave.

Mistress Garnet and Jason also rose, and within moments only Rebecca remained in the drawing room while Travis saw their guests out to their waiting horses. Standing by the window, she noticed Mr. Loyde remaining behind as the Garnets left. It would seem he wanted a few moments alone with Travis, she mused. Gently she opened the window a crack.

"I must say," Mr. Loyde was saying, "that I was quite taken aback when Rebecca chose you. I was hoping it might be me. But as it has turned out, I am pleased with her choice. I prefer a quieter, more stable life." He shook his head in a consoling manner. "And your wife does seem to have a propensity for searching out trouble."

"So it would seem," Travis agreed, his tone suggesting that she was wearing on his nerves.

Rebecca had to force herself to close the window quietly instead of slamming it down. She was seated, munching on a seed cake and sipping lukewarm tea, when Travis returned.

"And just what did you think you were doing?" he demanded, kicking the door closed, then coming to stand glaring down at her.

Refusing to be intimidated, she swallowed the bite of seed cake, took a sip of tea, then met his angry gaze. "I was attempting to discover if one of the two men in this room was my attacker. I assume we can exclude Mr. Wetherly from the suspects since he is in Gloucester or Green Spring or wherever Mr. Bacon has placed him."

"You are supposed to be trying to convince people that you believe your attacker to be a passing scavenger. You are not supposed to be putting your attacker on guard by asking a lot of questions about his past," Travis fumed. He had been pacing around the room. Now he came to a halt in the middle and stood frowning at her. Her near death last night had obviously frightened him much worse than it had frightened her. "If it weren't for this damn war between Bacon and the governor, I'd pack you off to England."

Rebecca practically jumped to her feet. "You, sir, would do no such thing."

"You forget yourself, madam. You are my wife. 'Tis my right to command and your duty to obey. If you do not give up this private pursuit and leave me to my own devices to discover the murderer, I shall most certainly pack you up, take you north, and send you to England on a ship from Maryland." The smile on his face became an impatient scowl. "Your safety is in my hands, and I will not allow you to continue on this dangerous path."

She did not doubt that he meant it. "What of Daniel?" she demanded.

"He will accompany you," he replied.

A sudden fear spread through Rebecca. "And then you will be free to act against my father."

"I will act against no man until I am certain he is the man I seek."

"On that point, sir, I trust you as little as you trust me. I'll not leave my father to face your self-righteous judgment on his own."

"Then I trust you will guard your tongue," he cautioned.

She drew a terse breath. "As you wish." Suddenly afraid she might say something she would regret if she should linger a moment longer, she strode out of the room.

Under his breath Travis cursed himself for having attached himself to a woman who was not only untrustworthy but as stubborn as an ass. Didn't she understand he was trying to keep her from harm?

Rebecca was halfway up the stairs when she came to a halt. Grudgingly, she forced herself to admit that she had spoken unfairly. Although she was certain Travis Brandt thought her father was the man he sought, he had proved himself to be an honorable man. In truth, he had not firmly labeled her father a murderer. And he was trying to protect her. It was her own impatience that had nearly gotten her killed. The self-directed frown on her face deepened. And that he did not think highly of her was her own fault. She could not let him think she was a complete jackass.

She returned to the sitting room and found him standing, looking out the window. His shoulders were slumped as if he were tired. Tired of putting up with me, she realized and wanted to kick herself for behaving so stubbornly. "I wish to apologize."

Travis whirled around to face her. There was suspicion in his eyes. "You what?"

"I behaved badly. You are right. I was putting myself in jeopardy when I had promised I would not. And I know you will not act against my father without proof." Having said her piece, she turned abruptly to leave.

As many times as he had told himself he wanted her out of his life, Travis knew it was a lie. Damn, how he missed holding her, laughing with her, talking to her as a friend. Reaching her before she could open the door, his hand closed around her arm, halting her retreat. "I wish . . ." he began grimly, then stopped himself. What could he say to her? He could tell her that if she were to promise never to lie to him again, he would accept her word because he wanted to believe in her. But there was her loyalty to consider. It did not belong to him but to her father. And what if Hadrian Riley was the man he sought? What then? She would hate him for what he must do. 'Tis better to leave it as it is, he ordered himself.

Rebecca waited, her breath locked in her lungs. He was studying her with an intensity that set her heart pounding. Would he give her a chance to redeem herself?

Releasing her, Travis took a step back. "For your sake and for Daniel's I hope you are right about your father," he said, then, turning away, strode back to the window and stood gazing out.

For a long moment Rebecca stared at his tall rigid form. For a brief instant she had thought there might be hope for them. But it was clear he wanted no part of her. And I want no part of him, she told herself. But the lie was thin, and deep within she felt a twisting pain of regret.

SIXTEEN

THE nights were the hardest, Rebecca decided. Lying in the same bed with Travis yet not touching. She told herself she wanted nothing to do with him. But memories of the early days of their marriage would arise to haunt her, and at those times she would wake wanting him so badly, her body ached. But pride refused to allow her to turn to him.

Tonight was one of those nights. She rose from the bed and walked to the window to gaze out at the shadowy landscape. He was stubborn, arrogant, self-righteous, she argued. She was a fool to feel any softening toward him. But as she gazed out at the night, she remembered the sound of his laughter and the mischievous gleam he would get in his eyes when he was teasing her. Her hands seemed to rise of their own accord and cup themselves in front of her as if she were accepting a gift. In her mind's eye she could almost see the small bouquet of wildflowers he had brought her. A tear trickled down her cheek, and she pulled her shawl more closely around her shoulders against the chill of the night.

Travis had woken when she left the bed. He lay gazing at her as she stood barefoot by the window. In the moon's eerie light she looked the image of a wild gypsy . . . barefoot, a long shawl wrapped around her shoulders, her thick black hair hanging in disarray around her shoulders and down her back. His wild gypsy woman. No, not "his," not in her heart. But she was his wife, and she was a passionate woman. She had warned him to keep his distance, and he had promised to do nothing against her will. But watching her, he wondered if she missed a man's touch. It is best to leave her alone, he cautioned himself. But he was not in a reasoning mood. He rose from the bed and crossed the room to stand behind her.

Rebecca was acutely aware of his presence. His breath played on her hair. In her mind's eye she could see him. He would be wearing nothing. He did not like to sleep clothed.

"You will catch a chill," he said softly as he lightly ran his hands along the lines of her arms to where her hands clutched the shawl closed in front of her.

She ordered herself to step away from him. He only wished to use her to satisfy his lust. But her legs refused to obey. "You are the one who is most likely to catch the chill," she heard herself saying and wondered how she could sound coherent when she was shaking so badly inside.

Travis's heart pounded more strongly. She had not pulled away from him. Releasing her hands, he circled one arm around her. With his free hand, he lifted her hair from her neck and, leaning down, kissed her warm, sweet-smelling skin.

Rebecca stiffened. Her gaze fell on the sturdy arm that held her pinned loosely against him. Along the length of her, the heat of his body penetrated the cloth barrier between them, tantalizing her with its warmth. Against her will, memories of his caresses ignited a fire within her. Have you no pride? she chided herself.

Travis felt her stiffen. He had promised himself he would not force her to accept him. But to his satisfaction, she did not draw away. Caressingly, he trailed his hand over her shoulder and downward. Gently he cupped her breast, and even with the shawl and her nightgown between them he felt the nipple harden. "We cannot deny our humanity," he said lowly in her ear. "We are a man and a woman. 'Tis natural to have needs."

His warm breath upon her skin was creating havoc with her senses. He drew her closer. She felt his strength as well as his warmth, and excitement surged through her.

Deserting her breast, Travis's hand moved lower over her belly, and he pulled her more tightly against him. How he had missed the feel of her! It was as if without her he had somehow been incomplete.

Rebecca's heart was pounding wildly. Her nightgown and the shawl became irritating barriers as her body hungered for his. Wanton wench! she screamed at herself. But it did not matter. She released her hold on the shawl.

A smile played at the corners of Travis's mouth. She had missed male companionship. He stepped back slightly to let the shawl fall to the floor. Then slowly, very slowly, he let his hands travel the length of her. His body moved with them and through the fabric of her nightgown he trailed kisses down her back and over her buttocks. She had the most wonderfully firm feel to her.

Rebecca's teeth closed over her lower lip to keep herself from screaming at the ecstasy his mouth and touch brought. At any second she was certain her body would burst into flame.

Finding the hem of her nightgown, Travis raised it. Bending low, he nipped her ankle, then kissed it. The taste of her skin was like a fine brandy. His mind grew intoxicated with desire. Like a thirsty man, he could not resist continuing the sampling. His mouth moved up her calf to her thigh.

Rebecca's breath was coming in small gasps. Every fiber of her being was focused on his touch. Her body trembled as his mouth moved higher. "Travis, please," she moaned, aching for him to claim her fully.

"Please what?" he demanded gruffly. He was kneeling in front of her now. His hands massaged her firm rounded bottom while his tongue teased her thighs. "Please stop? Do not try one of your lies with me now," he growled. "I can too easily prove it to be false." His hand moved between her legs to the very core of her womanhood. "Your body begs for mine," he said with triumph.

Her hands reached for the hem of her nightgown, and she drew it up over her head and tossed it to the ground. "I was not asking you to stop," she said huskily. She could not have fought him now if she had wanted to. Her body was too much in his control. But pride demanded that she not allow him to think for one moment that there was anything beyond her willingness to submit to him than pure lust. "We are husband and wife. It would be foolish for us not to seek what small pleasures we can from this unfortunate union."

He knew it was not fair, but her words irked him, and for a moment his pride tempted him to leave her. But it was only for a moment. Her body was much too inviting. He could not turn away now. " 'Twould be foolish," he agreed gruffly.

He continued slowly upward, tasting her as he went, until he renewed his acquaintance with each inch of her. It had been too long. He was having a difficult time controlling himself, but he did not want to rush.

Rebecca stood unable to move. His touch was sweet insanity. Her stomach muscles tightened, and her back arched toward him as he rose and his male readiness brushed against her. Very lightly she let her hand move from his shoulders down his chest to his hard flat abdomen. She smiled a womanly smile as her touch became more intimate, and she heard him suck in a gasping breath. For this moment, at least, Mr. Travis Brandt was in her power. But she was also in his.

Travis shuddered with pleasure. His mouth found hers and was welcomed.

Her mind in a fog of passion, Rebecca lost herself in the wild sensations stirring within her. Her tongue teased him, gliding in and out of his mouth. She wanted to be one with him so badly it hurt.

Travis could wait no longer. He wanted her now . . .

here. "Accept me, Rebecca." He lifted her, turning so that her back was against the wall.

Her legs parted. She felt him enter, and her arms wound around his neck for support as her legs wrapped around his hips. She had never felt so alive. Her whole body was aware of his possession and reveled in it.

For a long moment Travis stood merely enjoying the feel of her. No woman had the right to make a man feel such a need to be a part of her.

Her legs tightening, Rebecca began to move slowly, her body caressing his. Currents of excitement and pleasure surged through her.

Travis's hands sank deep into her buttocks as he helped her move. It felt so necessary, this union of their bodies. He wished he had more control. It had been dangerous to give in to this lust. But it was too late now. His mind forgot everything but the feel of her and the urgent primitive needs that drove them.

Fire raced through Rebecca's body. His thrust was deep, and she reveled in the force of him. Her mouth moved over his neck, to his shoulder, and she moaned against him as the pleasure he brought her grew too intense to contain. Her movements became more frantic.

"Look at me," he demanded, suddenly determined that she not forget who held her. He wanted no other man's image to fill her mind.

Rebecca lifted her head and opened her eyes.

They seemed almost ebony in the moonlight and Travis smiled at the desire he read in them. He had done this for her. No other man. "Say my name, Rebecca," he ordered, driving deep and strong.

"Travis," she breathed, gasping as her body trembled and then exploded in the blaze of fulfilled passion.

From deep down inside, Travis growled with satisfaction as he joined her in the mindless moment of supreme pleasure.

Rebecca clung to him, her breathing coming in pants as her body began to quiet.

They were both still now. Her long dark hair cascaded over Travis's face and shoulders. She smelled sweet and tasted salty. He felt himself leaving her, but he did not want to let her go. She has the kind of body that could own a man's soul, he thought. His jaw tensed. But she would not own his. He carried her to the bed and set her upon it, then walked around to his side, climbed in, and lay apart from her.

Rebecca lay clutching the covers up around her chin. They gave her warmth, but they did nothing to ease the aloneness that had come back more strongly than ever. She turned her head toward Travis. He was lying with his back toward her. In that moment she hated him for being able to remain so aloof. But she knew she would not deny him when he again wanted the physical pleasure her company could bring him.

As October drew to a close, news of Bacon's death reached them. He had died of dysentery, and the stories of the lice that had infested his body were legend.

"The rebellion will not last," Colonel Howard predicted with certainty. "Ingles cannot hold the men together. He does not have have their hearts as Bacon did. Besides, with no navy they cannot win, and the king's soldiers will be arriving shortly."

Rebecca knew he was right, and she prayed for Gyles Woods's safety. When news came that the governor had hanged Colonel Hansford, her fear grew. He had allowed the men who had served under Hansford to take a pledge to the crown and then sent them home. But rumors were that Sir William was in a rage that was close to being totally out of control. He could, at any moment, begin to demand that all prisoners taken be tried for treason and hanged.

With November the chill of winter had come to stay. But the cold outside was like a July day compared to the iciness of the atmosphere at their breakfast table, Travis mused, as he and Rebecca sat alone one brisk morning. He had been trying not to think of her constantly and of what they could have shared. But she was always on his mind. Each night he promised himself he would not touch her again. But the temptation was too great. He knew he pleased her. He was also quite certain that when he was gone, she would find a lover who would please her just as well. She was much too passionate a woman to live out her life alone. The thought caused him sharp discomfort, and he frowned. What she did once he was gone was none of his business, he told himself. "You have been in a very pensive mood these past few days," he said, breaking the heavy silence that so often hung between them lately.

She was tempted to reply cuttingly that she was surprised he had noticed her mood. It seemed to her that he had been trying to avoid noticing anything about her except for her body, which he had claimed quite often these past nights. But she bit back her words. She would not let him know that his indifference to her as a person stung. Instead, she said honestly, "I am worried about Mr. Woods."

The discomfort came again. Jealousy? Travis scowled at himself. He was determined to feel nothing for her. Her heart did not belong to him, and his would not belong to her. "Gyles knows how to take care of himself, and I instructed him most strictly that he was not to allow his observations of Mr. Wetherly to interfere with his own safety."

His voice was firm, but Rebecca saw the shadow of concern for his friend in his eyes. At least he is capable of caring for someone. He had begun even to show a restraint toward Daniel. She had meant to say nothing, but Daniel was quite upset. "Daniel spoke with me yesterday," she said stiffly. "He wanted to know what he had done to offend you."

Travis drew a tired breath. He was trying to do what he

considered best for all of them. "I have not meant to make him think he has offended me."

Rebecca glared at the man's obtuseness. "How could he not? You have avoided him for days now."

Setting aside his spoon, Travis met her gaze levelly.

"Daniel has grown very close to his father. If Hadrian should be the man I seek, Daniel, too, will hate me for what I must do. I thought it would be false of me to encourage his friendship when I may be forced to cause him great grief."

"'Tis only yourself you will bring grief upon," she assured him. Unable to bear his company any longer, she rose and left the room.

"I have already brought much grief to myself," he muttered as the door closed behind her and he was alone. He had for a brief time thought he had found a family. Now he was once again alone. Lines of concern wrinkled his brow. And he was worried about Gyles.

Rebecca strode into the drawing room. But she was too tense to sit and sew. She felt trapped. There had to be a way to end this. She stood staring out the window, only half conscious of the world beyond. Suddenly her attention was caught by a movement at the edge of the woods. A moment later a man stumbled out. His coat was torn, and one leg was crudely bandaged forcing him to use a heavy branch as a cane. "Gyles," she gasped. She nearly collided with Travis in the hall as she dashed wildly toward the front door.

"What the devil!" he demanded, following behind her

Ignoring him, she raced out of the house. "Gyles . . . Mr. Woods! We've been so worried about you," she said, reaching the limping man. Immediately she saw the blood staining his coat near his left shoulder and the ugly bruise darkening the right side of his face.

Still, he smiled a foxlike smile. "They left me for dead. Should'a known they couldn't kill Gyles Woods that easily."

"Good heavens, man, what happened to you?" Travis

demanded, reaching them and quickly placing an arm around the injured man to lend support.

"Wetherly and his cutthroat friends," Gyles explained as Travis helped him toward the house. "I came to warn you."

"Help Mr. Brandt get this man upstairs to one of the guest rooms," Rebecca ordered as Joseph came running to lend a hand. Seeing Philip at the door, she yelled to him to have Mildred boil some water and prepare bandages.

"You'd better be seeing to posting a guard," Gyles said, his voice weak from exhaustion and pain. "No telling how soon Wetherly'll be here. They's five others with him. They deserted the army and are heading toward Maryland. But they's raiding and stealing all the way."

"Post the guard and send out someone to warn our neighbors," Travis ordered Joseph. "Rebecca and I can get Gyles upstairs."

"Daniel!" Fear for her brother and her father raced through Rebecca. "He is with my father. Send someone to fetch them here quickly," she added to Joseph's orders from Travis.

Joseph quickly relinquished his position beside Gyles to Rebecca and set out to sound the alarm.

"I woke up a few days ago to find Wetherly gone and that bunch of hooligans with him," Gyles was saying as they helped him up the stairs. "I'd been thinking about leaving myself. I'd stayed because I'd given Mr. Bacon my oath, and I'm a man what stands by my word. But with Mr. Bacon dead, my oath was served and I've no quarrel with the king. Anyways, I followed. Their path was easy. They've been plundering their way across Virginia. Guess they figured they'd pick themselves up a bit of booty and go start new lives somewhere else. Anyways, when I realized they was heading in this direction instead of straight north, I knew they'd come here. Wetherly never hid his hate of you, Travis." He glanced toward Rebecca. "He don't like you much, either."

Again Travis found himself feeling a sharp pang of

jealousy as they laid Gyles on the bed and he read the
anxiousness on Rebecca's face. He remembered regaining
consciousness in Bacon's camp. For a brief moment he'd
seen a similar look in her eyes. But he doubted she would
ever look at him like that again. *She would probably be
relieved to see me so near death. Then she would be free,
and she wouldn't have to worry about her father's safety any
longer.*

"We must get him undressed and his wounds cleaned,"
she was saying, beginning to remove Gyles's coat.

The thought of her touching another man brought the bile
to Travis's throat. *Damn, he cursed this weakness he still
felt for her.* "I'll undress him," he said stiffly.

Rebecca paused to stare at him. *He actually seemed
jealous. Don't be ridiculous,* she scolded herself. *He cannot
wait to be free of you.* "Then I shall fetch the medicines."
Relinquishing her job, she hurried from the room.

When she returned a few moments later, it was to find
Gyles naked from the waist up. Dark bruises covered his
chest, and there was a knife wound that went deep in his left
shoulder.

Susan came in carrying the hot water, and Rebecca set to
work. The wound was not fresh, but he had treated it with
one of his poultices, and it looked as if it was healing
without an infection. Still, it was tender to the touch. "How
long ago were you injured?" she questioned, hoping to take
his mind off the pain she must be causing him.

"Two days ago." His words came out choppily, and she
saw his pupils dilate with pain. "I came up on them whilst
they were robbing a place a ways down the river. Tried to
help stop them, but they got me instead." He smiled. "But
they shouldn't have left me for dead. Should've known I
wasn't that easy to kill."

Rebecca was tempted to say she didn't know how he had
survived. It was clear his bruises were from being kicked. It
was a miracle he wasn't showing any signs of internal
injuries. Satisfied there was no infection building in the

wound, she applied some salve, then bandaged it. Finished with that task, she washed his torso. There was a definite tenderness over his rib cage. "You've a couple of broken ribs 'tis my guess," she said.

"Most likely you're right," he conceded.

Rebecca motioned for Travis to help. "It's best if we bind you."

Gyles nodded and gritted his teeth as they worked.

When they were finished, she sent for clean water.

It took every ounce of control Travis had not to show the envy he felt as Rebecca ministered to Gyles. 'Tis a very destructive attitude to have, he warned himself. Had he not promised both her and himself that he would leave her on her own to do as she pleased when his quest was finished?

Gyles's hands went to capture the tops of his pants as Rebecca turned her attention back to the bed. "I'll be taking care of my private parts myself, mistress," he said.

"You have to be stripped and the wound in your leg seen to," she replied impatiently.

"I'll take care of preparing him," Travis interrupted any further debate. When he was gone she could minister to other men, but he was not ready to stand by and watch. "Fetch one of my nightshirts for him."

Rebecca had the urge to point out that she had seen a man's body before and insist that she continue. But she saw the flush of embarrassment on Gyles's face made even more distinct by the paleness of his complexion and took pity on him. "As you wish," she conceded and went in search of the nightshirt.

She returned with it at the same time Susan returned with the fresh water. "You two will leave us," Travis instructed. To Rebecca he added, "I will call for you when 'tis time for you to see to the wound on his leg."

Rebecca waited out in the hall. Travis's dislike for her to see another man would have been enjoyable—even amusing—if he had cared for her. But he didn't. She told herself that it would not disturb her one small bit if he should need to minister to another woman. But even before the thought was out, her stomach knotted so painfully she was forced to call herself a liar.

She paced the floor until Travis opened the door and again admitted her. There was an anxiousness in his eyes that caused her to move swiftly toward the bed.

"Guess that poultice didn't do much good with the ball still in my leg," Gyles said as she came to a halt and looked down at the festering wound.

"He always did have the stamina of a mule," Travis muttered.

"Maybe you'd better give him a bit of brandy," Rebecca suggested. "This is going to hurt."

Travis nodded and Rebecca prepared her medicines. Half an hour later she had drained the infection, removed the ball, and cauterized the wound. To her relief, Gyles had fainted soon after her first incision. Now, as she finished wrapping the wound, he seemed to be sleeping peacefully. "Someone should stay with him," she said as she covered him and felt his forehead. At the moment he had only a mild fever. With any luck she had gotten out all of the infection and the fever would go away.

"I'll stay with him, ma'am," Susan spoke up. Then, flushing, she curtsied in a show of respect. "He's a right brave man to travel as he was to warn us," she added demurely.

Rebecca regarded her maid speculatively. She had noticed the anxiousness on Susan's face as the girl watched while Gyles's wounds were being doctored. She also recalled that Susan had shown a more than passing interest in the man when he had first come to Green Glen. At the time Rebecca had thought it merely Susan's unquenchable curiosity. But now she noticed that her maid seemed unable to take her gaze from the man lying on the bed. Recalling how Travis had, at first, fascinated her, Rebecca wondered if she should caution Susan and warn the maid to guard her heart more closely. Perhaps, but with Travis standing nearby, this was not the time. "That will be fine," she conceded and left the room.

"I'll check on the guard," Travis said as he accompanied her down the stairs. But even as his last syllable was being uttered they heard the sound of firearms.

"Get a pistol and sword from the study and go to Gyles's room and lock yourself and Susan inside," Travis ordered her.

"But what of Daniel and my father?" she questioned worriedly.

"Don't you worry none about us," Hadrian said as he and Daniel came out of the drawing room. "Daniel, you go with your sister and protect her," he ordered, shoving the boy toward the stairs. "I'll stand by Travis."

She had no time to react to the irony of his words as Daniel raced past her and Travis and her father moved toward the study to arm themselves.

Quickly following Daniel, she found the pistol and sword and ran to the room Gyles was occupying. The door was locked. "Open up, Susan," she demanded, pounding on the wooden barrier.

The sound of a key was heard, and the door swung open. Inside, she found Susan holding Gyles's hunting knife.

"After what he's been through, I weren't going to let him die easily," the maid said fiercely.

This was not the Susan that Rebecca knew. This was a woman fighting for a man. Travis's image loomed large in Rebecca's mind, and she rushed to the window. Below she saw him dueling with Wetherly. Her father was struggling in hand-to-hand combat with one of Wetherly's men. A wounded Joseph was coming to his aid.

Her gaze turned back to Travis. She knew Wetherly to be an excellent swordsman. Clutching the pistol, she raced for the door. She could not remain up here. Travis might not want her beside him, but at this moment that was where she intended to be. "Lock the door after me," she ordered

Susan. To Daniel, she added, "You stay and protect Susan and Gyles."

"I was told to protect you," he argued, following on her heels.

"Do not argue with me!" she snapped, and he froze in his path.

In the next instant she was running down the stairs. She reached the porch as her father and Joseph subdued their man. Paying them no heed, her attention rested on Travis. She could not bear the thought of him dead or even injured.

Wetherly smiled with confidence. He knew he was the better swordsman. He lunged at Travis, forcing Travis off-balance. In the next instant he had disarmed him. "You cheated me out of what was my rightful due, Brandt," he growled. "Now 'tis time for you to pay."

Please don't move, Travis, Rebecca prayed silently as she took aim and fired. But her fear of hitting him caused her shot to go wide. The ball whizzed past Wetherly's head.

Travis had never been one to miss an opportunity. Wetherly was distracted for only a moment, but it was a moment too long. Travis's fist caught him in the jaw and sent him sprawling. Before Wetherly could regain his senses, Travis's foot was on the wrist of Wetherly's sword arm, pinning it to the ground.

Rebecca retrieved Travis's sword and handed it to him.

"You have turned out to be a true scoundrel," Travis muttered, holding the point of the sword against Wetherly's throat.

Quickly Rebecca relieved Wetherly of his sword. Then grimly she surveyed the front lawn. Two of their men sat nursing wounds. Four of Wetherly's men lay sprawled upon the ground. Hopefully dead, she thought vengefully, recalling what they had done to Gyles.

Her gaze returned to Travis. He was staring at the ground as if he had seen a ghost. Then a hatred like none she had ever seen before etched itself into his features.

Her gaze followed his, and she saw it . . . a cameo

brooch, just as Travis had described. It had to have fallen from Wetherly's pocket when he fell.

"So it was you all along." Travis was looking at Wetherly now, and there was murder in his eyes.

Wetherly had proved to have the soul of the highwayman, but something nagged at Rebecca. "He could not have been the man who attacked me. Gyles would have told us if Wetherly had left Bacon's encampment. Besides, he did not know I was asking about the brooch."

Travis stood rigidly, his gaze never leaving the man on the ground.

Joseph, Hadrian, and the rest stood watching. Rebecca saw the questions on their faces, but the look on Travis's face kept them silent.

"Where did you get the brooch?" Travis demanded.

Wetherly was regarding Travis speculatively. "That brooch would appear to be very important to you. Do you mind telling a doomed man why?"

"It was in the possession of the man who murdered my mother," Travis replied grimly. He pushed the point of his sword more firmly against Wetherly's throat. "And I'll have his name."

"I want a horse and your word that I'll have a full day's start before anyone comes after me," Wetherly bargained.

Rebecca watched Travis anxiously. Clearly, it had grown easy for Wetherly to kill to gain whatever he wanted. If Travis let him go, Wetherly would kill again, and she knew Travis well enough to know that he would feel that blood on his hands.

"This one's coming around," Hadrian's voice broke the silence that had fallen over the assembly. "Maybe he can give us the answer you want."

Wetherly cursed under his breath. "Keep quiet, Noland!" he yelled.

Joseph and Hadrian were helping the hapless Noland to his feet. He looked dazed and frightened. "Where did you get that brooch?" Hadrian questioned the man. "You tell us, and we'll let you live long enough to face a trial."

" 'Twas at the house with the gaggle of kids," Noland muttered.

Travis's gaze narrowed threateningly on Wetherly. "Loyde?"

Wetherly smiled. "Isn't that a jest? There he was up on the pulpit preaching to us about how to act saintly and him a murderer."

"Charles, saddle my horse," Travis ordered a stableboy standing nearby.

"Mine, also," Rebecca added.

"This is my battle."

"I am certain that Mr. Loyde was responsible for Mr. Mercer's death. I, too, wish to see justice done." But it was not justice that interested her. It was fear for Travis that caused her to insist upon accompanying him. Mr. Loyde was a dangerous man, and she would not allow Travis to face him alone. Before he could say more, she hurried into the house to reload her pistol and load one for Travis.

It took her only a few moments. When she emerged again, Charles was returning with the horses, and her father and Joseph had their prisoners bound.

"We'll take these rascals to Colonel Howard," Hadrian was saying. "He'll see that justice is done."

Travis merely nodded, not taking the time for words as he accepted the pistol from Rebecca and swung himself into the saddle. He was already on his way down the road when she mounted and kicked her horse into a gallop.

As they rode up to the front of the two-story brick manor house, Loyde came out to meet them. He was holding Timothy, his youngest child, in his arms.

"I'm afraid your man got here only in time to get himself wounded by Wetherly and his men. He's inside being ministered to by my staff," Loyde said in polite terms. "I sent one of my men to warn the others."

Rebecca saw nothing but polite concern on his face. It still did not seem possible he was the man Travis sought.

"There is no need to warn others," Travis replied. "We have caught Wetherly and his men." His hand went to his pocket and pulled out the brooch. There was a deadly look on his face as he showed it to Loyde. "Wetherly told me he found this here."

Loyde squinted for a better look at the brooch. "I just bought that from Garnet." His gaze swung to Rebecca. "Is that the brooch you were asking about?"

Rebecca had to admit that he appeared to be honestly confused. So it had been Jason Garnet who had murdered Thomas? She glanced questioningly toward Travis.

"And these also?" Travis's gaze never left Loyde as he pulled a string of pearls from the pocket of his coat. "And this ring?" He smiled sarcastically. "You could not think I would be so stupid as to not check all of Wetherly's pockets as well as those of his men."

Loyde shrugged and his mask of innocent confusion vanished. In its place was a look of arrogant cruelty. "Who are you, Travis Brandt?"

"My mother was maid to the daughter of the Earl of Dormott," he replied.

"And you have chased me all these years." Loyde shook his head as if to say he found this a dreadful waste of time. "I am afraid your quest is not over." The hand he had been holding behind him came forward, and in it he held a pistol.

Travis did not flinch. "You only have one shot."

Loyde smiled and raised the pistol to the child's head. "But you are a decent man, Brandt. Could you sleep at night with the child's life on your conscience?"

Rebecca stared in shocked horror. He was threatening to kill his own child!

Timothy squirmed and cried, but Loyde held him.

"What is happening?" Mistress Hansone demanded, coming out of the house with two of the other children following behind. "Here, give Timothy to m—" Her words were cut short at the sight of the gun being held to the child's head.

"Get back inside and take the others with you if you do not wish the brat harmed," Loyde ordered.

"You would not harm your own son!" Mistress Hansone protested.

"Do not tempt me," Loyde warned.

"I knew there was a cold streak in you, but I never guessed it ran so deep," she said. The fear in her eyes told Rebecca that she believed him perfectly capable of harming the child.

"Get back inside," Loyde ordered once again.

Her complexion ashen, Mistress Hansone quickly ushered the others back inside.

But the eldest girl paused at the door to look back at Travis. "Do not let him harm Timothy," she pleaded.

"That's right, Brandt." Loyde's cruel smile returned. "The child's safety rests with you. I'm going to leave now, and if you follow, I promise you I shall kill him."

Rebecca studied Travis as he sat motionless, watching the man back away from them until he was around the house and out of sight. She knew it must be killing him inside to be so close to his quarry and yet not be able to act. "You were right about the character of the man you sought," she said, breaking the heavy silence surrounding them.

He did not look at her but continued to keep his attention on the spot where Loyde had disappeared from view. He knew he must have patience if the child was to have a chance. But he would not let Loyde escape. The man had cost him more than he could ever imagine. "I am glad it was not your father."

She saw the frustration on his face and could not bring herself to say that she had told him so.

Abruptly he kicked his horse into motion. "He has had enough of a start now," he said. "I doubt he will keep the child with him for long. That would only slow him down."

"No, you mustn't!" the eldest daughter screamed, racing out of the house.

"He knows your father well," Rebecca told the girl. "And we will do all we can to save your brother."

Travis gave her a look of thanks for her show of confidence, then continued around the house.

Rebecca followed.

From the stableboy they learned that Loyde had entered the woods to the west.

Travis was a quick tracker, and they picked up the trail almost immediately. They had gone only a short way when a child's whimpering caught their attention.

Timothy was lying on the ground, his leg twisted under him in an unnatural way. Clearly Loyde had simply tossed the child away as he rode.

"I suppose we should be glad he did not kill him," Rebecca said as she knelt beside the child and determined that his leg was broken but that he had no other serious injuries.

"He did not want to waste his ammunition," Travis replied, and she knew he was right.

He stayed with her, holding the child and talking to him gently as she set the leg. Timothy was a brave little soul and only screamed twice when she pulled on the leg to straighten it. As she bound it using a couple of sturdy branches and pieces of her petticoat, she marveled at how tender Travis was with the child, and a lump formed in her throat. He would have made an excellent father. But not for her children. He wouldn't have wanted that.

When she had finished, Travis helped her back into the saddle, then handed Timothy to her. "You take the child back. I'm going after Loyde. He'll not escape me this time."

Without thinking, she reached out and caught his arm. "Be careful," she said tightly.

He saw the fear in her eyes and wondered how she could feel any concern for what happened to him after all he had put her through. "I will," he promised gruffly, then added in authoritative tones, "After you have taken Timothy home, I want your word that you will return to Green Glen. I do not want to have to worry about you trying to follow and getting lost or injured."

In a polite but firm way he was telling her he did not want her with him. Suddenly embarrassed by her open show of emotion, she released his arm. "As you wish."

He might never see her again. He could not let her part from him on a sour note. "It is for your own safety."

She hated it when he was kind to her. It caused her to hope for things that could never be. Nodding her acknowledgment of his words, she returned her attention to the child. "Please let him return safely," she prayed quietly as she heard Travis ride away.

The other Loyde children came running across the back lawn to meet her when she returned to the house. Their grandmother stood frozen with anxiousness at the door.

"He's going to be fine," Rebecca assured the children as they crowed around her horse. Vince Jones, the overseer, came running with the children and took Timothy from her. "Be gentle," she cautioned. "His leg has been broken and he's bruised."

"I will, ma'am," the man assured her, carrying the child quickly to the house.

Rebecca looked back toward the woods. In her mind's eye she saw the cruelty on Loyde's face, and her chin trembled with fear. Travis knows how to take care of himself, she told herself, but the fear remained.

She stayed at the Loyde home only long enough to inform Mistress Hansone of Mr. Loyde's disreputable past. Then, assured that the woman and children would be looked after, she rode back to Green Glen. To her relief, the man they had sent to Loyde's house to warn him of Wetherly's coming had only been slightly wounded by Wetherly's men and was in good enough shape to accompany her.

That night she paced the floor. The thought that she might

never see Travis again plagued her. She told herself she should be glad to be rid of him. He would certainly be glad to be rid of her. But she wanted to know that he was safe. "Please keep him safe," she prayed over and over again.

SEVENTEEN

FOR the next two weeks Rebecca waited. Gyles's leg was healing well, and he talked of going after Travis. It was all she could do not to beg him to take her with him. She had to know if Travis was still alive.

She had fallen into the habit of wandering down by the river each afternoon. The weather was turning much colder. Hugging her cloak tightly around herself, she wondered if Travis was keeping himself warm enough. "He could at least send a message," she said aloud, the strain of her wait causing her nerves to grow brittle.

"He has been too busy dogging my trail," a familiar voice said from behind her.

In the next instant she felt a blinding pain as something hit her hard upon the head, and the world turned to blackness.

Rebecca awoke with a pounding headache. When she tried to move, her arms and legs were restricted. Opening her eyes, she gazed around her. She was lying bound beside a campfire inside a cave. For a moment confusion ruled. Then she remembered the voice behind her just before all had gone black. It had belonged to Mr. Loyde.

She shifted her head for a fuller view. The action caused a sharp jab of pain, and she groaned.

"So you're finally awake," her captor said with a nasty sneer.

She forced herself to shift in the direction of his voice and saw Theodore Loyde seated on a rock near the fire eating on a roasted rabbit. She frowned at him in confusion. "Why did you come back here? Everyone knows of you now."

He smiled. "I needed a bit of bait. I realized that Brandt would trail me until his dying day. Therefore, if I am to have any peace, I shall have to see that his dying day arrives soon."

He was going to use her to trap Travis! "You are a heartless man," she hissed.

He gave a shrug and took another bite.

Her stomach growled, but she would not ask to share his meal. "Are you not even going to ask what condition little Timothy is in—or if he survived?" she questioned, still finding it hard to believe that anyone could be so cold as to have no feelings for his own children.

He shrugged. "What happened to the brat is of no concern to me."

Rebecca stared at him. He showed no sign of even the smallest amount of remorse. "You are truly evil."

He laughed. "I will enjoy doing away with you once your purpose is served. You have caused me a great deal of trouble, Rebecca."

There was a malice in his eyes that caused her blood to run cold. "All the trouble that has been visited upon you is that which you brought upon yourself."

He shook his head, as if reprimanding a child. "None of this would be happening to you if you had married me."

Rebecca's stomach knotted as she recalled how she had actually considered that possibility.

Mr. Loyde took another bite of meat, chewed it, and swallowed. All the time he watched her thoughtfully. "You have thwarted my plans at every step."

"I have thwarted your plans?" she replied incredulously. "I was a stupid innocent who thought you were a strict but loving father, a pillar of the community, an honest man!"

"But you chose to marry Brandt, and after I had done

away with my wife to clear the path for us. We could have united Green Glen and River View into a profitable and enviable estate."

Rebecca stared at him in horror. "You murdered Amanda so that you could marry the widow of the man you had killed?"

"Amanda could be a nag. Besides, she had seen the brooch." He smiled. "Luckily for me I had the foresight to secure another in the event she had mentioned the brooch to anyone."

"I cannot believe you killed Amanda, too."

He shrugged, as if to say it was of no importance. "She never knew what was happening. She had a slight cold. I gave her her medicine each night. A little poison at first to keep her ill, then a final fatal dose." His smile broadened. "I thought I played the part of the bereaved husband very well. Not too many tears but just enough to make everyone believe I was holding myself under tight control."

Rebecca shivered. "You are truly the devil incarnate."

"I am merely looking out for my own best interests," he replied and returned his attention to his eating.

The pain in Rebecca's head was growing worse. Closing her eyes, she allowed herself to drift back into the darkness beyond conscious thought.

When she awoke again, it was cold. The fire was nothing more than a few smoldering embers. Forcing herself to lift her head, she looked around. She was alone in the cave. Her entire body ached. Her hands and arms were numb from being tied in a painful position behind her, and her legs, bound at the ankles, felt as if they were being pricked by needles. A gag had been stuffed into her mouth, and a rope around her waist was fastened to a large rock to keep her movements restricted to a small area near the fire. It took every ounce of willpower she had, but she managed to shift herself into a sitting position.

Attempting to ignore the numbness in her hands, she twisted her wrists, trying to loosen her bonds. They were

securely tied. Closing her eyes, she rested her head on her
knees. She could not allow Mr. Loyde to use her to murder
Travis. Her jaw set in a determined line. Lifting her head,
she looked at what remained of the fire. Reaching a
decision, she moved toward it.

Turning so that her back was toward the smoldering
embers, she carefully lowered her hands, hoping to burn the
rope enough to allow her to break her bonds.

Her wrist touched a hot coal, and she sucked in a sharp
breath of pain. Shifting slightly, she tried not to think of the
heat.

She had no idea what time it was, but it was day. She
could tell that by the sunlight finding its way in through the
brush masking the cave entrance. Tears ran down her
cheeks. The heat was too great.

Shifting away from the fire, she pulled on her bonds.
They were still secure. Her gaze turned to the rock to which
she was tied. There was a narrow jagged edge that jutted out
from the rest of the smoother surface.

In a slow painful motion she moved herself into position.
It took a couple of tries and a bloodied arm before she
positioned the rope correctly. Then, with what strength she
had left, she began to try to cut the rope on the rock.

The crack of a twig outside told her that someone was
approaching. Mr. Loyde, she guessed. Travis would have
been more silent.

Her guess was right.

"You will be pleased to learn that your beloved husband
is home," he announced as he entered the cave and replaced
the brush across the opening.

Travis was back at Green Glen!

"I guessed he was barely a day behind me," Mr. Loyde
was saying with a self-approving grin. "And I have set my
little plan into motion. I sent your loving husband a message
through Daniel. And I made it clear to the boy he was to tell
no one else."

Fear shone in Rebecca's eyes.

Mr. Loyde scowled impatiently. "Don't worry—I didn't do any permanent harm to your brother, just scared him a bit. I wanted to be certain the message got back to Brandt."

The words *no permanent harm* echoed in Rebecca's mind. She would kill Loyde with her bare hands if he had harmed Daniel in any way.

Loyde began to rebuild the fire, chuckling as if he found this whole situation amusing.

His confidence caused the flesh on the back of her neck to prickle. Surely Travis wouldn't be so stupid as to fall into Mr. Loyde's trap, Rebecca reasoned.

Travis sat listening to the message Loyde had sent through Daniel. The boy was holding himself stiffly, determined to get every word right. Loyde had cut a long thin gash in Daniel's cheek as a warning to Travis to take the message seriously.

Susan and Mildred had wanted to care for the wound immediately, but Daniel had refused to allow them to touch him until he had given Travis the message. Listening to the boy, Travis could not take his eyes from the trickle of blood still flowing from the wound. His stomach knotted in fear for Rebecca. She could already be dead. No! He would not believe that. He could not.

"And he says you must come alone," Daniel finished.

"You have done well," Travis assured the boy, giving him a pat on the shoulder. "Do not tell anyone else what you have told me. Now, run along and get that cut tended."

But Daniel stood his ground. "You will save her, won't you?" he demanded, his panic too near the surface to be hidden.

"I will save her," Travis replied resolutely.

Alone in his study he paced the floor. He had never meant to place Rebecca in any jeopardy. His hands balled into fists. He would give his life to see her walk through that door at this moment.

Staring out the window, he reached a decision. It might not be wise, but he would follow Loyde's directions exactly.

The next morning Loyde woke Rebecca before dawn. He cut the bonds around her ankles and jerked her to her feet.

Her head spun and her legs felt like jelly. She was starting to sink back to the ground when he slapped her hard. "If you want to live to see your husband one last time, you'll walk and you'll walk now," he threatened.

She was tired of being bullied. Besides, she was not so certain his plan would work if she was dead. Otherwise, why would he have kept her alive? "You have to give me a moment," she snapped. "To get some circulation back."

He glowered but gave her the time she needed.

When they left the cave, he led the way, using the rope tied around her waist to half drag her behind him.

Forcing her mind to clear, she watched for any chance to escape, but her legs were still weak, and spells of dizziness kept sweeping over her. Still, she fought her bonds, but she had not been able to cut them enough on the rock to gain her freedom.

When she was certain her legs could carry her no farther, they entered a clearing about twenty feet in diameter. A stake had been placed in the center, and he bound her to it. She could see his plan now. It was quite simple. He would be waiting in hiding and when Travis entered the clearing to tree her, Loyde would kill him.

"Now I must go sprinkle my crumbs and lead your beloved to this spot," Loyde was saying, as if he found this game very enjoyable. "In the meantime, you must hope that no hungry animal finds you."

Rebecca glared at him. Her mouth ached from the gag stuffed deep inside, but still she managed a few guttural sounds to let him know what she thought of him.

He laughed and waved good-bye.

* * *

Travis had spent the night at the spot designated by Loyde. Daniel had kept his word and not told anyone else of the message, but both Hadrian and Gyles had guessed Loyde had sent word through the boy. They had both wanted to accompany Travis, but he had convinced them that this was a matter he must deal with on his own. All through the night he had prayed that Rebecca was not already dead. Just the thought of her lifeless body caused a pain so deep it made him ill. In spite of all of his efforts to turn his heart away from her, he loved her. He wouldn't deny that any longer. "She has to be alive," he muttered aloud for the millionth time as dawn broke.

"Yes, she is," a voice said from the woods behind him.

He spun around, his pistol at the ready. "Where are you, Loyde? This is between you and me. Let her go!"

"Not just yet." Loyde walked out into full view.

Travis's finger closed on the trigger.

"However, should you kill me now, I guarantee you will never see her alive again," Loyde promised.

Travis eased his finger from the trigger. "Where is she, Loyde?"

"First I must satisfy myself that you have come alone," Loyde stipulated. "I have marked a path for you to follow. 'Tis pieces of Rebecca's petticoat." Waving Travis a farewell, he headed back into the woods.

It took Travis only a moment to find the trail. He debated over whether to follow the one laid out by Loyde or the one Loyde was leaving now. With all of the underbrush and leaves to hide Loyde's footprints, the marked one would be faster. He also knew that even if she was alive now, Loyde planned to kill her too. It was the man's way. Travis's expression became resolute. If he had to do it with his dying breath, he would save her.

Rebecca stood in the clearing listening for signs of anyone approaching. But she wasn't waiting patiently. She was fighting her bonds with all the strength she could muster. She was determined to warn Travis even if it meant her death.

She heard a twig snap to her right. That had to be Loyde. Travis would make no sound when he approached. Pain shot up her arms, and she felt the sticky wetness of blood on her hands as she worked more frantically against her bonds.

Travis approached the clearing slowly. He could see Rebecca tied in the center. He drew a relieved breath when he saw her struggling. At least she was not already dead. He knew Loyde would be lurking on the perimeter ready to ambush him. Carefully he began to make his way, trying to keep hidden by the trees.

A laugh filled the air. "You do not think I would be so stupid as to not keep a sharp eye out for you, do you, Brandt?" Loyde's voice rang out. "Lay your weapons aside and go to your wife, or I shall surely kill her now."

Rebecca tried to shout through the gag, but all that came out were a few guttural sounds. Don't expose yourself! she screamed mentally. With added frenzy, she fought her bonds.

Then suddenly she froze. It was Travis. He was walking right into the clearing. At the edge he stopped and set aside his pistol and sword. He looked bigger and more sturdy than she remembered. But pistols had brought down men larger than he was. The fates had never shone favorably upon her, she thought, preparing herself to meet death with him.

A shot rang out. Rebecca saw Travis flinch sideways as the ball caught him in the shoulder, but he did not fall. Another shot was fired. His torso jerked back. Clearly the ball had hit him full in the chest, but again he did not fall. Two more pistol shots filled the air.

Travis grunted as they hit their marks upon his chest. He was almost to Rebecca now. Sinking to his knees, he fell to the ground.

Rebecca stared in horror. Travis was dead. Tears began to

stream down her cheeks. A rage like none she had ever felt before swept over her.

Loyde came out of hiding and walked across the clearing. Reaching her, he laid his emptied pistols down. "Tears? A touching sight," he said cynically, pulling the gag from her mouth.

"You . . . you . . ." she sputtered, too furious to be able to put two words together coherently. Travis was dead, and she felt as if a part of her had been ripped away.

Loyde laughed.

It was the final straw. Her hands tightened around the stake, and she kicked at him with both feet. He was standing close enough that she caught him full in the chest.

"Bitch!" he roared, staggering backward.

Before he could regain his balance, Travis's hand suddenly came out and caught Loyde's ankle. With a jerk Travis sent him crashing to the ground. In the next instant Travis was on his feet. But Loyde was fast, too. He rolled away and in a catlike motion sprang back to his feet. In his hand was a dagger.

Rebecca stared in shocked disbelief. Travis wasn't dead!

Loyde lunged at him. Travis caught Loyde's arm, and the two men fell to the ground, locked in battle. Rebecca watched, still stunned. How could Travis have so much life left in him? Frantically she again worked against her bonds. Her wrists were raw and bleeding, but she did not notice the pain. At any moment she expected Travis to collapse, and she was determined to aid him. But her bonds were too secure.

Travis was on his back, and Loyde had the knife at his throat.

Travis could not die! She couldn't bear it. "No!" she screamed, her voice shrill with panic.

Loyde laughed as he prepared to finish Travis. Rebecca wanted to close her eyes, but she couldn't. Bile rose in her throat. Suddenly the men rolled.

Her scream still echoing in her ears, Rebecca watched,

barely breathing. For a moment it seemed as if Travis had
the advantage, then Loyde was on top of him again.

"Bastard!" she heard Loyde growl, and fear like an icy
hand gripped her. Then suddenly Loyde slumped forward,
the knife driven to the hilt through his black heart.

"This damn mail shirt is heavy. Slowed me down more
than I thought it would," Travis muttered as he shoved
Loyde off and slowly dragged himself to his feet.

Rebecca was staring at him. He wasn't even bleeding.
"Mail shirt?" she questioned as his words sank in.

"From your late husband's armory," he elaborated,
opening his coat and exposing the heavy metal covering that
had protected him. "Wore two layers. Good thing Thomas
was a stout fellow."

"I can't believe you just walked right into the clearing."
Her relief that he was all right gave way to the shock of
what could have happened. "What if he had hit you in the
head or the leg?"

Travis shrugged. "Life is full of chances one must take."
He could not tell her that his life would have meant nothing
to him if he could not have saved her. She wouldn't be
interested in hearing it, and he had his pride. Moving
around behind the stake, he paled when he saw her bloody
wrists. "I'm sorry to have caused this to happen to you," he
apologized as he quickly cut her free.

She wished he would take her in his arms and tell her that
he had been a fool and that he wanted her to stay with him.
But instead, he knelt and ripped a long strip of cloth from
her petticoat, then busied himself with binding her wrists.
'Twas a foolish wish, she chided herself.

As Travis worked, it took all of his control not to draw
her into his embrace and hold her. But he had promised her
her freedom, and he was certain she wanted nothing more to
do with him. Avoiding looking at her, he concentrated on
bandaging her wrists.

Rebecca's gaze shifted to the man who now lay dead on
the ground. " 'Tis over," she said with finality.

"Yes," he confirmed. "And now I must get you home."

She looked at him. Home. His home but not her home. Their bargain was finished.

When he started to lift her into his arms to carry her to his horse, she balked. She was afraid she might reveal how much he still affected her, and her pride would not allow that. "I can walk," she insisted.

Travis nodded his consent and led the way. He had wanted to hold her one last time. But it was best this way, he told himself. He had not been certain he could make himself release her once he had her in his arms.

The ride back to Green Glen was bittersweet torture for Rebecca. She sat straddled behind Travis and was forced to hold on to him for support. For the first mile she remained rigid, keeping their contact as limited as possible. But her body ached, and she was tired. Giving in to the urge to feel his physical closeness one last time, she relaxed and laid her head upon his back. It was stupid to feel this drawn to a man who thought so little of her. But she could not stop remembering the first days of their marriage. If she had not lied to him . . . But she had, and he would never trust her again.

Travis sat rigidly. He was acutely aware of the way her legs brushed against his and the soft rise and fall of her chest as she breathed. It was bittersweet agony to have her so close and yet know he must walk out of her life forever. But he had made a vow and he would keep it.

Suddenly shouts rang out. Looking to her right, Rebecca saw her father, Gyles, and Daniel.

"I was so worried I could not keep my promise to tell no one," Daniel blurted out as they guided their horses toward Rebecca and Travis.

"Where's Loyde?" Hadrian asked, glancing over his shoulder, as if he expected to see the man coming up from behind.

"Dead in a clearing a couple of miles back," Travis

replied. "I wanted to get Rebecca to safety. She's had a rough couple of days."

"You go ahead," Hadrian said. "Gyles and I'll take care of the body. Guess Colonel Howard's the man to present it to."

Travis nodded.

But before the men rode away, Gyles smiled at Rebecca. "I ain't never seen a man as worried about anyone as Travis was about you. Good thing you're safe. I don't know if we could have controlled him if you'd been harmed."

Travis tensed as if he was embarrassed, and she forced a smile. She would like to have believed his concern had been caused by caring, but she would not fool herself. It had been guilt and nothing more.

Daniel rode with Rebecca and Travis as they continued back toward Green Glen. She considered insisting on sharing her brother's horse, but she was too tired to dismount and remount. Besides, she was weak-willed, she admitted. She had not yet gotten over the shock of thinking Travis was dead, and she wanted this last opportunity to hold him near.

As they neared Green Glen, Travis sent Daniel ahead to alert the servants of their arrival and arrange for a bath to be prepared for Rebecca.

Her mind drifted back to a bath they had once shared. Tears welled in her eyes. Suddenly her jaw hardened and she straightened away from him. She would not cry over a man who was so arrogantly self-righteous and so unforgiving.

When they reached Green Glen, Travis insisted on carrying her up to their room, where the bath was sitting.

Susan was there standing irresolutely beside the tub. Clearly she was not certain if she was wanted.

Travis wanted to roar at her to leave. But he did not dare. If he helped Rebecca, he knew he would not be able to maintain the tenuous control he was now holding over himself.

Determinedly Rebecca ignored the feeling of desertion that filled her as he stood her upon the floor and left. Pushing him from her mind, she allowed Susan to help her and minister to her wounds. But later, as she sat in the bed she and Travis had shared, her body bathed, her wrists bandaged, sipping on a hot cup of tea, his image again filled her mind. Reaching over, she touched his pillow, and a bitter sadness filled her. She had half expected him to come in to check on her. But he hadn't.

"He's avoiding me," she said softly, forcing herself to face the truth. She took a bite of buttered scone. Even Mildred's hot bread tasted like sawdust. "He wants to be rid of me." Reaching a decision, she set the tray aside and left the bed. She would not spend another night in his bed. She would not even spend another night under his roof. Quickly she dressed herself, then went in search of him.

He was in his study seated at his desk reading over a document. "I thought you were resting," he said, rising to greet her as she entered.

He looked more tired than she had ever seen him. Tired of me and all the pretense, she told herself. Well, she would put an end to it now and forever. "I have decided that there is no reason to continue with this farce of a marriage any longer," she informed him. "I will pack a few things for myself and Daniel and be gone before nightfall. You can have the servants pack the rest of our belongings and send them to my cabin."

Travis had expected her to want to leave. He had just not expected it to happen so abruptly. 'Tis for the best, he told himself. In truth, he had been afraid of sharing a bed with her again. If he held her again, he might never be able to keep his promise to give her her freedom. "There is no reason for you to leave Green Glen," he replied. "I have just finished writing up a paper that will give you title to the property. 'Tis rightfully yours." He picked up the document and handed it to her. "With your permission I will remain in a guest room one last night and leave with Gyles in the morning."

It was truly over. A lump suddenly formed in her throat. "I am not so certain Gyles will want to leave," she heard herself saying. "He and Susan appear to have grown quite fond of each other." The lump in her throat grew. There had been a time when Travis had looked at her in much the same way Gyles looked at Susan. 'Tis past and dead, she told herself curtly. She shoved the paper back toward him. "I want only what we originally bargained for."

Travis frowned at her stubbornness. The only way to grant her the freedom she desired was for him to leave here and never return. "I have no need for Green Glen. Besides, you have paid dearly for it. By all rights it should be yours."

She could not deny his words, but she had her pride. "No, thank you," she said. Ripping the document in half, she let the pieces flutter to the ground as she turned and strode toward the door.

In two long steps Travis reached her and caught her by the arm. "Green Glen is yours," he said with firm insistence. "I shall leave a paper with Colonel Howard stating that is so."

Hot tears burned at the back of Rebecca's eyes. She wanted to scream at him that she cared nothing for Green Glen. But an admission such as that might cause him to guess how much he had hurt her. She had to get away from him before she made a fool of herself. Jerking free, she faced him boldly. "You may do as you wish," she replied, then, turning away, she again started toward the door.

Travis could not let it end this way. He knew she had to hate him, and she had every right to. But he did not want them to part with so much anger between them. "I admire your loyalty toward your father and Daniel. They are very lucky men. I envy them."

Rebecca stopped dead in her tracks. Stunned by his words, she turned to face him. "You envy them?"

For a moment a crooked self-conscious smile tilted one

corner of Travis's mouth, then disappeared to be replaced by a look of bitterness. "The reason I was so angry with you for lying to me was because I had wanted the loyalty for myself." Suddenly embarrassed by this confession, he turned away from her and, walking to the window, stared out. He half expected her to laugh at him.

But Rebecca wasn't laughing. She was watching him mutely, frightened by the confessions she was considering making. After all, he had not said he had learned to care for her. He had merely said he wanted her loyalty. But if there was a chance for them, she would not pass it by because of pride. "I did not lie to you because I felt more loyal toward my father and brother than I did toward you."

Travis turned toward her. He wanted to believe that more than he had ever wanted to believe anything in his life. His gaze narrowed upon her. "Why did you lie?"

There was no accusation in his voice. It was almost a plea. Rebecca drew a shaky breath as she met his gaze evenly. "I lied because I had begun to learn to care for you, and I was afraid you would turn against me if you discovered my father was still alive. Mr. Mercer had been very clear about my parentage being an embarrassment." Her back straightened. "And when you suggested my father was the murderer you sought, I had to stand by him because I knew he was innocent."

He had been a damn fool! "It is not easy for me to trust others," he said, watching her for any sign that she might consider forgiving him. "I know I have behaved badly. But if I were to promise to try to improve, do you think you could learn to tolerate me? Perhaps even learn to care for me once again?"

He looked so vulnerable. She had never thought he could be so humble. She wanted to rush into his arms, but the fear of being hurt once again held her still. "I would need to know that you truly cared for me."

It was not easy revealing himself so fully. But he would do anything to keep his gypsy. "Even when I felt betrayed,

I could not stop myself from wishing you still stood by me. And when I thought you might have come to harm, I would have made a pact with the devil to trade my life for yours."

Rebecca remembered Gyles's words in the forest and the panic in Travis's eyes. He did care.

The blue of his eyes darkened with a pleading warmth. "It is as if I am incomplete without you."

Tears began to roll freely down Rebecca's cheeks. " 'Tis the same for me," she confessed. "When I thought you had been slain in that clearing, it was as if my heart had been ripped from me."

Relief spread over Travis's features. Bridging the distance between them in two long strides, he swept her up into his arms. "I love you, Rebecca," he said against her hair, crushing her to him.

Lifting her head, she met his gaze with a mock reprimanding frown. " 'Tis not been easy, but I love you, too," she said.

Travis laughed, then his expression became solemn. "I shall spend the rest of my life proving to you that I am worthy."

Rebecca smiled under the heat of his gaze. "I shall enjoy that."

"And now 'tis time for you to be back in your bed," he said, lifting her into his arms and carrying her toward the door.

Rebecca's mouth formed a playful pout. " 'Twas very lonely up there."

Travis's mouth found hers. "Then I shall have to make certain you are not left alone this time."

The promise in his voice sent a rush of excitement through her. "That would be most kind of you, sir."

Laughing gently, he carried her up the stairs.

EPILOGUE

MAY came. The king had sent three commissioners to help settle the rebellion. It was made clear that Charles wished peace in Virginia, and he was willing to grant pardons to achieve this. But Sir William would not be quelled. His estates had been looted, his wealth severely depleted, and his authority seriously challenged. He was determined to have his revenge. Despite orders from the king that he return to England, Sir William delayed his departure. Throughout the winter he continued to hang the rebel leaders. Of Drummond and Lawrence, the two men who it was believed had actually drawn up Bacon's Laws, Drummond was caught and hanged. Lawrence, however, managed to escape to the northern colonies. And although the assembly repealed Bacon's Laws, new laws were drawn up that instituted the majority of the same reforms. But finally in April Sir William set sail for England and sanity again ruled in Virginia.

Rebecca lay, levered on an elbow beside Travis, watching him in the soft morning light.

"You look like a woman with something serious on her mind," he said, studying her gently. "Was there something in the letter you received from Susan that I should know?"

Rebecca smiled. Susan and Gyles had been married at Green Glen a month earlier and had gone back to Gyles's

345

homestead to begin their life together. "They are quite happy. But 'tis not them that was on my mind."

Travis traced the line of her jaw with the tip of his finger. "And what is on your mind?"

Rebecca's smile deepened, and a soft pink glow came to her cheeks. "I was thinking that I should warn you that you are going to be a father."

Travis laughed and drew her close to him. "I've known that for at least a week."

"You've known?" she demanded, pouting.

His free hand traveled possessively over her hip. "As part of my husbandly duties, I keep a very close guard over your body."

Rebecca could not help laughing. Trailing her hand over his chest, she leaned forward and kissed him lightly. "You are very good at performing your husbandly duties."

"I try to please," he replied, pulling her closer.

"You do," she assured him huskily.